MARLIN BEACH

ROBERTA L. GREENWALD

This is a work of fiction. Names, characters, places, events, and incidents are either the product of the author's imagination or are used fictitiously. Any resemblance to persons living or dead is entirely coincidental.

All rights are reserved. Reprinting of this book or sale is entirely unauthorized. No part of this manuscript may be reproduced, stored in a retrieval system, or transmitted in any form or by any means- electronic, mechanical, photocopy, recording, or any other – without the prior permission of the author.

Marlin Beach

Copyright © 2020 Greenwald, Roberta L.

All rights reserved.

ISBN: 9798670978712

I DEDICATE THIS BOOK TO THE COURAGEOUS PEOPLE WHO WERE A PART OF THE COR0NAVIRUS OUTBREAK OF 2020.

THE MASK

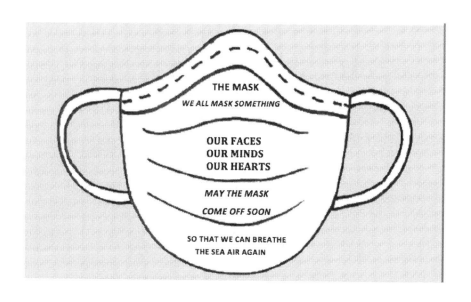

You rule the raging of the sea; when its waves rise, you still them.

Psalm 89:9

THANK YOU TO ALL MY FAMILY AND FRIENDS WHO HAVE ALWAYS ENCOURAGED ME TO WRITE THE NEXT BOOK.

MARLIN BEACH

CHAPTER 1

"Hey, Aunt Sarah, it's William."

"Well hello, William," Sarah replied with a pleased smile on her face, not hearing from her nephew in quite some time. "Long time, no hear. How are your classes going?"

"Everything is going well, but I do have a favor to ask. I was wondering once school is out this year, if I can stay with you this summer? I promise I will get a job," Will asked anxiously, already not expecting a good response from her.

Sarah sat down on the comfortable down-filled sectional that she custom designed, looking out at the glistening ocean in front of her, considering his words. "Are you sure Nan and G-Dad would want you to do that since this is your first summer home after being in college for only a year? Why not continue with your job at the movie theater? Nan said that you worked there last summer a few evenings a week, and that you seemed to enjoy it."

Will paced back in forth across the his dorm room floor at Towson University, kicking a dirty undershirt out of his way, realizing she made a valid point, and that's why he hadn't ask his grandparents in the first place. "So I guess I need to talk to them, huh?" he shrugged, knowing

Sarah was always the sensible one.

"That's what I would suggest."

He plopped down on his unmade bed with the dirty sheets that hadn't been washed in well over a month. *"I was hoping I could stay at your place with a couple of my buddies here at school? We would pay you once we get out job,"* he added with one last desperate attempt, hoping she would reconsider and change her mind.

Sarah stood again and began to take the stairs to the second floor to check on the twins who were taking their afternoon nap. She whispered as she spoke, not wanting to wake the active babies who kept her constantly busy and without much time to get things done these days.

"William, as much as I would like to say yes, I do not think it is feasible. You know Abby and Alex are only 9 months old, and I cannot entertain and keep up with your college friends with active toddlers on my hands keeping me very busy everyday."

Sarah opened the door slightly and peaked in at her sleeping cherubs, who typically slept for another hour before waking for another round of active playtime before she started dinner. She quietly shut the door again, wanting the extra moments alone to breathe and get some laundry folded. She tiptoed back down the steps, taking her seat again in the living room, where her laundry basket sat on the Brazilian cherry hardwood floor nearby, piled high with onsies and matching boy and girl outfits that everyone complimented.

"Do you think G-Dad and Nan will allow me stay at the Dancing Seahorse, since you can't help me out?" he asked with nervous anticipation, as his hand ran through his brown wavy locks, waiting on her response.

Sarah began to laugh and shake her head, knowing he was being persistent and that The Dancing Seahorse belonged to her too and she could put an end to that possibility real quickly, but it was a moot point. "I must go, but I think you should talk to G-Dad and Nan and see what they say. I wish you the best, William, and if things work out for you, I look forward to seeing you more this summer in Marlin Beach."

"Me too, Aunt Sarah. Me too."

William had adjusted nicely to life in Baltimore with his grandparents as his primary guardians and caregivers since his mother's death three years earlier. He attended the same high school as his mother, father and aunt Sarah. His father Dexter and his aunt Sarah were twins. He never met his father, who had died in a horrific, ocean riptide accident, shortly after getting his mother pregnant at a young age of 18.

Curiosity at age 16, led William on a journey from Birmingham, Alabama to Marlin Beach, Maryland to find his grandparents and aunt Sarah. Once he sought out and met Sarah, she refused to believe that it was even remotely possible - that William was her brother's son. Only through a series of events that transpired, was William found by his grandfather, Mike, and accepted into the family.

After his mother's illness and death, his grandparents - Mike and Nancy Miller - led the way in bringing healing to the family that William was now a part of. It was difficult to say goodbye to his half brother and sister – Jackson and Eva – and leave them behind in Alabama; but on the flip side he was relieved to be out of the evil grips of his alcoholic and abusive stepfather - Mitchell Robbins. Mitchell did not abuse his own children, but for William, being the son of Dexter William Miller - whose name he carried - life was filled with a series of threats, violence and actual physical abuse.

Once he moved to Baltimore and lived with Mike and Nancy, or G-Dad and Nan, as he so fondly nicknamed them, things were totally different and an exact opposite of what he had experienced up until that point living in Birmingham. He was pampered and spoiled, now growing up in an affluent neighborhood and not lacking in any way.

The house was spacious and custom built by Mike, who was a successful architect by trade with his own firm in Baltimore that Sarah was also part owner of. He built the house that featured an inground swimming pool when his children – Sarah and Dexter - were only in elementary school, not missing any detail of functionality and beauty inside and out. He also built a beach house in Marlin Beach, Maryland that was so fondly named – The Dancing Seahorse - around the same time that he was constructing the main family home in Baltimore.

The Dancing Seahorse was always used throughout the summer months when Sarah and Dexter were growing up. Nancy, their mother, was an elementary school teacher. Once the summer school break began, they would depart for Marlin Beach for the entire summer. Mike, their father, would arrive for long weekends and stay with the family, enjoying long leisurely days on the beach. In the early evening, Nancy would cook dinner as the children washed up and changed out of their wet bathing suits, and Mike would retreat to the back deck that overlooked the dunes and ocean, positioning himself in a rattan chair with a Tanqueray and tonic with lime in hand, ready to watch the sun set. The family would join him for dinners on the patio, taking in the last lingering moments of the day, watching the beachgoers who remained and continued to lounge in their sand chairs, as the seagulls squealed and dipped like bombs to the ocean floor below for a fish, and a kite floated lazily by - being dragged along by a spirited child. They were happy and content with their blessed lives living and working in Baltimore, and then retreating to their beach house in Marlin Beach.

But life as they knew it changed drastically after their son Dexter tragically died. The family rarely used The Dancing Seahorse in the ten years following his passing, and then it was almost sold, until a change of heart occurred when Sarah fell in love with Lance Snyder - once a lifeguard and then a realtor - chosen to sell the beach house for the Miller family.

Reluctantly, Sarah allowed Lance to change her whole world from the bitterness she harbored from the loss of her brother. With the building of The Dexter Resort and Spa in Marlin Beach – the architectural project that she was in charge of - a marriage to Lance and the discovery of William - her brother's only heir - life was a series of ups and down that were never ending.

Once Sarah and Lance were married, they built their own beach house – The Playful Starfish – which was an impressive architectural feat. Her professional life was flourishing, but she longed to have children after experiencing a miscarriage. Soon, her sorrow turned to joy when she found out she was pregnant again, and this time with twins. Abigail and Alexander became her priority, as she put aside her flourishing career for a few years, to lovingly care for her children.

William longed to know about his father. He could only get glimpses of his short-lived life through his mother, Claire, during private conversations about Dexter when Mitchell wasn't present. It would anger Mitchell that Claire wouldn't allow him to adopt Will and that his last name – Miller - was that of his birth father's. She kept a well-hidden, private box of memorabilia high up on a closet shelf in William's bedroom that they would look at frequently when they were alone, reliving the memories of her youth while Dexter and she were in high school together, showing Will pictures, school projects and other significant things related to his father that she had collected and valued.

Once William lived with Mike and Nancy, the family did their best to speak of Dexter whenever Will had any questions about him, showing him family photos, home movies that had been recorded especially during the holidays, and other mementos that brought his father to life for him. He chose his father's bedrooms both at the house in Baltimore and also in Marlin Beach, sleeping in the same bed that Dex had slept in while he was still alive. Somehow, this gave him a feeling of comfort and peace, almost sensing his father's presence in those rooms at times.

He made friends easily in high school once he was established in his new life in Baltimore, maintaining good grades and excelling in track. He graduated with honors and chose to go to the same college that his father had intended to attend - Towson University - but never got the opportunity to do so since he died the summer prior to beginning his schooling there.

With one year of college almost completed, William wanted to experience life in Marlin Beach, working and enjoying life as a nineteen year old. He had casually started to date in his senior year of high school, even experiencing sex for the first time the night of his senior prom with a pretty redhead who every guy wanted to screw. He became more serious about a few girls once in college, but he didn't want to be exclusive with any of them and he liked it that way. If all went as planned, the summer would hold great memories with a place to stay at the beach, a fun job, good times with his friends, and maybe a chick or two along the way. He knew he would ultimately say goodbye to any female at the end of the summer, realizing his primary focus once again would have to be on Towson and his studies. William was committed to doing well and graduating at the top of his class, setting for himself high goals and standards. He felt he had big shoes to fill and that the Miller family was counting on him to do well, since his father, Dexter, would never have the same opportunity.

William picked up his Western Civilization book and headed out of his dorm room. He picked up the pace and began to jog down the sidewalk. *Two more weeks of class and then hopefully everything will fall in place – A new job and staying at The Dancing Seahorse for the summer with my friends,* he thought as he hurried to class. *Now, I just gotta convince G-Dad and Nan of the same...*

CHAPTER 2

"Well hello, Sarah," Mike greeted cheerfully to his daughter and business partner who was on a hiatus from daily work at the office, and was only involved now for occasional projects because of the twins.

"Hi, dad. Thought I should call and check in," she offered pleasantly as she placed a tray of chicken under the broiler, and Abby and Alex played in their fenced-in play yard close by that Lance had put together and set up to keep them contained.

Mike was driving home from work, knowing Nancy would have dinner waiting. "All is well at the office. We miss you there, you know," he admitted fondly, reminding her of that almost on every conversation.

Sarah sat at the table, sipping from her chilled Chardonnay, looking at her giggling babies who were throwing toys at each other. "Play nice, you two," she scolded, before turning her attention back to her father.

"Children acting up?"

Sarah laughed, "It's constant, dad. And that's why I can't return to work on a full-time basis for awhile yet."

"I realize that, Sarah. My grandchildren are top priority right now, as we have discussed. And I know your mother and Lance feel the same way as I do."

"Yes, I realize how you all feel," Sarah smiled contentedly, as she looked lovingly at Alex and Abby. "Speaking of your grandchildren, I heard from William today."

"Oh, he called you?"

"Yes, he sure did. He wondered if I would allow him and his friends to live here at The Playful Starfish for the summer so that they can work and hang out. Which as we know interprets out to mean *partying*," she laughed.

Mike pulled into his driveway, stopping with a halt, considering Sarah's surprising words. "I hope you said no to him."

Sarah took another sip of her wine, pacing over to the window, glancing out at the sea that was fairly calm now compared to the week previous when a bad storm had passed through for a couple days. "Well of course I had to say no with the babies and all, but he still pursued the subject thinking maybe The Dancing Seahorse was another option."

Mike sighed deeply, not liking the thought of his grandson wanting to be alone in Marlin Beach for the upcoming summer season, even if it were with friends. He knew what teenagers could get into, and even though it had been years since Dexter had died, it still haunted him from time to time. If only he and Nancy would have never allowed Sarah and Dex to go to the beach at age 18 before college for a few days prior to their arrival at the beach house. *Maybe he would still be here today...*

"Dad, are you still there?"

"Yeah, I'm sorry Sarah. I was just thinking about what I am going to say to William when he contacts me about this."

"Even though you always tell me The Dancing Seahorse is partially mine, I feel it truly belongs to you and mom since I have my own place now in Marlin Beach. Of course it's also Will's beach house to use and enjoy, but I still believe adult supervision is in order. So feel free to let him stay there with his friends if you would like, but that is my stance on the subject and I would take that into consideration before you give him answer when he calls."

Mike walked from his Lincoln Navigator grabbing his briefcase on the way, before opening the front door with his key. "I will speak with your mother about this, but I agree with you that it isn't the best decision to allow him to stay there, whether William agrees or not. College students with their friends and the parties that they have can destroy a place rather quickly."

Nancy looked confused by the conversation Mike was having about William as he laid his briefcase on an overstuffed chair in their family room and approached her with a quick kiss to the cheek. The table was set and a chicken and rice casserole was cooling on the counter, ready to be eaten.

Sarah reached over the plastic play yard fence, scooping up Alex in her arms as he sobbed against her t-shirt, making her top wet with his tears. "I better get off of here. The twins are restless and Abby just bopped Alex on the head with a stuffed toy and he isn't too happy about it."

"Give them a kiss from G-Dad and Nan. Hopefully, it won't be too long until we get to Marlin Beach for a long weekend and see you and the family again."

"That would be wonderful if you could make it. Say hi to mom for me. I must go... Abby wants me to hold her now too," Sarah added with a sigh, feeling sheer exhaustion running through her from the weight of both twins now planted firmly on each hip, which had become an art form she had mastered in the almost 9 months of having two babies.

"Will do, honey. Talk to you soon..."

Nancy placed the casserole on a trivet in the center of the large farm table, adding a fresh tossed salad and a basket of hot dinner rolls, off to the side. She offered Mike his nightly, after work, gin and tonic, and poured a glass of red wine for herself.

"What is this conversation I overheard about William?" she asked with alarm, trying to be on the same page with Mike as she took her usual seat beside of her husband at the table.

Mike squeezed the lime into his cocktail, taking a long sip before responding. "William wants to go to Marlin Beach for the summer with his friends," he answered matter-of-factly, looking Nancy squarely in the eyes for her reaction.

"Absolutely not!" she remarked a little too loudly, reaching back in her mind and recalling her own painful memories of the last summer that they had together with their son before he died and was taken away at much too young of an age from the tragic ocean accident. She began to cry, wiping the tears from her eyes. "I hope you know I can't handle this. Will is all I have... If something terrible happens to him like it did to Dex, I don't think I could go through that again and survive."

Mike reached out to grab Nancy's hand, squeezing it a little too firmly but lovingly all at the same time. "Nancy, we can't keep him in a glass bubble and protect him forever from any harm that could come his way in life. You know the struggle I had getting your permission to allow him just to leave home and attend Towson this year. He can't always be under your watchful eye, dear."

Nancy grimaced at Mike, with fear etching her face. "He just turned 19, for heaven's sakes. He is still young and a naïve teenager."

Mike shook his head in disbelief, hearing variations of the same theme - excuse after excuse - many times over - since William had moved in with them, knowing Nancy was always setting up barriers where he was concerned. "If Dexter would have survived he would have been a father at age nineteen, you know, which *ironically* is the very same age that William is now!"

"That is horrible, Mike, that you would even say such a thing!" she bit out in disbelief, not caring to hear that line of reference being used in relation to her grandson.

Mike took another long swig of his nightly, tasty alcoholic beverage, trying to clear his mind. "I haven't spoken to William yet, but I am open to hearing his thoughts on the subject. He deserves that. He is levelheaded and hasn't given me any reason *not* to trust him. I did speak to Sarah though, and she has already informed him that her house is not an option this summer."

Nancy put down her fork, unable to believe the subject was still open for discussion. "First of all, I do not want him staying in Marlin Beach even if you do trust him. He has a job here that has worked out well for him in the past, working at the movie theater. Soon enough, he will be involved with someone and out of the house, so let's not rush things."

Mike began to laugh, putting down his fork before wiping his mouth with his napkin. "He is far from being *involved* as you say, and barely dates for that matter. He is more interested in just being a guy and hanging out with his friends. We can't shelter him forever, Nancy. *It's not healthy!"* Mike insisted, getting up from the table and retreating to the sectional in the family room with the rest of his drink in hand.

Nancy looked shocked and surprised by his reaction. "You barely touched your dinner, Michael, and I worked so hard to prepare it."

"I suddenly lost my appetite," he answered firmly, with tight lips.

"I'm sorry, Mike," she moaned, joining him with her glass of wine, hoping for his pity. "I love, William, and he has become my pure joy and comfort in the last few years. He has helped me heal and get past the pain of losing Dexter."

"And I love him too, and I understand where you are coming from," Mike consoled, while pulling her in close and kissing the top of her head. "But I will not suffocate him with my underlying fears of the past, concerning Dexter. He has his own life to live and it's our responsibility to set him free and allow him to live it with our blessing. *Does any of this make sense to you?*" He pleaded, with his own mist-filled eyes of pain from remembering the past.

"Yes, Mike, it does... as much as I don't want to admit it, you are always right where William is concerned. Now can we *please* finish dinner before Rascal jumps up on the table?" she giggled, knowing their cat had just pranced by them towards the kitchen, ready to be fed.

"Absolutely! Lead the way, sweet lady! And then a movie is in order after we clean up the kitchen together," he insisted, patting her backside suggestively.

Laugher filled the air as the pair took their seats again at the familiar table that was still there from the time that Dex and Sarah were young. After dinner and once the dishes were done, the promised movie was watched before Mike and Nancy settled in for the night.

They lay in bed entwined together after some serious lovemaking, with each one thinking of Marlin Beach and what the summer would hold for them and their grandson - William Dexter Miller.

CHAPTER 3

"Hey, G-Dad."

Mike looked up from a stack of blueprints scattered on his desk at Miller's Architecture, as his grandson's call took him away from the pressing business at hand, knowing he anticipated the call sooner or later in the next few days after getting the heads up from Sarah.

"Well, good morning, William. Everything going okay with school?"

"All is great," Will answered, as he made his way towards the cafeteria, ready to grab a late breakfast before his next class. "I wanted to talk to you about something though - unrelated to school, if I may."

Mike walked over to the large expanse of windows that overlooked the picturesque Inner Harbor of Baltimore, glancing out at a few lingering boats that were docked. *"And what would that be?"*

"It's about my summer break that is coming up. I've been talking to my friends here at school and we've decided that we want to live and work in Marlin Beach for the summer."

Mike silently shook his head, knowing Nancy was not going to be happy about any of this. "William, I understand your desire to do just that, but remember that you do have a pending job at the movie theater here in town. I'm sure they will put you back on the schedule and maybe even increase your hours, with just a phone call."

Will held a fried chicken tender sandwich in one hand, that he had just purchased, taking a few tasty bites. "G-Dad, you know that job is not the same thing as going to the beach and working. My friends thought that maybe we could stay at aunt Sarah's or The Dancing Seahorse, just to save some money on rent."

Mike sighed, not wanting to blow Sarah's cover that she had already contacted him about the situation. "I guess you could call Sarah and Lance and ask them if they are willing to take on you and your friends for the summer, if you would like."

"I already did that," William admitted sheepishly, taking a long swig of his soft drink in front of him. "But she said Alex and Abby are too young and she can't deal with the extra activity. So I was thinking that maybe we could stay at The Dancing Seahorse instead - if you are okay with us doing so."

Mike walked back to his desk knowing he needed to be diplomatic and not burst Will's dream of staying there for the summer. "You know, William, the beach house is not just mine. Nan owns it and so does your aunt Sarah."

"Yes, I'm aware, but aunt Sarah did say she's fine with us staying at The Dancing Seahorse as long as you and Nan are too."

"I will need to talk to Nan about all this, but I can tell you that chances are that she will want you to return home for the summer and work at the movie theater. But if by some miracle you or I can convince her to allow you to go to Marlin Beach, she will probably want you to find your own place for you and your friends."

William wadded up his sandwich wrapper, throwing it in the trash along with his empty drink cup, as he walked from the cafeteria feeling totally frustrated. "I guessed you were going to say all this. I love Nan, but she's gotta loosen up and let me breathe... if you know what I mean, G-Dad."

Mike began to laugh, leaning back in his desk chair, staring up at the ceiling with his hands clasped behind his head. "Yes, William, you are exactly right about Nan, but she loves you and wants you home safe and sound in Baltimore with us for the summer."

"I understand, but I'm 19 years old now and I just want to experience things without you guys always being around me. If I have any issues you know aunt Sarah and uncle Lance are in Marlin Beach, so I can always turn to them for help."

Mike paused, remembering life many years earlier when he was only nineteen. His parents were wealthy and allowed him to pretty much do whatever he wanted during his school breaks, so he spent lots of time at the beach without them. He frequented Marlin Beach quite regularly, going there every few days. He would drive from Baltimore with one or two guys that were his friends, being consumed with surfing and finding summer romance with seasonal waitresses from Ireland. Things changed within a couple years, when he and his buddies buckled down and began to find summer jobs in their own hometown, but that magical few summers stuck in his mind as being some of the most carefree and fun times of his youth.

Within a few years, Mike graduated from college with a degree in architecture. He met Nancy during that time and fell in love with her. She graduated from the same school with a teaching degree specializing in elementary school education. They both excelled in their chosen occupations, beginning a family of their own soon thereafter. With the building of The Dancing Seahorse, Mike had become very fond of Marlin Beach, even considering it a place he would want to retire one day until his son Dexter died, changing the course of his life forever.

"*G-Dad, are you there?*" Will asked. "You're not answering me."

Mike snapped out of his daydream of the past and came back to the present. "Sorry, William, I'm just busy today and I got a lot on my mind. I will talk to Nan after work and let you know what she has to say about this. If she agrees with what you have planned, I would suggest you start looking online for a job in Marlin Beach and try to find a summer rental there also. You may already have a difficult time finding something at this late date."

"Already a step ahead of you, G-Dad," he boasted proudly. "My friend Chris has an uncle who runs a hotel at Marlin Beach, and he told him that there are job openings in the restaurant as well as in valet parking. We can't get a place there to stay unfortunately, but my friends are all working on trying to find us housing. If this all works out, I want to leave for Marlin Beach as soon as school is out in a couple weeks."

"Please don't get ahead of yourself, William. I will get back to you as soon as I speak with Nan. Get to class now and I will talk to you later. Hopefully, you will hear from me before the day is up."

Will grinned, trusting that his grandfather always had his back. "I'm counting on that! I hope you can soften Nan up since it's obvious she wants me home working at the movie theater and keeping her company in my free time."

"You know her well," he chuckled, hanging up and shaking his head, as his attention turned back again to the blueprints in front of him. Mike paused, knowing he needed to keep his promise, setting his paperwork aside. He looked at his cellphone, dialing Nancy's number, which was his first contact in his call list.

"Hi Mike. Just got home from hot Yoga," she announced, dropping her gym back on the foyer floor, as Rascal ran up, wanting a scratch to his head. "What time do you plan to get home this evening? I was thinking pizza tonight, if that is alright?"

"Anything is fine, dear. I shouldn't be late, so plan dinner for around six o'clock."

"I will order the large special with extra cheese. Would you like a salad to go along with that also?" she inquired, as she dished out the feline's canned cat food into a pottery bowl with his name on it that was sitting on the kitchen floor.

"Sure... a salad is fine. Please ask for extra croutons and salad dressing though, because they forgot it the last time," he recalled.

Nancy smiled, pouring a glass of sweet iced tea over the crushed ice that she was very fond of. "Exercise class went well. My instructor was out sick, but Mindy stepped in and I think she honestly gave us a better workout this time."

Mike listened half-heartedly, knowing he was avoiding the inevitable. "That's great dear, but I'm sure you could teach the group yourself if asked."

Nancy paused to consider his words, knowing she had never been asked... resuming the scratching of her cat's head as he reached up on her knee with both soft paws in place. She stood, after Rascal was content and jumped down, running then to his liter box close by. "I guess I should shower and change. I will see you in a few hours."

"Before you go..."

"Yes?"

"William called me earlier and he is still questioning whether he can go to Marlin Beach for the summer with his friends from college."

Nancy abruptly sat down again with a thump, suddenly not liking the conversation and where it was leading. *"Mike, we already discussed this last night and you know how I feel about the subject. You should have told William the answer is absolutely no, and that he needs to stay here for the summer and work at the theater."*

"As we already discussed, Nancy, he's 19 years old. *You realize that he doesn't have to ask our permission and can do what he wants?*"

"But he cares and doesn't want to hurt either you or I - so that is why he is asking," she reasoned.

"Yes, you are right… he does care, so let's show him some mutual respect and give him that same consideration back. We will discuss this when I get home, and *please* don't forget to order the extra croutons and salad dressing."

Chapter 4

Two babies were crying in unison as Sarah changed Abby on the large, hand-made changing table, and Alex sat in his crib looking on with large puddles of tears staining his cheeks as well as the soft blue-colored sheets he was cross-legged sitting on.

"Daddy's home!" Lance announced with a pleasant smile, still dressed in his work clothes, as he leaned in to kiss Sarah on the cheek before rescuing Alex from his *jail,* snuggling him in close to his side.

"Been quite the day," Sarah commented in frustration as she finished up with Abby. She was dressed in gray leggings with a matching t-shirt, and her hair was pulled up on top of her head with a few lost wispy strands finding their way in front of her face that she tried to blow away, but kept landing right back where they started.

"Babies keeping you up again with their teething?" he asked matter-of-factly, as he changed places with Sarah at the changing table, ready to do his routine parental duty of changing his son's poopy diaper.

"Yes, and it's keeping me from the latest project at work that my father wanted my advice on," she answered with impatience, holding and rocking Abby in the rocking chair close by, trying to soothe her pain as she hiccupped and sighed against her mother's chest as she nursed.

Lance turned, smiling down at his incredible wife who was now a mother. He felt she was even more beautiful without her makeup and put-together attire, that was so much a part of her past trademark look and what he first saw a few years back at The Dancing Seahorse, when he was first asked to list the property for the Miller's. He joined her on the other matching glider rocker that they had so cleverly decided was a good idea to have two, giving them both a chance to rock the twins at the same time.

"We could get a nanny if you want to return to work, Sarah?" he offered for the umpteen time, patting Alex on the back as he comforted him over his shoulder, knowing that he needed to wait patiently on his turn to nurse next.

"I'm fine," she replied firmly, switching twins with Lance and positioning Alex on her other, still-full breast that had not been emptied yet by Abby.

Sarah had nursed the twins since birth and had only recently added supplemental formula. She slowly was introducing fruits and vegetables that she cooked and strained, and never gave them the jarred variety.

Lance paused, looking out the window with its raised wooden shade, noticing the calm sea off in the distance and the sun still shining brightly overhead. *"Why don't we take a walk after dinner on the beach with the twins?"* he suggested, trying to change the subject to something more pleasant and lighten the mood.

Sarah rose with her half slumbering son, who snuggled lovingly against his mother's chest, placing him back in his crib for a short nap, ready go downstairs to the kitchen where she wanted to make a meatloaf. *"By the time I'm done cooking dinner it may be too late for a walk,"* she whispered, as Lance placed Abby in her own crib, positioned on the opposite side of the nursery.

Lance wrapped his arms around his retreating wife's waist, holding her tightly against his muscular chest, as they stood together in the hallway outside of the twins' room that now had the door shut. He gazed into her sky blue eyes that always held him in their grasp. "No cooking tonight, sweetie. I brought home Chinese."

Sarah was thrilled and relieved that she didn't have to cook after all. *"I hope you didn't get the spicy Szechuan chicken again. You know what that did to my breast milk the last time and how the twins were up all night,"* she playfully reminded, as they made their way down the steps into the spacious living room together.

Lance laughed, remembering the sleepless night for all of them. *"Oh, don't worry, I didn't forget!* I ordered only the mildest things on the menu."

They walked hand in hand down the steps and towards the kitchen, as Sarah put the thawed hamburger back into the refrigerator to be used the following day. Lance removed the trays of assorted Chinese food from the oversized, paper bag that held it all, arranging each tray on the granite countertop for Sarah's perusal.

Sarah poured Lance a glass of chilled Chardonnay and then filled one for her. She was careful not to over-indulge since she was still nursing, but enjoyed a glass of wine several times a week on the advice of her pediatrician *that it was okay after they reached the six-month mark.*

Lance grabbed a couple of large aqua-colored plates from one of the custom-made kitchen cabinets, placing them on the counter alongside of the food. He chose a sampling from all of the containers, sitting on a barstool instead of at the table that over-looked the beach close by.

Sarah joined him, only dishing out some of the Moo Goo Gai Pan, white rice and an egg roll, finishing up with a bowl of the egg drop soup that contained no spice. "How was work today?" she asked, as she slurped the tasty soup directly from the bowl.

"Just fine. Been busy with several showings with the beach season kicking into full gear now. I also interviewed someone new who will assist us during the busy summer months. He's a college student who just graduated and he wants an intern job for the season."

Sarah stopped, putting her half-eaten egg roll back down on her plate, remembering her conversation with William recently. *"Guess who else wants a summer job at the beach?"*

"No clue," Lance replied, finishing up his second helping of pork fried rice.

"William."

"Your mom won't allow that," he answered succinctly, downing and finishing his bowl of sweet and sour soup, not even giving what she was saying a second thought.

Sarah laughed, jumping down from the barstool, ready to clean up her plate. *"You know my mother well, don't you?"*

Lance joined her by the sink, handing her his empty plate, bowl and silverware, before filling up his wine glass another time. "She is protective and I get it - since we are parents now too."

Sarah paused, wiping her wet hands on a dishtowel that was hanging over one of the double oven doors close by. She then walked to the deck, sliding back the hurricane force patio doors with Lance in tow, as she sunk into a comfortable deck chair that held an overstuffed seat and back cushion, sipping from her remaining wine.

"She doesn't want anything bad to happen to him at the beach, you know..." she explained eerily, with the distant memory of her brother's death still looming somewhere deep in the recesses of her mind.

Lance patted the top of her hand, thankful she had forgiven him for Dex's death. He had tried to rescue Dex from the ocean many years earlier, but unfortunately he lingered and died one week later in the hospital, which Lance too could never forget. For Sarah, to get past that hurdle of blaming him was big for her, but they had worked through it.

"I think it is a great idea for William to come to the beach for the summer. It will teach him some responsibility beyond going to college."

Sarah put her wine glass down a little too firmly on the glass table that was between them, staring at Lance in disbelief. *"He wants to stay here with his friends from college. I told him that was an impossibility with the babies!"*

"You could have asked me how I felt about this first."

"Lance, for heaven's sakes, I am at my wit's end now with the twins as it is, and I certainly do not want to deal with the shenanigans of young college students and what they pull during their summer break when they are here at the beach. You know from being in the real estate business what they can do to destroy rental properties!" she stated defensively, as she rose from her seat and grabbed onto the deck railing for support. She glared down at Lance who was still relaxing, sipping from his wine and looking up at his wife unfazed with a smile plastered on his face.

"Why are you getting so upset? I never suggested he live here. I was going to offer though to help him find another place closer to the boardwalk and the action. Sarah, *let's be real here. No one in that age group wants to camp out with people our age, even putting the babies aside, for the summer."*

Sarah sat back down again, trying to regain her composure. "That was *exactly* what he asked when he called and I told him no, and then I suggested that he talk to mom and dad and see if they would allow him to stay with his friends at The Dancing Seahorse instead."

"Either one of those places isn't good for them or us. I will find him a rental designed for college students. He honestly waited too long to begin all this, but I still have a few leads that no one else knows about which should *seal the deal* for the summer for him."

"I'm surprised, Lance, that you are so casual about all this. What if he gets into some sort of trouble here?"

"Then we will be a good aunt and uncle and help him out," he smiled, as he glanced again into her alluring pale blue eyes that were filled only with worry at the moment. "Let's get moving before the sun sets. I'm going to change into some shorts and a tee and then get the twins ready. *Are you going to join me or continue to fret over this?*" he teased, leaning down to kiss her softly on the lips before grabbing her hand and helping her from the beach chair.

Sarah walked with Lance to the kitchen again, sliding the glass patio doors back in place before securely locking them. "I did speak with my dad earlier and I could tell he had mixed emotions about allowing Will to be here in Marlin Beach for the summer also… and convincing my mother is going to be another story."

Lance placed his wine glass along with Sarah's in the dishwasher, turning to look at her with his arms crossed. "William is a good kid. It's time for him to take the next step and be away from your parents for the summer. He deserves to experience Marlin Beach just as you and I did when we were growing up. I'm sure he will always remember the lifetime memories he will be making this summer."

"Until I hear back from my mom and dad, nothing is for certain at this point and William may be spending his summer in Baltimore," Sarah answered realistically, still not understanding her husband's point of view, and continuing to hold to her own.

Lance smiled, reaching his arms securely around his lovely wife's waist, planting a long, passionate tongue kiss on her awaiting mouth, leaving her breathless for more. "It's time to change into some shorts and take our walk with the twins before we bathe them. Then we are going to go to bed for some long overdue, intimate lovemaking. It's been way too long you know…" he beckoned flirtatiously, as the twins cried loudly from the second story nursery, demanding to be picked up from their cribs once again.

CHAPTER 5

"Hello?"

"Nan, it's William," he began in earnest, sitting on the side of his unmade, extra-long twin bed that most dorm rooms were outfitted with especially for the tall students.

Nancy gulped, catching her breath, knowing the intention of the call. "Well hello, William. Everything okay with your classes?" she asked, as she proceeded to the family room where Mike got the signal *to turn off the evening news*, as she plopped down next to him on the sectional.

"Classes are fine, Nan. I take my finals soon and I know I will pass."

"I hope you can do more than pass," she gently scolded. "You are capable of A's, so let's hope you are maintaining you average."

Mike looked at Nancy seeing her nervousness increasing as the call continued. He reached out to pat the top of her hand, trying to calm her anxiety and reassure her that everything was going to be all right.

"I'm doing just fine with my grade point average, Nan. No need to worry. I study and I feel ready for my upcoming tests," he replied with confidence, getting up to grab a cola out of his mini fridge. "I want to talk to you about something else though, Nan. I was hoping that G-Dad would have already spoken to you and called me back," Will said with a little hurt since Mike hadn't done so as he promised. "My friends are bugging me nonstop, so I figured I should call you and just get the answer straight from you. I want to go to Marlin Beach for the summer and work there once my finals are completed."

Nancy immediately switched her cellphone speaker on at that point, needing Mike to join in with the conversation. "William, it's G-Dad, I'm sorry I haven't gotten back to you yet, but I needed some time just to think about things. I'm sitting by Nan and you are on speaker. *It's better we have a family meeting about this."*

"That's perfectly fine, G-Dad," Will answered, running his free hand through his unkempt hair. "What do you guys think? I need an answer since my friends keep asking me if we are staying at The Dancing Seahorse or not."

Nancy glanced at Mike, firmly shaking her head back and forth *no*, not being willing to change her mind about him staying there.

"William, you are over 18 and we can't demand that you stay here with us for the summer, but we do have a say so about The Dancing Seahorse. I'm sorry, but if you truly want to go to the beach you will have to find another place to stay. And beyond that, I would definitely communicate with your friends that are planning to go there with you, that everyone will need to have a job in place first so that the rent can equally be paid by all."

Nancy stared at her husband who was now firmly holding her hand. "I'm sorry to disappoint you, William, but we would like the freedom to stay at The Dancing Seahorse alone this summer if we so well choose to go to Marlin Beach for a visit."

"I get that Nan, but you have plenty of room also at Aunt Sarah's."

Nancy shook her head in frustration, not happy with Will's resistance and persistence. "This is true, but I enjoy my own place and the subject is closed!"

Mike winked at her and nodded his silent approval, giving her his vote of support with a *thumbs up* signal.

"So I would say you have your answer now. Plan to go to the beach for the summer – if you would like - but get a place to live in and definitely find employment first. *Please* remember to pass that word along to your friends that they will need to get jobs lined up. Also, you will need a security deposit to hold the place that you rent. Do you have any money saved yet?"

"I have $1500 in the bank."

"Well that's excellent!" Mike complimented, not remembering that his grandson had saved so much. "Reach out to Lance. He may know of something that will be affordable for all of you to rent. He may also know of people that are hiring for the summer. Any ideas on what you think you would like to do for employment while you are there, William?"

Will tossed his smashed soda can in the recycling bin, pondering his grandfather's question. "Hmmm…. been trying to figure that out. Hopefully, something fun and during the day. I'm hoping my roommates and I will all be on the same day schedule and then we can go out in the evenings and hang out."

The speakerphone was still on as Nancy gave the questioning eye to Mike again. "Well, I hope that works out for all of you. Not always easy to find day jobs at the beach that pay enough to cover the rent for the summer. Typically, it involves making tips from waiting tables in the evenings."

"I thought about that, but I'm still hoping to find a job working days," he answered unrealistically, thinking he knew more than his grandparents, as he spread peanut butter and jelly on white bread and headed out the door with the quickly made sandwich in one hand, slinging his backpack over the shoulder with the other.

"When will you be coming home, William?"

"Within two weeks, Nan. I need to get organized and bring things home from my dorm, and then I will need to repack for the beach. If all goes as planned, I will have everything in place by then."

"I hope you will be home for a least a couple days before you leave for Marlin Beach, so that I can make you a special meal or two," she offered sadly, suddenly resigning herself to the fact that he was leaving.

"Of course, Nan, I will be home for a few days. Don't worry, I'm not moving to California," he grinned as he took the last bite of his sandwich. "I'm sure I'll be seeing you guys a lot this summer when you stay at The Dancing Seahorse, since you'll want to check up on me and make sure I'm okay."

Mike and Nancy mutually began to laugh, realizing their grandson knew them well. As the phone conversation continued about Marlin Beach and all his big plans, they realized that Will had fought hard for what he wanted and had gotten his way.

"We love you, William," Nancy yelled over the speaker of the phone, not wanting him to miss her loving words before he hung up.

"As do I," Mike joined in.

"Gotta get to class now, but I will be in touch soon. And thank you, guys. I know this summer is gonna be a blast!"

William hung up as Mike and Nancy sat in silence for several minutes on the sectional, with her head leaning into Mike's embrace, just considering what they had just done and allowed. "We may live to regret this," Nancy stated solemnly, breaking away and looking seriously into Mike's eyes.

"Or we may come to realize that we did something wonderful allowing our grandson to have the time of his life this summer."

"I hope you're right, Mike. I truly hope your are right."

William sat in the cafeteria after class, waiting on his three roommates that he also considered to be his best friends, who planned to join him at the beach. Chris, Matt and Tyler were typical college students who partied first and considered classes and studying secondary, even with their parents' constant threats of removing them from the university if things didn't improve. William did seem to take things more seriously than his friends, still considering it to be a wonderful gift that he was living with his grandparents and able to go to Towson without having to pay for it. It greatly helped that he was a quick learner and retained knowledge easily, even attempting to tutor the others in his quad from time to time.

Christopher and Matthew were actually from the Baltimore area, but William had not know them prior to attending Towson, since they had went to a different high school from him. Tyler was from Fort Lauderdale, Florida and came north for college hoping to experience snow and skiing for the very first time in his life.

Unfortunately, the year had been unseasonably warm and there was barely a dusting of natural snow. They did attempt to go to a ski resort in the Western Maryland Mountains one Sunday in January, but the conditions were very icy and not favorable for beginner skiers who were just leaning. After the group ended up with wet ski clothes, from one too many falls, and Tyler experienced the pain of a sprained knee from the ski not popping off properly, it was mutually decided that it was time to pack it up and go back to Towson. Tyler had no desire after that to go skiing again after hobbling around on crutches for awhile.

They had grown close in the past year as roommates, hanging out after class and going to sporting events held at the university along with dorm parties that they would either attend or throw. One too many hangovers, and a girl or two in their room that had spent the night, was a year of transition and growth in areas that none of their parents had allowed or knew about up until that point when they were in high school.

William accepted his roommates' sorted behavior and even participated to some level when they threw their own wild parties, but he felt mildly aggravated all the same when the alcohol brought out violent traits in those present which reminded him of his stepfather Mitchell and what was done to him and his mother Claire in the past. He did not talk about his past life in Birmingham to any of them. Life for William started in Baltimore, as far as his friends were concerned. He had decided from the very start of them becoming college roommates, that there was no need to dig into that bad time of his life and what he had experienced with a drunken stepfather.

The three friends entered the busy bustling cafeteria that was filled with college students trying to catch a hurried meal before their next class, waving at William who was sitting off in the distance at a table not surrounded by others.

"Hey bud, why are you sitting over here in this lonely corner?" Matt teased, as the group joined him at the table, slinging their book bags off their shoulders and onto the floor.

William looked happily at his buddies, beaming from ear to ear, not paying any mind to Matt. "Cuz I wanted a quiet place to talk to you guys about the details of our upcoming few months that we will be spending in Marlin Beach for the summer!"

"What? Your grandparents agreed to let us stay at their beach house?" Chris asked excitedly.

The others sat in primed anticipation, waiting for the answer.

William paused to look at the group, hoping he could have

answered differently. "No, we can't stay at their beach house, but the good news is my grandparents are cool with me going to the beach now. All I got to do is reach out to my uncle Lance and I'm sure he can find us a place to stay at, since he is a realtor in Marlin Beach."

"Great!" they answered mutually, reaching over the table to *high-five* William.

The initial plans were set in motion and discussed over burgers and fries. William was to call Lance and talk to him about any potential rentals and maybe he would even suggest a job or two - if they were lucky. If all went as planned, Lance would be helping them out on both fronts, and William and his college roommates would be living and working in Marlin Beach very soon.

CHAPTER 6

Snyder's Beach Dreams Real Estate was a flurry of morning activity. Alison Snyder walked into her son Lance's office with a stack of file folders piled high in her arms. She placed them on the center of his desk as Lance looked up from his computer from the new listing he was adding to his already extensive list of other properties.

"Well good morning to you, mother," he greeted pleasantly, looking at the mountain of obvious work she had unloaded from her desk to his. *"Is this all of it?"* he asked with a smile, trying to be polite and knowing she rarely asked very much of him when it came to her work.

Alison sat down on the chair opposite his desk, crossing her leg over the other shapely one, sighing and catching her breath. "I'm sorry, Lance that I'm giving you so much to deal with along with your other responsibilities, but your father is insisting upon this Caribbean Cruise as you know."

Lance began to chuckle, rising to make his mother a cup of coffee from his Keurig. "Here you go, mother," he said with a pleasant grin that always melted her heart with his kind ways and handsome good looks. "Dad loves to sweep you off to some tropical island every year before the summer season takes off. Consider it a good thing that you can relax and not have to worry about Beach Dreams for ten days."

"I absolutely do appreciate the time," she replied, taking a sip from her tasty hazelnut blend that was always her favorite. "It's just that I hate to leave things and get out of the loop. You know your mother, Lance. I confess – I'm a workaholic!"

"No way," he winked, joining her now with his own cup of hot coffee, standing by the window that overlooked Old Bay Café across the street. "Dad worries about his health, as we both are aware. So take the time to relax because the busy summer season will be waiting on your once you get back."

"Lance, your father will probably out live all of us," she teased with a wink, setting her empty cup in the small sink near by.

"Probably so," he laughed. "I got a few things that are a priority this morning, and then I will look over the files and meet back up with you with any questions that I might have before the day is up. What time are you planning to leave?"

"I'm here until five," she answered simply, clicking her heels as she walked towards the hallway. "And then it's off to Old Bay Café for a quick dinner with your father before I pack."

Lance was busy and already focused on his computer and the task at hand. "I'll catch up later in the afternoon... " He waved.

"Sounds good," she replied from the doorframe, happy knowing that she could go away and Lance was in charge.

The ringing cellphone interrupted Lance's thoughts as he stopped to reach for it, realizing it was William trying to call. "Well hello, Will."

"Sorry, uncle Lance that I haven't called you lately. I've just been very busy with my classes and now I'm studying for finals."

"Hey, no worries. I was in college once too and I remember that time well," Lance replied, breaking away from his desk again and walking towards the window so that he could focus on the conversation. "So what's up?"

"I wanted to tell you what I plan to do this summer."

"Okay... Sure."

"I want to come to Marlin Beach and work until school starts again in the fall, and my three college roommates want to join me too."

Lance ran his free hand through his curly brown locks, already knowing the back-story from Sarah, but wanting Will to tell him anyway. *"Does G-Dad and Nan know of your plans?"*

"Oh yeah, they know..." Will confessed, laying on his bed and staring up at the ceiling. "I think G-Dad is okay with it, but not so sure about Nan."

Lance began to laugh, knowing how his mother-in-law was natured with her worrywart ways. "Doesn't surprise me any about Nancy."

"In case you hadn't heard, Sarah also knows about this. I did ask her if we could stay at your place, but she said that it wasn't a good idea with the twins."

"I'm sorry, Will, but I do understand where she is coming from. The twins are a handful right now and no one would be getting any rest if they heard you guys coming in late at night. Trust me, it's better if you get your own place."

"Yeah, I figured as much, but I was trying to save some money with the rent. I did ask G-Dad and Nan about staying at The Dancing Seahorse, but they shut me down on the option real fast. Nan thinks she'll be staying there a lot this summer, and I guess G-Dad will be joining her when he isn't working."

"Can't blame them for that. It's a great place and I'm sure they'd like to be around to see you but also Alex and Abby, and try to get in on all that Marlin Beach has to offer during the warm summer months."

"It's fine. I totally understand, but that still leaves me with the problem of finding another place, especially since we didn't arrange for a rental several months ago like all the other college students did. So that is why I am calling you. I was hoping you knew of something."

Lance returned to his desk, trying to think of any available properties that were unrented for the entire season. Typically, the rental properties that he knew of were for weekly rentals only and unfortunately did not rent to one tenant for the entire summer, since there was more profit in renting by the week. He also knew that his clients steered away from college students because they wanted to party and were known for destroying places - leaving dirty carpets and walls, broken toilets in bathrooms, and unworkable garbage disposals and dishwashers in kitchens after they departed. Unfortunately for the students, the security deposit was rarely refunded.

"I just looked at my available listings and I'm sorry that I have to tell you this, but I don't have anything at all right now."

William sighed, not wanting to hear the bad news that could end his summer hopes and dreams. "Wow, uncle Lance... I really didn't expect this."

"Yeah, I know, bro. My clients just do weekly rentals for the most part for families." Lance paced again to the window, lost in his thoughts as William rambled on about why he wanted a summer in Marlin Beach with his friends. He remembered his time lifeguarding at the beach and having a place to stay with the guards even though his parents lived there in Marlin Beach. *If only I could think of something...* he pondered as William droned on. *He needs a place big enough for him and his roommates and preferably on the beach.*

And then it came to him... The beach house that he and his parents owned and didn't typically rent out. It was actually the first home that he grew up in, before they built another place in Marlin Beach once he was in high school.

"You still there, uncle Lance?"

"Oh yeah, William. Sorry... I've been thinking about the situation and trying to come up with a solution, and I just may have!"

"No way!" Will answered in surprise, sitting straight up now in his bed, and waiting on the answer.

"Well, I can't promise you a 100% at this point, but I will talk to my folks today about all this. What I have in mind is a beach house my parents and I own here together. Actually, it's my childhood home when I was a youngster growing up in Marlin Beach."

Will walked out to the kitchen and grabbed a soda from the refrigerator, pulling back on the pop-top and taking a few fast swigs. "I never knew that you had another place?"

Lance smiled, reminiscing over the early days of his youth, playing on the beach and learning how to surf in the ocean out front of his family's beach house with his friends who lived or vacationed there. For the Snyder family, their beach house was a permanent residence, unlike the many others who would come and go as tourists, renting places for a week or more during the summer season. The house was fondly named The Happy Crab and truly Lance could attest to the happiness he felt from living there when he was young.

"Yes, it is in the family and rarely used. So let me get back to you in a few hours and hopefully you will at least have your lodging taken care of. What about jobs? Do you guys have that part covered yet?"

Will walked outside with his soda and a bag of chips, taking in the pleasant, spring May air and the bright sunshine that was beaming down on his face. "Not really... I know we sound totally unorganized. My one buddy has an uncle who works at The Dexter and he said we can all get jobs there being servers or doing valet parking if we would like."

"Well that's great! I got pull there too if you need it, and so does your aunt Sarah. If that is where you and your friends decide to work, I am sure that can be arranged according to what you are saying. But let me throw something else out to you, William. I need someone else to help me here for the summer at Beach Dreams, beyond who I just employed. I can't hire your friends, but I would be happy to hook you up with a job, if you don't mind hanging out with your uncle Lance."

William's eyes lit up, realizing how much Lance was doing for him. "I would love to work at Beach Dreams! You can teach me everything you know!"

"Whoa... I'm not sure I can pull that off in one summer," Lance laughed. "I would expect you to be in here early and work all day, but the good news is your evenings will be free for the most part. Can you handle that?"

"Yes, I can handle that!" Will insisted.

"I will teach you how to do listings and deal with rentals, and then there is the occasional time something comes up after hours. Are you up for that?"

"Anything you ask of me, uncle Lance, I will gladly do. I can' t thank you enough for all of this."

"Well let's not get ahead of ourselves just yet. Let me get an answer first from my folks about The Happy Crab, and then I will get back to you and we will talk about all the other details."

CHAPTER 7

It was four o'clock and Lance made his way to his mother's office, with a list of questions in hand about the files she had given him. Alison looked up from her desk with her readers perched way too low on the bridge of her nose.

"Do you have a minute?"

"Two for you," she rhymed, knowing in one hour her vacation was officially beginning and she could finally get some much needed R&R with her husband.

Lance laughed. "I can see you are ready to get out of here."

"I couldn't agree more, now that I have everything in order."

"Well, I only have a few questions."

"Let's hope the phone doesn't ring," she answered realistically, knowing that it was nearly impossible with the endless amount of inquiries they received this time of the year for rentals. "Hold your thought for one minute…. Patti, please hold all my calls. I'm in a meeting with Lance for the next few minutes."

"Sure, Mrs. Snyder," Patti the receptionist answered, as she continued to file her nails and look at a YouTube video of some crazy cat antics and their owners who were entertained by them.

Lance sat on the other side of Alison's desk ready to begin. "The Davis file - concerning the settlement time for their condo – I feel it's in conflict with the Wilson's in my opinion. I think we need to add an hour more between their closings just in case something unforeseen comes up."

"Noted." Alison concurred, making a notation in her planner.

"I will make the necessary calls and take care of this."

"Thank you, Lance, that would be great if I can cross one more thing off my list before I leave. *Anything else?*"

"No, that's about it, but I do have something of a personal nature that I wanted to discuss with you."

"Nothing serious, I hope?" Alison asked with concern, knowing the past hadn't always been kind to Lance and Sarah.

"Everything is fine at home, mother," he reassured. "It's about something else though. Do you remember William? Sarah's nephew?"

"Well of course, Lance! I'm not that forgetful yet," she teased, waiting for him to continue. "We had dinner with him at Old Bay Cafe and he's been at your house, correct?"

"Yes, mother. That is correct. William called me today asking if I could recommend a rental for him and his college roommates. He wants to come to Marlin Beach for the summer and work. I honestly couldn't think of any place or anyone who could help him out at this late date, and then it dawned on me that I did know a place."

"Oh? And what place would that be?"

"The Happy Crab!"

Alison stood, immediately straightening her light blue suit, making sure she heard him correctly. *"The Happy Crab?* I'm not sure your father would approve of that, sweetheart."

"Mother, how often is the beach house ever used?"

She nodded in agreement. "You are correct, we rarely use it, but occasionally we have provided it as a courtesy to someone who has a scheduling issue or may be here from a far distance and is interested in buying one of our properties."

"I know the deal with the place and I'm not trying to strong-arm you, but I do own The Happy Crab too and I would like to do William a favor if possible. It would mean a lot to him and too me also for that matter."

Alison studied her son, knowing he rarely rallied for something such as this or bucked up against her or John. *"How can I say no to you, Lance?"* she questioned with sincere motherly love, having a hard time refusing her only child that she adored.

"Should we discuss this first with dad?"

"No need," she replied, rising again to gather the last remaining things from her desk along with her laptop, placing it all in her briefcase with a bit of anxiety about leaving. "Your dad is only thinking about taking a vacation right now, and the more I think about it, he would want me to make the final decision about The Happy Crab anyway. You know he rarely gets involved in too much decision making anymore, Lance. That is, except for playing golf."

"Yes, I know mother. He would rather be swinging a golf club seven days a week than to make a major decision of any kind," he laughed, wrapping a free arm around his mother's shoulder and giving her a warm kiss goodbye. "Use your sunscreen and don't let dad drink too much," he playfully admonished, as he walked her towards the reception area.

"I'm leaving now, Patti. Please turn all my calls and correspondence over to Lance, along with any other pressing issues that need to be dealt with, until I return from my cruise."

"I sure will," she replied sarcastically, looking at Lance with a raised eyebrow.

Lance walked his mother to her parked BMW, bidding her a final farewell. "Enjoy the cruise. I know it's a *dad-thing,* but I still think you enjoy the whole thing even if you don't want to admit it."

"You know your mother well, don't you? Yes, I enjoy all the activities of the cruise ship, but mostly I enjoy my time alone with your father," she confessed, hugging Lance one last time, ready to leave.

"Good to hear. Now get going and have a good time!"

Lance returned to his office remembering William was expecting a call back. Even though he and his folks didn't really need the rent money for the Happy Crab, he knew that some sort of arrangement needed to be formulated and signed off on by Will and his friends, with the rental amount and rules clearly outlined.

"Let me see…." Lance contemplated as he chewed on the end of a pen, gathering the standard rent agreement from the printer and stapling several copies of it together. He reviewed all the edits, which included the rent amount of $1000.00 monthly, allowing a two-week grace period until it was due, with no security deposit. There was also a provision made eliminating standard housekeeping fees if they wanted to clean the place themselves, but if they didn't keep up with the weekly cleaning, a cleaning crew would then be brought in and they would be charged retrospectively at the going rate per hour for cleaning. Lance felt that what he had drafted was more than fair, and that no other landlord in Marlin Beach would be so generous.

He considered talking to Sarah first about the rental agreement, but he knew she would take a more conservative approach, suggesting he charge them far more than what he was proposing. She was not a fan of William's plan anyway, so he would keep the details to himself until everything was agreed upon and finalized.

Lance dialed the number that he had saved in his family contact list, with a response coming in immediately on the first ring.

"Hello?"

"Hey, Will, just getting back to you about The Happy Crab," he mentioned pleasantly, knowing this was a big moment for his nephew.

"Yes?" William replied, sitting on the edge of his seat.

"I did speak with my mother and I got her approval for you and your friends to stay at The Happy Crab this summer."

"Yesss!" Will yelled out victoriously, with a *fist pump* to the ceiling of his dorm room. "Thank you so much, uncle Lance!"

"You're welcome, William. But lets talk about a few things for a moment before we get ahead of ourselves," he replied sternly, trying to be the adult and reign him in somewhat even though it was tough to do so. "There will be a $1000.00 rent fee on a monthly basis. That is a bargain if you have checked elsewhere. I will not be charging you for utilities or cleaning, but you must understand that if the place starts looking shabby I will charge you a cleaning fee dating back to the beginning of our agreement based on current local rates."

William scratched his unruly brown locks, trying to digest what he was saying. "I know that the price is a bargain since most landlords want $2000 or higher, but the whole cleaning thing never crossed my mind."

Lance laughed, shaking his head in disbelief. *"It's not gonna clean itself, William.* You have three roommates. Between the four of you this shouldn't be a problem - if you keep up with things on a daily basis."

"Geesh, I'm not sure my roommates are gonna want to run a vacuum everyday."

"William, you misunderstood me. Daily chores involve washing up the dishes in the kitchen sink and taking out the trash. Also, keeping your laundry picked up in each of your rooms. On a weekly basis that would involve the actual cleaning of the beach house and that does include vacuuming, washing floors and scrubbing down the bathrooms. I will ask you one more time - *Does that sound like something you can handle?*"

"I guess so…. Haven't done much of this sort of thing since living with Nan and G-Dad. If Nan doesn't do it, the maid who comes in once a week does."

Lance began to laugh again, realizing Mike and Nancy had really pampered and spoiled William in the last three years. "It will be fine. I have all the confidence to believe that you and your buddies can figure this out and handle it. I'm giving you two weeks to come up with the $1000.00. Honestly, that shouldn't be too difficult if you all start working right away."

William sat quietly listening to Lance's words. He felt somewhat overwhelmed and even considered backing out, fearing his friends wouldn't live up to their end of the bargain and he would be doing all the housework himself. But the allure of Marlin Beach and what the summer could hold brought him back to his senses. "I think it all sounds great! I will talk to my friends just to confirm everything, but I think you got four new tenants!"

"I'll be waiting to hear back," Lance replied, hanging up and crossing his suntanned arms on the desk in front of him, pondering what he had just gotten himself into. *"God I hope this doesn't blow up in face…."* He admitted out loud with a sigh, as he grabbed another cup of coffee and then went back to work, putting in another new listing that had just come through for Beach Dreams.

CHAPTER 8

William picked up some fast food, knowing he needed to get back to studying since he had a final later on that evening in calculus. The next morning he would take his English exam and then it was time to pack and drive home for a few days, before heading to the beach.

His cheeseburger dangled from his mouth as he opened the dorm room door, hearing loud music on the other side. *"Hey, can you please turn that down!"* he yelled, as he threw the bag of food on the table, and his backpack on the floor by the kitchen table.

Chris got up to oblige him, joining him at the table afterwards. *"What's eating you? You seem tense."*

Will smiled, trying to relax. "Nah, its just that I got a lot on my mind with my finals. My grandparents will have a *conniption fit* if I don't do well on these final test scores for the semester."

"I hear ya," Chris admitted, taking a swig from a soda. "I have three more and then I'm done. I think my phys ed went well today."

"You can't count that as a real class!" Will teased.

"It's paid for, so it counts!"

"If you say so," Will laughed, squinting his brow in a questioning way.

"Any word yet on the place at the beach?" Chris asked, hoping for a good update.

"Oh, yeah... sorry I've been busy with studying and forgot to tell you. We did get the place that my uncle Lance owns, as long as we agree to the conditions."

"Conditions?"

"The rent amount and keeping the place clean."

"Isn't he rich or something? Tell him to hire a maid for us."

Will slammed his hands on the table. *"I don't think so!"*

"Aww... chill, bro. I was just teasing," Chris answered sheepishly, giving Will's shoulder a steadying pinch.

"Sorry, Chris. I just don't need my family on my back about us not keeping up with the cleaning of the place or other things."

"Not sure anyone at our age keeps up with a place at the beach. Isn't that asking a lot if we are paying him rent?" Chris rationalized, squishing his soda can flat and aiming it high in the air towards the trash can, where it missed and lay on the floor instead.

William stared at the metal drink can now lying on the kitchen floor that was oozing out a small puddle of the sugary syrup from the drink opening. "That is exactly what Lance is trying to avoid if he rents us the place."

"What do you mean? My soda can?"

"Yeah, Chris, that sticky, leaking soda can lying there on the floor!" he pointed. "The beach house has never been rented out to guys our age *ever,* and is typically only used by their friends and business

associates. He is really going out on a limb here to trust us that nothing crazy will happen. *Can you understand that?"*

"I guess so…. I know my parents would never allow us to stay at their place - if they actually owned a beach house. So what about the rent?"

"$1000 per month."

"Per guy?"

"No dumbass. In total."

Chris laughed. "It's an honest question. Well I must admit your uncle is being more than generous with us about the price for rent, knowing what I have researched about rental prices in Marlin Beach. *What's the catch?"*

"No catch. He just wants us to keep up with his place, so we will need to do some straightening and cleaning every week. I think that is more than fair."

Chris returned to the couch, turning on the TV. "Is this house big enough for all four of us?"

"Four bedrooms and two baths. So we'll all have our own room, but the bathrooms will have to be shared. And it's on the beach."

He grabbed the half eaten bag of barbeque chips off of the dirty, water stained cocktail table in front of him, stuffing a big handful of greasy potato chips in his mouth. "I gotta clean my room at home. I guess I can handle it."

William laughed. "Wouldn't know it from all the crumbs that just came out of your mouth and are now laying on the couch."

Chris brushed them aside onto the floor, sitting up straight with his arm thrown over the back of the sofa, looking at Will who was still busily studying on his laptop at the kitchen table. "I'm fine with the arrangement, but you gotta convince Matt and Tyler too."

"There is no *convincing* anyone," William answered matter-of-factly. "If they don't like the deal than we will find someone else who does. I need a nap before I take my test. We can talk later," he called over his shoulder, as he closed the door to his bedroom with his computer in hand, climbing in his bed beneath the covers, drifting off to sleep to thoughts of sand and surf in the near distant future.

Will awoke to the blaring of his cellphone alarm - 5:30 p.m. and only thirty minutes to spare until his class began. He grabbed a quick shower, trying to shake the cobwebs from his mind, knowing he needed to focus on the difficult calculus final he was ready to take, being warned by others, who had already taken it, that it was a challenge to get through. He slipped on his jeans that he had worn earlier in the day, choosing a clean Towson t-shirt that he allowed to hang loose. All three of his roommates were now hanging out in the living watching a funny sitcom that they had seen the reruns of many times before. He grabbed his backpack off the floor and found an unopened, full bottle of water in the refrigerator that rarely existed.

"Good luck!" Tyler yelled.

"Yeah, I need it," he grumbled back sleepily, as he made his way quickly out of the dormitory to the outside world of the campus, mingling in with the other students in a steady stream on the sidewalk who were also heading to their classrooms to take their finals.

William slid into his seat, looking at his cellphone one last time before turning it off and putting it away, having ten minutes to spare. *G-dad tried to call...* he realized, as he waited on his professor to enter the room and begin speaking. *Must want to know when I'm on my way home...* he pondered, as professor Lessinger began to address the class.

"You have one hour to complete the exam. Your actual calculator is permitted, but no calculations on your cellphone are allowed, which as you know has always been the rule of this classroom. As soon as you complete the exam, log out of your computer and you are free to leave. Your results will be sent to you through email within the week. Talking is not permitted," he reminded unnecessarily, since all present knew the consequences of doing so.

William logged into his computer, finding the problems to be challenging but fairly easy to compute and resolve. He felt a sense of ease after several questions were answered, knowing that he was prepared and that the studying had actually paid off. He jumped slightly as the first student rose to depart from the classroom, hoping it would have been him instead. Several more followed, and then finally he completed the last, *grand finale,* complicated problem. He breathed a sigh of relief as he turned off his computer and rose quietly - ready to exit the room. He smiled slightly and nodded a goodbye to professor Lessinger, happy it was his last time in his classroom. The nerdy, thirty-something, stereotypical math professor, with his tortoise shell brown glasses, nodded back at Will, before returning his attention to the remaining students who were struggling to complete the final exam.

William exited the math building, restarting his cellphone as he walked back towards his dorm. "G-dad, it William," he beamed happily. "I just completed my calculus exam."

"Great to hear!" Mike praised. "I'm sure you did well on it."

"I actually think I did," Will replied in earnest. "I didn't know what to expect, since a few others that I know who took his class in the past said the final was a killer, but I actually didn't find it to be so."

Mike reacted proudly. "That doesn't surprise me any, son. You are a Miller, after all."

"Yes, I am, G-Dad. Maybe one day I will be an architect too and work with you and aunt Sarah at Miller's Architecture."

"I wouldn't say no if you come to that conclusion."

"Ask me again in a few years after I take more math classes," he chuckled, feeling a sense of relief that the exam was finally over.

"Well, I wanted to check in with you, but of course Nan and I are anxious to see you. Any idea when you are leaving to come home?"

"The plan is for tomorrow. I gotta get out of my dorm in a few days anyway, but my last final is in the morning, and then I will pack up my things and be on my way."

"Nan will make you dinner."

"Tell her not to go to any trouble."

"That is impossible, William. You know your grandmother."

"Oh yes, I do," he replied, knowing she was always driven to do whatever she put her mind to, and there was no changing it. "I talked to Lance and he found us a place in Marlin Beach."

Mike looked through the sliding glass doors, seeing Nancy busily cleaning up the kitchen, as he sat at the patio table by the pool sipping on his Tanqueray, tonic and lime. *"Okay.... Didn't expect that so soon."*

"Me neither, but uncle Lance knows how to remarkably make things happen rather quickly. We are actually staying at his family beach house called - The Happy Crab."

"The Happy Crab, you say? I'm surprised John and Alison would agree to that. They have always been very selective with whom they allow to stay there. I don't think they even rent it out to the general public - if I remember correctly."

"He didn't act like it would be a problem to stay there. He even offered me a job at Beach Dreams working with him for the summer," he announced proudly.

Mike took another swig from his drink, realizing Nancy was losing this war of keeping William at home for the summer. "Well, it sounds like you have all the loose ends wrapped up. Do your friends have their jobs lined up?"

"They have a contact at The Dexter who has promised them jobs. I will remind them that they need to make sure this is definitely taken care of before we go to the beach."

"And the rent amount?"

"Only a thousand a month, and Lance is giving us two weeks to get the first rent check to him, and we don't have to come up with a security deposit either!"

Mike sat quietly pondering his words. It was obvious that Lance was bending over backwards to help William and his friends make their summer dream of staying and working in Marlin Beach a reality. "Well, that is great news, William!"

"G-dad?"

"Yes, Will?"

"You and Nan are always welcome, you know. You can always come to Marlin Beach for a visit and then we can meet up for dinner or hang out at the beach, when I have spare time."

"That sounds great," Mike answered sincerely, realizing his grandson - who was more like a son to him - was finally growing up and becoming a man.

CHAPTER 9

Will placed the last of the plastic totes in the trunk of his Jeep before slamming it shut. One more piss break and he would be on his way to the suburbs of Baltimore for a couple days.

"You back?" Tyler asked, packing up his own belongings, ready to put them in storage on campus since he was going to the beach instead of home to Fort Lauderdale for the summer.

"Just gotta pee before I hit the road."

"Hey, while you are still here, Chris just got off the phone with his uncle - Mr. McHenry - who works at The Dexter in Marlin Beach. He definitely has our jobs lined up. I'm probably going to be waiting tables along with Chris, and Matt is going to valet park cars. He said we could switch it up if we change our minds, but for now that is where they want us to start."

"Great! We all got our jobs figured out, so there's no stopping us now from going to the beach!" He reached out his hand and *high-fived* Tyler in the air, smiling broadly with the good news.

"He said that we should show up for an interview at The Dexter as soon as we get into town, since they need the help right away."

"Well, it sounds like it's a done deal then. Hey, I gotta run, dude. My grandparents are home and waiting on me. I will see you soon. Do you need a ride to the beach?" he asked as an afterthought, turning back before walking out the door.

"Nah, gonna catch a ride with Matt. Wish I had my own car here from Florida, but next year will be different," he grinned. "My parents said that since I made it a whole year with good grades they would allow me to have it back again. They plan to ship it up on the auto train once we go back to Towson in the fall."

"You southern boys. Always some complication to go to college up here," he teased, as he waved a pleasant goodbye to his friend and roommate who he would see again in a few days.

Will drove the twenty minutes from Towson, Maryland to Baltimore. As close as the cities were to each other he could have realistically commuted to class, but he wanted to experience campus life fully by staying in a dorm room and eating cafeteria food. He regularly thought of his departed father, and wondered if the very steps that he walked to his classes everyday would have been the same path Dexter would have taken. For William, attending Towson was like a pilgrimage. His only desire was to honor the memory of his father who had never gotten the chance to attend there.

Moving to Baltimore and living with his grandparents after his mother's death several years earlier, made his dad more real to him with the stories and photographs scattered throughout the house, along with sleeping in his room in the home in Baltimore as well as at The Dancing Seahorse. Sometimes, William thought he could hear Dexter whisper, especially in his sleep. The thought was always present in the back of his mind *to be disciplined and strong, and always do his best.*

He pulled into the driveway of the brick colonial with its well-groomed yard and gardens, situated in the affluent neighborhood of

Highland Estates. Mike's SUV was already in the driveway and Nancy's was nowhere to be found. He guessed it was tucked away safely in the spotless garage that was vacuumed on a weekly basis just like the rest of the house.

"Hello?" William yelled from the front door, peaking in his head with his arms full, carrying one of the plastic totes that was filled to over-flowing with a week's worth of dirty laundry.

"Coming," Mike answered with a happy smile and a mouth full of guacamole and chips. "Do you need some help?"

"My jeep is full so anything you can grab would be great!" he replied, unloading the plastic tub right inside the door of the spacious marble-floored foyer.

"Let's take care of this and get things organized before Nan notices the mess," Mike joked with an arm wrapped around William's neck.

Will laughed. "Nan needs to seriously relax."

"Absolutely! But not in this lifetime," Mike replied, shaking his head and knowing how his wife was natured, but loving her all the same for her other fine attributes.

Will placed a tote in his grandfather's arms and then grabbed one for him. Several trips later and the Jeep was totally unloaded, but now the foyer was full with an overflow of his stuff. They stood side by side with their hands on their hips, assessing the mess and what to do with it all.

"You're *finally* home, William," Nancy greeted, running over to wrap both arms securely around Will's waist before planting a big kiss on his cheek.

"Sorry about the mess, Nan. G-Dad and I are trying to figure out what to do with it all. Some of it I will definitely need for the beach, but the rest I won't need until the fall. And that big container over there is filled with my dirty laundry," he pointed, feeling somewhat guilty that he hadn't washed his clothes at school.

"Then put those items in the garage over by the wall and take the laundry to the laundry room," she barked out, much like a military drill sergeant.

"I didn't think you would want me junking up the garage."

Nancy looked at Mike, knowing what he was probably thinking as he grinned at her, waiting for her typical, over-reactive response. "It's really no problem, William," she replied sweetly, surprising them both. "Better in the garage than going up and down the steps to your room a million times, trying to find a place for everything there. This way in the fall, your totes will be ready to go and you can load them right back into your Jeep."

"Good idea, Nan," William praised, knowing he had already thought that one out for himself. "What's for dinner? I'm starving."

"We are having a Mexican feast! Meet me in the kitchen for nachos once you start a load of laundry," she added, walking away and back to her cooking.

Mike laughed. "Well I can see she wants that laundry done now. Not trying to hurt your feelings, but the foyer is starting to smell."

William joined in with his grandfather's laughter as they carried the overflowing tote to the laundry room. "Sorry G-Dad. It's been a week since I did my laundry. Studying and my exams took first priority."

"I get it, but Nan never will."

Will sorted the whites from the darks and dumped in a generous portion of blue liquid laundry detergent, before slamming the lid shut as the water filled up the washer. "You know I never sort out my clothes when I do my laundry at Towson. Thank God for color-fast detergent or I guess all my clothes would be pink and gray by now," he admitted, making small talk as his grandfather looked on.

"Well thank you for doing so here. We need to make Nan feel she has trained you well."

"Of course, G-Dad, I would never tell her any different," he whispered on the way to the kitchen with his grandfather.

"Did you start your laundry yet?"

"Absolutely, Nan. Wouldn't want you upset with me," he teased.

"I could never be upset with you, William," she answered lovingly, placing the large nacho platter that was piled high with all sorts of toppings, right on the counter in front of him. He greedily dug in with Nancy and Mike's help, feeling like he hadn't eaten in days.

"You outdid yourself, Nan. I don't think I can eat anything else," Will groaned, holding his stomach from consuming half of the chicken nachos.

"There is more food," she announced, as she went to the oven and removed a casserole of beef and cheese enchiladas and another with stuffed chili rellenos.

"You feeding an army, Nancy?" Mike asked, as the additional Mexican dishes were placed on the countertop along with what remained of the nachos.

"Of course not, Mike, but it is William's homecoming dinner after working so hard this year at Towson. If you can't eat anymore right now than maybe you will be hungry again later, and of course there's always leftovers for tomorrow."

"It won't go to waste, Nan," Will grinned. "But right now I think I will take a little nap and then maybe go for a swim, if that's okay?"

"Of course, sweetie. You must be exhausted from studying and taking your exams these last couple of days."

"Yeah, I am. Can I help you with the dishes before I go upstairs?"

"No, G-Dad and I can clean up, but I would like you to place your laundry in the dryer if you are up to it. I did hear the *beep* that the washer cycle was completed."

"Sure, Nan. And I'll go a step further and start my whites, *since I took the time to separate them,*" he teased, giving her a hug and kiss before leaving his grandparents to stare after him.

"It's sure good to have him home, even if only for a few days..."

"We'll see him a lot this summer, Nancy. He already told me that he hopes we will come to the beach and meet up with him. So don't worry, he's still your wonderful and loyal grandson - who wants to hang out with you."

Nancy brightened, happy to hear the good news. "I would like that. There isn't any reason I can't pack my bags and stay at The Dancing Seahorse all summer long and keep tabs on William."

"Now let's not go that far," Mike answered with some concern, wrapping his arms around Nancy and planting a soft kiss on her lips that tasted of a salty lime Margarita. "You know I would miss you not being here with me. Let's just plan on some long lazy weekends at the beach house. I can take off of work, since I have ample coverage right now with projects. We can see Sarah and the family and maybe I can play some golf with John Snyder too. Then we can meet up later for dinner with whoever wants to join us at Old Bay Café or have a picnic at the beach house."

"Sounds wonderful!" she gushed.

"After that we can have some alone time much later in the evening, enjoying the deck while we look at the moon and the star constellations over the ocean."

"Are you flirting with me, Mr. Miller?"

"Is there any doubt?" he teased, as he nuzzled her neck, making Nancy giggle with delight. She suddenly was looking very forward to her summer at Marlin Beach - just as much as William was.

CHAPTER 10

Sarah pushed the double stroller into the foyer of Beach Dreams, struggling to get it through the door without any help from Patti. *"Please let Lance know I am here,"* she requested, feeling exhausted as she tried to smooth her hair back into her high ponytail and regain her composure, as the twins took in the bright colors of the room that were catching their attention.

Rarely, did she show up there, but Sarah had just taken the babies for their 9-month checkup and now she wanted to surprise Lance with a visit, after just speaking with him.

"Sarah!" he greeted, being pleased that she and the twins were there, giving her a quick kiss to the cheek. Alex and Abby bopped up and down in the stroller at seeing their daddy. "I didn't expect you."

"I know…" she teased, "but I was in the area and I thought… what the heck. You know I don't get out much these days."

"Yes, darling, I realize this," he answered tenderly, as he led Sarah and the children to his office and Patti rolled her eyes and mimicked the group sarcastically.

"I thought maybe we could grab a bite to eat?"

He handed her a bottle of water from his mini frig. "Well I didn't expect that, but of course! Where would you like to go?"

"Across the street is fine. I thought maybe Alex and Abby would enjoy the happy hour music and we can look out over the bay while we are having our dinner. I can't remember the last time we did that, you know. I guess before I had the babies."

"Your choice, my love. I'm always open to Old Bay Café," he grinned, leaning down to pick up Abby and then Alex began to cry for someone to hold him too.

Sarah scooped in to grab her son from the stroller, and positioned him on her breast already wet with milk. *"No one will walk in here right now, will they?"* she asked cautiously, not wanting the staff to catch a *boob shot*.

"Not without knocking first. But you know, Sarah, you are turning me on immensely with that wanton picture of you in front of me," he teased, finding her more beautiful and irresistible being a nursing mother.

"You're twisted, Lance. Do you know that?" she replied with a raised tilt to her one eyebrow, shaking her head as if she was surprised by his comment, but loving it all the same.

Lance began to laugh, as he looked out the window and balanced Abby on his hip, trying to bounce and console her until it was her turn to nurse. "Perfect timing that you showed up now, because earlier I was swamped with work. Thanks for understanding that I couldn't join you at the twins' appointment. Is everything okay with them?"

"Everything is perfect," she answered, as they switched children and Abby nursed on Sarah's other full breast. "Dr. Keyser says they are right where they need to be in growth and their level of development. He does want me to introduce more solids now though."

Lance paused, knowing that Sarah struggled with the perfect time to introduce solids, reading many opinions from other mothers on delaying food introduction for as long as possible because of possible food allergies.

"Any shots today?"

"Not this appointment, but the next."

Again he knew of her feelings on delaying vaccines. Sarah wasn't an anti-vaxxer by any means, but she still was conservative in delaying the vaccines for as long as possible. Lance knew that was probably the real reason why she chose to stay at home much of the time with the twins instead of exposing them to other children with all their colds, coughs and snotty noses. Other than a mild cold probably related to teething, they were symptom free, so it was obviously working.

"I do have something to talk to you about that I think you would want to know. We can do so here or wait until dinner."

"Go on… you have my curiosity up now."

"Will has been in touch with me and I have agreed to rent him and his friends The Happy Crab."

"You can't be serious!" Sarah laughed, feeling astonished by his confession, removing Abby from her breast and rising to stand by Lance at the window. *"Do your parents know about this?"*

"Sure they do," Lance continued calmly, bouncing up and down with Alex and patting him on the back, hoping he would burp. "I'm just trying to do him a favor."

"A favor?" she gritted out, suddenly defensive. "I have my hands full now as it is with the twins! If anything bad happens it is all on you, Lance! I'm sure my parents are just going to have a fit when they find out about this!"

"Actually, they already know about it."

"Wow… so everyone knows but me?" she said, suddenly feeling frustrated and somewhat hurt that she was the last one to know.

"Honey, I was just trying to take some pressure off of you by not mentioning it until I knew for sure."

She stared at him, suspicious that he was telling her the truth. "I love William. He is my brother's son and my nephew. I just do not want any issues here at the beach for him or us – for that matter. You know how quickly things can go amiss when it comes to the ocean."

"Yes, my dear, I most certainly do know that," he answered, giving her a light kiss on the lips that made her melt and soften.

"When does he arrive?" she asked, placing the twins back in their stroller, ready to leave for dinner.

"Within a few days after he takes his exams and spends some time at home with your parents."

Sarah shook her head and laughed nervously. "I must say I'm a little taken back that all of this has been planned out behind my back. I get it that you wanted to spare me the grief of working things out for him, but all at once I feel like an outsider looking in."

Lance wrapped his arms around Sarah's slim waist, pulling her in closer to his firm chest, whispering seductively in her ear. *"You are far from an outsider, my love. You are my everything and some things are better left unsaid, if I can easily resolve issues on my own."*

She smiled back warmly, taking in his handsome face. "I guess so…. Just promise me you'll keep tabs on him and his friends throughout this summer. If they ruin The Happy Crab, we will never hear the end of it, and there will be hell to pay with your folks!"

"And with me…" he answered gently, leaning down to give her a deep tongue kiss that had her shivering with desire.

"I'm starving, Lance. I've been wanting crab cakes all day."

"Me too," he laughed, patting her backside and grabbing the stroller handle, wheeling the twins out into the hallway ahead of Sarah.

"I'm leaving for the day, Patti. Please take a message or forward all of my calls to voicemail if anyone stops by or calls."

"Sure," she answered absent-mindedly, already turning her attention back to her cellphone and the newsfeed that kept her occupied when Beach Dreams wasn't busy and her work was caught up.

They walked out into the balmy May air, sniffing deeply of the smell of seafood across the street. A faint sound of music filled the air as they strolled together with the twins across the street.

"Lance, why do you keep Patti around? She obviously doesn't care for you that much."

"It's just her way," he laughed. "My parents have had her here for 15 years. She is a fixture around the place and actually get things done once she files her nails daily," he laughed.

"To each their own. I would never allow her attitude at Miller's Architecture."

Lance wrapped an arm around Sarah's shoulder walking her and the twins into the bar area of Old Bay Café with the intention of saying hello to his best friend. "Is Mark here?" he asked the hostess.

"In the cooler getting some strawberry daiquiri mix. There he is...." She pointed, as Mark made his way back to the bar.

"Brother!" he bellowed, placing the plastic quart bottles on the bar and giving Lance a warm bear hug. "And you brought the family!" he happily proclaimed, knowing it had been way too long of a time.

"I sure did! Sarah was hungry for some crab cakes."

"On the house," he announced eagerly with a kind smile, leading his friends to the best table overlooking the bay before hugging Sarah and admiring the babies.

"Seriously, Mark, I will pay for dinner," Lance insisted, as Mark joined them at their table for several minutes before he returned to his duties.

"No way, bro. You have treated Maddie and I way too many times in the past. Consider it our gift since you haven't been to our house for dinner since the twins were born."

Lance felt embarrassed, realizing once again that Sarah was overprotective with the twins. *Mark has several older kids that could possibly get the twins sick...* she so frequently reminded him, when the invite was made for dinner at their house.

The early evening was perfect with Lance enjoying a Natty Boh and Sarah her one glass of white Chardonnay. Each dined on crab cakes, peanut fries and coleslaw as the two-man ensemble strummed their guitars and played oldies beach tunes. The sun began to set as the seagulls soared and squealed overhead, darting for fish and spraying water as one was found and snatched up from the bay. A blue heron strolled amongst the sea grass almost strutting to the beat of the music.

The twins slept, filling their lungs with the fresh bay air, feeling full and content from their specially prepared dinner of cooked carrots and grilled minced chicken, and mesmerized from the serenade of the singers.

Lance reached out to grab Sarah's hand, lost in the moment. "I didn't realize how much I missed this," he confessed with his sensual blue eyes that were aroused from the beer that he was drinking. "The way I'm feeling, I think desert will have to wait until we get home."

"I'm *very* okay with that," Sarah hinted with a saucy lift to her voice, rubbing his palm in small circles and turning him on even more so. *"Don't take long paying the bill, sweetie,"* she suggested with a wink, rising from the table and pushing the stroller towards the doorway with Lance not far behind.

CHAPTER 11

William rolled over and looked at the alarm clock of his father's youth that still sat on the nightstand beside of his bed. He stared with one eye, feeling tired and needing more rest. "Geesh, I can't believe it's 8 p.m. already."

He yawned and scratched his perspired hair, knowing he needed a shower, but decided to head downstairs to the kitchen instead for some of the promised Mexican dishes he had not touched earlier at dinner.

"You up?" Mike asked from the soft confines of the sectional in the living room, where he cuddled with Nancy who was snoring and resting her head on his side with his arm wrapped around her.

"Yeah," he replied softly, not wanting to wake his grandmother. "Sorry I slept so late, but I guess I was beat. Gonna just get some food," he explained, making his way to the kitchen and then back to the family room with a plate full of enchiladas and chili rellenos. He scooped in a couple big bites, swigging it all down with a Coke.

Mike began to laugh, waking Nancy in the process. "It's obvious you've missed Nan's cooking."

"Huh?" she said groggily, trying to understand what was going on as she sat up and yawned.

"Sorry I woke you, Nan," Will said guiltily, taking another huge bite from his plate.

"Oh…. William…. no problem. I wasn't really asleep anyway."

"Really?" Mike teased. "Maybe I need to record you in the future so you know what you sound like when you are not *really sleeping*."

"Michael, that is not nice!" she chastened, standing up to make herself look more presentable.

"Nan, it's fine. G-Dad is only teasing."

"Oh, I know all about his teasing," she remarked, giving Mike the stare down. "Let me take your plate, unless you want more to eat."

"No, I'm finished. I thought I would just throw my other load of laundry in the dryer and maybe fold the first, before I head upstairs and grab a shower."

"Too late, my boy. Nan *already* took care of your laundry."

"Michael, enough all ready!" she announced, feeling somewhat irritated by his teasing. "It was totally fine to help William out since he just arrived home and was napping."

"Thank you, Nan. I appreciate all your help with my laundry and by the way - dinner was great too!" He praised, trying to change her mood.

"At least someone appreciates me," she jested back, excusing herself before going off to the kitchen to do the final clean up.

Mike shook his head, looking at William. "Sorry about that. Nan's still tense about you leaving for the summer, but things will be okay," he whispered so she couldn't hear him in the kitchen. "I think I'm going to head upstairs myself in a few because I got a busy day in the office tomorrow. Unfortunately, our swim will have to wait until tomorrow evening, William, if you don't mind?"

"I figured as much. But I will be more awake by then after a good night's rest and a day of getting organized for the beach."

Nancy rejoined Mike and Will on the sectional, suddenly appearing anxious. *"When are you planning to leave, William?"*

"Probably in two days," he answered, scratching the top of Rascal's head. "Boy, it would be fun taking him to the beach with me."

"You say that now, but feeding and cleaning up after him with his liter box may change your mind," Nancy laughed. "He does well here on his own with our cat sitter stopping by when we go out of town, but I have never taken him away and would worry about his behavior."

"I guess… but if you change your mind I'm sure we can handle him at our place," William grinned, reaching down to pick up the friendly feline in his arms. "I think I'm gonna go upstairs now. See you in the morning."

"Sleep well."

"You too, Nan."

"Unless you're up early, I won't see you until tomorrow evening."

"Probably won't be up, G-Dad," he confessed, "So I will see you tomorrow evening."

William showered and laid in bed on his back with his arms crossed behind his head, watching the paddle fan circle round and round as the soft glow of the street lights slivered through the tilted wooden blinds. Rascal lay at the foot of his bed, keeping his feet a little too warm from the heat of his feline body positioned on top of the light cover. It was good to be home – even if for only a few days.

The morning arrived with Mike being at the office early as promised. Will's folded laundry from both loads was placed outside his bedroom on an upstairs hall credenza, waiting to be repacked or placed in his dresser drawers for use once he went back to school in the fall.

Nancy sat on the sectional with a cup of coffee in one hand and a romance novel in the other, totally consumed with her reading. She glanced up at hearing William the kitchen, peaking in the refrigerator for something to eat.

"I have you a plate in the microwave, sweetie," she offered; as she got up, ready to assist him.

"Thanks, Nan," he smiled, with his tousled hair hanging down over one eye. "Didn't expect a ham and cheese omelet this morning."

She grinned lovingly, grabbing a glass for orange juice. "I was going to make you pancakes too, but G-Dad said it was too much."

He knew he would have forced himself to eat them too if she would have gone to the trouble, but the omelet and toast sufficed. Two glasses of orange juice later, he stood and stretched, reaching high overhead to clear the kinks out of his neck from sleeping on a new pillow that was on his bed. "This morning, I'm going to work on organizing things that I will need for Marlin Beach."

"Have you thought about food? You are welcome to take whatever you would like from the pantry along with you."

Will sighed, not even considering that. "Nan, my friends and I are in college. Doubtful we will cook, but thanks for the offer. Maybe I will take a box a cereal and some chips with me, and some crackers too if you don't mind."

"Mind? Of course I don't mind! We can pack up a cooler of lunchmeat, fruit, eggs and other things too - if that helps to get you started."

"You're too good to me, Nan."

"I enjoy it, William. Always know that."

Nancy cleaned up the kitchen and then went off to her hot yoga class as William organized and filled up several totes he had emptied, already beginning to repack his Jeep before she returned home. As she pulled into the driveway and lifted the garage door, she was surprised to see Will busily packing his things back into the trunk of his car.

"Already loading your car?" she asked from her car window, feeling somewhat cheated for time with him again.

"Yeah, I think I'm gonna leave tomorrow after all. There's no sense in delaying things since I've gotten so much done today. The place in Marlin Beach is ready for us Nan."

Nancy walked with William from the garage into the house, fighting back her tears. "I was hoping for a few more days, but I guess…. I will see you…. soon?"

"Of course you will see me soon, Nan," William consoled, draping his arm around Nancy's shoulder and hugging her in close. "I'm just ready to get things underway, and to be honest, I'm excited now for it to happen."

Mike made it home by five and the three dined on the large quantity of Mexican leftovers, even though Nancy insisted on making something new. She did add another plate of nachos, which William heartily devoured for the second day in a row.

The pool heater was turned on earlier in the day so that they could enjoy the evening swim that had become a family tradition since William had came to live with them.

"I will miss swimming in the pool this summer," William confessed, as he floated lazily on his back in the warm water.

"Just try to get home more in the fall. I can keep the pool open through the end of October with the heater on, you know," Mike offered, as he hung on the edge with Nancy close by his side, watching William doing backstrokes.

"I'll try, but you know how wrapped up I get with things once I'm in school. There's never a lot of time for a visit."

"We understand, dear," Nancy piped in, always trying to do her best at putting her grandson at ease. "Maybe you can come back for a week or two before college begins again?"

"I'll see, Nan," he answered, not wanting to disappoint her again, looking at Mike who knew what he was up against.

"I think I have had enough swimming for the evening. Feel free to continue," Mike announced, walking up the steps on the shallow end.

"I'm ready too," Nancy added, finding Mike's hand who assisted her out of the pool, before she wrapped up tightly in her oversized beach towel that was waiting on a near by lounge chair. "I think I feel chilled and could use a cup of hot tea before bed."

"I think I will have a cup too."

"Mike that isn't like you to drink tea."

"I guess it okay to try something new from time to time," he joked as he wrapped his free arm around her waist, saying a final goodnight to William before departing back into the house.

William swam alone, gazing up at the starry night sky without a cloud in sight, enjoying the quiet lapping of the warm water. It was the last night of being at home with his grandparents. He could have chosen to stay with them for the entire summer, but instead he wanted to venture out and discover something new. Maybe he wouldn't like it and would venture back to Baltimore, but in the meantime, he would see what Marlin Beach had to offer and savor it for all it was worth.

CHAPTER 12

"I'm all packed!" William announced as he came back into the house after his third trip to the Jeep with his belongings.

"Take this lunch with you that I just packed," Nancy insisted, handing William a big plastic bag overflowing with food that looked like it was enough for ten people.

Will began to laugh. "Seriously, Nan. I can't eat all of this!" he shrugged with a grin, going through the content of the huge sack. "But I will take it with me and share it with my roommates, and I'm sure they will greatly appreciate it."

"That was my intention," she replied sweetly. "I also have the cooler packed for you, so don't forget that too. I filled it with lunchmeat, fruit, yogurt, vegetables, eggs and bacon. At least that will get you started for the first few days."

The subject has been discussed repeatedly since he was home, and he knew there was no reason to debate his Nan, because she would ultimately win. "Great! I will grab it after I use the bathroom one last time."

Hugs and cheek kisses were given and then he grabbed the very heavy cooler that his grandmother had filled to the brim, claiming that *it was no trouble to lift and that he didn't need her assistance.*

"I will call you guys some time later tonight after I'm settled. I know I gotta meet up with Lance and the others, so it may be awhile. And tell G-Dad I'm sorry I missed him this morning. I didn't expect him to leave so early."

"He needed to be at the office extra early since a project deadline was due today. He wanted me to tell you though to have fun and stay safe, and he will catch up with you later."

Nancy followed William out the front door as he placed the cooler in the back seat, which was the only remaining empty spot left in the Jeep, turning to give his grandmother one more hug goodbye. He could see tears forming in her eyes and worry etching her concerned face.

"Now Nan, everything is going be okay. You know we talked about all of this, and you will definitely see me as soon as G-Dad can slip away from his office for a few days."

"I know William, but now the time is finally here for you to actually leave, and I'm just feeling a little bluesy knowing you won't be home for the summer. That's all."

Will was at a loss for words, realizing that no answer would make her happy. "Remember to scratch Rascal's head for me everyday," he reminded, as he sat idling in his Jeep.

"Of course…"

"I will call you later, Nan…."

"Bye, William. Always know I love you…. and please stay safe."

"I know…. And I will."

William pulled away from the driveway, beeping several times at Nancy who was still standing and waving at the retreating vehicle. He was now pumped up and on his way to Marlin Beach, ready to think about the day ahead. As he drove around the Baltimore beltway, he thought of his grandmother and how at times she could be overbearing, but had only good intentions where he was concerned. He hoped she would get back to her normal daily routine and stop focusing on him.

He turned on the radio, singing to a top hit that was being played almost every hour about love that had gone wrong. His cellphone began to ring and interrupted the song - since it came through over his Bluetooth.

"Hello?"

"Are you on your way?"

"I am, uncle Lance."

"How was Nan and G-Dad today before you left?"

"I didn't see G-Dad this morning. He had already left for the office before I was even up... something about a deadline today on a project. But of course Nan was there to see me off."

Lance began to laugh. "I can only imagine that goodbye, and her not wanting you to leave."

He shook his head; focusing on the heavy traffic in front of him, ready to cross the Chesapeake Bay Bridge. "I wish she wouldn't get so emotional where I'm concerned. I love her, but boy can she be persistent and not take - *no* - for an answer."

"It's just her way, William. She honestly means well."

"Yeah, I know..."

"When do you think you will be here?" Lance asked, as he sat at his desk at Beach Dreams trying to multi-task and sort out his work and the overflow of his mother's, who was now soaking up the rays of the tropical sun aboard a cruise ship with his father.

"Depending on the traffic I would say 2 to 3 hours."

"That should be perfect timing. I got several showings on some properties before you arrive, and then we will meet up at the beach house and I will give you the tour of The Happy Crab."

"Sounds good, uncle Lance. I will let you know when I'm near Marlin Beach. Talk to you soon."

Will hung up, feeling content with his uncle's words as he rolled down the window, sniffing in the salty fish smelling air. The drive over the bay bridge was picture perfect. The sky was a shade of blue that was so vivid in its intensity that it almost hurt his eyes to stare too long, without a cloud present to even compete.

The traffic was moving at a steady pace, and there was no real back up to speak of that was causing any delay. He could see several large filled cargo ships floating lazily by throughout the bay on their way to drop off their goods to some unknown location. A few fishing boats were there also, bringing in their catch of the day of fish, crabs and oysters that would be sold to local restaurants and grocery stores, or to processing houses that would pick and harvest the crab meat or shuck and pack the oysters in clear jars.

William had come to love Maryland and the eastern shore, which was a display of nature at its finest with the bay with its shellfish and crabs and the ocean with its waves and shoreline. He had made friends and enjoyed Baltimore with its sports teams, and the tasty local food that typically featured Natty Boh beer, seafood and Old Bay seasoning sprinkled on everything.

The time he had lived in the south held happy and yet sad memories of his life spent with his mother and the family there. After her death from ovarian cancer, fate had brought him to Maryland to live with his grandparents afterwards. Nothing from his past could compare to what his life was like now. He thanked God everyday that he lived in Maryland and had a good life, changing his whole perspective of what his future could hold.

He saw the brightly painted building of Mom and Pops, a favorite produce stand of many, knowing Nan had already packed the cooler full of fruits and vegetables that would probably tide him and his friends over for the next week. Next, was a sign announcing that Marlin Beach was only 5 miles further down the road. Will felt adrenaline and excitement pumping throughout his veins, knowing that he was almost there. He crossed the bridge that entered the town, glancing at several jet skiers that were moving rather quickly, skimming over the top of the water with their engines roaring loudly behind them, and then passed the array of townhouses with their sunny roofs of yellow, blue and aqua, which greeted each visitor who came to the beach town.

William had arrived in Marlin Beach – the place of his summer destination! He looked towards his left at The Dexter Resort and Spa - the namesake of his departed father - where his friends would be working over their college break. The Dancing Seahorse, the beach house of his grandparents and aunt Sarah, was off to his right, and where he decided to pull off into the gravel driveway, just to gather his thoughts before he made his intended call to Lance.

The house was quiet and empty, waiting to be filled again with love and laugher from his Nan and G-Dad who he knew would be there soon, just to check up on him. As much as he acted the part that he needed a break from them and wanted his freedom to do his own thing for the summer, he was relieved that they would be at The Dancing Seahorse from time to time, just to make sure he was doing okay. *He could always retreat there, if his roommates were getting on his nerves and he needed a break,* he knew. Nan would always be available to pamper him and provide food.

He smiled at the house, already remembering some fond memories from the few years he had gone there with his grandparents. Sarah and Lance would join them, along with other guests that would get an occasional invite for dinner on the deck. William stepped from his jeep just to stretch and regroup from the long drive. The sea grass gently moved against the backside of the house, where birds nested and took refuge. He could also see glimpses of the ocean with its playful waves greeting him and welcoming him to Marlin Beach.

His cellphone was ringing again, as he snapped back to reality from the picture show of the beach spread out in front of him. "Matt, did you make it here yet?" Will asked, as he got back into the Jeep.

"On my way with Tyler now. We should be there in about two hours. I got a late start. Also, we just talked to Chris and he won't be in until around 5."

"No worries. I just got into town myself, and I'm gonna call my uncle now and go check out The Happy Crab before you guys get here. So take your time and I will see you soon. I also just texted you the address of our place where we will be staying at."

"Ok, bro. Can't wait to get there!"

"Yeah, me too!" Tyler added over Matt's cellphone speaker.

"Uncle Lance, I'm here…. Here in Marlin Beach," William announced proudly as he pulled out onto Beach Road, leaving The Dancing Seahorse behind until his grandparents' visited.

"Great! Perfect timing because I just finished up with my client. I just sent you the address of The Happy Crab, and I will be there in a few minutes to meet you."

CHAPTER 13

"*919 Pelican Way...*" William said aloud, memorizing the street as he read Lance's text, knowing this was his new address for the summer. As promised, Lance was in the gravel driveway in his Jeep looking preoccupied - on the phone speaking with someone else for the moment. Will waved as he parked beside him - Jeep beside of Jeep - one in black and one in red – the red one being William's.

When it came time for a car his only request was to have a Jeep just like his uncle Lance's *who he thought looked cool driving around in it*. Within a few months of living with his grandparents, he signed up for a driver's education class, took his driver's test and passed, and then got the Jeep for a present *just because he needed it for school, and it would save Nan time to do her own things if she didn't have to be his taxi service all of the time,* his G-Dad explained.

He idolized several men in his life, one being his G-Dad and the other Lance. Both men were of strong character with good drive and determination that made them successful in the business world, but lacking in violent tempers like his stepfather, Mitchell. He hoped he would never encounter Mitchell again in his life after the way he treated his mother, Claire, and him too for that matter. William didn't know what he would do if that time were ever upon him, and he honestly feared getting violent with Mitchell and out of control.

Lance finally hung up and flashed Will a pleasant wide-toothed smile, glad to see that he had arrived safe and sound. He climbed from his Jeep, meeting William by his car window. "Ready to check out your new place?"

"Am I? You better believe I'm ready!" William exclaimed, jumping down from the Jeep, meeting Lance where he waited in the driveway.

They stood for a moment pausing to look at the beach house in front of them. Not as impressive in design as the Miller's place - The Dancing Seahorse - and of course Lance's house with Sarah that she and her father had designed and was a showplace - The Playful Starfish - but still it held a simple beauty that felt welcoming and inviting.

The Happy Crab featured brown shaker siding with white trim and a tan shingled roof. A painted white deck with patio furniture that overlooked the ocean, displayed steps that led up to the deck, William noticed as Lance walked him around the property pointing out the main features. A shed off to the one side of the yard, and a wooden planked sidewalk, overlaid the sand that led out to the beach. A public shower for rinsing off was also near by.

"The place looks amazing, uncle Lance," Will complimented as they walked towards the front door.

"Glad you approve, but let's check out the inside first before you come to any conclusions," Lance teased with a wink, unlocking the door and flipping on the lights to a large expanse of a living room and a kitchen area that was fully furnished in front of them. A slight smell of mustiness, but not in an unpleasant sort of way, filled the air. Lance pulled back the blinds to the outdoor deck, sliding the glass doors open afterwards, allowing in the fresh sultry sea air which quickly masked any previous odor of being closed off and unused.

"Wow, this place is huge!"

"Much like The Dancing Seahorse, right?"

"Yeah, I guess so."

"Many beach houses were built this way then, with the thought that a common gathering area in the kitchen and family room would be appreciated. Vacationers always enjoy hanging out together to cook and dine, and also watch television or play a game, which brought about the concept," Lance explained, as he turned on the refrigerator, air conditioning and water heater.

"I get that since I'm sure my friends and I will be hanging out in both of these areas during most of our free time," Will grinned with excitement and anticipation, listening to Lance as if he were in a class room.

"About that…" Lance gently reminded, "Just remember you gotta keep the house clean. I know it will be tempting to start bringing in others that you meet, but you must follow the rules to keep things straight between you and I and your roommates."

"No worries, uncle Lance. I didn't mean anything by that. My friends and I know what you *expect* out of us, and as far as any visitors go, they will know about the rules too when they show up here."

"I hate to remind you, but the house doesn't only belong to me. It's my mom and dad's place also, and that is the only request that you *must* follow," Lance answered, trying to smile and lighten the mood. "Shall we proceed with the tour?" he asked.

"I'm ready!"

They walked down the hall to each furnished bedroom and also peeked in at the two bathrooms that were neat and clean and ready for use. "You may want to choose this bedroom, Will, since it is the largest and where my parents used to sleep. Can't beat having a king sized bed, and of course you have more than ample room for your clothes with a dresser and a chest of drawers too."

William smiled contentedly, taking a closer look at the beautiful master bedroom laid out in front of him. Beyond the assets that Lance pointed out in the cozy room, was a large expanse of windows with an additional set of patio doors that led out to the deck. He liked the sun shining into his bedroom, but also enjoyed hearing the sound of the ocean waves coming through his window or door if he left it open.

"I definitely want this bedroom! My friends may protest, but hey, I'm friends with the owner!" he laughed, *hi-fiving* Lance in the process. "We four will have to share the two baths, so they can't say I got an edge over them with that."

They proceeded back out to the main living area, making their way out to the deck as they continued to talk. "You may want to keep your set of patio doors locked in your room, or you may find an uninvited guest or two in there at some point."

William looked puzzled as they both leaned on the deck railing that overlooked the sandy beach and ocean in front of them. "I'm not following you."

Lance shook his head with a laugh. "Come on, William, you are now at the beach where everyone else on school break loves to come and hang out for the summer. Most students will not be as lucky as you to stay at a beach house directly on the beach. This could be a popular destination if you don't lay down the law about who is allowed to come here. Just a warning - you may find someone in your room when you least expect it if you forget to lock the sliding glass doors leading out to the back patio."

Will took in every word, picking up on the vibe. *"Ok... I get your point,"* he grinned, knowing he was referring to making out and even sex. "We had to set some rules too in our quad at school. My friends are pretty cool about respecting everyone's space, but your point is taken. We made it work at Towson with females. That's all can say."

Lance helped William unload his Jeep with all its containers and suitcases, placing the cooler's items in the refrigerator that had lowered significantly in temperature since they first arrived. William unpacked his bags and set up his toiletries on one half of the vanity counter, claiming that spot too before his roommates arrived. His cell rang just as he was finishing up. *Perfect timing...* he thought.

"Hey Matt, you almost here?"

"Just pulled in the driveway. Is that other Jeep your uncle's?"

"You got it. We are in the house unpacking. Come on in!" he suggested, as Lance followed him out the door to greet his friends.

They repeated the tour, first on the outside and then throughout the inside again. "I must get going, but I wanted to give you guys the keys and also the lease agreement for each one of you to review and sign," Lance instructed as he laid out the lease on the kitchen table along with the 4 keys for each one of them.

"Chris won't be here until five, but the rest of us can sign it now, if you would like."

"No, that's okay. I'll be back to get it in the morning. Take your time and review it," he offered with a kind smile. "Any questions you might have I can answer then. Also, here is a key to the shed out back," he explained, laying it on the table along with the other four keys.

"What's in there, uncle Lance?" Will asked.

"It has boogie boards and surfboards, chairs, umbrellas and some beach toys, and I think maybe a cooler or two. My mom probably has a bunch of Tiki torches in there also from the numerous parties she was always hosting. If you guys brought anything to store outside, feel free to do so; but if you use my things please just remember to return them to the shed and lock it up afterwards. Also, I only have two keys to the shed, so I'm leaving one here for your guys and I will keep the other -

just in case."

"*Just in case?*" William asked with a questionable look.

"Just in case you lose the other. Cheaper for me to keep the spare than to have a locksmith change the lock if you guys loose yours," he laughed, patting William on the back. "I gotta get going. Sarah is probably wondering where I'm at so long without calling her by now."

William walked outside with his uncle, following by his side out to the Jeep. "Thanks again, uncle Lance, for letting us stay at The Happy Crab. It's better than I imagined it would be. I know it is going to be a great summer. I can just feel it!"

Lance glanced knowingly at William from his car window, realizing he had a missed call from Sarah that he was waiting for. "You are welcome, Will. Just remember everything we went over and things will be fine. I want your summer to be fun and memorable for you and your friends. I'll be back by eleven tomorrow morning to pick up the signed lease agreement. Hopefully, that won't be too early and you guys will have gotten some sleep and didn't stay up all night," he grinned as he pulled away with a jovial gleam in his eyes, remembering his own fun times at Marlin Beach when he was younger, leaving William to stare after the black Jeep as Lance drove out of sight down Beach Road.

Will walked back towards the beach house realizing his dream of staying in Marlin Beach during his school break had actually come true thanks to Lance. He stopped to look at the outside façade of the house one more time, before joining his friends again inside. *"I really am one lucky dude!"* he said aloud with a broad happy smile; kicking up a few stones with his flip-flops, ready to begin his new summer adventure.

CHAPTER 14

As promised, Chris arrived at 5 o'clock with a two cases of beer stacked high in his arms, ringing the doorbell in the process. *"I could use some help here!"* he yelled out in irritation, as Matt opened the door and he walked right past him with his heavy load, dropping it off right inside of the closed door.

"You came well prepared," Tyler laughed, grabbing one of the cases, heading right for the refrigerator, and helping to unload each one of the cans.

William looked on, trying to sort out what was happening. *"What's up Chris?"*

"I'm here," he laughed, while bending down to pick up the remaining case of beer, ready to add it to the refrigerator once Tyler was finished stacking his.

"I can see that and I can also see you came ready to party," Will added somewhat sarcastically, remembering his past once again with his alcoholic stepfather Mitchell.

"We're at the beach, right? What else is there to do but drink and hang out?" Chris rationalized, looking around the room at the other three, trying to find room for his remaining beer cans that he placed in one of the produce bins on top of the salad that Nan had given to William.

Will took it all in, knowing that he had bucked heads with Chris at college in the past over too much drinking going on in the dorm quad, when they threw a party from time to time. Will wasn't one to seek out sympathy about his past life growing up in Alabama. They knew he lived with his grandparents but that was about it. There was no mention of his mother dying of cancer, or anything about his brother or sister or even Mitchell for that matter. He didn't want their questions, and it was easier to talk about his life from the time he started living with G-Dad and Nan and let it go at that.

Chris sat at the table after opening a can of beer, with a bit of it foaming out over the top of the can, landing on the clean table by the lease and the keys.

"Hey be careful!" Will warned while freaking out, hurrying to grab a paper towel and clean up the spilled beer before it hit the lease. He then removed it, along with the keys, to a foyer table by the front door.

"You got to calm down," Matt offered, grabbing his own beer and two more for Tyler and Will that he shoved in their direction on the table.

Will sighed deeply, looking at each of his roommates that were also his best friends. "I know we are here to have fun, but I am royally fucked if we ruin my uncle's house. We already went over all this before we got here. *Remember?*"

'Yeah, man, we remember. But for gosh sakes, Will, it's our first night here. Gotta chill for at least tonight. *Is that fair?*" Chris asked in frustration, already grabbing a second beer."

William looked quietly at the three, sliding his unopened beer can towards the center of the table, walking from the room and into his bedroom where he slammed the door shut, and locked it behind him. *"What the hell was I thinking inviting them here?"* he complained to himself, knowing he couldn't control what was happening in the kitchen. *"I'll be back in Baltimore within the week if this continues...."*

The three continued to sit at the kitchen table together, being at a loss for words, only sipping their beer and taking in the newness of the place.

"Now what?" Chris asked as he looked at Matt and Tyler.

"I'm not going home to Florida, that's for sure. If Will wants low-key activity here, then I will party elsewhere at a bar or something."

"That won't be easy since you're only 19, Tyler," Chris reminded, irritated with the discussion.

"What is your problem, Chris? Look around you. This place is great and William has a valid point!"

"Okay, I get it. I think I'm going to get some fresh air and take a walk on the beach. If you guys leave, can you please keep the door unlocked? I may lose my key in the sand, if I'm not careful," he laughed with a half-intoxicated belch, from drinking several beers and it was only 7 p.m.

"Better hope you remember what beach house you are even staying at," Matt yelled after him, as Chris headed down the wooden beach path away from The Happy Crab.

"Whatever, Matt. Don't worry about me."

Matt went back inside to sit in the living room with Tyler who had just turned on the oversized 60 inch TV that had been added to the beach house within the last year for the occasional guest who was fortunate enough to stay there. An overstuffed sofa in a pale blue fabric with two cozy inviting chairs in a pinstripe fabric graced the room, along with nautical themed area rug and an oak hand-hewed, square cocktail table in the center of it all. A paddle fan with a light that resembled a ship's lantern rotated slowly overhead, casting a faint cozy glow around the room. The patio doors were pushed back, allowing the ocean breeze to gently cascade in, with the sound of the waves echoing off in the distance. Overall, the college roommates knew they were lucky to be there for the summer on their first night at The Happy Crab.

"Whatcha want to watch?" Tyler asked, flipping the channels absent-mindedly.

"I think the Orioles are playing tonight."

"Yeah... sure," Tyler answered, finding the game and settling in.

Will reappeared, plopping down on the one empty chairs, rubbing the sleep from his eyes, yawning at the pair. *"Where's Chris?"*

"Took a walk down the beach," Matt answered, munching on some popcorn that was provided by Nan.

"By himself?"

"Awww... yeah," Tyler replied, looking at the three now present.

"Was that the smartest thing letting him go by himself? I'm sure he was drunk when he left, right?" Will asked with concern.

Matt laughed, putting his half-eaten bag of popcorn on the cocktail table. *"Come on Will, you gotta re...lax.* Seriously, man. Maybe Chris needs some time to think about how much of a dick he can be. If he fucks up, he will go home and then the place will be just be for us guys. Or we can ask another guy from school if he leaves. I'm sure someone would take his place in a minute."

"He's our roommate at Towson. Doesn't that count for something?"

"Yes, it does, but you know how he acts up there too. I'm not saying I want him to go home cuz we need his help with the rent, but I seriously don't want to see the two of you battling all summer."

"I'm fine with the rules," Tyler interjected, standing and clapping when the Orioles got a home run. "Better here than going back to Florida, listening to my parents hound me for a couple months."

Will laughed. "No one is going home, including Chris - just yet. I think I'm gonna try to find him though. I'll be back soon," he announced over the blare of the television. "Maybe we can grab a bite to eat on the boardwalk afterwards?"

"I'm game," Tyler replied before the door slammed shut, and William walked down the beach path trying to locate his friend.

Nancy sat curled up in the crook of Mike's arm as they cuddled on the sectional watching the Orioles game together. Mike drank his Tanqueray, tonic and lime and Nancy sipped from her stem glass filled with red wine.

"I'm surprised we haven't heard from William yet," she commented with a strained voice, looking at her husband in concern.

"I'm not," he answered frankly, focusing on the score and happy that his team was winning. "He probably is still getting situated and settling in to his new place. Maybe he is still waiting for all his roommates to arrive."

"But he promised to call, Mike. And he should keep his promises."

"Yes, sweetheart he did, but its okay if he decides to contact us tomorrow. Don't you think?" he answered, patting her knee and trying to speak reason to her.

"I guess so, honey, but I just wanted to make sure he is okay and is situated in his place."

"Now don't you think if he wasn't in his place yet, Nancy, that Lance would have called just to let us know?"

"Well that's true."

"Yes, it's true, silly," he replied, kissing her tenderly on the lips. "Now can we get back to some Orioles baseball? It looks like they are going into overtime."

"Oh, I can hardly wait," she answered, rolling her eyes.

Mike laughed, grabbing her and tickling her ribs. "You just can't stand being alone with me since William was just here. Admit it... " He whispered, nuzzling her neck playfully.

Nancy's eyes glistened with tears of happy emotion, laughing and gulping to catch her breath from the tickling that Mike had just given. "You know that is not the case... I cherish each day with you, Mike. I just want everyone safe and happy... that's all."

"You're a good woman, Nancy Miller. I picked the best when I chose you."

Nancy began to shake her head. "I think it was I who chose you," she teased, as she got up from the sectional with her empty wine glass in hand. "Rascal and I are going upstairs so I can read some more. I am almost at the end of my book and I can't wait to see what happens!"

"Be up soon," he called after her, as she climbed the steps to the second floor.

Mike could see his cellphone vibrating on the table in front of him. He glanced at the phone realizing it was William sending him a text. It wasn't the promised phone call, but he did get in touch before the day was over never the less.

"G-Dad, sorry it has taken me awhile to reach out to you. I made it to Marlin Beach this morning and met up with Lance. I'm unpacked and

my roommates have finally arrived. Been busy adjusting to the first day, but all is well. Tell Nan not to worry and I'm okay. Love you guys!"

"Good to hear that everything is okay. I will tell Nan you reached out. Stay safe and we will hopefully see you soon."

The game was still on and the Orioles were ahead. Mike had decided he would go upstairs and catch the final score later. Nancy was the priority now. He would give her the good news about William and put her worries to rest – at least for that one night anyway.

CHAPTER 15

"Hey Chris. Is that you?" William called from a distance, seeing a form that resembled his friend who was sitting close by the water's edge.

"Yeah, man. It's me," he hollered back over the roar of the ocean.

"You're getting all wet, dumbass," Will observed as he stood over him, watching the water run over his friend's shorts and then over his own feet.

"Trying to sober up... I drank one too many beers without eating first."

Will reached out a hand to help Chris stand. "It's okay. You were just celebrating because we finally made it here for the summer," he conceded, trying to cut his friend a break.

"I thought... you were... pissed at me..." he slurred out, feeling like he was ready to throw up. He glanced over at Will who was like a friend and a brother, walking shoulder to shoulder beside of him by the water's edge.

"Concerned... That's all. We have such a good thing going here with the beach house and we just got hooked up with jobs. I don't want to see any of us blowing it on something stupid."

"I get it, bro. And I'm sorry," Chris replied awkwardly. "I will watch what I am doing with the drinking. The last thing I want is to go back to Baltimore for the summer if my parents find out. If they ever know that I am drunk and then got myself in trouble because of it, there will be hell to pay!"

"Yeah, for any of us," William agreed, wrapping a supportive arm around his friend's shoulder, seeing the beach house in the distance. "Why don't you get a quick shower and change, and then we will all walk the boards and get a bite to eat?"

"Sounds fantastic!" he agreed, breaking free from the embrace. "I could use a big container of peanut fries and maybe a slice of cheese pizza."

"Me too! And maybe an ice cream if I'm still hungry."

"Always room for that!" Chris yelled, beating him in the front door.

The baseball game was concluding as William entered the living room. The Orioles had won in overtime 16 to 4 against the Oakland A's.

"Are we still going to the boards?" Tyler asked, still glued to the TV.

"I know Chris and I plan to as soon as he changes," William answered happily, glad he found his friend in one piece on the beach. He plopped down again in the comfortable living room chair. "I'm starving and I need something to eat."

Chris reappeared with his brown hair still wet and combed straight back. He had changed into khaki shorts and a clean Towson t-shirt, slipping into his flip-flops - taking William's lead. He suddenly felt refreshed and ready to go, shaking off his beer buzz.

"Are we leaving or what?" he barked out, making the group rise from their comfortable seats immediately and follow him towards the front door.

"Just grabbing my house key," William replied, taking one of the four keys and adding it to his key ring.

The others followed suit, each taking a house key and attaching it to their key ring respectively for safekeeping, before walking from the beach house as Will locked the door behind them. The walk to the boardwalk was only several blocks away as they passed by The Dancing Seahorse close by.

"That's my grandparents place," Will pointed out.

"That should be convenient if they ever come to visit," Matt grinned.

"What do you mean by that?"

"What I mean, bud, is free food! What you just brought from home won't last us forever!"

The group laughed, totally agreeing as they stepped up on the boardwalk ready to go the distance, as they mingled in with the other tourists ready to walk the boards.

They walked at a fast pace almost as if they were in a race, trying to go the couple miles to their favorite eateries as quickly as they could. Even though William had never invited any of them to stay at The Dancing Seahorse in the past, they were well accustomed with Marlin Beach, going there with their own families to vacation beyond *senior week* after they had graduated from high school. The exception being Tyler, who had only heard about the stories filled with good times at their favorite mid-Atlantic, east coast beach. He would only comment with stories of his own about south Florida where he grew up, not wanting to feel like the outsider, claiming it truly was the better beach.

Their favorite pizza shop was right in front of them, with a line of people already standing there waiting patiently for a slice or two when it was their turn. A cheap paper plate and a single napkin were offered along with the tasty Italian pie, dripping with grease and cheese on the top of a thin layer of red sauce. Three of them added pepperoni with the exception being Tyler who asked for only cheese, eating almost half of a slice in only one bite.

"*God, this is good!*" Tyler praised, finishing his ooey gooey first piece.

"*Nothing that good in Fort Lauderdale?*" Matt sarcastically teased.

Tyler shot him a glance, knowing what he was implying. "We got our good pizza shops too, Matt. But if I gotta stay here for the summer - this will do."

The group began to laugh, knowing the comparison was always going to be inevitable. Tyler was going to stand up for where he lived no matter what.

"Let's stop debating things and head up there for some fries. I can smell them cooking and I know you don't have anything this good in south Florida, or maybe even the whole state of Florida, Tyler," Chris interjected, winking at the rest of the group.

The famous French fry stand had a line even longer than what they had just experienced at the pizza shop, wrapping two buildings down the boardwalk. Each patron talked and laughed to those in their group who were waiting along with them, making the most of their time. It was all a part of the experience if you wanted the hot, peanut oil fries that Marlin Beach was famous for.

"I think I will get the largest size."

"*You're paying ten dollars?*"

"Yeah, it's our first night here, Matt. I'm celebrating!" Will excitedly announced, already getting his money out of his wallet.

The others followed suit, once again not wanting to be the odd man out with a smaller size just to save some money. They sat on a couple of benches overlooking the ocean, enjoying each hot and tasty potato strip that they sprinkled malt vinegar over.

"I don't get the no ketchup thing," Tyler interjected, as he stuffed a couple fries in his mouth at one time. "But they are delicious and no, we don't have anything like this in Florida," he conceded, looking like a beach boy with his very light blonde locks blowing freely in the sea air.

William began to laugh. "That says a lot coming from you, Tyler."

"We got things there that you guys don't have here."

"Name one!" Chris insisted, drinking the remaining vinegar from the bottom of the French fry cup before throwing it in the trashcan nearby.

"Well let's see… warm weather that rarely gets cold, Cuban food and hot babes on the beach - typically year round."

The group began to laugh hysterically, causing passersby to stare over in their direction as they *hi-fived* each other with Tyler's words, loving the part about the *hot babes.* As they got up to resume their walk again, Chris noticed a plaque on the back of the bench that he and Matt had been sitting on.

Dexter William Miller – Beloved son and brother.

"Keep dancing upon each wave – until we meet again."

"Hey, Will, look at this. *Close to your name, right?"* he pointed out.

Will paused, not sure he wanted to explain, staring blankly at the weathered plaque, while the others waited for him to answer. He looked at each one, finding it hard to begin. *"Aww… that was my father."*

"Your father? Why haven't you told us about him before?"

"Because I never met him. He was actually a year younger than I am now when he died here in Marlin Beach. My mother said he got caught up in a riptide, lingered in the hospital for a week in a coma and then finally died."

"Damn, bro, that sucks!"

"I'm not connecting?" Matt said, shaking his head. "He was 18 when he died and you never met him? How is that possible?"

"It is possible… " William answered irritably, as they began to walk again further down the boardwalk. *"What isn't there to understand? My dad was in high school and got my mother pregnant with me before he died. Yeah, its messed up and that's why I never mentioned it!"*

Chris wrapped a brotherly arm around Will's neck, knowing he was his best friend and always had his back just as he did earlier on the beach. "It's no big deal. Things happen and hopefully none of us will get anybody pregnant this summer," he laughed, trying to lighten the mood.

"Jackass!" Will yelled, breaking free and jogging a short distance away, with his friends standing still trying to figure out if he was mad or not. *"Let's hope Chris doesn't get anyone pregnant. Don't want any kid looking like his ugly ass!"* he teased, as the group of friends caught up to him laughing and relieved he was okay from seeing the bench. "I'm having ice cream and I think I've decided on chocolate and peanut butter swirl in a large waffle cone."

"Lead the way!" Tyler insisted. "We have great ice cream and gelato in Fort Lauderdale…. I'm just saying."

Everyone laughed, picking up the pace again, walking towards the brightly lite, swirling ice cream cone sign that was illuminated in the distance. They were more than ready for desert, rides and then some Skee-Ball competitions amongst friends.

As the roommates made their way back to The Happy Crab they were exhausted but content and happy. It still was sinking in that they were finally in Marlin Beach, staying at their very own beach house, directly on the beach. It was a great first day and life didn't get much better!

CHAPTER 16

"Anybody awake?" Lance yelled, closing the door behind him to The Happy Crab. The TV was still playing and Matt was on the sofa with his one leg dangling off of it and almost touching the floor. He had used the decorative aqua-colored throw to cover only his midsection that was minus any clothes except for his boxers. Open beer cans were sitting on the cocktail table minus coasters. A half eaten bag of chips was left out, laying on the granite counter top in the kitchen where a few chips had fallen out and a trail of ants had began attacking and eating them. Several cabinet doors were ajar and dirty dishes were piled high in the sink already. The fan swirled overhead and the patio doors were pushed back along with the screens, allowing for numerous flies to be buzzing on and off of the sleeping teen who had a trail of drool running down the side of his mouth. The air conditioning was struggling to keep up with the outside humid air competing for the same space. The place was fairly quiet, as Lance assumed that the exhausted, *over-partied* college students were now recuperating in each of their rooms.

Dressed and ready for work in his khakis and his Bream Dreams logo golf shirt, Lance wanted to pick up the signed contract and make his way into the office by eleven, since he was getting a late start from hanging out with Sarah and the twins that morning. He sighed and shook his head, pacing the living room floor in frustration that already held several discarded shirts from the young tenants. He wasn't sure how he was going to handle the situation from what he was witnessing. It was evident that the promises that were made had already been broken, and he was not happy with William or his friends.

He made his way back the hall to Will's room, tapping lightly on the bedroom door - without a response. He entered the unlocked room, seeing his nephew sleeping peacefully with his windows and the patio door open, and the covers completely covering him up to the top of his chin. Lance reached down and tapped him lightly on the shoulder.

"William, wake up. It's uncle Lance."

"Huh?"

"Will, I want you to get up now! I need the signed lease agreement and I would like to talk to you guys before I leave, since I'm already running late for work."

Will sat up, rubbing his eyes. "Sorry, uncle Lance, we were all up late last night and I guess we overslept."

"I can see that," Lance answered gruffly. "I'll give you a minute to wake up, and I will try to get your friends up too."

Lance left the bedroom, shutting the door firmly behind him, feeling his aggravation growing by the second. He proceeded to knock firmly on the other two bedroom doors, with the fourth being open and empty since Matt had decided to sleep on the couch in the living room instead. *"It's time for you sleeping beauties to get up now!"* he loudly announced while cupping his mouth with his hands, standing directly near Matt, rousing him from his slumber with a jolt. *"Meet me in the kitchen in five minutes or we are going to have a major problem on our hands!"*

Slowly, the three bedroom doors opened, with the weary, bent-over males appearing and then immediately exiting towards the two bathrooms for their morning emptying. Lance impatiently waited, as he tapped his fingertips repeatedly on and off of the tabletop, feeling like they were purposely delaying and taking too long.

Each one finally made their way to the kitchen and sat down at the table, quietly staring at their new landlord, trying to *gather their wits* with a few yawns and eye rubs. Lance shifted his weight, resting his elbows on the table in front of him, taking in each boy present. He cleared his throat, not really sure where to begin.

"I am William's uncle Lance, and your landlord for the summer while you are staying here in Marlin Beach. I stopped by to pick up the signed lease and to welcome you to The Happy Crab and to our beautiful beach town. But I must say, I am *very* disappointed to walk into this beach house today and find things in such disarray."

"Uncle Lance…."

"*Let me continue, Will,*" he said sternly, looking at him angrily like he had never seen before. "You will have your chance to speak, but I'm leading this meeting here this morning, and what I have to say - needs to be heard by all of you!"

William gave me his word that he reviewed things with you. He confirmed that he told you my conditions for living at The Happy Crab for the summer. "*Was there any confusion with my terms?*"

"No," they all replied in unison.

Lance stood up, slamming his hands hard on the table, making the dishes rattle in the sink. "*Then why the hell does my place look like this already? You haven't even been here for 24 hours and this is how it looks? Have you all lost your minds or what? Because if insanity isn't your plea, then maybe we will have to discuss when you plan to pack up and leave again for Baltimore or when you will be moving into another place here – and by that I mean within the day!"*

Each shifted in their seat as they looked at Lance with fear in their eyes and then to their laps, except for William who knew he had dealt with anger far worse than this with his stepfather in Alabama.

"May I speak now, uncle Lance?"

"Yes, you may, William… " He replied seething, sitting back down and breathing in deeply – just to clear his head.

"We screwed up. Plain and simple – no excuses. If you want us to leave I will be out by the end of the day and go back to G-Dad's and Nan's. I obviously can't control my roommates' actions and I shouldn't have thought for one moment that I could do so."

Lance shook his head, giving William a thorough eye-piercing glare, evaluating each of his words. "Well, you stated that very well, William. And yes, you obviously can't control you roommates, but can you honestly say you didn't create any of this mess yourself?"

Will lowered his head to his lap, pausing to answer before he made eye contact again with Lance. "Yeah, I'm equally as guilty."

The others sat quietly waiting for their ultimate punishment to begin of packing and leaving paradise, knowing William was taking the blame for them when he barely did anything to contribute to the poor state of things.

"Mr. Snyder?"

"Yes?" Lance answered, trying to calm down, looking over at one of the youth addressing him that he hadn't met yet.

"My name is Chris and I am a good friend of Will's. He isn't to blame for any of this. He honestly drank a soda and threw his empty soda can in the trash, watched a little TV and then went to bed. It was the rest of us who stayed up and partied. So don't make him leave.

Kick us out, but let William stay."

Lance studied Chris, considering his words, realizing how young they all were and how he acted at that age. "Thanks for being honest, Chris. That means a lot to me that you came clean about last night and what really happened here." Lance rose and leaned on the granite countertop, grabbing the chip bag and rolling it down before placing it back on the counter. "You guys made one hell of a mess and that was my number one rule – *Keep the place clean. How hard is that?*"

"Not so hard," Tyler answered, trying to kiss up. "I'm Tyler, by the way... from Fort Lauderdale, Florida," he offered with a pleasant, dentist lightened, white-toothed smile, getting up to shake Lance's hand.

The others rolled their eyes as they looked at each other, knowing what Tyler was up to. He especially didn't want to go back home for the summer to the heat and humidity of where he lived.

"I'm Matt," he added with a yawn, still trying to wake up. "I definitely screwed up and I'm admitting it."

Lance laughed, seeing the distinctive personalities of all of them. "Hey, I was young once too. I get it that you want to have some fun, but not at my expense. I own the place but so do my parents, and I can tell you they would kill me for allowing you to stay here if they saw this mess right now. My wife Sarah would be upset too."

"What can we do to make it up to you, uncle Lance?"

Lance looked at his watch and then at his cellphone that was vibrating from a call from the office. "I gotta get going, but I want the signed lease. Where is it?"

Each roommate looked at the others sitting around the table, perplexed to the answer he was seeking, except for William.

"I put it in the top drawer of the front foyer table. I figured we would all sign it today with you present. But under the circumstances, do you still want us to sign it?"

"William, get the lease and bring it here."

Will got up and grabbed the lease, bringing it over and handing it off to Lance. Lance laid it on the table along with an ink pen that he clicked and had ready. The group of young men looked at him in surprise and confusion.

"I need your signatures if you are going to continue staying here," he said with a half sincere smile. *"Consider this to be a final warning!* You get one more chance to make things right. *When I show up the next time, I better never see The Happy Crab in this condition again!"*

"When will that be, sir?" Chris asked awkwardly, not sure he could pull off what Lance was requesting from them.

Lance began to laugh, crossing his arms in amusement. "That's for me to know and for you to find out. So I would suggest you never screw this up again. The next time, I would make sure you pass my inspection if you want to continue staying here for the summer."

After each one signed the lease, William handed it to Lance and he tucked it safely under one arm as he reached for his cellphone. This time he answered it, realizing it was Patti calling about a particular problem at work that she could not resolve on her own. He waved and said his goodbyes to the group and was out the door, ready to give the boys another chance even if they truly didn't deserve it.

CHAPTER 17

The Towson University roommates sat together in the living room of The Happy Crab, trying to digest what was just said to them by Lance. It was clear that without some drastic changes they would need to pack up their things again and head back to each one of their perspective homes or find another place in Marlin Beach, which they probably couldn't afford.

Will got up and turned off the blaring TV and began to pace in front of his friends. *"Does anyone feel like they would like to go home under the circumstances?"* he asked, not wanting to have the conversation but feeling the need to do so.

"I sure don't," Tyler replied adamantly. "Florida is stinkin hot and buggy this time of year, and jobs are hard to come by since it's the off season."

Matt sighed deeply, crossing his arms in front of him, not wanting to consider that option either. "I wanna stay here, even if your uncle is being *hard-nosed* and a *dick*. After all, we are college students and guys for that matter. Isn't it pretty normal for guys to be slobs!" he laughed.

"Yeah, I agree," Chris echoed.

William sat again, shaking his head in disgust. "My uncle is not a dick, and I am *not* dealing with a whole summer of this battle with you guys! I don't care what you think is *normal* at our age. It's what Lance and the others want!"

"The others?"

"The *others* - meaning my grandparents, my aunt Sarah and Lance's parents. They expect us to be civilized adults and take care of this place!" Will answered in frustration.

Silence reigned for several minutes over the room, as each one considered what would be required of them for the entire summer with the beach house. Tyler was the first to speak.

"I have no problem with the rules. It is no different at my parents' house in Florida. And by the way, aren't we to meet with someone today about our jobs at The Dexter?" he asked, suddenly changing the subject.

Chris stood up, looking at the time on his cellphone and realizing it was already past noon. "Hey, we gotta hurry and get outta here since my uncle is expecting us around 1 p.m. We better get showers and change, and I mean fast! He warned me we are not to be late!" Matt yelled over his shoulder, already heading for the bathroom.

"So do we all have an agreement or not?" Will shouted out in frustration, as the others got up to scatter and disappear into their bedrooms, already dismissing the seriousness of Lance's words.

"Yes!" They mutually answered back from behind their closed bedroom doors, dodging a bullet of being kicked out of The Happy Crab for at least one more day.

Will drove down Beach Road on his way to Snyder's Beach Dreams Real Estate. He had quickly cleaned up the living room and kitchen after his roommates had departed from the beach house, not needing another surprise visitor while he was away checking out his new job. He had called Lance and they had agreed upon a 2:30 p.m. meet up time at the office.

He had showered and changed into a pair of tan khakis and had chosen a white collared polo shirt that he tucked into his pants, pulling his brown belt securely into place. He wore brown dress shoes that he slipped into, choosing a pair of tan socks that matched his slacks. He combed his damp wavy hair straight back, knowing once dry his hair had a mind of its own. William was handsome with a toned physic from running and swimming, with the same features as his dearly departed father with his steel blue eyes that pierced through to one's soul.

He maneuvered his car into the parking lot, pulling in right beside of Lance's black Jeep. John and Alison's cars were not present, since they were still away on their cruise. He walked from his Jeep, taking in his appearance one last time, making sure he looked presentable for his first day on the job.

Will opened the door to Beach Dreams, finding Patti speaking to someone on the phone. He waited patiently at her desk until she was done with the call, as she took him in from head to toe. Lance had not informed her that he would be arriving at the office, so she wondered why he was there. William had never been to Beach Dreams before. His time spent in Marlin Beach usually involved a vacation or a day trip for a party or a special event for one of his family members, never venturing to the office where Lance worked.

"*May I help you?*" she asked curiously, finding the lad to be quite put together and handsome.

Will smiled shyly, knowing she was staring a little too much. "I am here to see my uncle Lance if he is available."

"*Your uncle Lance?*" she asked in surprise, never considering that to be a possibility. She coughed slightly, trying to clear her throat, typically not being caught off guard or caring. She dialed Lance's extension, poking carefully at the phone's button with one of her long, *just-painted nails,* hoping not to chip it in the process.

"Hello?"

"Lance, you have company," she replied sarcastically, always being at odds with him from his past rejection of her years earlier.

"Did you get a name, Patti?"

She laughed, not wanting him to be the winner in any conversation. "He says he is your nephew if that helps."

"William?"

"I guess... he never told me his name."

Will looked anxiously at her, realizing she was being difficult. "My name is William, ma'am."

"Yeah, it's him," she replied, hanging up the phone before Lance could answer, returning her gaze to that one nail, making sure it survived without a chip, as she chomped aggressively on a piece of over-worked gum.

Lance appeared in the reception area, with a pleasant smile on his face, ready to welcome William and give him the tour of the place, being in much better spirits than he was at The Happy Crab earlier in the day.

"Well hello," he greeted acting pleased to see him, leading him away from the front waiting room and back towards his office. "Would you like something to drink?" he offered, as William took the seat opposite his desk.

"No, I'm fine. Just had a water in the car."

Lance made up a fresh cup of coffee, sipping from it deeply before beginning. "Sorry about this morning, but I felt it was better to get things off my chest before things got any worse."

"No need to apologize, uncle Lance. You were absolutely right and my friends needed to hear your warning. I spoke to them further once you left. They have promised me things will improve."

Lance paused to listen to his nephew, considering his words. "I hope so, Will…. I don't want to be a tyrant, but I got to enforce the lease whether you and your friends understand and accept my terms or not."

"Oh, I understand!" he quickly replied. "And my friends have promised me it won't happen again. If it does, they know we will all have to pack and leave - and go back to our homes, unfortunately."

"Good to hear that the message got through," he answered with his coffee mug in hand, getting up to pat Will on the back before continuing. "So you think you want to give real estate a try this summer?"

"Sure do!" William grinned, getting up to stand by Lance at the window that overlooked The Old Bay Café across the street. "Where do I begin?"

"I got other summertime help, but I think for now I am going to let you shadow me for a few days and then I will let you do some things on your own. How does that sound?"

"Whatever works."

Lance took in his appearance, approving of his attire. "Continue to come to work dressed as you are today, except I would like you to wear golf shirts with the Snyder's Beach Dreams Real Estate logo on them. I will give you a variety of colors and you can rotate them throughout the week. No flip-flops or shorts, please."

"Of course, uncle Lance. Do you need me to bring in my laptop?"

"No, we have several offices here equipped with desktop computers that I will have you use for now. There is no need to bring anything to work, but maybe your lunch," he smiled broadly with his sunny, wide-toothed smile.

Lance gave William a full overview of the building, showing him each office and introducing him to the three summer interns who were attempting to get their real estate licenses and hoping to work in the field full time in the future. They made there way back out to the front reception area, apparently disrupting Patti from the magazine article she was reading.

"Is there something you need?" Patti asked, acting annoyed, looking up at the pair in front of her desk now.

"I just wanted to introduce William to you, and let you know he will be working here all summer until he returns to college in the fall."

Patti paused, taking in William once again. "Are you wanting a career in real estate?" she asked somewhat inquisitively.

Will glanced at Lance, finding it difficult to answer since he was just beginning. "I'm not sure at this point. But maybe this summer of working here will help me figure that out," he grinned, making her heart skip a beat with his youthful good looks.

The phone began to ring, disrupting the awkward moment as Patti answered the call. "Snyder's Beach Dreams Real Estate. This is Patti speaking, how may I direct your call?"

Lance nodded at her, quietly whispering as they paused at the door. *"I will be out with William for a while on a showing. If you need me - please text or call and leave a message."*

Patti shook her head - *yes* - as they headed out, and rolled her eyes and smirked as an after thought, dismissing the two as she transferred the call - just as the phone began to ring again.

CHAPTER 18

William and Lance walked towards the parked Jeeps outside, with Lance opening his car door after a few beeps of his key. He motioned for Will to get in on the passenger's side and then quickly pulled out onto Beach Road.

"That Patti doesn't seem to be the friendliest woman in the world."

Lance began to laugh loudly as he glanced over at William who looked surprised by his reaction. "That's putting things mildly. She has been working for my parents for a long time and does a fairly good job. Although, I am not one of her favorite people," he admitted.

"And why is that?"

Lance sighed, not sure he wanted to disclose those details. It suddenly occurred to him that the summer was going to be interesting, with the possibility that many unspoken truths could be revealed, now that they would be working together.

"She liked me when we first met and I guess she had hopes that we would have became an item."

"I don't get it?" he replied in confusion, as Lance continued to drive

down the strip towards Delaware, looking straight ahead and concentrating on the road.

"What isn't to get? She wanted me to be her boyfriend and it wasn't in the cards. She isn't my type."

"Oh... I see. And you have had to work with her all these years since?"

"Oh, yes. Isn't that just wonderful?" Lance replied mockingly, *breaking into a good laugh.*

"Does aunt Sarah know about this?"

"Unfortunately, yes," he answered reluctantly. "It took some convincing that I wasn't interested in her and I think she finally realizes that," he grinned, parking the car in the small driveway of a beach house sitting on a narrow strip of land in front of them. "We are here...." Lance announced matter-of-factly, as he grabbed his briefcase and camera bag from the backseat. "This is a new listing I just acquired. I need to get some papers signed and then we will take measurements and photos of each room and also the outside of the place. When we finally go back to the office, I will show you how to input the data into MLS and we will make the listing live."

"MLS?"

"That stands for Multiple Listing Service. It is the standard of excellence for displaying all listings that every real estate office across the world can see and utilize".

"That's amazing!"

"It sure is," Lance said proudly, as they rang the doorbell.

Mrs. Garrison answered, looking well put together in her bright yellow dress and shiny black belt pulled snugly around her thin waist. She smiled as she invited both of them in. "I think I have the house ready for some lovely photos," she mentioned casually as she escorted Lance and William to the kitchen table for the required signatures on the listing contract. They waited patiently on her husband who was detained in the powder room for twenty minutes.

"Sorry about that," he confessed with a gruff embarrassed response, taking a seat by his wife at the table.

Lance smiled, knowing that sometimes it was better to remain silent. He handed each one a pen, pointing to where they needed to sign as William looked on, taking it all in.

Mr. Garrison turned his attention towards William, after Lance ended the formalities and gathered the signed forms. "And who is this young man – If I might ask?"

"I'm William Miller, sir - Mr. Snyder's nephew," he explained, extending his hand in the direction of the senior gentleman, shaking his in a warm and friendly sort of way.

"Well its good to know you, William Miller," he replied with his full set of dentures showing, suddenly lightening up from his cranky attitude of earlier which was probably an after affect of his chronic constipation that he was always dealing with on a daily basis, no matter how many laxatives he took to relieve it. *"Are you in the real estate business too?"*

"Just for the summer, sir," Will made clear, as Lance and the others rose from the table. "I'm in college at Towson University and my uncle gave me a summer job at Beach Dreams. To be honest, this is my first day on the job," he confessed.

"Well good for you, son," Mr. Garrison praised, patting William on the back. "I'm a Towson grad myself. Good school for business!"

William smiled and shook his head in agreement. "I think I want to pursue a business degree, but I'm still trying to figure that all out. Maybe working with my uncle this summer will help me decide."

Lance snapped numerous pictures as the group moved from room to room conversing. Mr. Garrison and William continued to talk and Mrs. Garrison pointed out notable key features to Lance along the way.

The inside photographs were completed as Lance paused to speak to the Garrison's again. "We are actually finished inside the house, and there is no need to accompany us outside. I will take a few additional pictures showcasing the beach and the exterior of your property, and then William and I will be on our way."

"When can we expect the listing to be made live?"

"Before the end of the day, Mrs. Garrison," Lance reassured pleasantly, smiling at her with his warm kind brown eyes. "I am sure you will have offers on the table within a few days. Your place is beautiful!"

"Well, thank you, Lance," Mrs. Garrison gushed, knowing she prided herself in the décor of their beach house. "Remember, if the potential buyers want to purchase any of our furniture, we are open to that also."

"I remembered you mentioning that," Lance concluded politely, walking with William to the rear of the house for the final outdoor shots.

A seagull cried overhead as Lance attempted to snap a picture with the bird floating lazily out over the ocean. The waves broke playfully on the shoreline and no one interfered with the tranquil scene, since it was by all means a very quiet and private beach, with only an occasional walker going by, even in the midst of the start of the busy beach season.

"I'm all set, William," Lance announced, as he replaced his lens cover before returning the camera to its case that was swinging back and forth off of his shoulder.

Together they headed back to the Jeep, waving a fond goodbye to the Garrison's who stood inside their patio doors watching their every move, as Lance backed out on the road.

"That didn't seem too difficult," Will commented, as Lance crossed back over the Maryland line towards Beach Dreams again.

"You're right. It wasn't, but imagine doing a couple of them in one day and then you have appointments set up with people interested in seeing multiple properties for the first time. It becomes a juggling act to accommodate everyone. That is why I need summer help."

"Wow, I didn't think about it that way!"

"It's ok, buddy. You just got a lot to learn about my business. That's all," Lance answered warmly, giving Will an understanding pat on the knee. "Let's get inside and I will show you how to put the listing in the computer now."

They walked together back into Beach Dreams, as Patti slid a piece of paper in Lance's direction. "You had two calls while you were out. One, from someone wanting to see several condos and the second from your mother."

"From my mother?" Lance answered her in surprise.

Patti glared at him, not wanting to go into any details, but knowing she needed to. "She said your dad got sick on the cruise and they may need to come home early. She wants you to call her," she replied in a monotone voice, putting her head back down and ignoring him again.

William and Lance walked down the hallway towards his office, taking their places again in the large spacious room, as he offered his nephew a soda and he brewed another cup of coffee.

"I must call my mother and will only be a few minutes. Feel free to use the bathroom or take a break outside. It shouldn't take long," he apologized, excusing himself to walk to another area close by where he could be alone.

"Sure, uncle Lance. I hope your father is okay."

"Well, thank you, William. We can only hope... " He answered with uncertainty, wishing for the same.

The phone vibrated on the bedside table where Alison Snyder was resting in a recliner beside of her sick husband. John had a fever of 101 degrees and was lying in the king-sized bed of their deluxe suite - tossing and turning restlessly in his sleep.

"Hello, Lance. Thank God you called," she whispered, trying not to disturb John.

"Is everything okay with dad?"

"Not really. He is very sick. The doctor thinks food poisoning, but they are still waiting on the lab results."

Lance scratched his head, trying to take it all in. "How about you, are you feeling bad also?"

"No, I am fine. But your father and I had different meals last night and something definitely did not agree with him."

Lance got up to pace, not liking the sound of things. "Is anyone else sick on the ship?"

"Yes, a few so far. They think it is the cream sauce that was served over broccoli or maybe even the steak, but they are just assuming at this point."

"So what can I do to help out?"

"There is really nothing, dear," Alison answered softly, looking at her sleeping husband who was perspired from heaving one too many times in the toilet. *"I just wanted you to know what was going on. The doctor is on top of things, but you know you father isn't in the best of health with his heart, and I thought you would* want to know."

"Absolutely, mother!" Lance answered, making his way back to his office where William was still waiting. "Well keep my updated. I got work to do and William is here observing things. I am ready to show him how to put in a listing."

"I almost forgot he was going to be in Marlin Beach for the summer, and obviously it sounds like you gave him a job at Beach Dreams. How does he like The Happy Crab so far?" she asked pleasantly with a whisper, not knowing the half of it and trying her best not to wake John.

CHAPTER 19

Lance glanced at Will who was sitting across from his desk looking bored, realizing his mother didn't need anymore on her plate under the circumstances. "He seems to be enjoying himself," Lance answered with a half-truth, bringing William back to the present. "Well I must go, mom. Everything is going smoothly here at Beach Dreams. Give dad my best and don't rush back on our account."

"Thank you, Lance, for taking care of things. I will keep you updated on your father if anything changes. I plan to be back to work next Thursday."

"See you then," Lance smiled, hanging up and turning his attention back to William.

"Are you ready to see how we put in a listing?"

"Absolutely!"

"Well bring your chair around and sit by me."

William picked up the fairly light accent chair, placing it right beside of Lance's desk, watching his every move. He showed him how to log in to the software that would upload the listing once completed. Each detail of the Garrison's property was included with room measurements, including features that a buyer would be interested in. The final step was to upload all the photos that were taken of the inside of the beach house along with the outside photos of the property that displayed the close proximity to the actual beach.

"One last step and then we make the Garrison's house *live* for everyone to see. I wouldn't be surprised if we have a contract within the week on their place," Lance smiled confidently, pressing the *save* button on the keyboard.

"So this is the process every time?" Will asked in interest, as Lance got up to make another cup of coffee that he was prone to over indulge in throughout his workday.

"It can vary, but for the most part, yes. After showing you this same process a few times, I would like for you to put in the listings. *Do you think you can handle that?"* Lance asked, sipping from his tasty French roast.

"I think so…. but what if I screw something up?"

"It's fixable. I will review your work and if I want to tweak something we will edit the listing. Pretty simple, really. Just don't get the price wrong," Lance winked, making light of the situation. "I'm sure you will be a pro within a few weeks."

"I hope so, uncle Lance. I know this is your business and I wouldn't want to do anything wrong."

"Stop worrying. Everyone has to get his or her feet wet at some point, when learning something new. Real Estate is no different," Lance explained as he patted William on the back. "By the way, Sarah called and would like to have you over for dinner tonight if you can break free of your friends for a few hours. What do you think?"

"What do I think?" William grinned. "Of course I would like to see

aunt Sarah and the twins! Are you sure it's okay? I wouldn't want to give her any extra work."

"I wouldn't have offered if I thought Sarah couldn't handle it. Pack up your book bag now and we will head over to the house. First thing in the morning though, you will have a full day tomorrow. So be here and ready to go by 8 a.m."

Mr. McHenry escorted the boys on a lengthy tour of The Dexter Resort and Spa. He showed them the two separate hotel buildings, convention center, top-rated restaurant and the Jeffrey Wells Aquatic Center that housed the indoor pool and health spa. He then proceeded to walk them outside so that they could take in the spacious grounds that boasted several swimming pools, tennis and basket courts, walking paths with lush tropical landscaping and decorative fountains, and of course the several parking lots with numerous spaces that were needed for all the guests and their vehicles.

"The resort is so big!" Tyler commented, as the group filed back into the business office, ready to hear about the several different jobs openings that they could sign up for.

"Yes, it is!" Mr. McHenry agreed, taking a seat at the large table spread out in front of him where the three stared back, waiting on his direction. "As you can see, this resort requires a lot of work to maintain such an operation, especially during the busy summer months when we are in full tourist mode. So where would you like to work?"

"I think I would like to work in the restaurant, uncle Jack."

Jack McHenry glanced at his nephew fondly who was his only sister's son. "Well Christopher, I can make that happen for you, but it isn't only a job of waiting on patrons and getting big fat tips afterwards – which it goes without saying that you can *never* demand or ask for. It also involves cleaning up your section, helping out with food prep and washing dishes too. Whatever the kitchen manager asks, you must comply with. *Do you think you can handle that?"*

"I think so ... I won't know until I try, but I think so," Chris answered hesitantly, knowing some more pressure was now being placed upon him besides - keeping The Happy Crab in tiptop shape to keep Lance off his back, and also needing to do his best at work so that is uncle remained happy.

"How about you guys? What shall it be - housekeeping, being a waiter or maybe parking cars as a valet – which one sounds appealing?" Jack Henry asked as he studied his nephew's friends' faces.

"I think I would like to try waiting tables also," Tyler replied. "I worked part-time in Florida when I was in high school for a diner on weekends. I used to help out with the breakfast shift."

"Well, that's great! We are always lacking in morning help here in the restaurant. Most college students coming here for the summer prefer jobs in the late afternoon or evening."

Tyler looked at Chris, concerned by his uncle's assumptions that he wanted the early morning shift, finding it difficult to respond. "Umm…. I can work any shift required of me, but if I had my preference… I guess I would avoid the early morning hours - at least for several days of the week."

The group began to laugh, including Mr. McHenry, knowing Tyler was caught off guard by his explanation and making things only worse the more he went on.

"It's okay, son," Mr. McHenry consoled. "I'm not the kitchen manager. If I had to guess, I'm sure she will want to know your work hour desires and then try to accommodate you, but I would keep an open mind to all of this," he warned, as he stood up, continuing to address the group.

"So two of you want to work in the restaurant. How about you, Matthew, what is your desire here at The Dexter?"

Matt sat back in his chair with his arms crossed in front of him, pondering the question. "I think I would like to valet park cars, and if that isn't a full time job, I am willing to do something else if needed."

"That is an excellent attitude, Matthew! This is just what we want to hear from our new hires at The Dexter Resort and Spa, even if you are only seeking temporary summer employment. Being open to helping anywhere in the facility and being flexible to that makes all the difference in the world. It makes the selection process easier who we will choose to be employed here," he preached, pacing the room with his speech.

"Uncle Jack, I think we *all* can be flexible with whatever you need us to do here," Chris interjected, looking at the other two for their approval at assuming responsibility for the group.

Jack smiled, understanding his nephew's statement and remembering he too had to impress someone many years earlier at Marlin Beach for a summer job. "Well that is a good mindset to have, Christopher, and it will definitely go a long way here, especially if you want to come back in the future to work here after this summer."

Chris, Matt and Tyler completed their withholding paperwork and other required startup forms, sliding them in the direction of Mr. McHenry, who placed them in a file folder.

"Your next step is a drug test that is required. Take this cup to the bathroom and urinate in it, and then screw the lip on top," he instructed, handing each one present a specimen cup. "When you are finished, I will retrieve the cup and label it before the next person goes into the bathroom. *Do I make myself perfectly clear?"* He asked succinctly.

"*Yes,"* they mutually answered together.

The testing procedure was completed as the group walked back into the office and sat down at the table again, waiting on Mr. McHenry who knew their results. He opened the door, smiling happily as he approached.

"Glad to say you all passed! I wouldn't have wanted to tell you any different," he added, as he thought he heard at least one sigh deeply in relief. "Just as a note, we occasionally do random retesting, so keep that in the back of your mind if you desire to be employed here all summer," he warned sternly as he tried to study the face of each college student, knowing that was typically not the case or enforced even though it could be. "Plan to get a call from your new supervisors tomorrow concerning your schedule and where you will actually work here at the resort," he advised, walking the group from the room they were in to the front of the hotel where the grand foyer was situated.

"Do you know what time we should be expecting a call?" Chris inquired.

Jack McHenry raised an eyebrow with a slight lift of a smile, knowing what he was asking. "Chris, if you are wondering if you can sleep in tomorrow and not answer the phone early, I would highly suggest that you be alert and ready for that call first thing in the morning! Many college kids want jobs here at The Dexter. You are lucky to have an uncle in such a position that I can look out for you and your friends. *Do I make myself clear?*"

"*Yes, sir!*" The three answered in unison, even though the statement was being addressed directly towards Chris.

"Well, then there is nothing else that needs to be gone over and covered at this point of time. Welcome aboard as new employees of The Dexter Resort and Spa!"

CHAPTER 20

"Hey, aunt Sarah!" William called out, as he and Lance entered the kitchen of The Playful Starfish where Sarah was busily turning barbeque chicken over for the last time in the oven as she brushed more sauce on each piece.

She put down the tongs, running over to give her nephew a warm, loving hug. "It's been too long," she gushed, looking him over at arm's length. "You look older to me," she assessed, taking him in from head to toe.

"It hasn't been that long!" he laughed, breaking free of her embrace, finding a seat at the large hand-made, boat-shaped, kitchen table. "Where are the twins?"

"Sleeping…." Sarah answered quietly. "And hopefully they will stay that way, at least for a few more minutes until I can finish dinner," she smiled, looking somewhat drained.

"I can help," Will offered.

"With the kids or dinner," Lance grinned, as he poured a glass of sweet tea, offering one to Sarah and William too.

"Whatever you need," Will answered with a laugh. "But I may be better at playing with Alex and Abby and keeping them entertained, than trying to make dinner for us."

"I would never ask you to do either," Sarah replied politely, always trying to be superwoman and do it all for her family.

Lance stared fondly at his beautiful wife who rarely chose makeup these days, but still tried to look attractive by combing her long, blonde locks back into her signature ponytail that she secured high up off her neck. She was dressed in a pink t-shirt and capris length blue jeans, and had on matching blue flip-flops. She was casual in attire, but feeling content and in good spirits most days even if she lacked in sleep. Sarah was a mother first to the twins – Alexander and Abigail - and then a wonderful wife to Lance besides. She was no longer a full-time businesswoman of the architectural world, taking a temporary leave of absence for a few years to raise her children, by common agreement with her father who she jointly owned the Miller Architecture Company with. She was a stay-at-home mother, now domesticated and also a woman of Marlin Beach - choosing to live close by its shoreline and enjoying the *salt life* immensely.

At one point after her twin brother's death, she would not allow herself time to be at Marlin Beach to vacation and never considered living there. The riptide accident was a sad reminder of how Dexter was taken out of her young life at only age 18. But a decade later, after falling in love with Lance and marrying him, everything had changed and she felt healed. The ocean was a part of her being once again, where she loved to reside and share a life with her husband and children.

The table was set with aqua blue dinner plates and lime green salad bowls, as Sarah lined up serving dishes on the granite countertop with the food she had prepared. She dished out the over-abundance of barbeque chicken on a large nautical themed platter, being accompanied by scalloped potatoes and fresh green beans, with a salad of mixed greens and croutons completing the fare.

Lance and William reappeared, each one carrying one of the freshly changed twins who were now smiling happily at their mother, trying to rub the sleep from their eyes.

"There you are!" Sarah gushed with delight at seeing her chubby cherubs who had just awoken from their afternoon nap. They giggled, jumping up and down in Will and Lance's arms, hoping their mother would hold them next as they reached out their arms in her direction. *"Not now, babies,"* she chided, removing the food trays off of their high chairs so that they could be strapped in.

"You can place them in here," she instructed, as the babies were put in their seats with their safety belts snapped into place, and then the food trays were locked over each one of the twins' laps. They cried as they waited on their food, with big teardrops falling down over their cheeks and landing on the plastic trays.

"Life is tough when you're 9 months old, right?" Lance laughed as he joined William who had already grabbed a plate and was helping himself to food on Sarah's insistence as she fed the babies.

"I can't remember," Will replied, half in jest. "But I know you and aunt Sarah are amazing parents."

"Well, thank you, William," Sarah answered, accepting his compliment, looking up from the half-eaten bowl of smashed sweet potatoes that she was spoon feeding the twins. "You may not feel the same when you see baby laundry all over the sectional that needs to be folded, and an overflowing diaper pail that needs to be emptied," she admitted, realizing how so much now was out of her control.

"Nonsense, Sarah!" Lance insisted, spooning in another bite of the tasty cheese covered scalloped potatoes. "Things are rarely as you describe. The twins are lucky to have you as their mommy."

Sarah's pale blue eyes moistened slightly from her husband's open praise. "I couldn't do it without you..." she confessed softly, looking at

Lance with an over-abundance of love in her heart for him.

"Dinner was great!" Will praised, feeling guilty that he was already finished and Sarah had still not eaten because of feeding the twins.

"There's plenty more," Sarah offered, getting up to finally make her own plate. "Please take some back to your roommates."

"I'll take you up on that, but I'm not sharing that delicious food with them," William teased, knowing once he placed it in the refrigerator back at The Happy Crab, it was open season for someone finding and eating it first. That was always the way at Towson too. He had come to learn that it required a tied plastic bag covering the container, with his name clearly marked on it with a black sharpie marker, along with a *do not eat* message, to get the word across and keep them out of his food.

The twins played happily in their play yard as Sarah brought in two large bowls heaped high with warm apple crisp and vanilla ice cream, giving one to Lance and the other to William, as they were engrossed in watching a movie about super heroes.

"Wow, am I full!" William announced, grabbing his stomach as he placed his dirty bowl in the dishwasher as per Sarah's request.

"You should be, since you had seconds," Lance teased, placing his empty desert dish in the dishwasher by Will's.

They all laughed as they made their way back to the living room to finish the movie and share some additional family time together. Will climbed in the play yard and lay on his back, allowing the babies to climb on top of his over-full stomach, making him groan out from the weight of them being on him. He lifted each one high in the air as they giggled down at him, with drool leaving their mouths and falling in his face.

"You little stinker!" he playfully yelled out, as he sat up taking Alex with him, as he lifted his shirt and gave him a *pink belly* with his mouth.

The baby laughed out in delight, enjoying the attention immensely, before William grabbed Abby, repeating the same theme, giving her the same *belly tickling* as her brother.

Lance and Sarah took it all in, glad that William was giving them a few minutes of reprieve before the nightly ritual began of baths, nursing and then supplemental bottles before going to bed - which could take several hours depending on the twins' moods. Lance typically helped out with the evening routine, but it was obvious that they babies preferred their mother at this time of their young lives. Sometimes, moral support was all that he could offer to Sarah when she was trying to put them down for the night.

"It's getting late, bro, and we start work early tomorrow, as you know," Lance reminded at 9:30 p.m., as he bent over to lift one of the twins out of the play yard. Sarah followed suit, grabbing the other as Will climbed out over the gated area, following them back out to the kitchen to grab his take-home, large goodie bag filled high with food containers.

"Thanks so much for everything," William said, trying to hug Sarah and Abby at the same time as Sarah held her.

"You are welcome, Will. I hope you won't be a stranger this summer. I know you will be busy with work and your friends, but stop in whenever you would like," she smiled and offered sincerely. "The twins obviously love to play with you," she added as they all walked to the front door to say goodnight and goodbye.

"I promise I will be back to play with the twins soon. Maybe I can even babysit for you guys and you can get a break."

Lance laughed, considering the possibility. " We will need to teach you how to change diapers first before that can happen; and for that matter, you may change your mind once you see how it's done."

"Don't be so sure of that, uncle Lance. Remember, I do have

younger siblings that I used to help my mother with," he replied realistically, suddenly feeling somewhat sad thinking about his mother again and his brother and sister who he hadn't seen in quite a long time.

"I'm sorry, Will," Lance answered, giving his shoulder an understanding squeeze. "I forgot about all that."

"We may take you up on that, sweetie," Sarah added, bending over to plant a sweet, gentle kiss on William's cheek, remembering to what he had been through with losing his mother.

"Thanks again for everything! It was a great evening," William called out from his car window, as he drove away in his Jeep, heading back to The Happy Crab for the night.

"You're back!" Chris yelled out over the blare of the TV, as Will unlocked the door with one hand, juggling his oversized bag of food with the other.

"Yes, I am," he smiled, as he placed each container on the counter, removing the lids to his roommates' inspection. *"Anyone hungry?"*

"You don't have to ask me a second time," Matt replied, making his way quickly to the kitchen before anyone else could get there first, grabbing a paper plate and a spoon, taking two pieces of the barbeque chicken and all of the sides.

Chris and Tyler did accordingly, eating as if they hadn't had a decent meal in days, cleaning out the containers entirely. William returned from the bathroom, viewing the empty containers in front of him now, shaking his head in disbelief that they all were empty.

"Seriously, you didn't save me anything? Not even one damn piece of chicken! You guys act as if you were starving or something!"

"We were! No one bothered inviting us for dinner!"

CHAPTER 21

The next couple of weeks were a time of adjustment to new work schedules and keeping The Happy Crab clean. The college students had only one goal - to do as little as they could to pass inspection on any of Lance's surprise visits. Only once since the initial warning did he need to remind the boys of the lease agreement clause of *maintaining the beach house or they would have to pay for housekeeping or move*.

William was learning the ropes at Beach Dreams and actually now putting in listings that Lance rarely found a mistake with before the *live* button was pressed for the real estate community to see. Will was not allowed to do the actual measurements of a property on his own, so Lance had to escort him there every time since he was not a licensed realtor. Lance would review the actual contract with the sellers or buyers and gain the signatures that were needed, while Will looked on trying to retain as much knowledge about the real estate business as possible. Together, they would measure each room at the properties - be it a condo, townhouse or beach house - taking a variety of photos inside and out with the amenity pictures being featured of swimming pools or workout facilities, along with gift shops and restaurants located close by. Lance typically would allow William to use the camera, realizing he had an excellent eye for capturing the perfect angle of each candid shot.

Chris and Tyler were learning to be excellent servers at their fast-paced award-winning restaurant, where they at times worked a double shift if asked. Matt was doing a superb job with valet parking the numerous vehicles that were always coming and going. Generous tips were being given to all, and in some ways William was jealous that he was not receiving the extra money that his friends were always bragging about from working at The Dexter.

John was still recovering from the flu that he was finally diagnosed with, not having food poisoning after all. Alison was only working part-time now at Beach Dreams so that she could stay at home and take care of her husband who seemed to be enjoying the extra attention. Alison's computer and phone were always on though, so her workload was no less stressful even though her office location had changed.

Lance was constantly busy trying to keep up with his daily workload, overseeing William and the three summer interns that had just gotten their licenses. At times, the new rookie realtors would stay on at Beach Dreams after their training, but most often they would branch out to another real estate agency away from Marlin Beach once the summer season was over.

Sarah stayed busy with the twins, happy to gain a few extra minutes alone with her husband after he was done working and they were down for the night. Lance typically came home exhausted, and there was always the debate back and forth who was the most tired after a day at the office during tourist season or staying at home being a full time mother to Alexander and Abigail. Sarah typically would win out with her full explanation of *stay-at-home mothers being under-valued and unappreciated and just as busy as someone working in an office.* Lance knew it was better to give in to her then protest too loudly where Sarah was concerned.

"Dinner was great, sweetie. How about a shower and then I will give you an amazing backrub?" Lance teased, rubbing and pinching Sarah's nipple playfully through her see-through dusty blue t-shirt.

"Umm... you got a deal," she purred, feeling warmth spreading between her legs already, knowing any opportunity for sex and intimacy without being interrupted by a crying infant, was a rarity these days.

They quietly climbed the stairs together hand in hand, not wanting to wake the twins, tiptoeing to their room before slowly easing their master bedroom door shut. Lance stopped to swoop Sarah into his arm, planting kisses down her neck that left her shuttering in delight.

"I hope... we can... pull this off..." she panted out, as he carried her to the bath area, removing her clothes quickly and his in kind, wanting only to be inside of her.

The pulsating hot water that was flowing from the multiple showerheads eased the day's worries, as Lance stood behind his wife working over her tired shoulder blades, as his erection grew increasingly larger. *"God, I want you..."* he beckoned with a ragged breath, as he easily slid her legs slightly apart.

He took her in the steamy over-sized shower, plunging deeply into her wet, slick cavern that was begging for more. They moved quickly against the other as Lance grabbed Sarah's breasts – one in each hand – bringing each nipple to a firm peak as he taunted and teased them by the skill of his well-versed fingers - who knew his wife well from their years of repeated lovemaking.

"Ah... oh..." Sarah screamed out in orgasm, over the sound of the incessant pouring water of the shower. Lance in turn yelled out, climaxing completely as his head bobbed back and forth against Sarah's back.

They turned to face the other - kissing and holding on, feeling depleted and fulfilled from their lovemaking, as the faucets were turned off. Only the sound of the remaining water droplets plopping and echoing loudly off of the ceramic tile floor could be heard as their breathing became normal again.

"We better dry off before the twins start screaming," Lance grinned, making Sarah's heart swoon again at the sheer sight of her handsome and tanned, chiseled man, who maintained his muscular physic from running on the beach almost daily before work, still slipping off to the gym for a mid-day workout if he had the chance.

They climbed into bed, now fully dressed in shorts and t-shirts, no longer able to sleep in the nude as was their habit before the birth of their children, because of the twins nightly reach outs. Lance cuddled and spooned Sarah, wrapping her securely in his arms, kissing the back of her still-wet, long blonde hair.

"You were amazing, darling."

Sarah turned to look lovingly into Lance's still-passionate, brown eyes that she could see in the dimly lit room, illuminated by the moon that was casting a soft glow against the windows that were free of encumbrances - with drawn-up shades and privacy forgotten.

"I am a lucky woman to have you. Do you know that?" she whispered, realizing how much she had come to love Lance over the years, especially now that she was a wife and mother.

"We are both lucky," he answered tenderly, kissing her lightly one more time on the lips. "We better get some rest. You know one of the twins will be crying out soon and waking us up."

"I know... but for now it is just us..." she said softly, clinging securely to her spouse. "Good night, Lance. I love you."

"I love you too, dear."

To their surprise the twins slept soundly, at least for a few hours...

It was midnight and Matt unlocked the door of the beach house, ready to call it a night, after parking the remainder of the vehicles at The Dexter. All was quiet except for the slight moaning he could hear coming from across the room in the direction of the sofa. Nude bodies were entwined, silhouetted against the slivers of moonlight filtering through from the vertical blinds of the patio doors. Pre-occupied with their activity, they were unaware that someone else what present.

"Hey bro, I'm home," Matt announced loudly, realizing it was Chris and his newest girlfriend that he had obviously picked up at The Dexter. Either it was a hotel guest or a fellow employee that he had developed a fondness for - if for just a routine hookup session. Matt turned towards the refrigerator, looking inside for a beer, giving them a minute to find their discarded clothes.

Chris and Mia sat up, fumbling to at least step into their underthings, as the slim and pretty brunette that worked the evening shift with him, re-hooked her bra in place and wiggled into her thong panties. Chris adjusted his briefs, walking to the kitchen while scratching his privates, joining Matt for a beer as Mia slipped on her sundress and sneakers, making her way to the table afterwards. She smiled boldly at Matt, knowing that they were caught in the act. Mia thought he was cute in his own way, and honestly was willing to have sex with him too.

Chris handed Mia a beer, sipping deeply from his own and then belching loudly afterwards, making her giggle and laugh. *"Chris, that's gross!"* she protested, rolling her eyes and placing her hands on her athletic hips in a saucy suggested way, looking in Matt's direction to see his reaction.

Matt shook his head, knowing her look and what she was hoping for. He had decided since the beginning of his college life with these guys at Towson, that he would not go after one of his roommate's chicks unless they were definitely not seeing them any longer - which was the general rule with all of them, and then he was still cautious -

not testing the waters yet or needing their wrath.

"I'm going to bed…. Have fun!" Matt yelled over his head, still with the beer can in hand, shutting his bedroom door behind him and locking it, just in case Mia decided to wander down the hallway in his direction.

He lay in bed thinking of Nicole who was his unofficial college girlfriend. She had promised to visit him in Marlin Beach if she could slip away from her summer lifeguarding job at the local swimming pool in her town, but so far she hadn't made any serious attempts to do so. He hadn't been with anyone else yet sexually at the beach, although several had tempted him.

The Dexter Resort and Spa, to Matt's surprise, was a hotbed of sexual invites from guests as well as other employees there. Even one of the male valets had made an intimate gesture, which he was totally turned off by, politely refusing, informing him that he preferred girls.

He knew Chris was a *male whore* at school as well as at the beach, and honestly wasn't sure about Tyler and Will's intentions for the summer at that point. As for him though, he would stick to the plan of making money and helping out with college tuition since his single mother was financially strapped and not fully able to pay for his education.

Matt awoke to a soft tapping after he had just drifted off to sleep, hearing Mia whisper his name, requesting the door to be opened for the third time. *Chris must be sleeping…* he surmised, ignoring her and placing the pillow over his head with a groan. *"God, will she ever stop! I have no time for this bitch!"* he softly growled out, before falling back asleep once again.

CHAPTER 22

7 a.m. and Matt rolled over to the shrieking beeping of his cellphone alarm clock. "Geesh," he exclaimed in frustration that he had to get up, knowing he was still tired from the repeated, persistent tapping on his door probably until 2 a.m. He only hoped Mia had left and Chris was no more the wiser by her intentions. The last thing he wanted was a debate this early in the morning over who was the guilty party, which he knew - he was not.

After a quick shower he slipped into his khaki shorts and a collared lime green t-shirt with The Dexter logo embroidered on the front of it, choosing a pair of clean white sneakers that allowed for a quick jog back and forth to the check-in area of the hotel after parking or retrieving a car. He combed his brown hair in place after shaving and placing a small dab of cologne on each side of his neck. Anything to get a good tip was his primary motivation, even if it meant smelling good for the female patrons who occasionally made a pass at him.

Matt entered the kitchen seeing his three roommates bustling about the kitchen, preparing or making due with what they could come up with for breakfast. Will was eating a bagel with cream cheese, Chris was pouring milk over a bowl of corn flakes, and Tyler was eating a cold slice of leftover pizza with a Coke to wash it all down with.

"God... why are you guys up already?"

"We're making plans," Chris explained.

"What sort of plans?" Matt asked, grabbing a frozen, pre-packaged breakfast sandwich from the freezer and popping it in the microwave before brewing some coffee in the one-cup Keurig maker.

"Par....tee bro!" Tyler yelled with a laugh.

Matt looked up after adding creamer to his coffee. *"When?"*

"Tonight!" Will smiled. "We invited a few from The Dexter and I also talked to a couple guys and one girl at Beach Dreams."

"Oh, boy... I'm not so sure this is a good idea with your uncle's random visits. *What if he finds out?"* Matt asked in concern, sipping deeply from his hot java and taking a big bite of sausage, egg and cheese on an English muffin.

"I told the ones that I invited not to say a word to Lance," Will explained, feeling confident that they would maintain the secret.

"No one will say anything on our end either - so he will *never* find out," Tyler added, throwing his greasy paper plate and now squashed-up empty soda can in the trash can.

"I invited Mia," Chris interjected, making Matt turn around and glare in his direction.

"Seriously? She is a pain in the ass!"

"Fuck you, Matt. She's great and I think I want to start dating her."

Matt shook his head in disbelief. "Better be careful before you come to that conclusion. She may not want to be totally exclusive with you yet. You may want to give it some time."

"Why ya sayin that? Something I need to know?" Chris asked,

looking suspicious and pissed off all at once.

Matt paused, not sure he wanted to reveal what he knew. "She kept knocking on my door last night until 2 a.m., wanting me to open it and let her in."

"You son of a bitch!" Chris yelled out, running around the other side of the table, knocking over a chair, ready to hit Matt with his balled up fist, straight in his face.

Matt ducked away from the blow, just as Tyler and William grabbed Chris on either side, holding him back from doing anything he would regret later.

"What the fuck, Chris! I don't want that ho!"

"Don't you dare call her a ho! *And why would she be at your bedroom door last night if you hadn't made a pass at her first?"*

Matt just shook his head again as he stared at his friend in disbelief. "I thought you *knew me* better than that!"

Chris just snorted in response and acted disgusted, not believing him for one moment.

"Have you ever known me to do that to any of you?" he asked the group, wanting to feel that they trusted him.

"Nah, bro, you're always straight," Will answered.

"Yeah, for me too," Tyler added, breaking away from restraining Chris. "Hey, I gotta get ready for work. Enough of this petty bullshit! I will be back later with my friends and some beer. Cam is over 21 and he can get us as much as we need as long as everyone chips in and helps pay for it, and I'm sure the others showing up will just bring their own. *The party is still on, right?"* Tyler asked, walking towards the bathroom.

"It is. That is, if Chris is still cool with things?" Will replied, looking at his friend intensely, still resting his hand firmly on his shoulder, trying to steady and calm him down.

Chris took a few slow deep breaths, trying to clear his head, glaring at Matt who was now in the living room sitting on one of the chairs watching some TV. "Yeah, let's do this. I won't be inviting Mia though," he added, glancing over at Matt and waiting for his reaction.

Matt turned, getting up and walking towards Chris, placing his cup in the sink first. "I don't give a shit if you invite her or not. She doesn't faze me in the least and I will have some of my own friends here tonight. So do what you want," he added with a sneer as he walked towards the door, ready to leave. "I'll get a tray of wings and some chips and dip. See you all later."

The door slammed behind him, leaving Will and Chris alone in the kitchen. Chris bent down to right side up the chair that he had knocked over with his temper, as William crossed his arms in front of him, just staring at his friend in disbelief.

"I know you like Mia, but maybe you should listen to Matt and keep your options open. Keep dating other people, bro."

"I'll think about...." he blurted out, not wanting to admit that his friends may be right.

"I can't be late for work. Lance is expecting me today at 9. He needed an extra hour this morning because of something Sarah had to do, but I definitely need to be at the office on time. I will see you after work and then we will have some fun tonight. Deal?" he grinned, reaching out to playfully pinch Chris's shoulder, trying to lighten the mood.

"Yeah, deal. I'm due in at The Dexter at 10. I'm only working until 4 today and then I will try to pick up a few things for the party. Gonna be a great night tonight. Not a chance of rain, you know."

"That's what I heard," Will smiled, walking towards the door with his backpack in hand. "See you later."

"Remember, not to breathe of word of this around your uncle."

"It's all good. Got it covered."

Tyler was the next one to leave, walking at a fast pace towards the door. "I'll see you at work and you better not be late."

"I'll be there soon," Chris replied half-irritated, knowing that being on time for work had been a problem so far. He placed his empty cereal bowl in the sink before walking to the bathroom and turning on the shower, trying to shake the fight with Matt from his mind.

The day progressed for the roommates. William was busy at Beach Dreams putting in a few new listings that Lance had laid on his desk. He waited for his opportunity while Lance was on the phone to quietly confirm with his co-workers - Devin, James and Harper - that the party was still on and that no one was to know that he was having it, especially Lance. Matt parked and retrieved cars non-stop, with a large convention just checking in, which kept him busy most of the day. Chris and Tyler waited tables mainly for the lunch crowd, prepping before the shift and cleaning up afterwards once they were gone. They then went the extra mile, assisting with the evening prep since someone had called in sick, even though they were free to leave for the day.

Each one of them, picked up a few things for the party, with Cam keeping his word to *buy the beer* once enough money was collected from the invited employees from The Dexter.

Chris was the one first home after work. He emptied the trash and washed the dishes in the sink, and wiped down the kitchen table and granite countertops. He tidied up both bathrooms and straightened the couch and chair cushions and made his bed, drawing the line at making the beds of the others. *Overall, the place would past inspection if Lance walks in about now - except for a few unmade beds,* he realized as he surveyed the cleaned up spaces of the beach house.

Chris changed into jeans and a black t-shirt and slipped into his black flip-flops after taking a shower. He looked in the mirror that was over the bathroom sink, self-appraising his appearance, wanting to look desirable to the soon arriving females who would show up for the party. He combed his brown hair as best he could, resembling Will and Matt's in color but not texture, since it was stick straight. He had hazel green eyes and a sprinkling of freckles across the bridge of his nose, with average looks. Unfortunately, he wasn't as muscular as his friends either, which he never put forth any effort to change. He typically chose the couch and a video game, or an occasional female companion over working out at the gym or running outside like the others did. His most appealing trait that set him apart was his outgoing personality which some described as "being the life of the party".

The front door opened with Will, Matt and Tyler coming in with their arms filled to overflowing with bags of food for the party, placing it on every available space on the clean countertops in the kitchen.

"Boy, the place looks nice!" Will complimented as he looked around, smiling at Chris who seemed to be in a much better mood now than he was earlier in the day.

"I figured that I owed you," Chris admitted with a sheepish grin, seeing his friends who were now walking around and checking out the clean rooms. "We are now officially party ready."

"Not until the beer arrives!" Tyler exclaimed. "Cam is trying to get a keg for the back yard along with some wine as we speak."

"Oh boy..." Matt replied with a shake of his head, still thinking about Lance showing up unexpectedly if someone at Beach Dreams didn't keep their promise.

"It's gonna be some night tonight. Our first summer party that we're throwing here at The Happy Crab!"

"Let's hope it isn't our last," Will laughed.

Chapter 23

Tyler wrapped a string of party lights with plastic margarita glasses - which he had brought from their dorm room in Towson - around the back deck railing. He then plugged them in, creating a warm and sensual glow that he was quite proud of and knew it would set the mood for the evening. He also placed a speaker on the deck, turning up the volume a little bit too loudly, with all the roommates hoping that the sound of the ocean waves would drown out the noise and not cause a problem with the adjacent neighbors. The other three guys spaced the Tiki torches - that they found in the shed behind the back of the beach house, filling each with oil and then lighting them afterwards, as the blue flames jumped up and swayed gently in the ocean breeze. Cam brought the promised keg along with a couple of boxes of cheap red and white wine, and some plastic red cups, knowing that the majority of females preferred the wine over the beer. *Anything to keep the girls happy and get them drunk with the promise of sex afterwards* was the goal of every male for the evening.

"*Hey, who wants the next beer?*" Cam yelled out from the sand below, as he bent over the keg with a red Solo cup, filling it up until the foam spilled out over the side, handing the next beer to some random guy that nobody seemed to know.

The uninvited *party people* came in droves, piling inside the beach house and hanging out on the back deck where the music was blasting much too loudly. The backyard was filled to capacity with the majority being college-aged summer workers who were waiting in line for a beer out of the keg or a glass of wine. Many did bring their own stash, breaking off into small groups, sitting cross-legged in the sand - drinking and smoking pot or consuming other drugs, having their own private parties with a few select friends joining them.

Will looked at Chris in concern. *"Who are all these people?* I only invited a few and I thought you guys did the same."

"Chill, bro," Chris insisted with a slightly intoxicated laugh, as he downed his third beer. "They are each paying us $5.00 a head, so what is the big deal? We are making more money than I make in a day waiting tables at The Dexter. Honestly, we should be having parties like thing on a regular basis if we were smart."

"Well that is *not* happening!" Will yelled over the loud boom of the music coming from the speaker that was now set to full volume. He moved towards the deck that had the patio doors fully pulled back, allowing in the ocean breeze but also a vast array of moths and mosquitoes, turning the volume down to a more desirable level. He pushed through the crowd, nudging forward to the deck railing, taking in the scene of what appeared to be 75 to 100 people, hoping that they were all over the age of 18. Beyond the ones wanting to get drunk and high, others stood around in groups talking and drinking, with some swaying and dancing to the music. In the distance, he could see two who were laughing and nude and purely void of caring, involved in lovemaking. They were out in the open and on the sand, near the water's edge, wildly bopping up and down and without abandon.

Matt joined Will by the railing taking in the scene at hand. *"I think we got a problem here, Will.* I just saw the deck lights go on at the neighbor's on the right a few minutes ago, and the guy over there was walking around in his backyard taking it all in. We better hope he doesn't call the cops on us."

"Fuck..." Will sighed, seeing Chris cozied up on the sand, fondling a girl through her sheer tank top, and Tyler pouring another beer out of the keg as he dragged a girl along with him towards the ocean for a late night swim. "I agree, this is getting out of control. I don't want anyone else showing up. We are at our max inside and out."

A set of arms wrapped around Will's waist from behind as he continued to lean over the deck taking it all in, turning to stare in surprise at a perky, petite cute blonde who smiled optimistically at her prey, hoping for a little action. *"Care to dance?"* she purred and taunted, clutching him tightly, as she pushed and rubbed against his shorts seductively.

"Ummm.... sure..." Will answered, being caught off-guard, as he grabbed her hand and walked down the steps of the deck, to the sand below, leaving Matt to stare in surprise.

"Now what?" he thought, as he stood alone taking in the whole crazy and yet happy partying scene, being the only one now trying to maintain and be a stable force and not throw caution to the wind.

Brooke held tightly, staring at Will with a saucy smile, looking into his steel blue eyes that suddenly held lust for the willing female, as they swayed barefoot on the sand, listening to music that only coaxed and aroused passion. He bent to kiss her parted lips, placing his tongue deeply inside her mouth, discovering her essence for the very first time, and liking the way she tasted.

He smiled at her, as the kiss ended, only leaning in again to repeat it several more times as his *hard-on* grew firmer, making Brooke look very pleased by what she knew she was capable of with a man.

"Why don't we go to my room?" he asked without hesitation, as his voice tried to regain some composure.

"I never thought you would ask..." she teased, leading him by the hand back up the deck steps passed Matt, who was now shaking his head in disbelief that Will was now caving, and he was on his own with the problem at hand.

"Gonna have some fun!" Will yelled over the blare of the speaker and in the direction of his friend with a happy grin, as he escorted Brooke into his bedroom and locked the door securely behind him. He also checked the lock on the patio doors that led out to the deck, making sure that no one could gain entry as he reclosed the vertical blinds – just as Lance had suggested when he first saw The Happy Crab.

As he turned he was somewhat stunned, but pleasantly surprised, that Brooke had already quickly disrobed – standing totally nude, discarding her very short blue jean shorts to the floor that were minus underwear, along with her sheer tank top that held no bra. Will was quick to follow, casting aside his blue t-shirt along with his boxers and khaki shorts.

Brooke took in his strong erection from his more than ample sized penis that she could hardly wait to have deep inside of her.

"Are you... on birth control?" Will breathed raggedly, as he fondled and kissed each of her taunt nipples.

"Of course silly.... Who isn't?" she teased, grabbing hold of Will's erection, already trying to place it inside of her as they stood together while the moon's light sliced through the blinds of the window.

He paused, regaining some self-control, walking towards his nightstand a short distance away and reaching for a condom. Will ripped open the packet with his teeth, stretching the sheer plastic over his dick before he turned back to Brooke, grabbing for her hand and falling on the bed along with her.

They kissed again repeatedly, as he crawled on top of the willing female, fumbling but placing his engorged cock in her small yet tight opening, thrusting repeatedly as they clung and rocked against the other.

"Ohhh... that feels sooo good!" she yelled out, as she whipped her head and hair side to side, making Will shutter and climax inside of her too, being encouraged by her words and wildness.

"For me too," he confessed, trying to slow down his breathing and regain his composure, looking at the pretty face of the unfamiliar female now lying beside of him. Will smiled and pushed back the wet blonde hair from her face that was perspired from their lovemaking. *"Where are you from?"* he asked in a tender, sincere way.

"Are you asking me where I live?" she asked, grabbing for her half drank cup of wine.

"Yeah," he grinned, propping up on one elbow to wait on her answer, as she downed the rest of her drink.

"Does it really matter?" she answered, setting her empty plastic cup on the nightstand beside of his, looking over at Will who was studying her intensely.

"It does to me..." he smiled.

She lay on her side with her knees pulled up, staring into Will's searching eyes that were well sated. "I'm from Hampton, Virginia. My relatives are from Maryland so that is how I know about Marlin Beach. My family used to come here when I was growing up, from time to time, on family vacations. I decided I wanted to work here last summer after I graduated from high school. This is my second summer hosting at The Dexter. A guy that works with me there invited me to the party."

"Would that be Chris or Tyler?" he asked with interest.

"Chris," she stated simply, getting up to redress into her short shorts and braless t-shirt that still had Will slightly aroused by her slim and trim body that no clothes could conceal.

"Oh, okay," he replied, taking her lead and dressing again also. "We better get back to the party before the beer is all drank," Will teased, giving her a quick kiss and a slap to her backside as he reopened the bedroom door to an overflow of people, with barely no room to move.

Brooke exited to the bathroom as William headed for the kitchen, seeing two of his roommates snacking on the last of the chips.

"We were looking for you, bro," Chris mentioned casually, now totally intoxicated, finishing another brew and throwing his red cup into the overflowing trashcan by the refrigerator.

"I've been busy," Will slyly admitted.

"I heard... Do you like Brooke?" Chris asked, hoping she would have chosen him instead, but happy for Will just the same since there were plenty more *babes* to choose from.

"Yeah, she's cool. We had a good time," he admitted, trying to act casual about it - like it was no big deal - as he grabbed a water from the refrigerator.

"Let me get you another beer," Tyler offered.

"Nah, I'm good. I gotta work tomorrow and I've had enough."

"Never enough, man!" Chris yelled over the blast of the music. *"It's summer and it's our official first party of the season!* You gotta be as hung over as the rest of us at work tomorrow," he laughed, slapping William a little bit to firmly on the back.

"Slow down, my friend. I'm good," he insisted, grabbing Chris's arms, trying to make his point, with a stern and yet kind smile. Will looked at his cellphone, realizing it was after 1 a.m. "I'm going to find Brooke and say my goodbyes. It's probably time to shut this party down for the night."

"What the hell, Will. Not until the beer and wine is finished!" Tyler yelled out.

"How is it even possible we still have any beer and wine left?"

Chris laughed, knowing Will was always too sensible for his own good. *"Cuz everyone brought more with them, dumbass!"*

Will shook his head, walking away through the maze of partygoers who had totally destroyed The Happy Crab inside and out. Empty red Solo cups with half-drank beer and wine were sitting on the cocktail and end tables, along with a scattering of crumbs from food that was carelessly discarded all over the couch and chairs, leaving them completely stained. A couple tried to make out on one end of the sofa without concern to their surroundings or the mess that they were sitting on. He noticed puddles of spilled liquid along with more food that was thrown all over the floor on the way out to the deck. The patio table and chairs outside were equally as cluttered with discarded cups, bottles and the half-eaten munchies that were offered. The beach was also a sad array of garbage and trash that he knew he would ultimately be responsible for picking up. Only one Tiki torch was still lit, with the others now dark from the fuel being used up. He sighed in frustration, feeling overwhelmed, and not knowing how to handle the situation.

Matt joined him again on the deck looking out over the mess in front of them. *"We got a big problem, Will.* I warned you something bad was going to happen, and now the police are here and they want to talk to the owner. I told them you were the closest thing to that."

"What the fuck, Matt! Why the hell did you tell them that?"

Matt ran his hands through his hair as they watched the partygoers scatter and run off like ants quickly down the beach - once the word was out that the cops were out in numbers in several police cruisers, parked on the street in front of the beach house.

Will and Matt turned towards the open patio doors leading into the house just as several police officers approached them from inside and the other officers joined them coming up the back set of deck steps. Only a few partygoers remained inside at that point, hiding under the beds and in the closets, hoping to avoid the inevitable.

"*Are you the owner of this house?*" One older cop asked as he approached William.

"No sir. I am not. I am the owner's nephew though, and I'm staying here at The Happy Crab for the summer."

The middle-aged officer studied William, trying to assess the situation, remembering he was young once too and did something similar many years before, as the other officers glanced around each room inside, not digging too deeply to locate the stragglers who were still hiding.

"*Does your uncle know you are having this party?*" he questioned.

"*Of course not!*" he responded much too quickly, realizing the end of his time at the beach was invariably over now just as quickly as it had begun.

The officer took out a notepad writing down a few key points as he proceeded. "What is your name and do you have anyone staying here with you?"

"My name is William Miller and these are roommates," Will continued, looking and pointing to each of his friends now present.

They too provided the necessary information that the officer asked of each - their name and their parents' names, as well as their home address and phone numbers.

"William, who owns this beach house?" Officer Gray asked.

Will glanced at Chris, feeling frustrated from the obvious reality of what was going on now. "My uncle's name is Lance Snyder. He owns

Snyder's Beach Dreams Real Estate here in Marlin Beach."

Officer Gray looked up from his notepad, studying the sincerity of William's words. *"Your uncle is Lance Snyder?"*

"Yes, that's him."

Officer Dan Gray realized he had a problem he hadn't planned on or expected. Lance was a good friend and a fellow volunteer EMT worker for Marlin Beach Ambulance that he also was a part of.

CHAPTER 24

"Hello?" Lance whispered, hoping not to wake Sarah, realizing it was Dan. *"Do you need me for ambulance duty tonight?"*

Officer Gray walked outside onto the deck and shut the patio doors behind him; with the four roommates looking on from the living room inside with worried looks plastered all over their faces.

"No ambulance duty, my friend. Sorry to bother you so late, but we have a problem at your beach house."

Lance sat up and rubbed his free hand over his eyes and then through his wavy brown hair, trying to make some sense of it all. *"I'm not following you. I'm here at my beach house and everything seems fine, as far as I can tell,"* he said glancing around the room. Lance slipped quietly from the bed, happy Sarah was still sleeping soundly.

"I'm not talking about The Playful Starfish, I'm talking about your other place that you rented out to the college students for the summer. Sorry bro, but it didn't dawn on me initially when I went there that it was your place, but I realize it now."

Lance tiptoed down the steps so as to not wake the twins, happy he found some clean clothes in the laundry room first that he could change into, slipping into a pair of jeans and a t-shirt, and finding his flip-flops still by the front door.

"*What the heck is going on?*" he asked, grabbing his car keys, locking the front door and heading out to his Jeep.

"Well…. I don't know how to say this, so I will just come out with it. There was a very large party at your beach house tonight and the whole place inside and out has been trashed - to put it plainly."

Lance sighed loudly and shook his head angrily as he drove down Beach Road going much faster than the speed limit allowed; totally in disbelief that William and his friends had not heeded his warning. *"You got to be kidding! Those assholes allowed my place to be ruined? Are they still there?"*

"*Oh yeah, they're still here,*" Officer Gray announced, turning from the railing and looking back into the living room to make sure his statement was correct. "I'm not sure what you want us to do about this and them. There are so many potential charges and fines we could slap on each one of them at this point - such as underage drinking, noise violations, destroying a rental property – you name it, the list goes on and on."

Lance pulled into the driveway of The Happy Crab seeing the scattering of red Solo cups, beer cans and glass bottles, paper plates, napkins and discarded uneaten food laying all over the yard and gravel driveway. A few beach towels hung haphazardly off the front porch railing and down the back steps that he could see in the distance, as he approached and walked up to meet his friend on the top deck where he was standing.

"*I can't fucking believe this!*" Lance shouted out in disgust and utter frustration, as he met up with Dan and then looked in at the group who had fear etched all over their faces at realizing who was now there.

"*What do you want us to do? Would you like us to arrest them?*"

Two police vehicles remained in front of the residence, with several officers still positioned out on the beach and in the yard close by The Happy Crab, while one stood inside guarding the college students. The few remaining partygoers still hid under the beds and in the closets, breathing heavily and hoping they would not be discovered as the interrogation continued in the living room. Several neighbors stood outside talking and being nosy, making it pretty evident that it was them who called and complained about the party.

"I'm not sure at this point, but I do need to go inside and talk to everyone present. *I guess it's time to let them know I'm not all fun and games,*" Lance replied with a fuming, unbending resolve, knowing he didn't like to feel this upset.

The patio doors were slid back and Lance and Office Gray entered the room, approaching the group of guys who were sitting on the soiled sofa and two chairs waiting for their sentencing. Lance glared at William, finding it hard to begin.

"I can not believe what you have allowed to happen to my house and property! I have gone out of my way to be kind and gracious to all of you, and yet you took advantage of me and now look at my place!" Lance yelled, slamming the overflowing trashed-filled cocktail table, making a few more cans of the half-drank beer slip to the floor, causing it to be even more wet and stickier than it was before.

Will, Chris, Matt and Tyler jumped at the action, with their eyes wide in fright, not knowing what to say or do.

"I take full responsibility for all of this, uncle Lance," William began, looking timidly at him, hoping that he wouldn't get violent.

"Was it only you allowing this party?" Lance questioned sternly, knowing that was not the case.

Will looked at his friends, hating to *run them under the bus*, and remaining silent with an answer.

"William are you hard of hearing? Again, was it only you allowing all this?" Lance gritted out, getting angrier by the minute.

Will rose from the sofa, standing in front of Lance as Officer Gray and the other police officer looked on from the kitchen area. "I speak only for myself. Do what you will to me. I will go to jail tonight or pack and leave. Whatever is decided for me," he added, bending his head in embarrassment and shame.

Lance looked at the other three who remained silent, aggravated with them that they were having a hard time being as brave and straightforward as William. He shook his head in disgust at them, shaking them from their silence and cowardliness.

Chris stood up, walking over to stand beside of William. "I was involved too. My friends were invited here and things got out of hand."

"Out of hand! That's putting it mildly, wouldn't you say?" Lance laughed sarcastically, looking around the soiled room that needed a total cleaning now.

"Yes, sir. I was wrong and I'll admit it. I will leave tonight and go home - back to Baltimore."

"Why do you think that is even an option at this point? You may be spending the night in jail."

Chris looked up at Lance, staring at him squarely in the eyes, terrified by his words. "My parents are gonna kill me."

Lance just shook his head, looking at the other two - Tyler sitting shirtless on one of the two chairs, and Matt on the sofa, just quietly taking it all in. *"How about you guys? Do you have anything to add?"*

Tyler and Matt joined the others, standing in a semi-circle with them now, knowing they too needed to speak up too.

"I don't want to go to jail," Tyler admitted with his head bent.

"Whatever happens, happens," Matt said realistically and without fear. "I'm not candy coating this. You warned us already about your place and we definitely screwed up again. *Don't I get one call though if I go to jail?* I think I will need to call my mother," he mentioned without hesitation, looking in the direction of Officer Gray.

"Yes, you do get one call if we take you to jail."

Lance looked at Dan, his words still resonating, trying to decide what to do with the roommates and the situation. "As I see it we have two distinct problems here – my house and the destruction of it and the underage drinking. I did not destroy my home so it should not be my responsibility to clean it up or pay someone else to do so. Therefore, I want all of you to take care of this mess, and I mean tonight yet whether you get any sleep or not! Once everything is picked up and put in trash bags, you will need to vacuum and scrub down every single wall and surface in this house, then you will proceed to the deck, yard and driveway where there better not be one trace of any scrap remaining. *Do I make myself clear?"*

"Yes, sir!" they all said in unison, as if answering to a drill sergeant.

"And then once that is all done, I will make my final decision about sending you home. I can not address the drinking situation and I think Officer Gray needs to speak with you concerning that."

Lance glanced at Dan motioning for him to rejoin the group as he crossed his arms defensively in front of him, taking a firm stance as his friend started where he left off.

"As Mr. Snyder just conveyed, you will totally clean up his property inside and out and when he feels the work is done, I will return here to speak to you about what will be happening next. Normally, I would be escorting you to police headquarters right now, but since I know Mr. Snyder, I will provide him the courtesy of having his property cleaned up first. This debacle is costing him a night's sleep as well, which I'm sure is not making him very happy," he mentioned while glancing over at Lance who was now pacing and looking totally irritated, realizing he was away from his comfortable bed, Sarah and the twins.

"You got that right, Dan!" he answered, having a hard time calming down with the hours of unexpected supervision he now had ahead of him. "Things will be fine here and I will handle this. I will be calling you in a few hours - once the beach house is presentable."

"We will be waiting on your call," Dan replied with a nod in Lance's direction, taking his exit then with the rest of the police officers now in tow.

Lance looked at the guys who were waiting his further instructions, looking at his watch and realizing it was already 4 a.m. "I think you all know where the trash bags are located and the cleaning supplies and vacuum. I am slipping away for a while to grab a cup of coffee and a bite to eat. I hope when I return things will be looking a lot different. *Do I make myself clear?*"

"Yes, sir!" the group again answered.

"*I meant what I said…. Not a single thing better be out of place when I return or there will be hell to pay!*" He added as he headed for the front door. "*And you may want to tell any of your remaining friends that are still here and hiding - to either help out with the cleaning or leave before I get back!*" Lance gritted out, slamming the door behind him, making a few more beer cans fall to the floor.

CHAPTER 25

With the warning from Lance and once the coast was clear, the few remaining stragglers climbed out from their hiding places and departed without so much as a word - to help clean up or a thank you for not blowing their cover.

William looked at his friends sadly, leaning on a mop handle as the remainder of the trash was placed in the last of the 30 large black trash bags where the rest were already filled and outside waiting for garbage pickup. "I washed all the floors and walls," he mentioned to Chris and Tyler, ready to toss the last of the dirty water off of the back deck.

Matt reappeared from one of the bathrooms with a toilet brush in hand. "I totally cleaned up both of the bathrooms. Not a spot to be found. I can assure you of that!"

The group moved towards the kitchen, realizing the table, counters, cabinets and appliances hadn't been cleaned up and washed down yet.

"*I thought you had this, Chris?*" Will questioned in frustration, realizing the kitchen had somehow been missed.

"Sorry, bro, been busy helping Tyler pick up all the trash inside and out. I can do it now though," he offered, feeling a bit overwhelmed with all the work, especially since he was tired and hung-over as was the rest of them.

"Let's all get on it!" Will demanded, beginning to draw more water and dump additional cleaner in the bucket. "Lance will be here soon and we don't want him to discover a problem," he added as he rung out his rag, trying to wash down the cabinets quickly.

The group of guys joined in, completing the tasks set before them. They each grabbed a granola bar, walking as a group around the beach house, making sure all the beds were made, although the sheets were filthy dirty with sand, dirt, food and alcohol and needed to be washed as soon as they could get around to it. But for now, they could conceal that problem, knowing all the other tasks were completed.

"What are we going to do about the couch and chairs?" Matt questioned, once they came back inside from checking out the yard, driveway and beach that was now presentable.

"Good question," William pondered, trying to think about the situation logically, looking over the upholstered furniture and flipping over a seat cushion to see if it were any more presentable on the other side. "I guess we will have to hire someone to clean it because I don't want to ruin the fabric by trying to scrub it ourselves."

Matt placed his hands on his hips surveying the scene. *"How could we have been so fucking stupid for this to have happened?"*

"Things just go out of control, bro," Chris answered.

"I didn't invite that many people," Tyler tried to rationalize.

"It's always like this at parties. You guys know that from Towson. You put out the word about a party and everyone you invite shows up, and then they bring a few friends, and then it gets batshit crazy with too many people!"

"Does anyone know what happened to all the money that we collected? We could use it to pay for the cleaning of the furniture and the rest could go towards our fines," William suggested.

"I think someone took it," Tyler reluctantly confessed, not wanting to admit that he saw a guy run off with it when he was pouring himself the next beer out of the keg, that he had stopped counting, after ten.

"How do you know that?" Chris asked, scrutinizing him for the answer. *"Who was it, Tyler?"*

"I'm not sure, but I did see him dancing with Mia, after she showed up later on in the evening."

"That bitch was here? I didn't see her!" Chris blurted out, still hurt by her lack of affection for him.

"Yeah, I saw her too," Will added, knowing the subject matter was still touchy for his friend. "Look, we'll figure this out about Mia when we get a chance, but for now let's just be ready for Lance and the cops when they show back up soon. It may be a good idea to start packing. You all know he's going to want us to leave the beach house one way or another - before this day is up."

"God, I don't want to leave Marlin Beach yet. Summer is just getting started!"

"We have no one to blame but ourselves," Matt interjected realistically. "I will just go home and start working there. There's no sense in beating this dead horse. We screwed up and Lance already gave us one last chance."

The front door suddenly swung open with Lance standing in the doorway along with Officer Gray right beside of him. They walked in, looking around as they approached the boys, sniffing the air.

"Well I must say it certainly smells better in here," Lance smiled, seeming to be in a slightly better mood with a *to go* cup of coffee in hand, after just having an early morning breakfast of an omelet and toast at The Seabreeze Diner.

"We cleaned everything up," Will said, speaking for the group, as they walked from room to room with the boys following close behind.

"Yes, you did," Lance acknowledged with his thorough inspection, looking under each bed for any stragglers left behind.

The outside of the beach house was surveyed also, with only a few beers cans discovered under one of the sea grass patches nearby in a dune area. Lance passed them off to William without a word, as Will clutched them in each hand as the walk continued. They stood in front of the 30 bags of trash that were now lined up, one by one on the sidewalk, as William placed the remaining crushed cans inside of one.

Lance snapped a picture of the garbage bags with his cellphone, turning to look at Dan. *"I think it is time to go back inside and talk about business."*

Everyone present proceeded back up the deck steps, stopping in front of the soiled furniture in the living room once again.

"This is a problem... My parents had this furniture professionally upholstered. My mother is *still dealing* with my sick father and I can tell you she doesn't need to know about her dirty furniture, or for that matter, what else happened here at The Happy Crab last night! *So what are you going to do about this?"*

"Can we pay you to replace it?"

Lance laughed heartily, knowing the furniture was probably worth at least $5,000. "I don't think you guys have enough money saved up between you for doing that at this point. But we will start with a rug and upholstery cleaning company that I use in my real estate business and see if they can resolve it at a reasonable cost, and then you will reimburse me for that expense. If that isn't an option, than I will need to notify your parents and they will have to come up with the money to replace the items. *Do I make myself clear on that subject?"*

Everyone shook their heads – *yes* - agreeing and not wanting to make the situation any worse with Lance, as Officer Gray took over next. "I would like you to follow me to the kitchen where we can go over a few things," he advised as the group moved in that direction. He gave them permission to sit as they all looked in his direction, waiting for him to continue. "Mr. Snyder and I just shared breakfast together and had a discussion about what occurred here last night. You are very lucky that you have a landlord who is a very kind and understanding man, and in your case – William – he is your uncle. Most, would want to press charges against you. You would be fined severely and forced to leave the property. But that is not the case with Mr. Snyder," he added, looking in Lance's direction, making sure that he was representing him properly as he had directed. "So as it stands, he just wants you to reimburse him for the cleaning of the furniture at this point. If the fabric does not look presentable afterwards, you will have to pay to have the furniture reupholstered or replaced. So now on to the underage drinking and other issues."

Each roommate at the table looked at each other, scared for the news and fearing the worst.

"This is not normal that I would be proceeding in this way under the circumstances, but once again because Mr. Snyder has asked for leniency where you are concerned. Therefore, I am *not* taking you in and arresting you."

The group of roommates breathed in a big sigh of relief at the news, as Officer Gray continued.

"Mr. Snyder and I both feel it's in the best interest of all parties concerned that you do community service for a time period of 80 hours for Marlin Beach ambulance as well as the local animal shelter. Let me make myself perfectly clear here, if any further partying or incidents occur at The Happy Crab or at another beach house in this town - that your name is attached with - I will not seek out the advice of Mr. Snyder and you will be arrested and removed from Marlin Beach and pay a substantial fine. Again... *Do I make myself perfectly clear?"* he warned, looking at each one present.

"Yes, sir," they all agreed again, feeling relieved to have been granted that light of a sentence.

"Where will we live at if we are continuing to stay here in town to do community service?" Tyler asked.

"I am allowing you to remain here," Lance answered softly.

William looked up in disbelief at his uncle who stood close by. *"You would do that for us?"*

Lance smiled with his kind brown eyes, remembering his college days and the crazy times he had with his friend Dan who was then a lifeguard along with him at Marlin Beach, as they had discussed earlier at breakfast. "Yes, William, I will do that for you and your friends. You tested the waters another time with me and now this is definitely your last warning – no ifs, ands, or buts about it!"

"Thank you, uncle Lance, and thank you Officer Gray."

"You're lucky to have an uncle like Lance. I would have called your parents at this point, but thanks to him you got off pretty easy if you ask me."

"I know...." Will smiled, knowing he was blessed to have Lance in his life. "Can we keep our jobs?"

"I would certainly hope so," Lance laughed. "Since you will need to figure out how you will pay for this furniture if it doesn't come clean. After all, it's worth a few thousand dollars!"

"Oh my God... a few thousand dollars!" Matt breathed out loud. "Let's hope it's cleanable or we're in big trouble!"

"You got that right!" Lance said, patting Matt a little too firmly on the back. "Talking about work, I think you guys need to get ready and get to your jobs today. And that goes for you too, William. See you soon!" he waved as he and Officer Gray left the premises, with the group being given a final reprieve – offered only by the skin of their teeth!

CHAPTER 26

"Hello, Nancy. It's Jennifer Fisher calling."

"Well hello, Jennifer. This is a pleasant surprise," Nancy offered with a smile, taking a seat on her family room sectional with a cup of coffee in hand.

"I'm trying to reach William. The message I am getting says his cellphone number is no longer in service."

"Oh my…. He changed it in the last couple of months when he got a new cellphone and carrier. Something about a better plan and rate… I believe," she mentioned casually, trying to remember the details. "I'm sorry he didn't inform you of that."

Jen sat at her kitchen table in Birmingham, Alabama on a Saturday morning, sipping from her own cup of coffee, enjoying the quietude of being the only one in the house for a few hours before her niece and nephew got back home from soccer practice.

Jennifer shook her head, realizing William probably had better things to do than to remember his aunt, brother and sister from his past. "I was hoping to visit this summer. Eva and Jackson keeping talking about William and wanting to go to the beach. I figured it may be time to introduce them to Marlin Beach since they have never been there before."

"Well of course you are welcome to visit! I know William would love to see you!" Nancy extended pleasantly, assuming that to be the case. "William is working and living in Marlin Beach this summer. He is helping Sarah's husband, Lance, at his real estate company."

"Well that's wonderful!" Jennifer beamed. "It doesn't seem possible that he is old enough to work in real estate. I sure do miss the time we used to spend together when he was a boy living in Alabama."

Nancy sighed, trying to be sensitive. "Well that is very sweet, Jennifer, and I'm sure he misses you too. So what is new with you and the children?"

Jennifer got up and paced the room, not sure she was ready to fill Nancy in on all the details quite yet. "Not much... still doing accounting when the kids are in school, and then the rest of the day is filled with homework, sports and on Sundays we go to church as a family."

"Well that is wonderful! I am glad things are working out so well. How old is Eva and Jackson now?" Nancy asked, as Rascal jumped up on her lap for a head scratch.

"Eva is 13 and Jackson is 11. I can't believe I have one teenager and one not so far behind. Where do the years go?"

"I totally understand. In less than a year William will be 20. That seems impossible."

"Yes it does..." Jennifer answered in a far-off, distant sort of way, remembering a time just a few short years ago when her sister Claire was still alive and raising all three of her children - in Birmingham with her husband Mitchell.

"So I will reach out to William and have him give you a call. I would give you his cellphone number now, but I am not in the habit of doing so without asking first, even though I am sure he wouldn't mind."

"I totally understand, Nancy."

"So about William and Marlin Beach... " Nancy began, sitting back down on her sectional with a refill of coffee and a slice of banana bread in hand that she had just baked. "He has three roommates and he is staying at a beach house not owned by us. You can still come to Marlin Beach though, and stay at our beach house - The Dancing Seahorse – if you would like. Mike and I would be happy to join you there if you can make it. It will give us an excuse to finally get to the beach this summer and visit William ourselves," she offered sweetly.

"Nancy, you are being very gracious, but I would not want to inconvenience you and Mike."

"Nonsense! We have ample space and would love to see you again! When do you think you would like to visit?"

"I was hoping in two weeks if that is possible?"

"I think that would work perfectly, but let me review things with Michael and then I will get back to you," Nancy replied, as she glanced over at her husband who had just come in from the backyard, where he had been catching up on the phone with Sarah about some upcoming projects with Miller's Architecture.

"Thank you, Nancy. I will be awaiting your call," Jennifer answered, hanging up the phone. She sat at her table sipping the remaining coffee that had gotten cold, thumbing through a catalog that held brightly colored pictures of beach attire. *"I guess I will need to order a new bathing suit or two if this trip to Marlin Beach works out,"* she said aloud as she closed the magazine. *"And maybe several things for the family too..."*

"Who was that on the phone?" Mike asked curiously, bending down to give Nancy a warm kiss as he joined her on the sectional.

"You will never guess," she smiled pleasantly at her beloved. "It was Jennifer Fisher - William's aunt from Birmingham!"

"Oh yes... I remember her. I'm not that old and senile yet, Nancy," he laughed and teased. "Why did she call?"

"She was trying to reach William. He obviously failed to give her his new cellphone number, because when she tried to call the old number the message said *it was no longer in service.*"

"That boy... He knows better," Mike replied, shaking his head.

"He's not a boy any longer, Michael, and sometimes I wish he was."

Mike paused, realizing the truth of Nancy's words. "Yes, that is obvious since he is choosing Marlin Beach over us this summer. He has been very quiet, don't you think? I guess that is a good thing and means he is probably very busy with work."

"I certainly hope so," Nancy responded with some hesitation. "I would think he would let us know if he were in any sort of trouble."

Mike reached out to grab Nancy's shoulder giving it a firm but loving squeeze. "Your grandson is just fine. He is learning to be a man and make his own decisions in life. I am sure Lance and Sarah have been keeping a watchful eye on him. She didn't mention anything unusual to me in our conversation just now."

"Well, I certainly hope so....." Nancy spoke, repeating herself again, feeling uneasy even with all the reassurances that Mike was giving her. "So Jennifer would like to vacation in Marlin Beach in a couple weeks. I extended an invite for her and the children to join us at The Dancing Seahorse as long as you can slip away from work for a few days. What do you say?" she inquired warmly, grabbing her husband's hand while looking fondly into his eyes, waiting for the answer.

"Well, Nancy, you surprise me. You honestly are feeling all right about sharing the beach house with them? I know we spent time with them during Claire's illness and death, but it has been a few years now and what would be talk about?"

"For heaven's sakes, Mike! We would talk about William and life in general! Will hasn't seen his aunt or his siblings in three years and I find that totally ridiculous! What better way to get reacquainted than with relaxation in a chair by the ocean or maybe some fun on the boardwalk?"

"I understand, but don't you think we should ask William first?"

"Yes, of course! Call him and let him know about Jennifer's plans to visit Marlin Beach in two weeks, and don't forget to mention that he needs to call her since he never provided her with his new number."

"Anything else?" Mike laughed, realizing he obviously wasn't getting a choice in the matter.

"You can let William know that his Nan loves and misses him."

"I will definitely let him know," Mike winked, getting up to make the call right away.

"Hello?"

"William, how are you?"

"G-Dad... I'm sorry for not contacting you for a while now. I've been meaning to call you but things have been so busy with work," he lied, not wanting to fill him in to his newest dilemma. "Everything okay with you and Nan?"

"Oh yes, everything is fine. I just thought it was time to check in and see if I could do anything for you, or if you needed anything since I plan to be in Marlin Beach soon."

"How soon?" Will quickly asked in concern, not wanting his grandfather to know about his bout with the law.

"How about in two weeks? *Is that too soon?*" Mike probed, realizing his grandson probably didn't want to make time for his G-Dad or Nan with his work schedule and the obvious beach house gatherings and other things that he and his roommates got into.

"G-Dad, I'm sorry. I didn't mean to come off that way. Of course you are welcome to visit any time you want, but as you know I don't have any extra rooms here for guests to stay - since every bedroom is taken."

"I'm a step ahead of you, grandson. It goes without saying that I would be staying at my own place when I come to Marlin Beach for a visit. You should know that."

Will breathed a sigh of relief – honestly knowing it, but hearing the words spoken gave him peace of mind that his grandfather was not trying to intrude upon his privacy. Maybe Mike would never need to know about the recent *summer party gone wrong event* and also the community service he was now forced to participate in.

"How is Nan?"

"She is fine and she sends her love, and of course she misses you."

William smiled, knowing his grandmother was always there for him. "Tell her I love and miss her too, and I look forward to seeing you both hopefully soon."

"Nan will also be joining me in a couple of weeks, so you can see her then - along with three others."

"Three others?"

"Yes – the three others – Jennifer, Eva and Jackson – who by the way you need to call and update with your cellphone information."

William sat down firmly on the edge of the bed, not expecting the news that his family from the past in Birmingham wanted to visit. It felt as shocking as the community service sentencing that he was being forced to comply with and complete. *"They are coming here to Marlin Beach for a visit in a couple weeks?"*

"Yes, sir. That is what I just heard from Nan. *I hope you are okay with that?"*

"I think so…. yeah… what can I say since the plans have already been put in motion by Nan," Will resigned with some reluctance, knowing his grandmother's plans could rarely be reversed once she made up her mind about something.

CHAPTER 27

William found his aunt Jen's information in his contact list and decided to call her call back the next morning. Maybe he could stall her from showing up for several weeks more and get the community service sentencing out of the way first.

The phone rang several times and Will was quite prepared to leave a lengthy message that would buy him more time, but she answered just before the beep of the voicemail began.

"Hello?"

"Aunt Jen, hello. It's me, William."

Jen had just finished vacuuming the living room and thought she heard the faint ringing of her cellphone, as she turned off the vacuum and ran to the kitchen to answer it.

"Well hello there, William! I didn't recognize your number. *Did you change it?*" she asked, making light conversation, already knowing the answer from Nancy's explanation of earlier.

"I did change it a few weeks ago and I'm sorry I didn't let you know sooner. I just was busy at college with my exams and now I'm here at

Marlin Beach living and working – which I'm sure Nan already mentioned."

"Yes, she did mention that to me and it's quite okay that you haven't called. I remember those busy days of college and having a summer job. *But please tell me how you've been?*" she asked sincerely, sitting at the kitchen table after grabbing a bottle of cold water from the refrigerator, ready for a long conversation with her nephew.

Will lay back down on his bed, blankly staring at the ceiling, being at a loss for words. It had been several years now since he had seen his aunt Jennifer or his siblings – Eva and Jackson - and somehow it felt like another lifetime when he was living in Birmingham and around them.

William's mother, Claire, was dead and his stepfather Mitchell might as well be, since he detested him so much after what he had done to his mother and him with the physical and mental abuse they both suffered at his hands. Will was free from Mitchell and happy with his life with his Nan and G-Dad. His mother's last gift of love was to have him live with his grandparents in Baltimore, as was stated in her *Last Will And Testament,* that she had written and had authorized by an attorney before her death.

Jennifer, was his mother's sister, and Will was happy that Claire had also made provisions before her death that Jennifer would raise Eva and Jackson instead of Mitchell as long as he was in rehab or continuing to drink and exhibiting signs of violent outbursts. Will had hoped and prayed for the best since he never heard of any further episodes after he moved away. He felt that no news was good news and he trusted that his siblings were safe and well taken care of just as he was also.

"William are you there?" Jennifer asked breaking into his thoughts, since he never responded back as she rambled on.

"Sorry, aunt Jen, I was just thinking about how long it has been since we last spoke, and it's been even longer since I have seen you. Matter-of-fact... the last time was the day after my mother's funeral when I moved away," he reminded her sadly.

Jennifer paused, recalling the sad time now too. "I'm sorry, William, that your mother is no longer with us. I miss her very much."

Will felt the tears welling up in his eyes, not wanting to add that to his list of anxieties at the moment. He had learned to suppress his mother's memory and place it deep in the recesses of his mind so that he could cope on a daily basis and not grieve for her all of the time. Now thoughts of her were there again, and it was better left in the past. "Aunt Jen, I do need to get to work and I would love to chat some more, but we may need to continue this conversation again sometime soon," he announced, as he sprung from his bed and opened the patio doors attached to his bedroom, walking out to the deck and glancing at the beach with a few beachgoers already setting up their camp for the day.

Jennifer shifted, taking a swig of water before answering. "Oh, I'm sorry. I didn't mean to hold you up. But before you go, I was wondering if you would mind if I came Marlin Beach for a visit in two weeks? Eva and Jackson are giving me no peace about about missing you and wanting to see you again. I spoke with Nancy and she says we can stay with her and Mike at their beach house - The Dancing Seahorse."

Will sighed deeply, breathing in the fresh, salty sea air, trying to clear out his lungs and his thoughts. He wanted to tell her no, but how could he? She wasn't the problem, his stepfather was. She had obviously set her life aside to raise his half brother and sister and honor his mother. *A vacation at the beach is definitely something Jennifer deserves!* He realized. As much as he resisted, William missed them too.

"Sure, aunt Jen. I may not be around all day with work and other things going on, but I will do my best to see you guys as much as I can. Just let me know when you are showing up, and I will try to adjust my schedule."

Jennifer began to smile, feeling happy with his words. "Well thank you, William. I know Eva and Jackson will be counting the days until we see you again! I will call Nancy back and let her know we spoke, and then I will text you all the details."

"Sounds great! Say hi to Eva and Jackson for me and I will see you guys in a couple weeks."

"Can't wait!" she replied, hanging up with her nephew and spinning around in circles with her arms outstretched with a big smile on her face, overjoyed with the news. She was looking so forward to the much anticipated beach trip that was long overdue, and now it was becoming a reality.

Will walked from The Happy Crab feeling like his head was ready to explode from so much on his mind. He was showered and dressed and hurrying to make it to work on time at Beach Dreams. His aunt Jennifer's phone call had set him back some, and he didn't need Lance's wrath coming down on him again if he arrived late. It had mutually been decided that he would only work a few hours after the major cleanup from the party, but today was a different story and Lance expected a full 8 hours on the clock.

"Nan?" he smiled from hearing her voice, as he rushed down Beach Road, going a little too fast, on his way to work.

"Well hello, William. I miss you!" she answered, happy to finally hear from her grandson. "How are you doing?"

He wanted to tell her the truth of what was happening with his community service sentencing, but he just couldn't. He knew it would disappoint her and break her heart, and she would insist that he come back home to Baltimore to be with her for the summer.

"I'm doing great, Nan. Sorry I haven't called sooner. There is just so much always going on," he confessed, knowing that was enough information to give her at this point. "I just wanted to give you a quick call while I'm driving to work. I heard from aunt Jen and she told me about her wish to come to Marlin Beach in a few weeks with Eva and

Jackson, and that she spoke with you about all this."

"She didn't have your new phone number so I guess that is why she reached out to me," she answered matter-of-factly as she sat on the sectional brushing Rascal, trying to pull out a hairball from his stomach that got in the way of her task.

"I understand," he replied, driving into the back parking lot of Beach Dreams, pulling in right beside of Lance's Jeep. "I just wanted to let you know we touched bases and I'm cool with them visiting. I hope it's not putting too much on you and G-Dad though, with your offer for them to stay at The Dancing Seahorse."

"I'm happy that they want to come for a visit! It's giving me an excuse to get to the beach with G-Dad in a couple weeks. I'm always finding other things to do here at home and never make time to relax and get away and take a vacation. This way, I can see Sarah, Lance and the twins and you too! And G-Dad can finally get some golf time in with John Snyder."

"Well, I'm glad you are finally taking a break and getting away, Nan. I can give you some money to help out with food once they arrive if you would like." he added, walking past Patti who was on the phone and deep in conversation, ignoring him totally.

"For heaven's sakes, William. I definitely do not need any help from you to entertain them! You keep your money and enjoy yourself."

Will paused, not knowing how to answer her, realizing that mindset *of enjoying himself* had already gotten him in more trouble than he had bargained for in the short time he was in Marlin Beach. He walked past Lance's office as he waved at him, seeing him on the phone obviously with a difficult client by the tone of the conversation.

Will sat at his desk, turning on the computer in front of him, realizing the others he shared the office space with were not present and probably out on showings. "Nan, I must go. I am at work now and

Lance will be tracking me down in a few minutes."

"Of course, dear. The last thing I want to do is get you in trouble with Lance," she quipped, as her devoted cat jumped from her lap to the floor. "I will fill you in on the details of our trip when we know more in a few days. Take care and we will see you soon," she added as she hung up the phone.

Will logged in to the MLS, typing in all the specs for the three-bedroom, oceanfront condo that Lance had just listed.

"Cutting it a little close, aren't you?" Lance mentioned with a smile, poking his head in from the doorframe. Will was happy to see that he had calmed down and his mood had obviously improved from a day ago, but he still expected him to tow the line and wasn't giving him any slack where work was concerned.

"Yeah, I'm sorry, uncle Lance. First my aunt Jen called from Birmingham and then I was speaking with Nan. It has just been a busy day so far," he admitted, realizing that he had barely come up for air since the craziness of the party.

Lance laughed. "Well I must say you haven't had a moment's rest obviously dealing with the law, and then your aunt and grandmother, and now work."

Will stopped what he was doing, running both hands through his wavy brown hair, just sighing deeply from his statement. "You don't know the half of it... My aunt Jen now wants to come to Marlin Beach in two weeks with my siblings for a vacation. She plans to stay at The Dancing Seahorse with Nan and G-Dad, and I'm not sure how I will juggle that - especially now that I have community service."

Lance paused, shaking his head at Will as he clicked his tongue. "*I guess you should have thought about all this before you decided to have that wild and out-of-control party. You do got a dilemma on your hands and I hope no one but me figures this whole thing out.*"

"I know I don't deserve this, but please…. don't tell anyone, especially Nan and G-Dad," William begged with fear etched all over his face.

CHAPTER 28

The Uber driver blared two long beeps on his horn, before resorting finally to calling. "Ma'am, I'm out here waiting."

"Oh, I'm sorry. I thought we said 9 a.m. and not 8:30."

"Got here early, but I can wait if you would like."

"Please don't leave," Jennifer requested, as she walked towards Eva and Jackson's rooms where she found them still shoving in the remaining items into their over-packed suitcases. "We'll be out in a fifteen minutes," she explained.

Eva looked at her aunt while sitting on top of her suitcase, attempting to zipper it shut. "I'm all packed," she beamed, jumping off the secured suitcase and wheeling it out to the living room. "Just gotta get my pillow and cellphone," she added as she ran back into her bedroom.

Jackson had already figured out that he would be next with the inquisition, so he hurried to complete his packing and placed his suitcase by his sister's.

"You already, Jack?"

"All packed, aunt Jen."

"Great! Me too!" she replied, wheeling her suitcase out with the others, finding her purse and cellphone along with a jacket that she felt she may need on the airplane, if the air conditioning became too cold.

The three of them pulled their suitcases out to the curb as the Uber driver stood and waited by his car, and then loaded each bag into the trunk of his sedan.

"I'll sit up front and you guys can get in the back," Jennifer directed, as the kids climbed into the back seat of the four-door vehicle.

The Uber driver paused to look at his cellphone and then at Jennifer who was now sitting to his right and as close to the front passenger door as she could, confirming their destination before he pulled away from the house. "You wanna go to the local airport, right?" he asked, glancing now at Jen who apparently seemed uncomfortable being in the car with the stranger.

"Yes, I do, sir. Our flight is in 2 ½ hours so we should have plenty of time," she smiled awkwardly, realizing that now they had an extra 30 minutes on their hands since the Uber driver showed up too early.

"Where are you flying too?" the inquisitive, thirty-something man with the offensive body odor asked, glancing over at Jennifer, taking her in from head to toe, making her slightly shutter and feel somewhat uncomfortable with his staring.

"Visiting my husband in Alaska where we plan to move soon," she lied, making Eva and Jackson giggle in the back seat. Luckily for her, they had kept quiet and did not blow here cover, only being half interested with the conversation.

"Why is he there and you are here?" the nosy driver questioned, continuing to pry and stare occasionally at Jen, as he drove and wiped his dripping nose with the back of his hand.

Jennifer looked out the car window and sighed, not wanting him to continue with his prodding. She turned back to look at him, searching for a worthy answer. "I had to get the children through their school year first. My husband is in the military and he had to leave Birmingham quickly because he was on an emergency mission."

"What branch?" he persisted, not caring that he was being rude.

Jennifer turned to look over the back seat at Eva and Jackson, winking as inconspicuously as she could at them, giving them the signal to go along with her story.

"I know you guys miss your daddy, but the good news is by tomorrow we will all be back together again."

Eva placed her hands over her eyes, pretending to cry loudly, as Jackson patted her arm telling her not to cry. Jennifer winked again at them, continuing with the farce. "You're doing a great job being brave and your daddy would be so proud of!"

Jennifer turned her attention back to the Uber driver. "Sir, I'm not trying to be rude, but the subject of my husband, which of course is my children's father, is upsetting to them since we haven't seen him in quite some time. I just came to find out that he had a recent accident in Alaska that I'm not free to discuss the details of with you. So I would appreciate it if we can let it go at that."

"No worries, ma'am," he said tensely, turning his attention back to his driving, as he coughed and cleared his throat, spitting a wad of phlegm out of the window that he had just opened, grossing Jennifer out even further.

Within minutes they pulled into the departure area of Birmingham-Shuttlesworth International Airport. The Uber driver placed the three suitcases on the sidewalk, addressing Jennifer as they began to walk away, dragging each one of their bags behind them.

"Ma'am?" he yelled loudly over the blare of traffic.

"*Yes?*" Jennifer answered reluctantly, turning back to look at the Uber driver one last time before entering the airport.

"I always appreciate a great review," he requested, with a broad grin that displayed a few teeth missing.

"Ok… sure," she hesitantly answered, knowing she had no intentions of ever doing so.

They approached a kiosk that automatically pulled up their flight information as Jennifer showed Eva and Jackson what she was doing as she typed in the requested information. Out of the machine, the printed baggage stickers appeared for each of their suitcases. Once the labels were affixed securely around the handles, they wheeled them to the next available agent who confirmed their identification and then loaded each one of their bags on the moving conveyor belt in front of them.

"You're all set," the female agent acknowledged.

"Now what?" Jackson asked eagerly, since this was all new and his first time to fly.

"You need to go this way," the agent pointed, "and then go through security and then on to your gate."

"I'm hungry," Jackson announced with a grimace, looking at Jennifer while the agent was still talking.

"Jackson, we have plenty of time to eat," she answered firmly, looking at him and then back at the agent who the boy had interrupted.

"Sorry about that. My nephew and niece have never flown before," she explained apologetically.

"I totally understand… next!" she announced loudly, already

instructing the people behind to approach her with their bags, dismissing Jennifer and the kids, wanting them to now move along.

They made it through security, removing their shoes and placing them in a plastic container along with their backpacks and phones and Jennifer's purse and cellphone, retrieving them on the other side of the x-ray machine.

"What was that all about?" Eva asked, as she slid back into her sneakers and looked questionably at her aunt.

"It's to keep us safe," Jennifer explained as they walked away towards their gate.

"How does that keep us safe?"

"Well, Eva, unfortunately there are bad people in this world who would like to hurt us and they can do bad things on airplanes."

"That isn't happening to us today, is it, aunt Jen?" Jackson prodded, looking at her with slight worry in his eyes.

Jennifer smiled reassuredly at both her niece and nephew as they continued with the long walk to their gate. "Of course not! The x-ray machine is used to make sure no one has a gun or knife or something dangerous like that with them which they could potentially take on board of an airplane."

Jackson was already distracted seeing a burger stand off in the distance. "Can we eat now?" he pleaded, already moving in that direction.

"It's only 10 o'clock. You are hungry already?" she laughed, knowing this was typical for him most days.

"I only had a bowl of cereal at the house," he moaned.

"And 2 packs of Pop-Tarts," Eva added, rolling her eyes.

"That was a couple hours ago and I don't care, I'm starving!" he insisted, trying to work Jennifer again with his *puppy dog* sad expression, knowing Eva was no help.

Jennifer laughed. "Ok, Jackson, we won't starve you any longer," she conceded, walking into the burger joint in front of them, placing an arm around her niece and nephew as they walked up to the counter. "Get whatever you would like, since we won't be eating again until we arrive in Baltimore."

One hour later the boarding call was announced and Jennifer, Eva and Jackson took their seats on the plane with Jennifer sitting in a row directly behind them, having to share it with a gentleman already typing away on his laptop that was placed on his lap. She briefly smiled at him and then glanced at her cellphone one last time before turning it off for the flight.

Jennifer had several missed calls. One, being from Nancy who she had already called back while they were still waiting in the airport after eating their burgers. She gave her the update, letting Nancy know that they would be seeing them within several hours. The other was from the cat sitter who was confirming the daily schedule, and the last was from Mitchell who wished her and the children well on their vacation.

She would need to text them all once she landed in Baltimore and her phone was turned back on. She listened to the flight attendant addressing all the passengers on board how to *properly fasten the seatbelt and what to do in case of an emergency*, as she pointed towards several exit doors with her arm out-stretched. Once the stewardess completed her presentation, Jennifer closed her eyes, ready to take a quick nap, suggesting to the children also that it was a good idea for them rest on the flight before they landed. She fell asleep with a pleasant smile on her face, clutching one arm to the other with her jacket in place since the air conditioning was too cold - thinking of sand and surf, and a week's adventure in Marlin Beach.

CHAPTER 29

"You're all set!" the young man informed Jennifer as he handed her back her credit card. "Let's proceed out to the parking lot and you can do a fast walk around to make sure everything looks okay, and then you can be on your way to the beach!" he informed with a bright smile, escorting the group outside to the car rental parking lot.

The three walked towards the shiny red, Mustang convertible as they pulled their suitcases behind them, stopping to stare in pride along with the car representative. Jennifer did a quick perusal of the vehicle finding only a small scratch on the bumper, which was noted.

She always wanted to own a convertible and a red Mustang one at that, but found it to be too impractical – especially because of the Alabama winters that occasionally brought snow. If that occasional snowstorm did occur, she knew driving to work might be a problem. So she settled for a more practical 4-door sedan that had front wheel drive, that gave her peace of mind not only for her commute, but also for driving Eva and Jackson around in comfort and safety. Now she had a week of carefree living at the beach, and she would allow herself a few glorious days of freedom and abandonment from the norm - and that included the vehicle she would drive.

"Here are your keys and I hope you have a great time in Marlin Beach!"

"Well thank you very much," Jennifer answered sincerely, as she loaded the three suitcases into the trunk and Eva and Jackson climbed into the back seat as per her insistence. "I will return here in a week and drop it off."

"Absolutely! See you then," the young worker waved as he walked away, back into the car rental building attached to the airport.

"Why can't I sit up front?" Eva questioned, as she clutched the headrest of the front passenger's seat from behind.

"That's not fair!" Jackson argued, beginning to fight with his sister.

Jennifer turned to stare at her niece and nephew, giving them an *eye of warning* that they had come to recognize as pushing her over the edge. "Why you are both in the backseat is for this very reason! *I will have no arguments over who is sitting up front, and that one was up here longer than the other!* My purse and other things are here anyway on the front seat. Just be content that you are going to the beach finally to see William!" she announced irritably, lowering her head and breathing deeply while saying a silent prayer for safety, just to clear her thoughts before pulling away. She checked her directions, realizing she had a three and a half hour journey ahead of her.

Growing up in Baltimore, Maryland held fond memories for Jennifer. She grew up in a religious family where her father was a pastor and her mother was at home tending to the household. She was close to her sister Claire and the two would play inside and out for many hours during the summer months when school was out. Several times the family did go to Marlin Beach, but her father preferred a mountain getaway to the busy bustling crowds that were drawn to the ocean community.

As Jennifer drove away from BWI Airport, they passed by Annapolis where numerous sailboats where scattered throughout the water, and then they approached the majestic Chesapeake Bay Bridge. As she stopped to pay the toll to cross the double spanned bridge, Eva and Jackson looked out of their open car windows in awe and fascination as they began their journey crossing the 4-mile span. They had never been to Maryland and had only heard the fond stories of the beloved places that both their aunt Jennifer and their mother Claire had lived at or visited as youth.

Jennifer drove across the lengthy bridge pointing out a large cargo ship drifting lazily by in the water below. "This is the Chesapeake Bay. Can you smell seafood in the air?" she asked, feeling light-hearted that her vacation had finally begun.

"*I can!*" Jackson announced, as the bright sun beat down on the group. Jennifer had released the roof of the convertible while they were stalled in the middle of the bridge from the slow movement of traffic that was also heading for Marlin Beach, with all in the car being fascinated as it collapsed and disappeared before their eyes.

"Wow, this is so cool, aunt Jen!" Eva said in fascination, looking around at the car that was now minus its roof. "I feel like I'm almost standing on top of the bridge."

"Don't get any ideas," she laughed, finally feeling the weight of stress from weeks of grinding work - from the end of the busiest time in tax season - lifting off of her shoulders.

The Mustang made it again to solid ground, as the children looked behind them at the Bay Bridge that was now fading away in the distance. Jennifer drove past several small towns, as her phone began to ring. "Hi Nancy," she smiled, placing her cellphone on speaker so that she could hear the call and drive at the same time.

"Did you make it safely to Baltimore?"

"Oh yes! The flight was wonderful and we are now on our way to

Marlin Beach as we speak. We should be there in two hours according to my GPS. Do you need me to pick anything up before we arrive?"

"I think we are fine. Mike and I stopped at Mom and Pops and picked up some produce for dinner tonight. I hope hamburgers on the grill and corn on the cob are okay?"

"That sounds perfect! I would like to take you to dinner this week as a thank you for allowing us to stay with you at your beach house."

"We are very happy to host you and there is no need for that. I'm sure you will want to treat William, Eva and Jackson to the boardwalk or maybe other activities, so don't worry about anything else."

"Well thank you, Nancy, that is very kind of you and Mike."

"I'm hearing a lot of wind on the phone. Is it windy where you are at?" Nancy asked.

"Not really. I just rented a convertible and I have the top down. I'm sorry for having you on speaker, but I know the traffic law of Maryland is for hands free driving. Would you like me to put the top back up so that you can hear me better?"

"Of course not, dear. It really isn't that bad," Nancy answered, realizing now she shouldn't have mentioned it. She walked out to the deck where Mike was sitting and looking out over the beach, joining him on the other rattan chair close by, reaching out to grab his hand. "Well, we will see you soon. Please drive safely."

"Thank you. See you soon."

Mike looked at his wife, who was more than ready for company, having each room tidy and the refrigerator and pantry amply stocked with food for the incoming guests. "When will they arrive?"

"I'm guessing around 5 o'clock?"

"So I have two hours to relax?"

"More like an hour since I want to have the grill started before they get here."

"Why the rush?" Mike asked, looking at Nancy with slight confusion, not ready to break from his last moments of quiet on the deck alone before their company arrived.

"I'm sure they will be hungry when they get here, Mike. You know how children can be. And then maybe we can take them to the boardwalk afterwards?"

Mike patted the top of his wife's hand. "Maybe we should reach out to William first and see if he still plans to join us for dinner, and then we can decide what we will do afterwards."

"I tried to call him already, but it went right to voicemail. He seems to be very distracted lately and rarely answers the phone when I call."

Mike got up to walk to the railing as Nancy joined him. "Honey, he is living the dream right now. Summer and the beach take a front row seat to us. Things will be different when he is back in school and then he will have fewer distractions."

"I certainly hope so. He just seems so preoccupied with other things now, even with his job at the real estate agency. He has grown up so much in the past three years."

They stood together silently watching a boy with a kite that had a long tail, rising and falling with the ocean breeze. It took them back to an earlier time when their son Dexter would do something similar and now he was no longer with them. Now their grandson, William, was becoming a man and not the child that they first met who wanted to run and play on the beach and pull a kite along also.

Mike leaned forward and kissed Nancy tenderly on the lips, making her blush.

"What was that for?"

"Just a reminder that we will always have each other, even when things change. Remember, you have two young guests coming that have never experienced Marlin Beach or The Dancing Seahorse. You know you are at your best when you can entertain and make our company feel welcome."

Nancy could feel tears welling up in her eyes with her husband's kind words. "That is so sweet that you would say that. We definitely don't get here enough, Mike. I'm glad that Jennifer and the children are giving us a chance to do so now."

Mike's cellphone began to ring as he picked it up off the patio table. "William! We've been waiting on your call!"

"Sorry, G-Dad, I've been swamped at work," he lied, driving home for the final time from community service with Marlin Beach Ambulance. Lance had thankfully saved his ass once again, putting in a good word with the ambulance company and getting his community service assigned there, which he had fully completed in only two weeks. He had put aside work at Beach Dreams - with Lance's permission - so that he could focus in on his 80 hours of community service, knowing Jennifer and the kids were arriving today. He was exhausted from another full day of answering the phones and washing down the fire engines and ambulances.

"Jennifer and the kids will be here within two hours. Are you up for joining us for dinner tonight or do you have other plans?"

Will yawned, pulling into the driveway of The Happy Crab, realizing his other roommates were still not home and probably busy at work. "Sure, I will be there. I need to get a shower and change and then I will see you soon."

"Looking forward to it!" Mike replied, walking down the deck steps towards the shed. "We're grilling out and we'll probably eat around

5:30 or six if that helps."

"I will be there as soon and then I will I help you with the grill."

"Sounds like a plan," Mike answered, happy to know that William would also be joining them. He wheeled the grill out to the driveway making sure it was cleaned and had enough propane – being more than ready for a barbeque.

Chapter 30

Jennifer pulled into the gravel driveway of The Dancing Seahorse and could see two men working side by side – Mike with a barbeque turner in one hand placing the cooked hamburgers on a large tray that William was holding.

Will smiled as he realized who it was, as the car doors opened and Jennifer, Eva and Jackson ran towards him - ready to give him a big hug. "Hey everybody," he grinned. "I better take these burgers in the house and then we can say our hellos," he explained.

"Nonsense!" Mike insisted, grabbing the tray away from William. "I can take these inside. Say a proper hello first to everybody!" Mike suggested with a smile, leaving the group to be alone.

William stood for a moment dumbfounded, just staring at the family he had left behind three years earlier, realizing his siblings had grown up some. Immediately they approached and mutually wrapped their arms around him, stunning him in the process by their affection.

"Willy, we missed you!" Jennifer gushed, kissing him tenderly on the cheek as she continued with the group hug.

"Me too…" Eva added bashfully.

"I've been playing with your toys," Jackson admitted with a sly grin.

"Well I'm glad you are getting some use out of them, Jack," William grinned, patting his younger brother playfully on the top of his head. "Let's get inside because I think Nan has dinner ready, and then I will help you unload the car afterwards."

The family made their way up the steps of the beach house and entered to a room filled with delightful smells of citrusy candles. A full array of picnic foods sat on the counter, ready to be eaten. "Well you're finally here!" Nancy beamed, wiping her hands on a dishtowel and walking towards the living room to greet everyone.

"Thank you so much for allowing us to stay," Jennifer immediately offered, after they hugged. She then handed Nancy a bottle of wine, not being an expert by any means on a decent brand or year. "This is just a little thank you for your hospitality. It's all that we've been talking and dreaming about since we knew that you had invited us to your beautiful beach house."

"The pleasure is all ours," Nancy answered sweetly, accepting her hostess gift. "I hope you are hungry since we have a feast prepared," she directed with a smile, leading them to the kitchen to see all that was offered and laid out on the countertop in front of them. "As you can see - plates, napkins, silverware are over there. Help yourselves and then you can either eat inside at the table or go out to the deck and dine there," she pointed towards the outside patio. "I also have sodas and water in the cooler" she added, wanting to make sure everything was covered.

"May I go to the bathroom first?" Eva pleaded, feeling half embarrassed for asking and looking slightly uncomfortable.

"Follow me, Evie," Will smiled, trying to ease her worries, escorting her towards the hall bathroom.

"I need to go too," Jackson insisted, following right behind the other two.

"It was a long flight and then we got right on the road with only one break," Jennifer explained. "Your home is so lovely," she complimented, looking around at the custom kitchen and the large expanse of a living room spread out in front of her, with the deck and ocean beyond that.

"Mike designed it," Nancy bragged.

"It was many years ago..." Mike replied humbly, looking at the women in front of him. "It was something Nancy and I decided we wanted shortly after we were married and had our children. It's been a place of retreat for us that unfortunately we don't get enough time to enjoy anymore with our busy lives in Baltimore."

"Whose fault is that? I am always ready to pack up and stay in Marlin Beach for an extended weekend."

Mike shook his head and smiled, knowing Nancy stayed fairly busy too with all her local activities at home. "If you say so, dear," he conceded.

The children reappeared, ready to dig into the offerings, realizing they were suddenly hungry after their long journey. They grabbed a plate and piled it high with burgers, corn on the cob, potato salad and baked beans. Each decided to eat outdoors at the patio table on the deck, as they took their seats and ate hungrily of the picnic fare.

"The view is specular here," Jennifer noticed, looking out over the large expanse of beach with its lingering array of beachgoers who were still relaxing and enjoying the sand and surf.

"We are very blessed. To be near the ocean is wonderful in itself, but then we have the dunes right in our backyard too - with wildlife and birds always scurrying to and fro. We are constantly entertained," Nancy explained.

"*Can we go swimming now?*" Jackson asked William suddenly, already bored and looking over the deck railing.

"It's getting kinda late for that, buddy," Will explained, making an excuse, knowing the children didn't need to be introduced to the ocean at nearly 7 p.m. for their first time. "But tomorrow is to be sunny and a fine day for hanging out at the beach. I promise I will come back and show you how to boogie board then." He could still recall his first time at Marlin Beach getting in the ocean, just several years earlier with Lance and Sarah who were his water coaches.

"*Are you leaving us?*" Eva implored. "*You're not staying here tonight? I thought you were staying with us,*" she moaned.

Will looked at the adults present, searching for the right answer. "Evie, I'm living here this summer and have my own place to go home to. But I promise I will come back first thing in the morning and hang out with you all day. Maybe we can even go to the boardwalk in the evening after the beach."

"*What's a boardwalk?*"

Will laughed, realizing this was all new to them with new things to experience just as it had been for him a short time ago. "It is a super fun place filled with games and rides and ice cream!"

"*Can't we go now?*" Jackson begged.

Jennifer stepped in to bring order back to the group. "Eva and Jackson, we have had a very long day, and I for one am exhausted! We are here for a week and I promise we will go to the beach and the boardwalk - but not tonight. I want to help Nancy clean up the kitchen and then I want to relax the rest of the evening."

"No need for that," Mike interjected, getting up along with Nancy to gather the dishes and head towards the kitchen. "Visit with William for awhile and then we will get your suitcases and show you where you will be sleeping."

"Well, thank you, Mike."

"No worries," he called over his shoulder as he pulled the patio doors shut behind him, giving them some alone time and privacy once again.

Jennifer smiled at William, being the first to speak, finding things somewhat awkward as she tried to make small talk. *"So you are staying here for the entire summer?"*

"That is my plan, as long as Lance allows me to continue to stay at his beach house."

Jennifer looked puzzled. *"I'm not following?"*

Will smiled and shook his head, feeling slightly ashamed. "My friends and I are typical college kids and we like to party a little too much at times. Lance wants us to keep the place clean and has asked us not to have parties. We have already been warned more than once. If we are told again, my time in Marlin Beach will be done for the summer and I will have to go back to Baltimore to live and work until school begins again in the fall. Lance has cut us a break on the rent and I honestly couldn't afford to live here if he kicks us out."

Jennifer reached out to place a hand on Will's arm, looking into his steel gray eyes. "You are very lucky to have a beach house to stay in like you are doing. Your mother and I were never allowed to come to the beach to work and have fun for the summer. *Never take this for granted!"* she thoughtfully warned.

"I know, aunt Jen, but it's not only me living there. As hard as I try, my roommates want to do things their own way. It's like that at Towson too. They're my friends, but I can't control them."

She smiled understandably at him, remembering her earlier years. "I get it... just try your best. Make your mother proud. She isn't here now and I made her a promise to always watch out for you."

Will dropped his head, taking in her words. He was happy that his siblings were busy playing games on their tablets, oblivious to their conversation. *"Why has it been so long since I've last seen you guys?"* he questioned, confused by here lack of presence.

Jennifer paused, looking at her distracted niece and nephew who were in her care. "I don't know... so much has happened and time has a way of just getting away from us. I wanted you to get adjusted to your new life living with your grandparents in Baltimore, and then you started college. In all fairness, this transition was all new for me too – having to watch and take care of children for the first time in my life, and dealing with your mother's death."

Will looked into Jennifer's eyes that were now moist with tears. "I get it, aunt Jen. I'm not trying to judge, but I have really missed all of you. Life has been great for me with Nan and G-Dad, but you guys are my family too - and at times it has been tough, especially around the holidays."

"I'm sorry, William. I will try harder in the future to visit and stay in touch, and you are always welcome to come see us too."

"It's all good. Seriously," he answered, getting up to stretch his arms high overhead and get the kinks out, looking at his watch and realizing it was now close to 8 p.m. "I probably should leave soon. Gotta do some laundry when I get home. And aunt Jen, will you please do me a favor and not mention the parties to Nan and G-Dad. I will never hear the end of it if they find out!"

"I understand," she smiled knowingly. "You have my word – I will keep our discussion to myself."

Mike slid the patio doors back again, as Nancy carried out a tray with ample sized portions of hot fudge sundaes with whipped cream piled high that she had so lovingly prepared. "I have desert!" she announced proudly, placing the tray in front of the group.

"Oh boy!" Jackson exclaimed. "My favorite!"

Each claimed a dish of the decadent, hot fudge ice cream treat that Nancy was known for, lapping up each bite as they enjoyed the last rays of a brilliant sunset off in the distance.

Will placed the suitcases in the two bedrooms, ready to leave. "I'll see you guys in the morning. Be ready for a fun-filled day!" he winked, giving each a hug goodbye.

CHAPTER 31

The smell of pancakes and bacon filled the early morning air at The Dancing Seahorse, as soft knocks were heard on each of the guest room doors. Jackson sat up straight in the bed that had originally been occupied by Dexter and then later by William. Eva shared the other room and bed with her aunt Jennifer. The room they slept in had always been designated as Sarah's, but with the building of The Playful Starfish her possessions, for the most part, had been removed and the room was used primarily for guests now.

"Wake up, guys. I'm back!" Will announced happily. "Nan is making us breakfast and then it's off to the beach," he added, before making his way back to the kitchen to join his grandparents.

"It sounds like you mean business," Mike mentioned half in jest, looking up from reading his Baltimore Sun, at his grandson who he was very fond of and missed - from not seeing enough of lately.

Nancy poured Will a cup of coffee, before adding to her own cup and Mike's. "Do you want us to join you at the beach or do your prefer some time alone with your family?"

Will reached out to pat the top of his grandmother's hand. "Of course I want you at the beach today. *It's a family day and I want everybody there that is a part of my family!"*

Nancy was touched – picking up on the sentiment. "Then I guess I better pack a cooler after breakfast and Mike you will need to get the umbrellas and chairs together out of the shed," she instructed.

"We'll all pitch in, Nan, or we can buy lunch. I'm not suggesting that you go to any trouble today. You already made dinner last night and now breakfast for everyone."

Jennifer, Eva and Jackson joined the others - still dressed in their pajamas and getting in on the tail end of the conversation.

"I don't mind treating today," Jennifer offered with a smile, as they found a seat around the table that held clean place settings.

Nancy placed a large stack of pancakes and bacon in the center of the table along with syrup, butter and orange juice. "Thanks, Jennifer, but we always pack a cooler for the beach, and then we can decide together what we will have for dinner."

"I want to go to the boardwalk that Will told us about yesterday."

"Jackson, let's have some manners here this morning," Jennifer scolded, giving him the *eye*.

"I'm sorry, aunt Jen," he replied, taking a big bite of the syrup-filled pancakes. "I just really want to get on the rides and have some fun."

William began to laugh, patting his brother on the back. "It's okay, buddy, I get it. I like the rides too! As long as everyone is up for it, why don't we go to the boardwalk for dinner?" he asked the group.

"It's fine with me," Mike answered.

"And me too," Nancy agreed.

"So you get your wish, Jack. After the beach and showers we will go off to the boardwalk!" Will promised, giving his word to the cheers and applause of Jackson and Eva both.

Every pancake and piece of bacon was eaten and the coffee pot was emptied. Nancy and Jennifer cleaned up the kitchen and Mike and Will organized the shed that had not been done in close to a year.

"Wow G-dad, there's lots of cobwebs in here."

"Yeah, I should probably spray in here for spiders," Mike considered as he fished out a large cooler, beach chairs, umbrellas and boogie boards, handing each to William that he then placed together in a pile outside of the shed for their walk to the beach. They washed out the cooler with the hose before taking it inside to Nancy to be packed with some tasty snacks that she typically chose for every outing.

She closed the overstuffed cooler, putting several bags of pretzels and chips in a large duffle bag beside of it. "I'm ready to go!" she announced to the group who had now changed into their bathing suits. The cooler was wheeled outside along with the duffle bag of snacks and another large duffle filled with beach towels and suntan lotion.

"Grab a chair or something else," Mike suggested pleasantly, as everyone present joined in to help. They made their way to the shoreline, which was only a short distance away, forming a caravan line with all of their belongings.

Will led the group, going straight to the spot where his family typically liked to sit. Mike set up the umbrellas, and William unfolded each sand chair placing them under the shade of the umbrellas with the cooler close by.

Nancy found the suntan lotion, applying it first, before helping Mike by rubbing some on his back. She then tried to rub down William's back too, but he felt embarrassed with the others looking on, insisting *he had it covered*. Jennifer searched for her own suntan lotion in her overstuffed beach bag, begging Eva and Jackson to hold still long enough for her to cover them well enough to her liking.

"*You're burning my eyes!*" Eva yelled, as the SPF 30 suntan lotion got slightly into her one eye.

"I'm so sorry, honey. Here's a beach towel," Jennifer offered, as Eva tried to wipe the stinging sensation from her sore eyes.

Will looked on, amused by his siblings resistance to having the suntan lotion applied, but feeling sorry for Eva's predicament all the same. He was anxious to begin the first lesson that would make them ready for boogie boarding, trying to remember Lance's words to him only a few short years ago. *"Are you guys ready to get in the ocean yet?"*

"Yes!" Jackson yelled.

"And you, Evie?"

"I'm ready, but a little scared," Eva confessed, looking at Will with wide eyes that were no longer hurting.

"Well that's a good thing, Evie, to have respect for the ocean," William continued, patting the beach blanket that was now spread out, asking them to join him on it where he sat cross-legged. "Look out there at that big ocean. You can't see any land on the other side like you can with a lake. Right?"

"Yeah..." Evie answered, looking out at the water timidly.

"That's because it's not small like a lake, but very, very big - ending at another continent. And it starts out shallow by the sand - here at the shoreline - and then gets deeper and deeper the further out you go."

Jackson scrunched up his nose, not liking the conversation so far. *"Are we going to be safe out in the deep water?"* he asked, feeling perplexed.

Nancy looked at Mike in concern, questioning whether William was doing a good job of explaining things. "You will be fine with Will looking over you," Mike smiled reassuredly. *"Can you both swim?"* he asked, wanting to make sure that was a given as he looked at Jennifer for the answer.

"Yes, they can, Mike. Eva and Jackson have had lessons at our local YMCA, and in the summer months the local pool offers swim classes 5 days a week, which they participate in."

"Great to hear!" Will praised, jumping back into the conversation. "We are not going out far. So don't worry about all that, Jack and Evie. We will stay close to shore today and you can get used to the waves that at times try to pull you down. Also, the ocean water contains salt and tastes horrible and will burn your eyes if you open them."

"That sounds horrible!" Evie moaned, not sure now that she wanted to go in after all. "My eyes were just burning with suntan lotion. I don't wanna go through that again!"

Nancy began to laugh, shaking her head at William. "Don't scare them, dear, or they will sit on the beach for their whole vacation."

"Nothing doing!" Jackson yelled, as he got up to walk towards the water's edge with Eva now in tow. William was quick to follow, standing side by side by his siblings as the rushing water ran up over their feet, making Evie jump from the jolt of the temperature.

"It's cold!" she exclaimed.

"Yes, but it is also hot outside today, so it will feel good once you get used to it," Will answered reasonably, trying to calm her down.

They stood together for several minutes allowing the ocean surge to run over their feet. Will broke free, walking further into the water, instructing them as they stood on the shoreline watching him. "I want you to turn your back on the waves like I am ready to do and put your arms straight out and it will carry you in to shore. Tuck your chin to your neck and keep your arms close to your head, and all should be fine." A small wave approached as Will demonstrated what he wanted them to do, riding it in to shore. Eva placed her hands over her mouth, squealing in delight as she watched William, and Jackson jumped up and down against the foam of an incoming breaking wave, hooting and hollering as he went by.

"Can we get in yet?" Jackson insisted, as William made his way back over to them.

"Not quite yet, buddy. We got more to go over first." Will grabbed the boogie board that he left laying in the sand close by, ready to give his next lesson. "I want to show you what step number two will look like once you master body surfing." He took the strap that was attached to the boogie board and wrapped it around his wrist, securing the Velcro fastener before wading out a short distance into the water as he patiently waited. Eva and Jackson stood together, side-by-side, watching from the shoreline.

A wave finally broke, lifting Will high into the air above its arch, with the rushing water pushing the board and thrusting him towards the beach. *"Wheee...!"* he yelled and laughed all at the same time, as he slid to a stop right in front of Eva and Jackson's feet. *"That was great!"*

"I want to try that!" Jackson yelled, reaching down to claim the boogie board.

"Not so fast, Jack. By tomorrow all three of us will have our own boogie boards, but for now its time to body surf and get used to salt water in your eyes and mouth, and let's hope you don't swallow too much of it or it may make you sick."

"I don't plan to," Eva grimaced, making a tight seal with her lips.

"Me neither," Jackson agreed, shaking his head in disgust.

Will laughed, wrapping an arm around each one of them as he led the brother and sister pair into the surf that broke with small playful waves. They jumped over each whitecap and finally began body surfing into shore, giggling once they reached the dry sand.

The adults watched from a short distance away, as they lounged and talked in their low-slung sand chairs, under the welcoming shade of the umbrellas. Each one had a drink in hand, digging their toes into the warm sand as they discussed the plans for the evening ahead, taking in the progress of the children and the other beachgoers in front of them. It was a laid-back, blue-sky, calm-ocean, summer in Marlin Beach kind of day – and no one lucky enough to be there had a care in the world.

CHAPTER 32

Three drown rats trudged tiredly through the sand, back up to the beach camp of adults where the snacks had been just brought forth from the cooler a few moments earlier - waiting to be eaten.

"Are you hungry?" Nancy asked, looking at William and the others, as she handed Jennifer a plate of cheese and crackers.

William laughed. "Seriously, Nan. You must know we are starving after that workout!"

"I want some!" Jackson yelled, reaching for a bottle of water from the open cooler in front of him.

"Manners, Jackson!" Jennifer demanded for another time, constantly having to remind him to choose a different way of acting.

"Sorry, aunt Jen, but I'm hungry and thirsty after all that."

"It's okay," Mike offered with a kind smile, helping Nancy fill up a couple more plates of snacks for the starving swimmers, handing the first one to Jackson. "How was the water temperature out there?"

"Freezing!" Eva answered, hugging herself and shaking for affect.

"It wasn't that bad," Will laughed as he shook his head, taking a big bite of cheese on top of a cracker, stuffing the whole thing in his mouth at once. "Actually, it's an excellent day for getting in the ocean. No undertow to speak of. The lifeguards should have it pretty easy today."

Nancy listened to the words, drifting back once again to that fateful day many years earlier when the undertow was not as calm and forgiving as it was now... taking Dex from her. She shook her head slightly and shuttered, bringing her back to the present.

"Maybe a little rest is in order?" she suggested, looking worriedly at Jennifer and Mike, only desiring now to keep the children far away from the ocean and safely on shore with them.

Will studied his grandmother, knowing her well and sensing her fear. She had that typical look of alarm and despair etched all over her face that was usually present when they would visit The Dancing Seahorse for a vacation and actually go to the beach. Her anxieties would always surface when she watched one of her family members enter the water.

"I know that I'm tired," he said, winking in Nan's direction, giving her some peace of mind for at least a little while. Will found a beach towel and collapsed on it, belly down. "Don't let me sleep too long since we plan to go to the boardwalk later," he told the adults, closing his eyes and falling off to sleep quickly. Eva and Jackson followed suit, placing each of their towels on opposite sides of William, not having any trouble joining him in slumber.

Jennifer looked on at the sleeping trio who had now been resting for way over an hour, smiling contentedly at the scene. "You are very fortunate to have your own beach house, you know. If I was so lucky, I would drive here every weekend to hang out."

"Everyone plans for that until you own one," Mike answered realistically. "But life and responsibilities always seem to pull one away from fulfilling that desire."

"We found more time when the children were younger. I used to spend my entire summer here with Sarah and Dexter while they were on their school breaks and when I was a schoolteacher. Mike would join us here on the weekends," Nancy added, looking at Mike with a reminiscent smile.

He reached out to pat the top of her hand. "Yes, you are right, dear. We did make it more of a priority then as we should now."

"Well, I want to thank you again for your hospitality. We are very appreciative of the time that you are taking out of your busy schedules to be here with us. I know Eva and Jackson are having the time of their lives."

"You have thanked us enough," Mike insisted, handing Jennifer another bottle of the chilled water from the cooler, and taking one for him and Nancy. Will rolled over, blocking his eyes from the sun.

"Got one for me, G-Dad?" he asked, sitting up and arching out his back in a stretch from lying too long in the sand.

"Sure, Will," Mike answered with a smile, handing his grandson another of the bottles of water. "Maybe its time to wake the others if you want to get to the boardwalk at a decent hour yet today?" he suggested.

Will nudged them, as they stirred and groaned, not ready to end their afternoon nap. They sat up, squinting with half-opened eyes.

"You wanna keep laying there and sleeping or do you want to get cleaned up and go to the boardwalk?"

"I want to go to the boardwalk!" Jackson yelled, suddenly jumping up and wiping the sand off of his legs with the beach towel, ready to run towards the beach house.

"Not so fast," Will called out with his hands cupping his mouth. "Get back here, Jackson. Everyone needs to help out and get everything

back up to the shed and house before we get our showers and leave for the boardwalk."

Jackson turned around, running back to the group. "Sorry. I'm just excited to go to the boardwalk for the first time," he explained, looking at his aunt and fearing her reaction.

"We understand," Nancy soothed, placing a beach bag in Jackson's hand and a sand chair in Eva's.

The rest of the things were claimed and carried as the caravan made their way back up to The Dancing Seahorse. William and Mike washed the sand from each item with the outdoor garden hose, before replacing them neatly back into the shed. The beach bags needed to be emptied out into the laundry room so that Nancy could later wash the beach and bath towels after the showers were taken.

Everyone showered and changed their clothes for the evening, ready to go to the boardwalk. "Better grab a jacket," Nancy urged, finding hers in the hall closet on the way out the door. The others complied upon her insistence, but were not quite ready yet to put theirs on as she had already done, tying them around their waists instead.

The walked the couple blocks where the boardwalk began, seeing the train station in front of them. "Are we riding the tram, G-Dad?" William inquired.

"Of course!" Mike replied, approaching the attendant's window as the others waited a short distance away. "I need six round trip tickets, please," he requested with a smile, handing the young woman his credit card. She passed the tickets and his credit card back through the window, along with his receipt.

"Have a nice evening," she offered, as Mike walked away, giving a ticket to each one in the group. Will assisted Jennifer and Nancy onto the tram, as the children jumped up on their own, and Mike followed. Each one found a vacant seat, sitting close together. Soon, each trolley car was filled with passengers and the tram's engine was turned on and began to move slowly down the wooden boardwalk, gaining momentum as it chugged along.

"This is really cool," Eva exclaimed, as the train passed by souvenir shops, motels and eateries.

"It sure is, Evie," Will agreed, reaching over in the seat to wrap a protective arm around his little sister who was sitting right beside of him. "Pretty neat, right, Jack?"

"I love it!" Jackson answered with merriment flooding his eyes. *"Where are all the rides?"* he asked William, being extremely impatient at his young age.

"Look ahead," Will pointed, seeing the Ferris wheel off in the distance with its bright lights flashing as it circled.

"Oh boy. I can't wait to get on that! Can we ride that one first?"

"Don't get ahead of yourself, Jack. We normally do that ride last... before we go home for the evening," he replied, knowing it was somewhat of a family tradition with Mike and Nancy to do so.

Nancy smiled warmly at Mike, happy that William had become so much a part of their lives and knew the routine. *"Aren't you hungry?"* she asked, looking at Jackson, trying to change the subject.

"I guess so, but can't we go on rides first?"

Jennifer glanced at Jackson, knowing he was always keeping her on her toes. *"We will eat first and then do the rides. I for one am hungry."*

"Me too," Eva added, smiling and agreeing with her aunt. The tram stopped at the other end of the boardwalk by the Life Saving museum, which was the final stop and where the last remaining riders had to exit.

"That was fun, now let's get dinner," Jennifer expressed taking charge for the group, as they all agreed and walked towards the busy French fry stand nearby.

"Why so many people?" Jackson inquired, looking innocently at his aunt for the answer.

"Because the French fries are delicious!" she giggled.

They stood for what seemed like an eternity to the children, finally being first in line. Mike made his way up to the front of the group, barking out his request loudly to the guy taking his order. *"Five small and one medium,"* he said, once again handing over his credit card with Jennifer trying her best to pay and Mike shaking his head – a firm *no*.

Each one was handed their own individual container, with Mike and Nancy being the exception and sharing theirs. Eva and Jackson didn't understand the lack of ketchup and made a face when William sprinkled Malt vinegar on top of his. They proceeded towards a famous pizza stand where Jennifer insisted once again that she would like to pay, with Mike finally agreeing to let her to do so.

After dinner, the rides and Skee-Ball were to follow, along with many arcade games that produced cheap prizes of stuffed animals that no one except for Eva really wanted or cared to carry for the rest of the evening. An incandescent swirling ice cream cone could be seen ahead, as the group happily approached the desert stand, each choosing their special flavor which once again Mike paid for and *would not take no for an answer* this time around from Jennifer.

They walked towards the Ferris wheel after finishing their cones, proceeding forward and waiting until it was their turn to take the next seat. A *carnie worker* waited close by, securing and locking the bar down over them before pushing the seat forward so that the next one in line could get on. Nancy sat with Mike and Jackson squeezed in quickly beside of William, leaving Eva to stand and stare in disbelief as she waited now with her aunt. She thought she was riding with William instead of her brother, as they had discussed on the way to the ride.

"Don't worry Evie, you will ride with me the next time!" Will yelled out and promised over the lively, pre-recorded organ style music, that was constantly being played, not wanting to disappoint her.

Jackson looked out over the side of the seat, taking in the view of Marlin Beach and the tiny people walking on the boardwalk below. *"We are up so high, Will,"* he whispered, fascinated with what he was seeing.

"Yeah, we sure are buddy," he answered with a broad smile as he wrapped an arm around Jackson's shoulder and hugged him tight, enjoying the day immensely with his family.

The moon shone brightly, sending a beam of light across the ocean, as the waves broke against the shoreline, and those fortunate enough to see it from that viewpoint took it all in - as the organ music played on.

CHAPTER 33

"Hey, where have you been, bro?" Chris inquired of William, after grabbing a beer from the refrigerator and taking a big long swig.

"I told you my family was visiting from Alabama. You *never* remember things," Will sighed, shaking his head.

"Oh…. yeah…. my bad. There's just so much going on with community service and working. *How are you pulling everything off?"*

Will laughed, grabbing a beer also, before sitting at the kitchen table with his friend. "I already finished my community service. Lance was great and worked things out for me with Marlin Beach ambulance, and I powered through it all in only two weeks."

"And work?"

"I'm taking a break from that until my family leaves town. I just want to focus my time on hanging out with them since I haven't been around them in three years."

"Must be nice having a rich uncle who can fix things for you," Chris mocked sarcastically, getting up to grab another beer for him and Will also.

"Yes it is! What can I say – are you jealous?"

"Of you? Well maybe I am from time to time," Chris honestly confessed, socking Will playfully in the arm. "At least with what you got going here in Marlin Beach. Hey, did you know Lance showed up today and he was looking over the beach house again?"

"What time was that?"

"I would say around noon."

"I hope you guys had the place cleaned up."

"We finally passed the test," Chris grinned. "Just a little trash he commented on, but other than that - he *finally* seemed pleased."

The front door opened and in came Matt and Tyler with several girls in tow along with Brooke, who were all dressed in short shorts and halter-tops, looking slightly intoxicated from wherever they had just ventured.

"You guys missed a great party!" Tyler commented, as the group of partygoers made their way towards the kitchen. Will glanced at Brooke who was intently staring and smiling in his direction, obviously giving him signals of interest again.

"Where was the party?" Chris curiously asked, getting up to place the remaining beer from the refrigerator on the table for everyone to drink and enjoy.

"At our place," Rachel giggled, slightly belching in an unladylike manner.

Rachel, Mia, Brooke and Amber were roommates for the summer much like William and his friends, except that they did not all attend the same colleges. Brooke and Mia attended the University of Maryland and Rachel and Amber attended Penn State.

Rachel and Brooke were first cousins that had always wanted to work and live together at Marlin Beach, so a plan was formulated and a place was found with the assistance of the cousins' mothers who were sisters. Unlike William and his friends who had an easy time with cheap rent thanks to Lance, the girls had to come up with $2000 a month between them for their place. Three of them worked as waitresses at The Dexter, and thanks to their good looks they typically made enough tip money to easily pay the rent. Brooke was the hostess at the Dexter, getting compensated with a higher hourly amount, since she rarely made tip money like the other ones did.

Brooke slid her chair close to Will's, whispering in his ear playfully. *"I thought you would have called me by now,"* she purred sweetly while batting her eyelashes at him.

Will smiled, looking downward at the fullness of her well endowed breasts, that were begging to be touched with her taunt nipples showing through her see-through, white camisole top.

"I've been busy with cleaning up my mess from the big party we had here and hanging out with my family," he plainly commented, knowing none of them helped to clean up.

Her hand rested on his blue-jeaned thigh that was concealed under the table, making William slightly jump in surprise as she made her way up to his crotch and started massaging his penis. He readjusted his position as the others in the room were slowly disappearing and trying to get cozy.

Will locked eyes with hers, sending Brooke a silent message. He grabbed her hand and walked from the kitchen towards his bedroom, as she looked back triumphantly at her friends set on their own male and intentions.

The bedroom door opened and shut quickly, as Will pinned Brooke up against the back of it, kneading her breasts intentionally through her t-shirt, sending shivers down her spine as he kissed her deeply with his tongue that met her own.

They undressed without restraint, just like they did the night of the party, falling on top of the half-made bed. Will's fingers plunged deeply into her wetness, tasting them afterwards and groaning in delight. He proceeded downward, planting kisses on her nipples and then her stomach before finding its intended goal between her parted legs. His tongue teased her opening as he mouthed her clitoris, making her orgasm with repeated waves of delight as Brooke's head thrust from side to side from the ecstasy of it all.

Will climbed on top of her with his penis hard and erect, entering her with one swift movement, making her hips arch upward to meet his own. He clutched her buttocks while rocking repeatedly - in and out - inside her warm and wet opening that sent him over the edge with his own heated release.

"Oh my God, that was so sweet," he sighed, looking at the beautiful, contented nymph beside of him.

She giggled, darting her tongue out of her mouth playfully, ready to do it again. *"It's my turn to go down on you."*

Will laughed, perspired from their spirited workout. "You may want to give me a little time to recover from all that."

"We have all night. I'm not going anywhere unless you want to kick me out," she said coyly, as she mimicked Will's move of earlier, kissing his sleek wet nipples and trailing open tongue kisses down his stomach to his semi-rigid penis and balls, that she licked and fondled and moaned over, arousing William once again very quickly, much to his liking and surprise. She allowed him to come in her mouth as she sucked and swallowed every last drop of semen from his engorged shaft, making him pull her head away from the intensity of it all.

"No more..." he begged, knowing she was the best he had ever had. "Come up here and lay with me," he requested, pulling her up to join

him under the covers.

She smiled contentedly as he spooned her protectively, as they lay entwined together, ready to fall sleep. Brooke slept and Will could still hear the faint sounds of groaning and movement coming from the other bedrooms of his roommates who were also lost in ecstasy - immensely enjoying their evening with their female friends who visited.

Slivers of daylight peaked through the blinds of the window as Will rolled over, patting the bed where Brooke had once been sleeping, realizing she was no longer there. She reappeared, having used the bathroom, smiling as she slipped back under the covers, nuzzling into his chest and turning him on again.

"What time is it?" he asked, reaching over to look at his cellphone.

"Time to do it again," she giggled playfully, reaching for his dick.

"Hmm..." he moaned, realizing he was falling under the spell of her sexual prowess. *"We gotta make this quick because I got to get up and get going this morning,"* he whispered. "Family stuff... that's all."

Will rolled Brooke on top of him, knowing she was very willingly to oblige him. She positioned his cock inside of her vagina that was already wet with anticipation. She moved up and down slowly with her eyes closed, as he studied her very toned body that he was very much turned on by and wanted. He began to match her rhythm as they began to move against the other, sending them both over the edge with *delightful morning sex*.

They faced each other afterwards, body to body, with the covers pulled back, as Will wiped away the damp blonde hair from Brooke's beautiful face. "Wow, what a night and morning," he confessed tenderly to her. "I really must get a shower now and get going. I will call you though – if you would like."

Brooke sat up, studying him, as he lay nude on the bed. "I like you

William. *Of course I want you to call me, silly,"* she smiled sweetly, leaping from the bed and retrieving her *barely-there* bra and panties, and shorts and t-shirt too - dressing quickly and switching gears. "I need to get going also. I have an afternoon and evening shift at The Dexter. Have fun with your family," she wished with a peck kiss on his lips, before she disappeared from the room.

Will could hear Brooke talking to her friends who had just made their exit from his roommates' bedrooms. She had knocked on their doors, trying to wake the girls up since she had driven the car that was their ride out of there for work that day.

They were all in the family room together looking for their shoes, pocketbooks and cellphones as Matt and Chris echoed in with comments of their own, trying to lend their assistance. Tyler was the only voice William did not hear, and he figured that he had remained in bed not caring too much about saying goodbye to his bed companion of the evening, which didn't surprise him any.

With the items found, the females left The Happy Crab. He could hear laughter and talking and then kisses goodbye, as Brooke's four car doors opened and then shut loudly, with silence reigning once the vehicle had driven away. Matt and Chris were heard bragging, after coming back into the beach house, arguing over who had the *better lay* which had Will smiling that he knew he truly did – and there was no debating that.

Will sat for a moment on the edge of his bed just scratching his head and pondering the situation, realizing he was beginning to have romantic feelings for Brooke that he didn't see coming. He knew it wasn't the smartest thing to pursue since they would be going their separate ways at the end of the summer - once they were back in college. *I have other occasional love interests at school and maybe this is just a summer fling, but if feels good all the same,* he considered, as he leaped from the bed, hurrying off to the bathroom for a quick shower before returning to his family at The Dancing Seahorse.

CHAPTER 34

"I'm back!" Will grinned, dragging in his backpack with a change of clothes tucked neatly inside for any planned activity after the beach. He was already dressed in his board shorts, ready to boogie board the day away with his siblings.

Nancy smiled, walking over to give William a hug and kiss on the cheek, noticing something especially different in his demeanor. *"Good morning, Will,"* she said at arm's length. *"You seem extra chipper this morning."*

"That's because I'm here with you, Nan," he winked, bending down to give her a return kiss on the cheek.

Nancy laughed, being overly fond of her grandson ever since she began to raise him a few short years prior. "No, its something else."

Will was not one to talk, especially about his female conquests. *There is no reason to tell anyone about Brooke at this point - if ever,* he pondered as he proceeded to the stove to dish out some eggs and bacon that his grandmother had just prepared. "Where is everyone this morning?" he asked as he poured some coffee into a large mug and joined Nancy at the table.

"G-Dad is playing golf with John Snyder and Jennifer and the children walked to the surf shop down the street. She promised to buy them each a new bathing suit."

"Oh, okay. I hope they still plan to go to the beach today since that was what I had planned," he casually mentioned, taking a big bite of toast and strawberry jam.

Nancy refilled her coffee and then joined Will at the table again after washing and drying the last of the dishes left in the sink. "Oh yes, they are definitely planning on the beach today, although Jackson mentioned the boardwalk again."

"We just went there last night," Will replied, not sure he was ready for another round of the rides so soon. "Maybe we can play some board games tonight or watch a movie instead?"

"I would ask them, dear," she consoled, patting his arm. "I may skip the beach today and just read on the deck if you don't mind."

Will looked up from his empty plate, staring at the beautiful lady who was more like a mother to him now than a grandmother since his mother's death. "Aunt Jen likes your company, Nan. She may get lonely if I am in the ocean with Eva and Jackson for the majority of the afternoon and she is sitting on the beach alone. *So will you reconsider?*" he asked sweetly with a handsome smile, having her wrapped around his finger.

"Oh William, I can never say no to you, do you know that?" she giggled, getting up to take his dirty plate to the sink, washing it up quickly and then retuning it to the cabinet nearby. "G-Dad thought that maybe we could all go out to dinner tonight to Old Bay Café. He was hoping that maybe Sarah, Lance and the twins could join us, along with John and Alison."

Will got up to relax with Nancy in the living room as the ocean balmy breeze drifted in from the open patio doors. "I'm surprised John is playing golf today with G-Dad. According to Lance, it has been touch and go with that flu he came down with when they were on their cruise. I guess he must be feeling better?"

"Yes he is, and that's why your grandfather wanted to invite them. As much as he and Alison have routinely eaten there, they haven't been back in several weeks since the virus hit him. Alison is lucky she never came down with it, especially since it affected John so badly. With his heart issues, we were all concerned for awhile."

"I knew something was up since Alison rarely has been coming in to the office, and she seems to be working from home the majority of the time."

"Is Lance getting along okay without you this week?" Nancy inquired pleasantly, still sipping from her coffee mug.

"Lance claims he is fine without me," Will answered matter-of-factly, suddenly feeling somewhat guilty for taking off a whole week from Beach Dreams with Alison being out also.

The door opened wide with two happy children laughing and talking loudly as they ran into the room with their arms filled with shopping bags. Jennifer shut the door behind her, following the others into the living room with a bag of her own.

"Look at what I got!" Jackson beamed happily, pulling his brightly colored orange and green striped board shorts and matching rash guard shirt from the plastic bag that had the surf shop store logo stamped on the front of it.

"Wow, those are cool, Jack! And how about you, Evie – what did you get?"

Eva more gingerly removed her beachwear from the bag, smiling at her older brother for his approval as she held up the two-piece bathing suit and cover-up for him to see.

"Well, that is very pretty, Evie," Will complimented, even if he wasn't really sure what someone her age liked. "I like the pink with the flowers."

"Oh, we got new sunglasses too!" Jackson added, removing his lime green ones from his bag and then reaching in to Eva's for her pink ones.

"Keep your hands to yourself!" she screamed at her younger brother, as she snatched her new sunglasses away from him.

"I was only trying to show Will," Jackson moaned.

"Now let's get along," Jennifer scolded as she held her own bag. "It's been a full day already and it's only a little after 12," she mentioned, looking at her watch.

"Who's ready for the beach?" William over-emphasized, getting up to take the empty mugs to the kitchen sink.

"I am!" Eva and Jackson yelled out in unison.

"Did you want some lunch first?" Nancy asked, knowing she had just cleaned up from breakfast.

"We just ate before we came back. We passed a burger stand along the way."

"Happy Jacks?" Will grinned, looking in his aunt's direction.

"Yeah, just like my name," Jackson boasted proudly.

"That's a great place to get burgers," Will informed, as he helped Nancy fill up the cooler with drinks and a few snacks. "We are planning to go out to dinner tonight after the beach if that is okay with everyone?"

"I want to go to the boardwalk again, Willy."

William paused to look at his young brother, realizing how magical and new everything was to him since he was experiencing Marlin Beach for the very first time. "Buddy, I don't think we will have time to go back to the boardwalk tonight since we're going out to dinner, but don't worry, we'll get back there several times yet this week."

"I like the boardwalk too," Eva chimed in.

"Of course you do," Will answered, making Jennifer and Nancy share a moment of understanding with the exchange. "I say you put on those new bathing suits and we hit the beach. How does that sound?"

"Ye...sss!" Jackson answered, running for his bedroom with his new clothes in hand, as Eva followed right behind, making a beeline for the bathroom and shutting the door loudly.

"Did you get something new?" Nancy inquired, being interested.

"Just a sundress for dinner," Jennifer smiled. "I already have a bathing suit that I ordered online before we left Birmingham so I was all set with that. I decided on the dress because it was on sale."

"Wonderful!" Nancy answered, trying to make her feel good.

The group made their way to the beach, with the cooler and the other things pulled out from the shed again. William quickly set up the chairs and umbrella before he and the children hurriedly took off for the ocean in front of them. They splashed and jumped over the first few waves, feeling the exhilaration of the cold water making content with their overly warm skin.

"It's so cold!" Eva shrieked, as a wave plowed into her.

"You'll get used to it just like you did yesterday!" William yelled back. "Dive under and totally get wet," he instructed, as Eva willingly did so and Jackson mimicked the move afterwards.

They played in the waves, body surfing into shore for around an hour before sitting on the shoreline all in a row, panting and trying to catch their breath as the waves continued to roll up over their feet.

"When can we use the boogie boards, Will?" Jackson asked for another time.

"I think you guys are ready now," William grinned at his younger siblings. "Let's go back up to Nan and aunt Jen and say hi and then we will grab the boards and get back in."

"Yeah!" Jackson yelled over his head, running the distance back up to the beach camp where the ladies were sitting in the shade under an umbrella, each holding a water bottle.

"Are you having fun?" Jennifer asked, behind the protection of her sunglasses.

"Yes!" Eva exclaimed. "Will is taking us boogie boarding finally. He says we are ready!"

"Would you like a snack first?" Nancy asked, trying to be the perfect hostess.

"Not now!" Jackson insisted, bending down to claim one of the three boogie boards that William had brought from the shed. Sarah had purchased them several years earlier when William first moved in with Mike and Nancy, visiting The Dancing Seahorse for the first time as a new member of the family. He could still remember her kind gesture and how she and Lance had taught him about the ocean and how to be safe when riding the waves. Now it was his turn – almost like a rite of passage – to teach his siblings all that he had learned from Lance and Sarah.

In no time, Eva and Jackson had mastered the boards, being like fish in water. Wave after wave the three ran with their boogie boards in hand, swimming through the fast moving current of the water and then turning to ride each perfect wave into shore. Nancy and Jennifer applauded and cheered, taking pictures from their low-slung sand chairs, as they watched the show in front of them, enjoying every moment of it.

Nancy did become somewhat concerned after awhile that the three were out in the ocean for quite some time without an obvious break. She stood up from her beach chair even though Jennifer remained in hers, hoping to give the group a signal; but it seemed to go without notice as they laughed and played, paying her no mind as she inched closer to the shoreline with her hands placed defensively on her hips.

Nancy gave up after a while, turning and walking back to Jennifer who was still sitting and relaxing in her sand chair. "I guess they aren't hungry," she said, making an excuse. "They will be starving by dinner time."

Jennifer smiled, realizing Nancy was worried. "It's so wonderful how William is teaching Eva and Jackson to boogie board, and also that he is spending so much quality time with them. They will always remember this week."

Nancy sighed, realizing Jennifer made a good point and she was acting selfish wanting them to come in out of the water. "You are absolutely right, Jen, and with that said I think I'm going to take a little nap and try to unwind."

"Now that's a good idea!" Jennifer agreed, reclining in her sand chair also, feeling confident that William could handle things.

As the ladies rested, William, Eva and Jackson had a boogie board competition seeing who could go the furthest into shore. Nothing else mattered to the happy trio – just riding the next wave and being the winner.

CHAPTER 35

"I need to make a reservation for this evening at 6 p.m."

"For you and Mrs. Snyder?"

"No, Mark. More like twelve," John Snyder coughed out gruffly, over a whirl of cigar smoke that he exhaled as he spoke. "The Miller's are in town and they have company visiting that will be joining us also, along with Lance, Sarah and the twins."

Mark the bartender, smiled, happy to know that the restaurant's regular – John Snyder - who was almost like a fixture around the place, was feeling much better and would be there that evening along with his wife and the others – which of course included his best friend, Lance Snyder and his family. "I will have your regular spot overlooking the bay ready for your group."

"Just make sure you have enough tables for us. I hate to be crowed in as you know!"

"Of course, boss!" Mark answered enthusiastically, knowing John Snyder always wanted to have VIP treatment when he arrived, and he definitely deserved it - being there typically five or six days out of the week before he got ill.

Mike and Nancy, Jennifer and the children along with William, met up in the front foyer of Old Bay Café just as the door swung open to Lance and Sarah pushing the twins through the narrow doorway of the restaurant in a two-seat baby stroller.

"You made it!" Mike smiled, happy to see Sarah and the others, as he leaned forward to give her a tender kiss on the cheek.

"Wouldn't miss it," Sarah answered, hugging her mother and William in the process, before turning her attention towards Jennifer and the children. Her expression spoke of mild confusion, as if she were trying to recall something or someone.

Jennifer smiled, reading her mind. "I'm not sure if you remember me from high school. My name is Jennifer Fisher," she offered, extending her hand towards Sarah's for a handshake. "I am Claire's sister."

Sarah slightly shook her head, feeling somewhat embarrassed, not remembering her anymore than her sister Claire from high school. She had only casually met Claire when she showed up at Dex's funeral. That much she recalled. "I constantly had my nose in my books back then," she offered in way of an excuse, trying to set Jen's mind at ease as she shook her hand.

Mark appeared in the foyer, *high-fiving* Lance as soon as he saw him. "If you are ready your tables are waiting out by the bay. John and Alison are already seated," he announced to the large group who followed him through the maze of other patrons who were dining inside the crowed restaurant. A small ensemble of three played in the bar area, strumming and singing beach tunes that the place was famous for.

"Well it's about time!" John Snyder bellowed as he stood up, while everyone in the large group found a place around the three tables. "I already ordered some crab dip and shrimp as starters," he continued, not caring what they would have chosen. "Feel free to order whatever you would like when our waitress comes back, even though I would

highly suggest the crab cakes. Dinner and drinks are on me!"

Jennifer stood up also at that point, looking down the way at John since she sat at the other end with Eva and Jackson. "Mr. Snyder I would like to buy dinner tonight for everyone if that is okay?"

John glared at her, trying to assess the situation of who she was exactly. "I appreciate the offer, but as I stated – dinner is on me."

Lance walked up to his father's end of the table, encouraging him to sit as he squatted down to speak with him quietly. *"Dad, the lady is Will's aunt Jennifer, and those are his siblings Eva and Jackson, from Birmingham, Alabama. They are here for a week on vacation."*

John laughed as he looked at his son in amusement, knowing he was trying to resolve the situation as best he could. "I think Mike mentioned something of that sort on the golf course to me today, but to be honest, I was focusing more on my golf swing at the time," he admitted. His attention then turned back to Jennifer who had finally sat down and was staring blankly at him, trying to figure out who the overbearing, older man was all about. *"Welcome Jennifer and family to Marlin Beach and to Old Bay Café,"* he nodded as he raised his glass of Natty Boh in her direction. "I am Lance's father and a regular here, and as I was saying – dinner is on me."

Sarah intentionally made eye contact with Jennifer, trying to save face and be kind to her, knowing she had no clue of how brash and unmoving John Snyder could be as she leaned in to talk to her. *"There is no sense arguing with John. Pick up the tab at some other point while you are here,"* she suggested, making everyone else at the table that knew John well agree and shake their head - *yes*.

Introductions were made all around, with Jennifer and the children meeting John, Alison, Lance and Sarah for the very first time. The twins slept peacefully in their stroller, having been well fed before leaving home. The appetizers were served as drinks and dinners were ordered. John once again reinforced his normal suggestions of Natty Boh beer and Crab Cake dinners. The children chose chicken strips with fries, but for the adults John's recommendation was chosen, except for Nancy who always ordered the fresh fish - which always led to a debate between John and Nancy as to why she did so.

"Are you enjoying working for Beach Dreams this summer, William?" Alison made a point of asking since she sincerely wanted to know, as the dinner plates were cleared and desert was ordered.

"Most definitely," Will replied. "Lance has been a great teacher."

"Yes, he is," Alison agreed warmly, looking at her son lovingly. "I plan to be back in the office next week more regularly, but as I'm sure you already heard, I've been home with my husband helping him through his illness."

"Nonsense!" John roared. "I told you, Alison, that I would have been fine by myself! You always make such a fuss when you are home, and to be honest – I'm quite self-sufficient."

"Yes, you are dear, but I wanted some time at home with you," she answered sweetly, knowing he couldn't have made it without her but would never admit to it.

Key lime pie and sundaes for the children were served, as the group broke into intimate conversations – John and Mike with Alison and Nancy, and Lance and Sarah with William and Jennifer, as Eva and Jackson played a game on their phones.

The music played on as the Tiki torches were lit, once the sun dipped low on the horizon. Waterfowl played in the reeds and sea grass, as several seagulls flew overhead, plunging into the bay water for their dinner. It was a scene that the Snyder's never tired of, and one of the main reasons that they patronized the Old Bay Café Restaurant almost on a daily basis.

Mark reappeared, taking several minutes to talk to Lance and

Sarah. "It's been forever since we have last seen you guys. We gotta make a point of getting together one evening, and maybe we can even take in a band again on the boards."

Lance and Sarah agreed, with William even offering his babysitting services. As hugs were given the group departed, thanking John one last time for the marvelous dinner as he lit up another cigar - not quite ready to leave just yet as the others were.

"You are most welcome," he barked out, waving the smoke away as he spoke. "Enjoy the rest of your trip and make sure you take in everything Marlin Beach has to offer."

"Who wants to play Scrabble?" Sarah asked, after nursing and having the twins fall unexpectedly back to sleep in her parents' bedroom.

"We will!" Eva and Jackson answered in unison.

Sarah counted the heads, realizing there were eight present. "Why don't we pair up and two can play together on one rack?"

"I will play with Jack," Jennifer offered.

"And I with Evie," Will chimed in.

"Mom and Dad, you should be partners, and Lance and I will be the last team. How does that sound?" Sarah inquired of everyone who was sitting around the kitchen table.

"Sounds perfect, aunt Sarah," William smiled, enjoying the family time immensely and the wonderful day that they had all shared together.

The tiles were shaken in the bag as everyone drew their seven, with Jennifer and Jackson going first. There were several spelling challenges along the way, but in the end Eva and Will won the first game. Two more games were played late into the evening, with Lance and Sarah winning a game and Jennifer and Jackson winning the other.

"Sorry, mom and dad, that you didn't win at all," Sarah consoled with adoring love for her parents, as she helped clean up the kitchen with its empty soda glasses and a bowl of popcorn that Nancy had popped in the microwave.

"It's fine, dear. As long as everyone had a good time your father and I are happy," she honestly admitted, giving Sarah a big hug as they walked back the hallway to her bedroom. She helped Sarah change the babies and return them to their stroller as they began to cry from being roused from sleep again.

"Oh boy, we may have our hands full tonight," Sarah said, looking at Lance with concern in her eyes.

Lance shook his head and sighed, knowing the drill. "Let's hope they conk out again before we get to the house."

Everyone laughed and hugged as the group made their way out to the driveway to say goodbye to Lance and Sarah and the twins.

"We had a great time and it was so nice to meet you, Jennifer," Sarah offered, as she spoke from Lance's Jeep window while the car idled. "And you two... Eva and Jackson," she added warmly, wanting to include them. "If you have the time, Lance and I would love to have you come to our house for dinner before you leave."

"Well, thank you," Jennifer answered, touched by Sarah's kindness. She had felt an instant attraction to her, wishing now that they had met in high school and had became friends back then with the ease of their conversation now. "I'm not sure of our plans but I would like that."

"You are invited too," Sarah said to the rest present, looking at her parents and then at William. "Let's make it in a couple days though. I think they are calling for rain later in the week and it will give you something to do since it won't be a beach day."

William smiled as he took in the exchange, climbing in his Jeep after saying his goodbyes also. He realized his Alabama family had made an unexpected connection with his family from Maryland that he never dreamt was even humanly possible.

CHAPTER 36

As promised, Lance and Sarah did host a dinner party at The Playful Starfish when the rain arrived two days later. Lance barbequed and there was game playing that featured Scrabble again. When the days were sunny the beach with boogie boarding and the adults sitting under umbrellas was the top priority. The evenings were filled with the boardwalk on back-to-back nights with rides, games, food and souvenirs.

Will had showed Jennifer, Jackson and Eva his beach house and Mike and Nancy had insisted that *they wanted to come along and see it too.* His roommates were at work and once he was inside with his family, he realized the place needed straightening up. Excuses were made as he picked up a few dirty shirts, tossing them in each of his friends' rooms as they walked around The Happy Crab together. He was glad Lance wasn't a part of the group or there would be hell to pay.

Now it was the last full day of activities before Jennifer and his siblings were leaving for Alabama. Will was sad that they were going, feeing the time had gone by much too quickly, and he honestly wasn't sure when he would see them again. He hoped that it wouldn't be another three years as it had been before their visit. As he pulled into the gravel driveway of The Dancing Seahorse he could see Eva and

Jackson already pulling the beach items from the shed, including the boogie boards. They ran in William's direction as he closed the door to his Jeep, coming up to greet him.

"Will, you're finally here!" Jackson exclaimed energetically. "It's our last day and we are trying to get an early start. Nan already has the cooler packed and we've been waiting on you!"

"Well let's do some boogie boarding," he laughed, playfully tousling through his younger brother's hair. William had his bag thrown over one arm as Eva and Jackson tried to hug him close with the other. "I should go inside just to see if Nan and G-Dad need any help before we go to the beach," he suggested, as he walked up the stairs with his siblings following right behind him now.

William opened the door to the beach house just as Jennifer, Mike and Nancy were on their way out with the cooler and beach bags in hand. *"You made it!"* Mike exclaimed. "We've had some anxious children waiting outside who didn't want to wait any longer on you," he said with a humored shake of his head. "So its perfect timing that you showed up when you did."

"Glad I did. I'll race you to the beach!" William yelled, grabbing a couple of sand chairs and boogie boards as he jogged at a pace so that Eva and Jackson could catch up easily, making them believe that they stood a chance of beating him.

"I got here first!" Eva yelled triumphantly, as she dropped the umbrellas on the ground.

"You sure did, Evie," Will grinned. "I never can beat you as hard as I try."

"Yeah, right," Jackson said with a roll to his eyes. "Anybody can beat her," he insisted, mockingly pointing at his sister.

"Then why didn't you, Jack?" Eva answered defensively, somewhat

hurt with her hands on her hips.

The last of the beach caravan caught up, immediately setting up their camp for the day with William's help. Suntan lotion was applied as the anxious children grabbed their boards, ready to tackle the waves.

"Can we get in now, Will?" Jackson asked impatiently.

"I'm ready if you are!" Will grinned, with his boogie board in hand, ready to make the dash. "G-Dad, do the count."

"Sure! On your mark, get set, go!" he yelled, as the three ran into the ocean, jumping over the oncoming waves with their boards in hand.

The adults stood up for the count, watching the group as shrills came from Evie from the impact of the cold water that she needed to get used to once again.

"Go under, Evie," William always encouraged, as he plunged beneath the salty water, feeling the cold himself.

The children continued to play in the surf as Mike, Nancy and Jennifer relaxed and passed around bottles of chilled water from the cooler.

"We hate to see you go," Nancy admitted, taking a sip from her bottle of ice-cold water.

"Oh, I know…" Jennifer sighed. "The days have gone by so quickly. The thought of going back to work next week doesn't sound fun at all."

"Yes, for me too… " Mike resigned, trying to give her some comfort. "But duty calls, as we so well know."

"Unfortunately, yes I do," Jennifer replied, shaking her head sadly with the realization that her vacation was almost over.

"Well, we hope you will come back soon. I know William has really enjoyed his time with you and the children."

"And us with him, and also with the both of you," Jennifer added with sincerity. "The time spent with you at The Dancing Seahorse has been absolutely wonderful and memory making."

"You are always welcome here, Jennifer."

"I appreciate that, Nancy."

The children played in the surf for several hours more, finally breaking for lunch. Sandwiches had been packed, along with chips and fruits, and chocolate chip cookies that Mike had just picked up earlier that morning at the bakery, when he was also purchasing the bagels for breakfast.

Beach blankets had been spread as Eva and Jackson plopped down under an umbrella, ready for a nap. Jennifer glanced in William's direction as he sat on a sand chair next to her, looking out over the ocean and taking in the other beachgoers playing and frolicking in the waves.

"Are you up for a walk?" she asked pleasantly.

"Sure, aunt Jen," he answered, seeing that Eva and Jackson were already asleep. "Better do it quickly though before those two wake up and want round two on the boogie boards," he grinned, pointing his chin in their direction.

They excused themselves, whispering to Mike and Nancy that they would be back within the hour, and *to keep Eva and Jackson out of the ocean until they returned.*

The ocean waves ran up over their feet as they strolled close to the shoreline, enjoying the sun and the surf immensely as they walked together conversing.

"I will miss you, William," Jennifer confessed, looking at her nephew with her large sunglasses in place, before turning her attention to a speed boat with a loud roar of an engine that was bouncing up and down off of the ocean filled with tourists that was flying by.

"Yeah, me too, aunt Jen," William answered sadly. "We must make a point of not allowing so much time to go by again without seeing each other."

"You are absolutely right," she replied, patting the sand for Will to sit down with her a short distance away from where the waves were breaking. "I need to speak with you about something important."

"Is everything okay?" he asked in concern, as he joined her in the warm sand.

Jennifer paused to remove her sunglasses, wanting to make full eye contact with him. "Well, that is a matter of opinion. But, I would say everything fine, but I am not sure if you will agree."

Will's heart began to race, fearful his aunt had become ill just like his mother had. He slid his hand over towards hers that was resting in the sand. "Aunt Jen, you aren't sick are you?" he asked anxiously.

"No, Will," she smiled. "I'm not sick, so please don't think that."

"So what is it then?" he implored, running his hands through his wet hair as he continued to stare at her, waiting for the answer.

Jennifer cleared her throat, finding it hard to begin as she turned her attention back towards the ocean, looking away from her nephew. She took a deep breath before she continued. "Three years have passed and a lot has happened since you left Birmingham. As you are aware, your mother made me the legal guardian of Eva and Jackson."

"Yes, aunt Jen, I know this."

"Please let me continue," she pleaded, needing to finish what she had started. "But her instructions were also for Mitchell to resume dual guardianship with me - if and when he was sober and able to do so."

William's face reddened as she spoke Mitchell's name, not sure where she was going with things. *"So did he?"*

"So did he what?"

"Did he become a dual guardian to Eva and Jackson?"

"Yes, William, he did."

"I can't believe that bastard would ever be sober enough to be a parent to them. I hope he isn't hurting them!" Will yelled out in anger. *"So help me God I will kill the bastard if he ever hurts them or you!"*

"Calm down, William. He doesn't drink anymore," she explained, turning her attention back to him. "He is not the same man you remember. Rehab has changed him. He grieved for your mother while he was there and then came home ready to be a father again. He now attends church regularly and has been working steadily for quite a while now. We are all very happy together."

"What in the hell does that mean? We are all very happy together?" he gritted out in disbelief. *"Why hasn't someone told me about this up until now? Evie and Jack haven't said anything to me about any of this!"*

"I thought it was best that they didn't discuss this with you until I had the chance to speak with you first."

William looked painfully at Jennifer, feeling very destroyed and distraught by her revelation. *"So you waited until the end of your vacation to tell me this? Seriously, aunt Jen, what were you thinking?"*

Jennifer stared in silence at her handsome nephew, not sure that she wanted to continue. "I just wanted to spend some quality time with you first since it has been so long... we all missed you, William," she admitted, reaching out to grab his hand again which he quickly pulled away out of her reach. He acted as if a wasp had just stung him, which she sadly noted and regretted.

CHAPTER 37

Will began to get up from the sand, ready to make his way back to the others.

"Please don't get up yet! I have something else to share with you," Jennifer explained, looking at him and guarding her eyes from the sun since her sunglasses were still off and lying in her lap.

William reluctantly sat down in the sand again beside of Jennifer, not sure he wanted to hear any more. *"What else is there to be said? You just told me Eva and Jackson are back with Mitchell, and I'm sure they are living at his house now instead of with you. Isn't that the case?"*

Jennifer cleared her throat, not sure she wanted to continue. "Yes, they do stay with him, but they also still stay with me part of the time."

Will shook his head, finding the whole conversation totally unnerving. *"Okay, I get it. You guys have some twisted arrangement. Can we leave now?"*

"Not just yet... " She whispered, looking downward towards the sand, where a pair of cast-off, forgotten goggles lay, washed up on the shore. "Mitchell and I are in love and plan to be married."

"Oh my God! Have you lost your ever-loving mind?" he yelled out in her direction over the roar of the ocean, this time rising up off of the sand and not willing to stay there any longer.

Jennifer rose quickly, replacing her sunglasses as she caught up, walking briskly beside of him, trying to explain. "William, it has been three years and things just happened.…"

"Obviously," he sarcastically gritted out, looking at her in disbelief, feeling he was experiencing a bad dream. "What about my mom and what he did to she and I? Doesn't that count for something?"

"He is sorry for all that, William. People do change you know. Doesn't he deserve a second chance?"

"Hell no!" he yelled out, as he started to pick up the pace even more so. *"If you want to ruin your life and also the lives of Jack and Evie then I can't stop you, but don't say I didn't warn you!* I can't be a part of this, aunt Jen. I wish you the best. I would appreciate it if you would allow me a few minutes alone with everyone, to say my goodbyes and give Jack and Evie a hug before I leave."

Jennifer began to cry openly, removing her sunglasses once again to wipe her eyes with her cover-up as he stopped and stared at her. "William, please don't leave me this way. I love you and I am not trying to hurt you. *Please… believe me,"* she moaned sadly, feeling defeated.

"Too late," he answered plainly, blinking back his own tears. "Please just give me five minutes lead time before your return. That is all I ask… " He pleaded.

"Sure… if that is how you feel. What do you want me to say to your grandparents once I return since we aren't leaving until tomorrow morning?"

"That is totally on you, aunt Jen. I will make an excuse that something came up and I had to cut the day short. I am not trying to ruin the last few hours of your vacation."

Jennifer began to openly weep, causing William to feel uncomfortable since several people near by were staring. *"Aunt Jen, get ahold of yourself. People are watching us!"* he informed as he reached out to give her a slight hug, trying to comfort her. "It was great seeing you guys. Safe travel homes and please stay safe, and keep close tabs on my little Evie and Jackson."

"I will…. And I love you, William," she answered simply, as he began to walk away, leaving her to stare at his retreating form with its hunched over shoulders.

Will turned briefly, pausing with her words. *"Me too, aunt Jen,"* he softly replied with tears of disbelief in his eyes, feeling his heart break and shatter again in a million pieces, bringing back the sad past that he thought was a distant memory and was forever behind him.

Nancy and Mike sat together enjoying the last lingering rays of sun as Eva and Jackson awakened from their beach naps, sitting straight up and looking simultaneously around for the others.

"Where's Will and aunt Jen?" Eva questioned.

"We were wondering the same thing, dear," Nancy smiled, trying to act polite and answer the questioning teen.

"Eva and I were hoping to get back into the ocean for a little while longer since we're leaving early tomorrow," Jackson explained.

"I think you should wait on William to do that, Jackson. I am sure he won't be much longer."

William trudged through the warm sand, finding his anxious siblings with their boogie boards in hand. "Hey guys, I gotta run," he announced firmly, making Mike and Nancy look at each other and question what had changed since William was planning to make a full day of it.

"I thought we would take everyone to the boardwalk one last time tonight as we discussed," Mike interjected, looking at Will in confusion.

"Thought so too, G-Dad, but things have come up and I can't keep that promise now."

"Why not?" Eva and Jackson questioned sadly, as their young impressionable eyes pierced William right through to his soul with disappointment for changing his mind on their last night there.

"I just can't, guys. *I'm sorry.*"

"*Can you at least take us boogie boarding one last time?*" Jackson moaned out in frustration.

"Sure...." Will reluctantly agreed, now seeing Jennifer walking towards them.

"You're back!" Nancy exclaimed cheerfully. "Did you and William have a nice walk and chat together?"

Jennifer glanced over at Will rather sheepishly, feeling somewhat ashamed now for ruining the day. She grabbed her beach towel, wiping the sweat from her brow, trying to change the subject and not answer Nancy. *"May I have a water?"* she asked. *"I think I overdid it and I am feeling somewhat flush."*

Mike immediately jumped up, grabbing a bottle of the ice-cold water from the cooler, as he handed it over to her and relocated the chair further under the shade-giving umbrella. "Here Jennifer - sit and relax. I think you will feel better once you are in the shade and have something to drink."

"Well thank you, Mike," she answered, as she obliged him and rested in the chair, drinking from the water bottle, trying to remain quiet and calm under the circumstances.

"Aunt Jen can we go back in the ocean one more time today before Will leaves?" Jackson begged, still holding on to a boogie board and brushing the sand back and forth with his feet, acting impatient. "He says he can't go to the boardwalk tonight."

Jennifer glanced over at Will, realizing the plans of going to the boardwalk for the evening had now changed. *"You're leaving?"* she questioned, with hurt registering all over her red face, as she tried to cool off, hoping he had changed his mind.

"Something came up," he lied, brushing aside his own sand. "But I can take Evie and Jack out for a few rides before I go - if that is okay?"

"Whatever you would like, William," Jennifer replied softly and distantly, realizing things were suddenly now different since her confession about Mitchell, after such an amazing week in Marlin Beach.

"Come on, guys. I'll race ya!" Will yelled over his shoulder, as he grabbed his boogie board for the final time, jumping through a few small oncoming breakers, with Eva and Jackson not far behind.

They played in the surf, laughing and riding the waves into shore, along with several others who lingered and ventured into the ocean water, attempting to have the same fun. The adults watched from the shoreline, enjoying the last remaining moments of seeing William, Eva and Jackson together as pictures were taken. Jennifer felt tears of sadness and regret welting up in her eyes and was glad her sunglasses concealed them from Mike and Nancy's view, wishing now she hadn't mentioned things to William.

The lifeguards blew their whistles, announcing the end of their day, guarding the beaches and ocean in front of them. As they jumped down off of their tall stands, they began to drag the heavy, wooden, platform structures through the sand, further away from the ocean - since a storm was forecasted throughout the night.

The summer workers that were hired for the rental of umbrellas and chairs, were also busy gathering up any remaining items that were left after the patrons had departed from the beach for the day, stacking and piling everything high in a large wooden container, before finally shutting and locking the lid.

The beach had only a few stragglers remaining, typically sitting together in small groups enjoying any lasting rays of sunlight while sneaking a beer in a koozie - since alcohol was not allowed to be publicly drunk on the beach. As long as there wasn't any trouble and the people indulging were over the legal drinking age, the police turned a blind eye to the obvious.

The dripping wet trio returned to the others, still dragging their boogie boards behind them, with at least Eva and Jackson announcing how much fun they had just had to the adults. William made it known again that he needed to leave, as reluctant goodbyes and hugs were given by all. Jennifer timidly approached, reaching out to embrace him too, as William indifferently patted her at arm's length, pulling away quickly and making an excuse that it was time for him to depart.

Mike and Nancy noticed the strained indifference of William, and could sense something was terribly wrong now between him and Jennifer. It wasn't the time or place to discuss it in front of the children, but something had obviously come up while they were on their beach walk together. It was definitely worth a discussion later - when young ears were not listening.

Will grabbed his backpack and looked one last time at each of his family members who he dearly loved. *"It was so good seeing you all. Safe travels home... "* He muttered, with pain etched in his steel blue eyes, as he looked one last time at his aunt Jennifer who was now crying openly and trying to wipe the tears from her eyes - even with her sunglasses still on.

He ignored the obvious, heading up the hill, past the dunes and The

Dancing Seahorse, towards his Jeep so that he could leave and drive away from the madness. He slammed his fists on his dash as the car idled, thinking of how angry he felt by his aunt's betrayal not only towards him but his dead mother's memory. All he wanted to do now was run away from the nightmare and forget about Jennifer being with Mitchell, and go back to his summer life of working and having fun with his college roommates. There would always be the next party and meeting and fucking another hot girl, and that was enough to end the frustration that he was now feeling.

"Why are you so sad, aunt Jen?" Eva questioned in confusion, as Mike and Nancy remained quiet and avoided adding to the strained conversation, gathering up the beach items instead - ready to walk back up to the beach house.

"Just sad that we had to say goodbye to William – that's all," she answered, giving an excuse that she hoped they would accept and not continue to question her about.

The group made their way up the hill towards the outside hose where they washed off the chairs and the umbrellas before replacing them back into the shed. Their legs and flip-flops were next to follow, getting a dousing too before returning to the house for a regular shower.

Nancy and Mike made the most of the last evening - being the kind people that they were - taking their Birmingham visitors one last time to the boardwalk for food, rides and a special adventure out on the pier to watch the fishermen casting out their reels. Jackson jumped up and down with excitement as several pulled in large fish that he took cellphone pictures of to show his father once they were back home.

As they returned to The Dancing Seahorse at the end of a very exhausting day and evening, Eva and Jackson were more than ready to go to sleep and not insist that they needed to stay up just a *little while longer* as they had done on previous nights when William was still with them.

Nancy and Mike sat together on the deck relaxing, staring out over the sea, gazing at the bright moon with the ring around it and the twinkling stars overhead. Mike sipped from his favorite cocktail of Tanqueray, tonic and lime as Nancy clutched her glass of red wine close to her chest. Jennifer slid the heavy patio doors open, walking out to stand by the railing, closing them behind her as she looked at the contented pair. "I hope I'm not intruding?" she asked sincerely, as she gazed at her gracious hosts of the week.

"Not at all," Mike reassured, patting the seat close. "Sit here, my dear, and take a load off. If you would like something to drink, Nancy still has the bottle of wine sitting out on the counter."

"I'm fine, thank you," she answered, suddenly beginning to cry openly again.

"For heavens sakes, Jennifer, what is going on?" Nancy asked with uncertainty, at seeing her cry yet another time.

Mike silently waited for her response, knowing something was terribly wrong and it probably had to do with William.

"I am not sure where to begin…. so I will just come out with it. *Mitchell and I are getting married and William is not happy about it!"*

CHAPTER 38

Mike quickly gulped down a large amount of his drink, making him cough several times in the process from Jennifer's shocking revelation. *"You got to be kidding... Right?"*

"I would never joke about something this important."

"Now everyone calm down," Nancy insisted, trying to be the voice of reason, as she patted Mike's arm. "Jennifer, can you please explain to us how this even remotely happened?"

Jennifer took the offered seat nearby and breathed in deeply of the sultry night air, before beginning her story. "I never expected this to happen, but it did. As I'm sure you already know, Claire gave me full custody of Eva and Jackson in her Last Will And Testament before she passed away. She also made a stipulation in the will that if Mitchell made changes in his life he could share in the custody with me if he stayed sober and employed, and proved to be a fit parent again. So we jointly took on the task after he completed rehab and was released. I was not immediately drawn to him in a romantic sort of way," she confessed, shifting her legs to cross one over the other. "But we began to spend a lot of mutual time together with the children - sharing outings and meals along with their sporting events. Things just naturally began to happen. We even attended church together on Sundays."

"Well that is all wonderful, dear, but what about his *horrible temper*?" Nancy interjected a little too dramatically, remembering William's stories.

Jennifer nervously laughed, realizing Mitchell's reputation of the past was not anything easy to deal with now. *"He's a changed man... that is all I can tell you.* I would never sign up for the abuse my sister had to deal with," she said realistically with her head bowed and her hands clasped together on her lap.

"How do you know he won't retreat back to that sort of thing once the two of you are married?" Mike asked in concern, as he laid his finished cocktail glass on the small table in between him and Nancy.

Jennifer took a deep breath again before she began, finding the whole conversation quite difficult but necessary. *"Who can be sure about anything in life?* I do believe God can change a person though. As you know, my father was a pastor while we lived in Baltimore. I saw many people during my childhood, while being raised in the church, change miraculously after attending the services."

Mike was now the one to sigh, not wanting to be the realist and break her hope of redemption. "Jennifer, I understand your positive spirit, but you got a lot at stake if Mitchell slips up and begins to drink again. He may even stop attending church at some point."

"He won't!" she insisted, standing back up at the railing, clutching it from behind as she looked at the pair of *doubters* in front of her. "He loves me and the children and has promised he will *never* go back to his old ways! *In the three years that I have been around him, he has always been consistent with his behavior.* We have even spoken to our minister about everything and he has given us his blessing to go ahead with the marriage after having a few counseling sessions together."

Nancy pursed up her lips after finishing her wine, sliding her empty glass beside of her husband's. "Jennifer, as you know I was a school teacher for many years. I saw children that were destroyed from being in homes filled with drugs, alcohol and abuse. It was horrible to deal with! Many times the children were even removed from their homes to protect them, and I was the one giving them hugs instead of their mommies and daddies. Even years later, I cannot erase from my mind the horrible stories that those *little ones* shared with me. *My heart breaks for these scarred children, and William was unfortunately one of them!*"

"Yes Nancy, I know! *But Mitchell deserves another chance, whether you or Mike or William understand any of this!* No one is perfect, but he is trying now and working on things daily. He cannot change the past, but he can go forward and try to do better in a new marriage - having the love and support of his family around him. I had hoped that William could be a part of this, but if he chooses not to do so, then that is his choice. I know he is an adult and sometimes it is harder to accept things like this when you are older."

"*That is putting it mildly...* " Mike replied distantly, remembering his grandson's sadness when he first came to live with him and Nancy and how heart-broken he was from losing his mother and saying goodbye to Eva and Jackson.

"*Would you like me to find a hotel and leave tonight?*"

"Of course not, dear. We are not mad at you, Jennifer, and besides the children are sleeping," Nance reassured, walking over to give her a hug and stand beside of her by the deck railing. "It's getting late and I know you are leaving early. Maybe it's time to call it a night and we should all sleep on this. After all, this revelation may take some time to think about and reason on by all of us – since we just heard the news for the first time today."

Mike rose, gathering up both glasses as they walked into the living room together. "As Nancy just said, we are not upset with you Jennifer, just surprised at the unexpected development of things. That's all," he reasoned, trying to calm her down so that they all could sleep.

"I understand," she conceded. "I guess if someone shared a similar story like that with me I would have my guard up too. I know you are just looking out for me and the children," she warmed with a smile.

"We would hope that you knew that, but we also want you to be happy too," Nancy offered with sincerity, as they walked towards the kitchen.

"Thank you, Nancy," she smiled, giving her another heartfelt hug. Mike stood off to the side, remaining silent and thinking about how this was affecting William - who truly was his main priority.

As Jennifer disappeared into her room and climbed into bed, Eva was fast asleep and she was soon to follow. Nancy and Mike retreated to their bedroom also, having a harder time falling off to sleep as they pondered all that transpired.

"It's been quite the day... " Nancy breathed.

"Yes, it has. I'm concerned for William," Mike confessed as he held his wife closely. "I saw the look on his face when he left the beach and he surely wasn't happy. Now that I know what is going on, I'm concerned about his mindset."

"Well of course you are concerned. I am too, for that matter. *Who would have expected any of this?* But Mike, you know our life has been a series of this sort of thing. Sarah is a prime example of someone having to heal from the past, and look at her wonderful life now being married to Lance and having the twins. Things could have gone a totally different way if she hadn't let go of her bitterness from losing Dexter and stopped blaming Lance for his death."

"You're right, my love, but William has to reach that same conclusion. He is a rational, sensible guy with a good head on his shoulders. I am sure he will come around and accept this in time, or go on without any of them in his life in the future."

"Let's hope for everyone's sake that he can work through these difficulties. The children could loose so much valuable time from not being together as siblings, if William can't get past this. What amazes me though is that Eva and Jackson didn't let this slip to William or to us while they were here this week. You know children, they have a difficult time keeping things like this quiet."

"I'm sure Jennifer gave them strict orders to keep it to themselves."

"I guess so... but I'm still surprised."

Mike changed positions, nestling and spooning Nancy in his arms as he turned on his side. "I think it is time for sleep. The alarm is set for 6 o'clock. Jennifer needs to get on the road early so she makes her flight on time."

"Yes... dear... I know...." Nancy answered dreamily, as she drifted off to sleep.

Six a.m. and the alarm blared out it's consistent series of beeps until Mike sat up and stopped the endless noise. "Time to get up," he yawned, looking at his wife who was turning to stretch with half-opened eyes.

"I'll make some coffee and get out some dry cereal and milk."

Mike slid on a pair of jeans and a t-shirt, walking out to the living room to find Jennifer dressed and already sitting on the couch, looking out at the cloudy, rain-filled sky. She smiled as he entered the room.

"Sorry if I woke you."

"No, you didn't. I had the alarm set."

"I know I need to get the children up now, but I just wanted a last few minutes to be alone and take in the beauty of your beach house and the wonderful scenery in front of me."

"I understand," Mike smiled sincerely. "Jennifer, as Nancy and I said last night…. we are not mad at you…. just concerned, that's all. You are always welcome back for a visit – here, or in Baltimore – either one. William will get passed all this. I am sure the initial shock of the news just surprised him."

"Well, I am truly sorry that he is upset… " She said sincerely, as Nancy joined them, still in her pajamas and housecoat.

"I was going to make coffee and get out some cereal before you left for the airport."

"Don't go to the trouble. Honestly, I was planning to get Eva and Jackson up now and we will be getting on the road in a few minutes. We will just stop along the way and pick something up."

As the group hurriedly packed and said their final goodbyes, they thanked Mike and Nancy once again for allowing them to stay at The Dancing Seahorse, showing them the time of their lives for one week in Marlin Beach. Jennifer and the children waved from the Mustang – now with the roof up because of the rain that was continuing to fall, pulling out onto Beach Road. They passed The Dexter and then drove across the bridge where an early morning fishing boat was chugging along slowly. They passed the small Eastern shore towns with their produce stands and then crossed the Bay Bridge. The rain had finally stopped and the sun broke through the clouds, making the drive more pleasant.

Soon, they arrived back at BWI, ready to drop off the rental vehicle and make their way through security, ready to go back home to Birmingham, Alabama. Jackson was already begging for a second meal, which was typical for him, as the attendant announced that their flight was boarding in only ten minutes.

As the plane pulled away and climbed high in the sky, Jennifer stared down through the clouds at Baltimore below, seeing traces of the Chesapeake Bay off in the distance. It was bittersweet leaving, knowing how much she had enjoyed her vacation in Marlin Beach, but she knew Mitchell was waiting on the other side – ready to welcome her home.

CHAPTER 39

The brakes of the plane squealed to an abrupt halt, stirring Eva and Jackson from their sleep, as well as Jennifer who was having a romantic dream about Mitchell that she was surprised and yet embarrassed over.

"Welcome to Birmingham-Shuttlesworth International Airport. It is sunny and 82 degrees," the flight attendant announced pleasantly, as everyone gathered their belongings for their departure from the plane.

As they wheeled their suitcases from the baggage claim area to the outside, Jennifer's phone began to ring, after just turning it back on. "Yes, we are coming outside now. Look for us at B10," she informed, as she stood waiting by the curb with the children.

Mitchell parked the car with his 4-way flashers on, running around quickly to make his embraces and then throw the suitcases into the trunk. "Hurry and buckle your seatbelts," he quickly mentioned, looking over the back seat with a heart-felt smile at Eva and Jackson. "Missed you guys," he admitted, looking at his children and then at Jennifer with obvious love. He pulled away from the curb, blending in with the other traffic, exiting from the airport.

"*It's good to be home,*" Jennifer whispered as she leaned in, as the distracted passengers in the back seat were already in another world and looking at their *turned back on* cellphones, discovering what they had missed on their return flight.

Mitchell nodded, trying to keep a sharp eye on the heavy traffic in front of him. "I hope you had a good trip?"

"It was wonderful! Lots of good beach time."

"William taught us how to boogie board!" Jackson interjected, breaking into the adult conversation that he was not supposed to be paying attention to.

"And we went to the boardwalk!" Eva added.

"Oh, yeah," Mitchell grinned, glancing in the rearview mirror at his children. "Well I'm glad you had fun and I can see you all got *very* suntanned!" he laughed, as he glanced again at Jennifer. "I hope you used your sunscreen!"

"Plenty of it! Matter-of-fact, we used up every bit on the last day."

Mitchell gazed at Jennifer boldly, making her blush. "I was thinking that maybe we could order in some pizza tonight, and then you can share more *intimate* details about the trip later?" he playfully grinned.

"Of course," she replied, fluttering her lashes flirtatiously at him.

Jackson and Eva were involved in playing a game on their phones that they regularly competed in against the other. It wasn't any secret to them that their father was in love with their aunt Jennifer and planned to marry her one day, so the front seat exchange came as no surprise to them.

As Mitchell pulled into Jennifer's driveway, he walked her to the front door of her home with her wheeled suitcase dragging behind him. *"I'll see you soon?"* he asked, bending down to give a sweet kiss.

She smiled back, with only contentment beaming from her face. "I want to shower and change, and then I will drive over to your house a little later, sweetie."

"Are you going to spend the night?"

"I would love to, but I think I will pass with work tomorrow."

"See you soon," Mitchell replied, placing her suitcase inside of the front door. "Pepperoni with mushroom okay?" he asked, half in and half out of the door.

"Of course!" she called out, already walking back the hallway with her suitcase in hand. Mitchell shut the front door behind him, skipping a step off of the porch on the way back to his car.

Eva and Jackson had the windows down and were yelling at each other, making him stop and stare at them as he leaned his head into Jackson's window. "What would the neighbors think if they heard you acting like this?"

"Sorry dad," Eva replied. "Jackson is just so bratty at times."

"Who are you calling a brat?" Jackson challenged, giving his sister a dirty look.

Mitchell climbed into the front seat, turning around one last time before he pulled away. "You just took a nice vacation and now you are home again and fighting? I am very surprised. That's all..." he said with a slight shake of his head.

"We're sorry," they both answered in *singsong* fashion.

Mitchell turned on the radio, cranking the music up loudly, breaking the fighting mood of his children as they sang each word to one of their favorite tunes. He drove home in silence, thinking of the evening ahead with Jennifer back in his arms. She had become the stabilizing force that had made him want to be a better man and father, encouraging him to stop with his destructive and abusive behavior. He loved the woman and she made his life worth living, allowing him to heal and work through his past failures and mistakes that he regretted.

William shut off his computer at the end of his workday, walking into Lance's office and plopping down in one of the comfortable chairs opposite his desk. Lance was busy speaking on the phone to an interested client who sought out a bayside townhouse in the area.

"I think we have a few possibilities, Mr. Haskell. I know of several here and maybe a few more in Delaware. Let me do some research and I will get back to you tomorrow morning - if that is okay?" Lance paused, listening to the long explanation from the potential buyer who wanted to come to Marlin Beach within two or three days to see a few ideal properties. William impatiently waited as he glanced around the room taking in all the nautical artwork hanging on the walls, looking irritated. *"I understand your desire to get a place, but as you know the summer season is in full swing and places have been going fast. So I will contact you in the morning,"* Lance concluded firmly, as the call ended.

He smiled, turning his attention back to William. "Some people just don't know when to hang up," he laughed, shaking his head. *"What's up?"*

Will sighed, not knowing where to begin. "I got everything done today that you wanted me to do."

"Great!" Lance answered, with his sunny wide-toothed smile, weaving his hands behind his head, as he leaned back in his computer chair, studying his nephew and sensing something was bothering him and didn't have anything to do with work.

"I need to talk to you about a personal matter," Will admitted, with a look of despair and frustration on his face.

Lance leaned forward, resting the chair back on all four wheels again. *"You okay?"* he asked in concern.

"Not really," he said with a downward glance. "It's about my aunt Jen. We had a conversation yesterday while we were together on the beach that has me really upset. She told me that she and my stepfather, Mitchell, plan to get married. *I just don't know how the fuck this could have happened!"* he exploded, with tears stinging his eyes.

"William, such language!" Lance replied curtly, somewhat surprised by his nephew's tone. "I thought your stepfather was out of the picture and your aunt Jen was raising your brother and sister alone?"

"Yeah, I thought so too, but I guess a lot has changed in the last three years - that no one bothered to tell me about until yesterday. I can't believe she waited until the end of her time here in Marlin Beach to announce this to me. *I am so angry with her!"*

"Understandably so," Lance answered sympathetically, getting up to stand by the window as he looked over at William who was ready to break. *"So what can I do to help you with this?"*

Will locked eyes with his kind uncle and friend, who he admired greatly. *"Just listen to me, I guess..."*

"Always, buddy," Lance smiled, walking over to grasp Will's shoulder with a reassuring squeeze, before joining him in the matching overstuffed chair that was next to his. "William, you're a grown man now and out of that house. *You can't control what is going on there."*

"I get that, but what about Eva and Jackson? I don't want them to get hurt by that asshole!"

Lance remained quiet, not wanting to call him out again about his cursing - just allowing him some time to vent.

"Aunt Jen says he is a changed man. She claims rehab and going to church has made a *big difference* in his life, and that he doesn't drink and do the violent things that he used to do. He's working again and from what she says - *they are one big happy family out there in Birmingham,*" he added with a sad, distant look of despair.

"I would think you would be overjoyed with knowing that."

"Seriously, uncle Lance? He can change going forward, but what about what he did to my mother and me in the past? He can't change that!"

"No, he can't change that, but you can change how you feel about that," Lance answered wisely, looking steadfastly at William. "You have a great life now. Why would you want any less for your siblings, your aunt Jen and for Mitchell too - for that matter? Everyone deserves to find happiness in this life. And as we so well know, life is fragile and uncertain…."

William looked intently at his uncle, knowing he was always rational and made good sense with his advice. "I just thought this was a closed door that I never had to walk through again."

"Have you talked to Nan and G-Dad about this?"

"Not really. The last time I was with them was that day at the beach when I had just heard the news from my aunt Jen. All I wanted to do was leave and not deal with any of this!"

"That's very understandable, but now that Jennifer and the kids have left and are back home in Alabama, you can freely discuss the situation with Nan and G-Dad and let them know how you feel. It always pays to hear more than one opinion."

"I guess you're right… " Will warily admitted, running his hands throughout his brown wavy hair fretfully. "Thanks for your time. You gave me something to at least think about," he waved, leaving Lance's office just as confused as when he came in.

CHAPTER 40

"Hello?"

"Hey, Brooke, it's William. I was just wondering what time you are getting off of work and if you would like to hang out tonight?"

"Will," she smiled happily, pleased that he finally called. "I just got home - since I worked the breakfast and lunch shifts both. I would love to hang out. What did you have in mind?" she asked, standing nude in the bathroom ready to take a shower, as she looked at her reflection in the mirror of her tight, firm body that she was so proud of.

"How about the boardwalk? I thought it might be fun to just walk and get on some rides. We can do dinner too if you would like?"

Me likie you getting inside of me... she thought naughtily as she listened to his suggestions for the evening. "Of course we can do that! Outside of a couple times when I first arrived this summer, I haven't been to the boards since."

"Great! Dress casual cuz I'm wearing shorts and a t-shirt. Maybe we can walk down to the beach too and just relax for awhile."

Brooke smiled again, running a brush through her long blonde hair that she was planning to wash and allow to air dry afterwards with its natural waves. "I'll meet you at The Happy Crab in an hour. How does that sound?"

"I can pick you up at your place."

"No bother. I'll meet you at your beach house. That way we can walk and not deal with paying for parking at the inlet."

"Sounds great! See you soon!" Will replied, hanging up and walking inside to where his roommates were chilling in the living room with their cold beers in hand.

"We're heading to Delaware tonight to hear the band *The Nuts And Bolts*. They're doing an outdoor concert. Any interest in going along with us?" Chris asked, as Will paused on the way to his room to drop off his backpack.

"Thanks for the invite, but I got other plans tonight with Brooke."

Mutual approval and *hoots and hollers* exploded as the group of college roommates applauded Will's move forward with the beautiful vixen with *high fives* in his direction, since it was a rarity that he planned an actual date with any girl.

"I didn't see that coming," Matt remarked snidely with a wink.

"Why not? I've seen her a couple times."

"Yeah, after a couple beers and when she shows up here to have sex with you," Tyler remarked realistically, with a raise to his eyebrow.

Will laughed, shaking his head at his friends. "So shoot me for liking her. I got no time for this! Enjoy the band and I'll catch up with you guys the next time."

"You better, bro. There's only a few more weeks left until we say goodbye to Marlin Beach and we're back in school again," Chris reminded, as Will disappeared into his bedroom and shut his door. He thought of Jennifer and Mitchell one last time before dismissing the terrible situation, wanting to shut out any negative thoughts before focusing in on his date with Brooke.

As he stood under the hot, pulsating flow of the shower, he allowed it to soothe his tight back and neck muscles, trying to relax and unwind. He thought of Brooke, undressing her perfect nude body, which made his penis harden at the memory of doing so in the past. If the evening went as he hoped, they would be carefree and enjoy the boardwalk and all it had to offer, and then it would end being in each other's arms with very fulfilling sex afterwards. He lingered, yanking on his member several times before orgasming in the shower with the warm water still cascading playfully over it, not desiring to be over anxious as soon as he saw her.

Brooke pulled into the gravel driveway of The Happy Crab dressed in very short white jean shorts, a black low-cut tank top that tied seductively in the front – showing off her cleavage - and black flip flops. Her light blonde hair was hanging loose and moving freely in the breeze. She carried a small black purse with a long strap that she carried across her body, and it bumped off of her one hip playfully as she walked up to the front door and knocked.

Will answered with a pleased, happy smile at seeing her looking as sexy as he remembered, greeting Brooke with a big hug. *"You look amazing,"* he complimented, escorting her inside for everyone present to stare at and admire from the living room where they were all relaxing and watching a ball game.

"Hey Brooke," Chris called out, taking a big swig of beer. "Have fun tonight with my bro."

She giggled, looking at William playfully. *"I will try... "*

The guys all silently looked at each other, feeling envious, knowing William was one lucky *son of a bitch* to have won her affection.

"Are you sure you guys don't want to join us?" Matt asked, before they were ready to leave, assuming Brooke's roommates would end up with the rest of them.

"No, we're good," he answered, wrapping an arm possessively around Brooke's waist, wasting no time to get on their way. Will had brought his backpack, filling it with a beach blanket and a couple of waters in case they ventured down to the beach, which he hoped for since it gave him an excuse to make-out with her.

They climbed up on the boardwalk where it began, pausing to look at the tram in front of them. *"Would you like to ride or walk?* Your choice," Will offered.

"Let's walk. I want to see everything, "Brooke smiled pleasantly, as Will grabbed for her hand, walking closely by her side.

There was much to see along the way, with vacationer's perched out on their balconies looking down at all the tourists who were walking on the boardwalk beneath them. T-shirt and souvenir shops, along with food and candy stands at times featured a pushy employee standing out front barking out a cheap deal or offering a tray of samples, trying to allure the passerby's just to come inside for a *deal too good to be true.* Occasionally, they stopped to take in a street musician or watch in fascination someone quickly painting a picture of a pretty scene with spray paint. Pizza and fries were chosen, as they ate and admired the sand art sculptures that had been created by some talented locals. Brooke took a few pictures, snapping some *selfies* with William in cute poses, before insisting on the rollercoaster as she clung tightly to his side as it went up and down - making her nauseous. They finally finished up with each having a large ice cream cone, knowing their date was not complete without it.

"Why don't we walk down to the beach?" Will asked with a suggestive smile, as he devoured the last of his ice cream cone in one single bite. "I just want to snuggle with you and watch the waves."

"Me too...." she sighed, pecking him playfully on the lips.

They walked hand in hand towards the beach, removing their flip-flops in the process, trudging through the deep sand together. Will removed his bag from his shoulders and spread out the beach blanket, inviting Brooke to sit with him. They leaned back on their elbows taking in the beautiful view of the ocean and the rolling waves that were coming in to shore near the pier. It was finally getting dark and no one was nearby, granting them at least some temporary privacy.

Brooke snuggled close to Will's side, as she stared up into his smoldering eyes that were ablaze with passion. His lips met hers for a soul-searing kiss that left them both weak. *"God, you're always amazing,"* Will breathed into her hair, as she purred like a contented kitten against him, being pleased with his words.

She reached up to kiss his slightly parted lips, finding his tongue that soon entered her mouth. He swirled it deliciously against her own, for the next series of heated kisses that left her breathless as he undid the string to her top and grabbed for a breast, playing with her nipple openly, not caring about anyone else on the beach.

The make-out session went on for quite a long time, with all rational reasoning of someone seeing them or even caring, leaving their senses. Laughter and several people talking and walking past them some time later, broke them from their trance, making them sit up and adjust their apparel.

Will looked at his watch realizing it was still early and his roommates were probably not home and away at the concert. "Do you want to get into anything else or go back to my place now?" he asked, hoping she was ready to leave.

She smiled, reading his mind and wanting the same thing, getting up to brush the sand off of her buttocks that were slightly exposed, riding up from her short shorts. William took it all in, as he brushed the sand from his shorts and t-shirt also, folding up the blanket quickly and placing it back in his bag that he swung over his shoulder.

"Let's take the tram back. It will be faster that way," she winked, leaning forward and standing close and rubbing up against William who was now hard and ready to explode.

He smiled knowingly, as he grabbed her hand and they ran back up to the boardwalk, flagging down the tram that was a short distance away. The bumpy ride back to the beginning of where the wooden platform began, was not quick enough for either of them as Will helped Brooke down and they continued their walk at a fast pace back to The Happy Crab.

No cars were present, which made William smile. They were truly alone and he was more than pleased. He opened the door to the beach house, turning on the lights to a swirling ceiling fan overhead and pushed back patio doors that were never closed and locked, that he needed to remind his roommates about one more time.

He escorted Brooke to his room, shutting and locking the door behind him, just in case the partying group of friends returned sooner than he expected. He pressed her up against the back of his bedroom door, reaching in to pull out and expose one of her luscious breasts for another time. His lips leaned down to find the taunt nipple, taking it in his mouth and pulling and suckling deeply of it, tasting the salt from being outdoors which made her moan. Brooke was lost with the feeling, begging William to take her to his bed, which he was more than eager to do.

Their clothes were hurriedly removed as Will immediately plunged deeply into her wet cavern – wasting no time - giving no thought to *safe sex* and condoms. They mutually climaxed loudly together, as they lay perspired and exhausted from the fierceness of it all.

Brooke turned on her side, leaning up on one elbow, gazing at William who was still trying to catch his breath. "Amber just texted me, and we probably have another hour until they get back," she teased, reaching her hand below to his limp penis, massaging it as she spoke.

"I can't get it up that quickly, babe," he admitted, feeling somewhat embarrassed and wanting to please her. Brooke lowered her head, sliding down to the depleted shaft, working her magic as she sucked and licked it back to life. William felt the blood begin to pump and coarse throughout his cock – awakening it once again from her oral massage. He was totally blown away by how quickly he could be turned on again by her. *"Come here, you..."* he beckoned, bringing her back up to his lips. *"It's my turn,"* he challenged, as he moved down to her throbbing triangle of lust that was begging to be touched. His lips and tongue found their intended goal, as he savored her taste that he craved, thrusting his tongue in and out of her vagina, making her scream out savagely in delight.

Will was totally hard again as he took her this time with slow, deliberate stokes, watching the gleam of cum and her wetness mixing together in an intoxicating blend. He reeled with pure carnal desire, shuttering violently as he exploded within her with one final, deliberate, determined thrust, only hoping she was telling the truth about being on birth control. He collapsed on top of her, knowing that even with her best attempts to make him hard again after this - he was done.

He fell asleep, still being inside of her as she slept too, only awakening after hearing the sound of laughter and the door slamming loudly some time later. Will abruptly sat up, realizing his roommates were back home for the evening.

Brooke lay like a wanton pixie with the waves of her blonde hair cascading down over her breasts as she smiled contentedly up at William. "Your door is locked, sweetie," she reminded, making William feel good by what she called him.

"Yeah, I know," he answered, crawling off of her and retrieving his underwear and shorts from the wooden floor close by. "But if they are drunk who knows what can happen," he grinned playfully, pushing his still damp hair back from his face.

Brooked laughed, retreating from the bed and finding her own clothes. "I guess I better say hi to the roomies – both yours and mine – before I go. I got an early breakfast shift again tomorrow."

Will wrapped her in his arms one last time before they left the room, kissing her tenderly on the lips as the moon sliced through the vertical blinds. "I'm falling for you, Brooke."

"Me too," she whispered, as she returned the affectionate kiss.

"It may sound like we're back in high school, but will you consider being my girlfriend?" William grinned, waiting for her answer.

"I already thought I was the girl you were seeing this summer."

"Yes, this is true, but I was hoping for beyond the summer. Maybe we should try to make this last even once we are back at college."

CHAPTER 41

Jackson grabbed the last slice of the pepperoni and mushroom pizza from the now empty cardboard pizza box, consuming it in just two bites.

"My word, Jackson," Mitchell gently scolded, looking at his son with a humorous grin of delight. *"Where do you put it all?"*

"In my big belly," he pointed with a laugh, patting his overextended belly at everyone at the table for effect.

"You're such a pig!" Eva exclaimed, rolling her eyes at her younger brother from his always-gross behavior.

"Settle down, you two," Mitchell insisted, clearing the now empty glasses from the table, along with the Parmesan cheese and hot pepper flakes.

"What did I just miss?" Jennifer smiled, looking at the children.

"Just Jackson being a pig," Eva announced for the second time, making Mitchell laugh and shake his head at her.

"Why don't you guys go outside for awhile and get some fresh air before bedtime?"

Eva and Jackson ran from the house, slamming the door to the kitchen behind them, leaving Mitchell and Jennifer alone. They walked together to the living room and sat on the sofa where Claire once lay dying, as Mitchell grabbed the remote and turned on the local news. He reached over, pulling Jennifer close, as he kissed the top of her head lovingly.

She smiled at Mitchell with contentment etched all over her face. *"It's good to be home and back in your arms,"* she confessed as he swooped down for a series of deep and passionate kisses that stirred Jennifer's heart and her senses. *"What if the children come back in?"* she asked with concern, not wanting to make their *make-out session* seem too obvious.

"What if they do?" he answered softly with his searching brown eyes that were passionate with lust and love, returning to kiss her willing mouth again.

Mitchell was middle aged with a mature look, still having a full head of salt and pepper hair and a slightly over-extended belly that hinted of a lack of exercise. He was handsome in his own way, but looked hardened and older than he should, probably from his over-indulgent use of alcohol in the past.

Jennifer was plain but pretty with fair skin that now hinted of blotchy red patches instead of the uniform tan that she was hoping for while away on vacation in Marlin Beach. She kept her hair cropped short in a cute chin-length bob hairstyle and wore little to no makeup to speak of. She had maintained her build over the years and looked younger than her actual age, even though she was in her fifties just like Mitchell was. She never married or had children of her own, devoting her life instead to a career in accounting.

It surprised her when Mitchell showed an interest in her within a year of Claire's death. Claire had been Mitchell's wife and Jennifer's sister, and Claire had been the older and the prettier of the two sisters. It still amazed Jennifer that Mitchell would want her now, after barely speaking to her or noticing her during all the years that Claire was still alive and married to him.

Court ordered rehab, along with shared custody with Jennifer, was a good thing for Mitchell. It brought out new determination in him to make some permanent life changes. With a vow to *never drink again* and to be given a second chance with a new job as a maintenance supervisor, he miraculously transformed his life into becoming someone respectful once again in the community. Jennifer was there to witness the transformation, as she began to spend mutual time with him and the children on family outings or when they would attend church together.

It was never expected, but slowly Mitchell and Jennifer began to like each other and then finally love grew and blossomed between the pair. When he presented her with an engagement ring one winter evening after the children were sleeping, she was stunned but overjoyed with happiness, agreeing to marry him and become his wife.

Jennifer cried tears of joy as Mitchell placed the gold band with its modest-sized diamond on her finger, causing her to stare at it for some time in fascination that she was finally *engaged* for the first time in her life. She had given up any hope of ever being married, and then suddenly everything changed.

Mitchell swooped her up in his arms that special night of placing the ring on her finger, quietly carrying her to his room where they made passionate love for the first time, even though Jennifer protested that *they should wait until they were actually married*. It had been too long though for either one of them - since they had last had sex with someone - and desire overtook any rational thought of abstinence until marriage. Regular intercourse now occurred on a weekly basis, once Eva and Jackson were definitely asleep, but Jennifer still felt guilty that they were doing something morally wrong before their wedding day.

Before the trip to Marlin Beach, a large discussion took place between Jennifer and Mitchell concerning their engagement and the wearing of the engagement ring in front of Will and the others. The conclusion was that Jennifer would leave the ring at home, making it somewhat easier for her to explain things at her own pace while on vacation. Mitchell was initially not happy with Jennifer's decision, but he realized in the end it was best for all concerned.

Convincing Eva and Jackson of the same, was another hurdle. They were instructed to keep quiet while in Marlin Beach and not breathe a word to William or anyone else, for that matter, about the relationship between Jennifer and their father. They were given strict orders that if they left it slip about the engagement, their phones would be taken away for an unspecified period of time once they were back home in Birmingham. Their cellphones were their lifelines to their friends, and that was reason enough to keep quiet and maintain the secret.

As they cuddled on the couch, Mitchell lovingly looked down at his fiancé, pausing to catch his breath. *"So did you finally tell everyone we are engaged?"*

Jennifer sat upright, breaking free from Mitchell's embrace. "Yes, I did… but it didn't go over so well with William."

Mitchell laughed out self-consciously. *"That doesn't surprise me in the least. What did he say?"*

Jennifer gulped, not wanting to injure his pride or feelings any further. *"I'm not sure you want to know."*

"I can handle it, sweetie. I realize he is hurt by the old me."

"Yes, he is… " She answered softly with downcast eyes. "He just doesn't believe you could have changed so much. I tried to explain everything to him, but he's having his doubts."

Mitchell sighed, taking a minute to gather his thoughts. "I guess I can understand his apprehensions. I didn't like the *old me* either. But I am a changed man - thanks be to God!" he answered humbly, with a mist now covering his eyes.

"Maybe you should talk to William. I don't know how we can arrange this, but it may make a difference if he hears things coming directly from you. I must be honest though, he is being very closed off," Jennifer confessed, reaching out to grab Mitchell's hand. "He feels that even if you have truly changed, you were not that same man for him and his mother, and that is something he can never get past and forgive you for."

Mitchell shook his head sadly, remembering the way he used to be, wishing he could go back and somehow change time, and do things differently. "I made my peace with Claire before she died. We talked in the hospital and she knows I was sorry at the end. William wasn't there to witness that, but I'm telling you honestly - it did happen."

"Maybe you need to tell him," she answered softly.

"Maybe I should…." Mitchell replied, reaching out to pull Jennifer back again into his arms. "Give me his number and I will call him and try to explain things. *But I need to make something perfectly clear - no one, including William, is standing in the way of us becoming husband and wife!"* he stated with intensity, as he began to kiss her passionately again.

The kitchen door burst open with Eva and Jackson running back inside, panting for air as they tried to catch their breath after a rambunctious time of playing outdoors with their friends.

"Ga…ross!" Eva yelled out in disgust with a wave of her hand, at seeing Mitchell and Jennifer kissing.

"You can say that again!" Jackson agreed, snarling up his lips at the enamored pair on the sofa, as he wiped his dirty hands on his jean shorts.

"Time to get cleaned up and ready for bed!" Mitchell snapped out at his children, trying to change the subject as he and Jennifer left the sofa and walked hand in hand out to the kitchen together.

"Maybe it's time for me to go home," she whispered, as both children showered in each of the bathrooms.

"Stay with me tonight. I've missed you and I can't go another night without being inside of you," Mitchell insisted, nuzzling her neck seductively.

Jennifer felt a familiar heat spreading down between her legs, making her melt by Mitchell's touch. He cast a spell over her that she was unable to say no to.

"I didn't bring anything to change in to for work in the morning, so I will have to leave especially early so I can go home and get ready there."

He smiled seductively at her, fondling one breast as his hand played with it through her t-shirt, rubbing her nipple to hardness. "However long you can stay here will be wonderful," he breathed against her ear, causing her to shiver.

"Ok… " She finally surrendered and agreed to, with only devoted love for him outlining her face. "But you must behave until Eva and Jackson are asleep. *Understood?*" she grinned playfully.

"Anything you say, darling," he answered back with a knowing smile, breaking free of the intimate embrace as Eva and Jackson ran from their showers to their bedrooms, interrupting the moment of bliss that they both shared.

CHAPTER 42

As Mitchell drove to Birmingham-Shuttlesworth International Airport he clutched the steering wheel with a contented smile. He recalled the passionate love making that he and Jennifer had just shared the night before, giving him the courage and determination to do what he was about to do.

Jennifer had slipped off at five-thirty, leaving Mitchell to attend to Eva and Jackson and make sure they were packed and ready for the church bus that was to pick them up at 7 a.m. for several days. They were more than excited to see their friends again that they had met the summer previous at church camp.

With the children gone, Mitchell was going to be alone in the house for his own week of vacation, knowing Jennifer was back at work and he would only see her in the evenings. He could not shake the conversation of the night before when Jennifer admitted that William was not happy about their engagement. It kept him awake and restless throughout the night, as Jennifer slept peacefully in his arms and he came up with a plan.

There was still availability on a flight to Baltimore, and without too much thought he purchased a round trip ticket, packed a duffle bag and texted Jennifer a brief explanation.

Hey sweetie,

I am going out a town for a couple days for work. I will try to contact you when I can, but I will be quite busy with a project that needs my attention, so I guess my vacation is unfortunately delayed. Last night was amazing and I miss you already. Talk soon.

Love and kisses,

Mitchell

Several hours later, Jennifer glanced at her cellphone that she kept well hidden in her desk drawer, being busy with a quarterly tax return from an important business client. She was stunned to realize that Mitchell had actually left town – since the children were away for a few days at church camp and would give them a chance to be alone - which barely ever happened in the time they had been dating. She shook her head slightly in confusion, not having the time to analyze things any further with her overwhelming workload that she was trying to catch up on from her time of being away on vacation.

The plane skidded to a stop and the announcement was made by a perky female flight attendant that it was sunny and 84 degrees in Baltimore as she welcomed everyone to the city. Mitchell hurriedly slipped from his seat and grabbed his carry-on bag in the overhead bin above, making his way through the throngs of busy travelers. He stepped into the office of the same car rental business that Jennifer had used, renting the most economical car offered. He programmed his GPS, being unfamiliar with the area or the drive ahead of him, as he maneuvered his way out of Baltimore/Washington International Thurgood Marshall Airport into heavy lunch hour traffic of the Baltimore beltway, on his way to Marlin Beach.

William stared at the large stack of file folders on his desk that Lance had so conveniently passed off to him even before he had arrived at the office. *Each one would have to be entered into the computer, which will take up the better part of the morning,* he realized as he typed away. Snyder's Beach Dreams Real Estate was having a very profitable summer so far, with the majority of the properties that were listed being sold within a week or two from the time they were made *live* on the Multiple Listing Service site. Will hoped in some way he had contributed to that success even with his lack of real estate knowledge and the limited time he had been there working.

Lance peaked around the door frame of William's office with his coffee mug in hand, looking ready to tackle the long day ahead with a pleasant smile greeting him. "I see you found the stack of files that I left for you?"

"Oh yeah... uncle Lance... I did..." he answered matter-of-factly, trying to focus on the task at hand.

"Will, I just wanted you to know that you have greatly helped me this summer. I am very pleased with all your efforts," he praised, taking a long swig of his coffee with hazelnut creamer. "Matter-of-fact, my mother wanted me to share that with you also."

William stopped, looking up from his work to take a minute for his uncle and friend. "Well, that means a lot, uncle Lance. I never realized that the real estate business involved so much work and effort."

Lance began to laugh. *"What did you think – that I just drank coffee all day long and talked to people on the phone?"*

"Something like that," he grinned, getting up to stretch his arms high above his head from being hunched over the computer. "And I figured you had to show a few properties. But I never dreamt there would be all the other work that we do – especially with the legal part with the contracts and closings."

"And keeping everyone else straight in the office with the new agents as well as you keeps me on my toes too," he winked.

"I realize that now, especially with what I put you through with The Happy Crab," he admitted, taking a seat again at the desk.

"That situation is behind is now. How is everything else going though?" Lance inquired, as he took the extra seat nearby Will's desk.

William took a moment to think, swiveling his desk chair in Lance's direction. "Everything is going okay. No more wild parties at The Happy Crab, and for the most part my roommates and I are keeping up with the place."

Lance smiled, remembering the challenge of doing so when he was at that same age. "I know school will be back in session soon. Do you plan to go back to G-Dad's and Nan's for a few days first?"

William paused, having not considered that the end of his summer break was quickly approaching. "I guess so…" he answered, suddenly thinking about Brooke and not wanting to say goodbye to her.

"Is something bothering you?" Lance asked in concern.

Will shifted in his chair, not sure he wanted to share about his love life, especially if Lance told Sarah and then it got back to Nan and G-Dad. "I have really enjoyed my summer – even the community service part of working at Marlin Beach Ambulance and getting to know everyone there – but I also have met a girl."

"You have…?" Lance responded in surprise, with his eyes filled with wonder, since Will had kept his special secret quiet and well guarded.

"Yeah, her name is Brooke and I really didn't see this coming. I think I have feelings for her that go beyond a summer fling."

"Bud, most of us don't see *love* coming. It typically sneaks up on us and bites us in the butt. *Have you told her how you feel?"*

Will cleared his throat, still finding it hard to open up. "I have… and surprise of surprises she seems to feel the same way about me," he confessed with a pleasant smile.

"Well good for you," Lance replied, getting up to pat William on the back. "Does she live nearby or is the distance going to be a problem?"

"Actually, no and yes. She lives in the southern part of Virginia but attends Maryland, so I think it's workable. Time will tell once we are back in school, but at this point we have agreed to exclusively date each other."

"I would like to meet her and I'm sure your aunt Sarah would want to also, before you leave Marlin Beach for the summer. Feel free to invite her to our house for dinner once you speak with Sarah about a good day and time."

Will paused, not sure he was ready to introduce her to the family just yet. "I sorta want to keep this to myself, uncle Lance. I just don't need Nan getting hurt feelings because I have a girlfriend. She still thinks of me as a little boy."

Lance began to laugh as he hung back by the doorframe, ready to leave the room again. *"She isn't that bad, William.* She knows you are a man now and will have a girlfriend sooner or later."

"I hope so… I don't want to break her heart."

Lance shook his head, recalling Nancy's overprotective ways even in the early days of his relationship with Sarah. "Consider it a good thing. She just really loves the members of her family."

Lance slipped away, leaving Will to think about Nan and how kind and supportive she had always been to him from the very first moments he met her. She was more than a grandmother – she was his friend.

The door creaked open to Beach Dreams, as Patti looked up from the e-book she was reading on her cellphone. *"May I help you?"* she inquired of the stranger who had just walked in from the outside, looking somewhat weary as he stood by the counter.

"Yes, I am here to see William Miller. *Is he available?"*

"He should be. If you have a seat I will make sure he hasn't stepped out for lunch yet," she stated in her typical, dry callous manner, trying to call his office phone in the process. "He is on a call right now. If you can wait a minute, I will walk back and let him know he has a visitor. *Was he expecting you?"* she pried with a slight sneer.

"Probably not... " He answered with a nervous twist to his lips.

Patti preceded back the hallway, tapping her long painted nails rhythmically on the doorframe, waiting for William to end his call with a female client that he was trying to get further clarification from as he put in the data for her listing.

"Do you need something, Patti?" Will asked, sensing her impatience.

"You have a guest out front."

"Did you get a name?" William questioned, realizing that rarely happened, rising from his desk chair to join her.

"No, I didn't get a name," she rudely responded, as she turned to walk in front of him and continued to explain things. *"But I came back here to your office to let you know he was here, since you were busy on the phone,"* she added curtly, as she proceeded back to the front waiting area of Beach Dreams.

William was not far behind her as he stopped dead in his tracks, staring in total shock at the stoic face from his stormy past - sitting there and waiting. *"What the hell are you doing here, Mitchell?"* he yelled out in disbelief, as Patti jumped to attention from the exchange.

Mitchell stood up and smiled reminiscently, remembering the little boy that he raised, who had suddenly become a man. "I came here to talk with you. I think its time we go over some things that you may want to know about."

"I have nothing to say to you!" Will gritted out angrily, concerning Patti even further as she dialed Lance's number and whispered into the phone receiver *that she needed his help.*

Lance entered the front foyer, witnessing the exchange, ready to protect his nephew. *"What is this all about?"* Lance asked in confusion, looking at them both for the answer as he walked over to stand beside of William.

Will breathed deeply, trying to gather his thoughts. "Uncle Lance, this is Mitchell. The one that I told you about from Birmingham, Alabama!"

Lance's eyes widened, knowing now who was in their presence. *"I see…. What brings you here, sir? This is a place of business and I do not want anyone that may enter after you, witnessing all of this and being exposed to this obvious craziness!"*

Patti quietly stepped off to the side, totally engrossed in the conversation, finding it far more interesting than any of the suspenseful romance novels that she was so attached to.

"I come here in peace. I never intended to create havoc here at your office. I just need to talk with William. His aunt Jennifer has shared with me his concern over our engagement and I just thought it may be worth the time to explain a few things to him."

"You have nothing to say to me that will make any difference!" William blurted out with a red face, making Patti look on in surprise

since Will never raised his voice in front of her.

Lance reached out to gently squeeze Will's shoulder, trying to calm him down. *"It may have made more sense to call first before you just showed up here in Marlin Beach. Don't you think?"*

Mitchell shook his head, knowing that was the logical choice. "I do not have William's phone number and I had some vacation time. So I decided to fly here and deal directly with this."

"You have no right to think you can do this to me! I am not a part of your household anymore and I won't deal with your crap!" Will stammered out in frustration, briskly walking out the front door and slamming it behind him, making the award pictures rattle on the wall as Patti grabbed for her chest in surprise.

CHAPTER 43

The three that remained in the front foyer - Lance, Patti and Mitchell – stared at the front door after William departed, anticipating that he would return right away. Instead, he got into his Jeep and pulled away quickly from the parking lot and merged onto Beach Road, choosing to run away from the situation at hand.

"That son-of-a-bitch!" he muttered out loud, as he slammed the dash with one fist. *"The nerve of him showing up here!"* he continued with a sting of tears in his eyes, feeling confused and defeated as he left Lance holding the bag. He considered calling the police, but knew Beach Dreams didn't need any more drama from Mitchell's surprise visit. He felt angry with Jennifer too that she would reveal to Mitchell the details of his summer life in Marlin Beach. *How dare aunt Jen tell Mitchell where I work!* He pondered miserably, as he drove to parts unknown, not caring where he was really going.

Will pulled off onto a side street somewhere close to the Delaware line, parking his car and walking towards the beach after throwing his socks and shoes in the trunk of his car. He didn't care that he was dressed in his dress khaki pants, as he slightly rolled up each trouser leg. He walked for some distance along the shoreline as the waves playfully lapped against each of his exposed calves with ocean water and sand.

He shook his head and closed his eyes, breathing in deeply of the sea air, trying to clear his senses and shattered thoughts as a seagull dipped and squealed close by, making him jump.

After several minutes of walking, William stopped dead in his tracks, as he gazed up in the sky at the cumulus clouds with the seawater still rushing up over his bare feet. He squinted with one hand, realizing his sunglasses were still in the car, knowing he couldn't run away from the situation any longer. He turned, heading back up the beach in the direction of his parked Jeep, knowing it wasn't fair to make Lance deal with his problems alone.

"Why don't you come back into my office?" Lance suggested with a fake pretense of a smile, as he led Mitchell back the hallway, away from Patti's nosy glares and stares.

"I am sorry to inconvenience you, Lance. It's Lance Snyder, correct?" Mitchell asked, as Lance pointed and offered an empty chair.

"Yes, that would be my name," he smiled, trying to ease the tenseness of the room. "How about a cup of coffee or a water? I'm sorry I don't have any food to offer you."

"A cup of coffee would be great! I had an early morning flight today."

Lance provided the coffee from his Keurig, making one also for himself. He sipped from his tasty brew, studying the stepfather of William, now sitting directly across from him. "I do not condone outbursts like William just displayed, but I must say I do understand his reaction after seeing you for the first time since his mother's death – especially after what he has shared with me about his past. *Why on earth would you be so bold to come here?"*

Mitchell sighed, trying to gather his thoughts, still feeling tired from his lack of sleep from the night before. "I am a changed man - plain and simple. I no longer drink and I've held down a steady job for three years now. I also attend church regularly with my family. *That evil man that William once knew - no longer exists."*

Lance looked on, trying to formulate his response as he considered what Mitchell just shared. "Hmmm…. I applaud you for making positive changes in your life, but what about the past and how you affected William and his mother for that matter? *Do you think that can now suddenly just disappear from Will's mind?"*

Mitchell dropped his head, staring at the floor, before looking back up and locking eyes with Lance. "If I held on to the past and the man I was back then, I would have probably committed suicide by now. But through lots of counseling, I have learned to go forward and not have *rear view mirror thinking."*

"Rear view mirror thinking?"

"I've learned to never look backwards - as if you were looking in the rear view mirror of your car – focusing on the past instead of driving straight ahead with your thoughts and plans. I know I must only focus now on going forward and forgiving myself, as God has chosen to forgive me first."

Lance considered his words, sensing the genuineness of them. "So you seem to be at peace with your past, but how do you convince everyone else of the same?"

"Time has a way of healing things. Jennifer, Eva and Jackson have seen consistency in me and they have forgiven me of my past mistakes. We are a happy family," Mitchell explained. "Over time, I have fallen in love with Jennifer and I have asked for her hand in marriage. We both desire to get married."

Patti interrupted the conversation, paging Lance's office phone. "You have a call on line one, Lance."

"Take a message, Patti. I am in a meeting."

"You may want to take this call," she insisted, as he shook his head in frustration by her persistence.

Lance parked the call, rising from his desk. "I will be right back. I must deal with this phone call."

"Would you like me to return to the reception area?"

"No need," Lance smiled with his kind brown eyes, walking from his office and back to William's to answer the phone there. "Thank you for holding. Lance speaking, how may I help you?" He greeted.

"Uncle Lance, it's me, William. *Is Mitchell still there?*"

"Yes, Will, he is still here. I've been speaking to him in my office."

William sighed in utter frustration, running one hand through his unruly wind-blown locks from his beach walk, trying to keep the other hand on the wheel. "I'm sorry he is disturbing your workday. *Please just tell him to leave!* If he is insisting on speaking with me, just give him my cellphone number and I will come up with a convenient location outside of work to speak with him later."

"No need for that, William. Just get back here and we will all talk together in my office. I think it may be good that I am here as a neutral party to keep things under control."

"I'm really sorry for my outburst earlier. You know I typically don't act like this, but Mitchell brings out the worst in me."

"No need to explain," Lance reassured. "When you get here, just come straight back to my office. There is no need to give Patti any sort of explanation if she starts prying."

"Thanks, uncle Lance. I owe you."

"You owe me nothing. You are family and we are here for each other during the good times but also the bad. You always have my support."

Tears began to form again in William's eyes. He knew he was truly blessed to have Lance looking out for him in life.

Patti remained quiet as William walked silently by her with his head bent low. She was already pre-occupied with filing her nails and flipping the channels on the TV that was attached to the wall nearby, finding her favorite soap that would now keep her entertained.

Will reluctantly opened the closed door of Lance's office, hearing the muffled conversation of the two men before he entered. Mitchell turned with a start as William entered the room, walking right past him and choosing to stand by the window instead of sitting in the empty seat nearby. He stood defensively with his arms crossed in front of him, being on guard as he glared down at him.

"Have a seat," Lance suggested with a pleasant smile, pointing to the empty, over-stuffed upholstered chair beside of Mitchell's. William reluctantly sat down, wanting to only pull it further away, but hesitating to do so. "I think we need to establish some ground rules here."

"And what would they be?" Will asked in concern.

"No yelling, cursing or leaving," Lance stated clearly and firmly, looking at each one and waiting for their answer.

"Of course," Mitchell answered civilly and calmly.

William glanced over at him, having a hard time believing he was agreeing to the terms. Something was different about him or he was playing an excellent game of deception.

"What do you say, William?" Lance asked again.

"Yeah... sure... whatever works... " He agreed, doubting Mitchell's sincerity. Will assumed he would probably screw up and his temper would flare before the conversation was over anyway, and Lance would see the real him.

"I can leave if the two of you would like, but I think it's in everyone's best interest if I am here to mediate and keep the peace. If something is interpreted incorrectly, I can jump in as a calming force."

Will considered Lance's words, realizing it made good sense what he was suggesting. "I have no problem with you staying here, uncle Lance."

"Me neither," Mitchell added.

"So Mitchell, I would like you to express to William what you shared with me earlier while Will was away."

William refused to look at Mitchell as he began, looking at the floor instead. "What I shared with your uncle is that I am a changed man." William looked up again, glaring at Mitchell and ready to explode, but holding back as was requested. "I no longer drink and I have been working for nearly three years now steadily. I also attend church and I am respected again in the community."

"Will, do you have anything to say to this?" Lance asked, as William sat with a blank look of disbelief and frustration etched all over his face.

"What about my mother, Mitchell? Did she ever see you sober and going to church when she was suffering and dying of ovarian cancer?" he gritted out angrily.

"No, she didn't… unfortunately," he confessed with pain and sadness outlining his brow. "I was horrible to her and you both. It was just an outward display of the sadness within me."

"Oh, what a crock of sh…. " Will started, then backed off from the curse word. *"How sad do you think I was? My mom was dying and I was the only one there to protect her from you!"* he said in despair, feeling the tears stinging his eyes again.

"I was very, very wrong! I know that now."

Will rubbed both of his watery steel blue eyes, locking them with Mitchell's stormy brown ones. "I'm glad you are doing better. *Honestly, I mean that...* " He said quietly. "But my mom never got to know about any of this. *How can I stay true to my mother's memory by just forgiving you now?*"

Mitchell took a deep breath, wanting to be clear with his words. *"The last day of your mother's life, I was allowed to go visit her by police escort. It was tough on me to say goodbye to her. Whether you believe it or not, I dearly loved her."* Will shook his head, not caring to hear Mitchell's proclamation of love. "I asked for her forgiveness and she then asked something of me," he explained.

"What was that?" Will asked, now interested.

"She asked that I become a changed man - that I get my life together and stop drinking. She wanted me to attend church again and go there with the family - just like we did when you were younger. *She did say she forgave me!* I have tried my best to honor her and do everything she requested."

"Maybe so... " Will answered frankly. "But I wasn't there to hear or verify any of this. So how do I know if it's all a crock, and you're making this up and it's not really true?"

"Doesn't her Last Will and Testament speak for itself?" Mitchell reasoned.

Lance joined in at that point, remembering something from the past that Sarah had shared with him after Claire died. "I do remember Sarah going over the will with me. Even though a provision was made for her to potentially help raise you - William - she didn't feel it was her place to do so. She felt your grandparents would do a much better job since she was overwhelmed at the time with Miller's Architecture. I know the discussion also came up about your siblings. Your mother wanted your aunt Jennifer to raise Eva and Jackson, but she also had come to the conclusion that Mitchell could jump back in again to help parent if he ever got his life back on track."

"I know all about this! I read the will too before I moved away to Baltimore," William replied with a sad shake of his head. *"So obviously you and aunt Jen did begin to co-parent and then you guys started to like each other,"* he stated sarcastically.

"Yes, that sums it up pretty well," Mitchell smiled sincerely, noting his disdain. William took a few deep breaths and looked away, trying to clear his head.

"So what do want from me? You hated my mother because she wouldn't change my last name to yours or allow you to adopt me!"

"I can't deny that either," Mitchell admitted sadly.

"I'm adult and it doesn't really matter anymore at this point. I never plan to go back to Birmingham anyway. Marry aunt Jen and stay sober, and you better never hurt Eva and Jackson or I will have to step in. That is all I ask…."

"Jennifer and I want your blessing, William. We want to try to put the past behind us and have you attend our wedding. You can be a part of our family too."

William stood up, running his hands again through his hair, nervously laughing out in response. *"Oh, what a pipe dream! Attend your wedding and be a part of your family? Seriously?"*

Mitchell looked up as William hawked down over him, trying to remain calm in the midst of the chaos. "Yes, that is what I would like. I felt it was important enough to come here in person and discuss this with you."

"Did aunt Jen put you up to this?" he gritted out.

"She, or no one else for that matter, knows I'm here."

Lance cleared his throat, breaking into the conversation, having his fill of the anger. "William, you say you are a man. Well I think it is high time you start acting like one and take the high road. No one is perfect in this world, and take it from me - we all make our mistakes!"

CHAPTER 44

William looked at Lance, somewhat hurt and utterly surprised by his remarks. "Wow, uncle Lance, I never thought I would hear you speak to me like that. You know everything I have shared with you about my past."

"Yes, I do, Will, but I have also told you about my past and how people that are in my life now did not want to forgive me either because of your father's unfortunate death. Imagine my life now minus Sarah and the twins. If she wouldn't have come to her senses and stopped blaming me, we could be at an impasse just like you and Mitchell. Let's just say that chances are I would have met and married someone else by this time without her forgiveness, and you wouldn't be in my life either."

"Gosh… I never thought about things that way."

"Well you need to," Lance replied realistically, looking in Mitchell's direction and trying to lend a supportive force as he sat quietly listening to the conversation.

Mitchell rose from his chair, addressing William before he departed. "I would like to give you my cellphone number. I plan to stay the night and then leave tomorrow for Birmingham again. *Maybe we can meet up later for dinner if that's possible?"*

William was prepared to say no, but Lance flashed him a warning glare that was unexpected. "Okay, you win…. I will meet you for dinner. Give me your number and I will put it in my phone. I need to go home and change first, but let's say 7:30. Does that work?" he asked, typing in Mitchell's cellphone number.

"It will be my treat," Mitchell smiled happily, feeling relieved by his sudden change of heart. "Pick the nicest place on the beach!"

"That would be The Dexter," Lance chimed in, not giving William any leeway to change his mind.

William was taken back with the suggestion, immediately thinking of his friends and running into Brooke, especially if he encountered her and the others while they were working and they were dining. "I can't expect you to put out for a place that expensive."

"I insist!" Mitchell answered, as he reached out to shake Lance's hand goodbye and then William's. "I will see you at 7:30 at The Dexter. By the way, could you also recommend a good place to stay for the night?"

"The Dexter fits that bill too!" Lance added, making William gulp and cough with his words.

"Well thanks for the suggestion. Hopefully, there will be a room available and I can get cleaned up before we meet for dinner," he mentioned in passing, leaving William to stare on in disbelief as he left the office.

"Seriously, uncle Lance?"

"Just enjoy your evening. Sarah wants me home early," he sidestepped and threw in – just trying to change the subject - while packing up his briefcase. "She wants dinner and drinks on the deck and a movie later after the twins are in bed. I will see you tomorrow, and I'm expecting a full report about your evening with Mitchell," Lance nodded, as he walked past him at a fast pace out of the room.

"Geesh, what just happened?" he questioned, scratching his head. Reality set in that he still had a few hours to finish up before the end of his workday, and then he would meet up with Mitchell for dinner. *"Who would have thought?"* he continued to ponder, walking back to his office, ready to finish up the stack of listings that were half way done.

Mitchell Robbins pulled his rental car into The Dexter Resort and Spa semi-circle, directly in front of the hotel. A handsome valet attendant was there to greet him as he rolled down the window of his still idling vehicle.

"I'm checking in and would like my car parked, please?"

"Of course!" Matt answered, reaching for his keys as he opened the driver's door. "One minute and I will have your claim ticket, hangtag, and a check-in information sheet that you will need to fill out before I am allowed to park your car," he added with a pleasant smile, as he excused himself to retrieve a clipboard and the form.

Mitchell quickly filled out the necessary documentation, handing the clipboard back to Matt. "I think I filled out all the information correctly?" he inquired.

Matt reviewed the form, asking to see his driver's license for verification. "Alabama? You came a long way to visit with us, Mr. Robbins," he smiled, handing his ID back to Mitchell afterwards.

"I'm here to visit a relative," he replied dryly, feeling the valet was prying somewhat. "Matter-of-fact, he will be meeting me for dinner later."

"Well, enjoy your dinner and have a great time in Marlin Beach and here also at The Dexter! We have a first class restaurant with great views of the ocean."

Matt drove off with the rental car as Mitchell entered the spacious foyer of The Dexter Hotel as the automatic doors opened in front of him. Mr. McHenry was checking in another guest as he approached the front desk with his overnight bag in hand.

"Good afternoon!" Mr. McHenry greeted pleasantly, as Mitchell proceeded forward and was next in line.

"I need a room for the night."

"One night?" Mr. McHenry inquired, as he glanced down at his computer and searched for room availability.

"Yes, only for tonight will I need a room, and it is only me - so anything is fine."

Mr. McHenry smiled, trying to assess the traveler's needs. "I have a nice room on the fifth floor with a queen sized bed that overlooks the ocean. How does that sound?" he asked, looking up from the screen.

"That will work," Mitchell answered kindly, ready to hand him a credit card. "Do I need to make a reservation for dinner here?" he inquired as Mr. McHenry handed him back his credit card along with his receipt and room keys.

"Yes, I would recommend that you make a dinner reservation since we are in tourist season and the restaurant can fill up rather quickly in the evenings," he suggested. "If you walk down the hall," he pointed, "you will find the dining room directly ahead of you."

"Thank you," Mitchell nodded, turning one last time to look at the grandeur of the lobby before he strolled away. He took notice to all of the luxurious surroundings as he proceeded down the glassed hallway that overlooked the beach in front of it. No expense was spared with

The Dexter's beautiful marble floors and elegant wall coverings and paintings. He passed by the oversized clay pots that were filled with palm trees and lush tropical foliage, as well as an indoor pond filled with koi fish and a trickling waterfall. He could hear the soft playing of music as he entered the reception area of The Dexter Restaurant and Lounge, taking in the large expanse of the dining area in front of him.

"Good afternoon," Brooke greeted pleasantly, as Mitchell approached the hostess stand. "Would you like a table?"

"I would like to make a reservation for tonight at 7:30," he explained with a slight smile, as she looked over her pending reservations for the evening.

"How many are in your party?"

"Just two of us."

"Yes, I do have a table available. *May I have your name, please?*" Brooke questioned sweetly, waiting patiently for the answer, as Mitchell acted distracted and glanced around the room. He now remembered the significance of the place – *it was named after Dexter Miller, William's birth father* - who had always been the strained presence in his marriage even if he had died tragically as a teenager. *"Sir, may I have your name?"* Brooke probed a second time, breaking him from his trance.

"I'm so sorry. It's been a long day of travel," Mitchell answered her with an excuse, shaking the cobwebs and sad memories of the past away from his mind, bringing him back to the present. "My name is Mitchell Robbins. I would prefer a table by the window - overlooking the ocean - if at all possible."

"Of course," Brooke replied with a cheery smile. "We will see you at 7:30 - table for two, by the window and overlooking the beach."

"Thank you, very much," he replied with a wave, as he turned and walked away.

"That was strange… " Brooked mentioned to her friend and roommate, as Mitchell retreated back down the hallway and out of her sight.

"What was?" Mia asked, as she joined Brooke by the hostess stand and removed her apron.

"That guy who was just here was staring around the dining area, looking like he was a million miles away…. "

Mia laughed, swinging her apron over her shoulder, ready to leave for the day. *"And how does that makes him any different from all the others crazies coming in here?"*

Brooke laughed and shook her head. "Yeah, I guess, but he just seemed to be overly distracted and bothered about something. That's all… "

"Who cares!" she replied. "When you're done working why don't you meet up with everybody unless you are doing something with Will later."

"He hasn't asked me to do anything tonight, so that should be fine. What are the plans?" Brooke asked, as she stacked the menus and placed them back on a shelf nearby.

"Maybe we will go over to Jessica's place. I would prefer going over to Will's so that I could try to hook up with Chris again, but you know how strict his uncle Lance has been with the parties. He definitely has screwed up our summer with all his rules."

Brooke just shook her head, knowing how much her roommate enjoyed her intimate encounters with way too many guys. "Things just got way out of control. You know that."

"Whatever," Mia said, dismissing her friend's practical side and

rolling her eyes. "Stop acting so damn mature," she laughed, pinching her in the ass. "I will see you later. Text me when you are finished working. Okay, chickie?"

"Sure, silly," she giggled as Mia skipped away, happy her shift was finally over.

Brooke folded the remaining clean linen napkins that had just come out of the dryer from the back laundry facility of the restaurant, and made sure the silverware was stocked and ready to go for the upcoming evening rush of patrons that were expected. The reservations were totally booked now for the evening, and only with a cancellation would someone find an available table if they were lucky.

Will pulled his Jeep into the front entry area of The Dexter - a little too quickly from rushing - seeing the smiling, friendly face of his friend. He threw his keys in his direction as he leaped from the vehicle. "Hey, Matt, I'm running a little late. Can you park the Jeep for me, bro?"

"Sure," he grinned, catching the keys mid air, and then running for the open car door that Will have left ajar. "Are you meeting your grandparents for dinner?"

"No... they're not in town right now. Just someone else …. " He yelled over his shoulder, as he slid away through the automatic doors, seeing Mr. McHenry waving in his direction after noticing that it was him.

He jogged down the hallway towards The Dexter Restaurant and Lounge, being five minutes late after waiting on Tyler to get out of the bathroom so that he could shower. Outside of the restaurant, stood Mitchell, staring out of the glass walled windows in front of him. "Sorry I'm late. My roommate was tying up the bathroom," he laughed, trying to catch his breath with his hands planted on his knees.

"No worries. We have a table waiting."

The two walked side by side into the front reception area of the restaurant as Brooke stood by the hostess stand ready to seat them.

"William?" she said in total confusion, looking wide-eyed at him and then at the distant stranger of earlier that caught her off-guard.

"Yeah, we are here for dinner."

Brooke looked at each one, trying to figure out the connection. *"Right this way,"* she directed with a sweep of her hand, not having a clue but acting the part of a gracious hostess. She walked them over to their table, leading her lover and the distant stranger that made her feel uncomfortable to the table for two - right by the window with the magnificent ocean view.

CHAPTER 45

"Get whatever you would like," Mitchell offered with a sincere smile, looking over the expansive menu of offerings that he rarely dined on except on special occasions.

Will had forgotten to turn off his cellphone and realized his blunder when a text message just came through. He reached for the buzzing device, extracting it from his khaki shorts, seeing that it was from Brooke who was watching his every move from the hostess stand with Rachel now standing beside of her. "Sorry Mitchell," he offered with his head bent, trying to read what you wrote.

Who is that with you? Brooke pried, not understanding in the least.

William quickly texted her back before shutting off his phone. *A relative… I will explain later.*

Brooke smiled at her boyfriend, accepting the answer as she greeted the next group of dinner guests who were waiting to be seated in the over-crowded dining room. As she made her way back to the hostess stand once again, Rachel was still standing there, waiting for the details.

"So did you figure out who that man is with Will?"

"He says he's a relative. Hey, your table over there is looking for you. One is holding up their empty glass. You better get over there before Mrs. Perry sees you. I heard she gave a write-up to Amber last night after a group of customers complained that she was never nearby to offer refills on their drinks."

"Yeah, yeah," Rachel threw out, rolling her eyes. "Who in the heck is she going to get to work here now, since summer is almost over?"

"Don't be so sure of yourself, Rachel. She has locals here that she can turn to if we decide to quit."

"Got it!" she stated curtly over her shoulder, as she walked towards the group of people who were motioning for her to refill their toddler's sippy cup with milk.

"So what would you recommend?" Mitchell asked after Amber approached the table and was ready to take their orders, dropping off a hot basket of rolls along the way. She smiled and stopped to think as she looked at William who she knew was dating Brooke, and wondered herself about the mystery man seating with him.

"We are known for our seafood and steaks," she mentioned cheerfully, as she assessed the middle-aged man who was now studying the menu.

"I think I will have the combo platter," he decided, pointing to the expensive dinner selection on the menu. "The one with the filet and the crab cake."

"How would you like your filet cooked?"

"Medium rare."

"And your sides?" she asked politely, as she wrote down his choice.

"Caesar salad and a baked potato."

"Sour cream and butter?"

"Sure! That would be great!" Mitchell smiled.

"And what would you like to drink?"

"Sweet tea with lemon will do."

"Very good. And for you, Will?" Amber continued, turning her attention back in his direction with her pencil and notepad ready.

"I'll have the same," he smiled with very tight lips, knowing Amber was waiting for an introduction that he wasn't sure he wanted to make.

"And something to drink?"

"I'll have what Mitchell is having," he nodded, trying to make her disappear quickly with their order.

"Okay…?" she answered, staring at both of them awkwardly.

"Amber, this is my stepfather, Mitchell Robbins," Will finally confessed. "He's from Birmingham, Alabama and he is here in town overnight. We wanted to have dinner and catch up. Maybe you can let the others know too… if you don't mind," Will explained, feeling somewhat irritated after noticing several of his roommates now standing with Brooke and her friends by the hostess stand.

"Oh… yes…" she replied uncomfortably, making her way back over to the others at the hostess stand who were waiting for answers.

"So who is he?" Chris asked.

"You of all people should know since you are Will's roommate," Amber challenged, feeling somewhat put off by William's brashness.

"I don't have a clue. Will has the tendency to keep his business to himself," he shrugged.

"He says his name is Mitchell and that he is here overnight, and get this – Will says he is his stepfather."

"No way!" Chris exclaimed in surprise, mostly hearing about his grandparents and Lance and Sarah, and now just recently about some of his other relatives from Alabama and his dead father Dexter that the place was named after.

A matronly woman with her gray hair pulled back into a tight bun, approached the hostess stand with her arms full with a heavy load. She carried a large tray of silverware and napkins that she dropped down loudly on the table close by, causing a sudden stir. When the wait staff had down time they were to assist in the folding of the dinner napkins along with organizing the silverware which they typically avoided doing until Mrs. Perry scolded and threatened to fire them. "I would suggest you get back to your customers immediately if you want to continue being employed here at The Dexter. There is no time for this idle chitchat!" she stated firmly, looking at the group who were clustered together, gossiping and wasting time.

"Sorry, Mrs. Perry. It's just that our friend, Will, is over there with his stepfather for dinner, and we didn't know he had a stepfather."

"That is no concern of yours, Brooke!" Mrs. Perry barked out, turning her attention back to the napkins. "Whoever is not busy at the moment needs to fold these napkins and focus again on work! I am needed in the kitchen and I better not find you huddled together here when I return to check on you!" she warned as she turned to walk away, disappearing behind the swinging doors of the kitchen area.

Amber stood nearby typing in the food order for William and Mitchell as the others dispersed and got back to their customers. She filled up two large glasses with ice and sweet tea, placing them on a tray with a dish of lemon slices on the side. "Sorry for the delay," she mentioned, as she placed each glass in front of them along with the lemon slices. "Your dinners should only be a few minutes," she added as she walked away.

"She seems nice," Mitchell commented, trying to figure out the connection.

Will sighed, diverting his eyes to his lap, trying to gather his thoughts. "A lot of my friends got jobs here for the summer. As you already figured out, I work at Beach Dreams but the rest work here at The Dexter."

"Oh, I see… Life at the beach… " Mitchell chuckled, taking a swig of the sweet tea after squeezing in two wedges of the lemon. "I have never been to Marlin Beach, if you didn't know. Your mother used to tell me how nice it was, but unfortunately we didn't vacation here."

Will paused and shook his head slightly in frustration. *"Yeah, I know… remember I lived with you and always wanted to see where my father grew up."*

Mitchell remained quiet, just studying William. "I'm sorry, William. I realize that you always wanted to know more about your dad. I hate to admit it now, but I guess I was always jealous about the whole thing. I just wanted you to like me and accept me as your father. I always felt I couldn't compete with his memory."

Will remained indifferent as he bit into a coconut roll that he had chosen from the overflowing basket of the famous delectables in front of him. *"You made my life a living hell! Do you recall that?"* he gritted out, suddenly feeling not hungry as he placed the half-eaten roll down on the small plate in front of him.

Mitchell crossed both arms on the table, leaning in as he answered. *"If there is one thing my counseling and my church has taught me is to not sugar coat things. I screwed up majorly and for that - I am sorry. I am just trying to be as honest as I can be now, why I acted the way I did when you were living in Alabama as a child under my roof."*

"Why now, Mitchell? What difference does it make if I like you or not at this point?"

"I do not want to quote scripture to you, William, but the Bible says that God has called all men to be at peace. Not a day has gone by since I have gotten my life together, that I have felt convicted about the past and not having things right with you. I had to do this."

Will began to nervously laugh, shaking his head sadly in frustration. "You want me to leave you off the hook after what you did to my mother, don't you? Even after what you did when she was dying and you knocked her down and beat me up?"

"Yes…. I am asking for your forgiveness… "

Will slammed his hands on the table, making the silverware jump and several families seated close by turn to stare at what was happening. He immediately realized his blunder as he tried to regain his composure, speaking quietly through his clenched teeth. "You want this all to go away, but my mother never got to witness you as a changed man. How is that fair?"

"She asked me that last day I was with her in the hospital to change. That was her dying wish – to get my life together and go to church. She only wanted me to be sober and a good dad to all of you."

"I've done fine, Mitchell, without you! My life now is with G-Dad and Nan. I've never missed you – ever!" he declared, still with clenched teeth. "Eva and Jackson, yes, but never you!"

Amber reappeared balancing a large tray high up on her shoulder. "Your dinners are ready," she announced with a bright smile as she placed the heavy tray on the stand nearby, ready to serve them. Amber placed the hot steaming plates of steak and crab cakes in front of Mitchell and then William, and then waited patiently close by until they tasted the steak, making sure that they were cooked the way they had requested. "Are your steaks to you liking and do you need anything else at this time?" she asked, looking at each one attentively.

"My steak is cooked perfectly and I need nothing else at this moment," Mitchell answered courteously with a sincere look.

"I'm fine too, Amber," William lied, not really thinking about the food in front of him, placing his steak knife and fork back on the table.

"I will be back with refills for your tea."

"Thank you," they both answered as she turned to leave with the tray and the fold up stand.

Mitchell paused and bowed his head as he breathed a silent pray for the food, as William looked on, filled with anger and disbelief over Mitchell's sincerity. He reopened his eyes, smiling kindly at William. *"Dig in,"* he invited, as he cut into his steak and popped a big bite in his mouth.

William stared at his plate and the beautiful presentation in front of him. The Dexter never disappointed in providing a first class meal, and periodically he and his grandparents, along with Sarah and Lance, had dined there on special occasions in the past.

"What are you majoring in?" Mitchell asked, as he took another long swig of his iced tea.

"Business. I'm not sure at this point what I want to do with that degree. That is why I'm trying real estate out this summer."

"That's fantastic that your uncle Lance is giving you the opportunity."

"He's a good guy," Will answered, as he finished off his steak. "He hooked me and my room mates up with a place to stay at also. I owe him a lot."

Mitchell smiled knowingly, realizing Will had matured a lot since he left Alabama. "I am happy for you William – now that you have your father's family in your life. Obviously, they have been very good to you."

"Yes, they have…" Will answered, finally feeling less on edge. "Look Mitchell, I know you came here to make peace. This is all so crazy for me. I hope you can just try to understand that."

Mitchell nodded, finally finishing his own plate of food as he wiped his mouth afterwards with his linen napkin. "I do get it. I know I am asking a lot out of you, but I still feel it is for the best that I'm trying to make amends. Your mother Claire would want this also."

"Do you honestly think she wanted you and aunt Jen to ever get married?" he asked half sarcastically.

Mitchell paused, considering his words. "She wanted me to be happy and Jennifer makes me happy. Of course she wanted happiness for all of us. *So I'm asking again, will you come to our wedding?"*

"I need to sleep on this. How about we talk again before you leave tomorrow?"

"Of course," Mitchell answered, as Amber reappeared with the ice tea pitcher in hand, ready to refill their glasses.

"Anyone for desert? We have chocolate pecan pie and strawberry cheesecake - that was just made today."

"None for me," Mitchell smiled, shaking his head. "And for you, William?"

"No, I'm good," Will answered, glaring at Amber once again, feeling totally embarrassed and uneasy. He knew his nosy friends would all want answers before the evening was over, and he wasn't sure he wanted to provide them.

CHAPTER 46

William pulled his Jeep into the gravel driveway of The Happy Crab. He realized he beat his roommates' home. *Maybe they will party elsewhere tonight,* he hoped as he changed out of his dress khaki shorts into some stretchy athletic ones instead. He sat shirtless watching TV in the living room on the sofa, downing a beer as the ocean breeze cascaded in from the open doors. He grabbed his cellphone off of the cocktail table to see if he had any messages, and realized he had forgotten to turn it back on. Repowering it back up made his phone chime out several text messages from Brooke and Chris both.

"Are you going to call me?" Brooke questioned.

"Yo, who the heck is the dude?" Chris wanted to know.

He answered Brooke that he was home and had his phone turned off, just as the door opened and Chris walked in, having his shirt slung over his shoulder from the very humid, warm evening that they were experiencing.

"You never answered me," Chris complained, walking towards the kitchen and grabbing a beer from the refrigerator.

"Get me one too while you're at it," Will yelled, as he brought over a couple and took a seat on the chair - handing him his second one of the evening.

"I texted you about the dude you were with."

"Yeah… my stepfather, if you really need to know," Will answered blankly, taking a big swig of his brew.

"I don't get you, Will. We have been friends for a long time now and you never share things with me concerning your past. I had no clue that you had a stepfather. What's up with the lack of information?"

Will stopped drinking to study his friend before answering. *"I seriously don't have to tell you all the fucking details of my life. You know that, right?"*

"Wow…. What set you off? I think it was a simple question. I'm honestly somewhat hurt. I have told you a lot about my family."

Will began to laugh, feeling the calming affects of the beer making him begin to relax. *"Yeah, you are an open book, much like a female who has to spill her guts about everything!"*

"Oh yeah?" Chris answered, wrapping Will's head in a headlock. "I've had no complaints in the past."

"No one wants to hurt your feelings," Will teased, standing up to break the constraint. "So you want to know all the details, then I will tell you. I used to live in Birmingham, Alabama before I knew you. My mother died and then I left the town, moving to Baltimore to be with my G-Dad and Nan."

"God, bro, your mother died too?" he asked in stunned surprise, shocked that Will had kept something that significant quiet.

"Yes, she did… and it's not any easier to talk about it today than when I first met you. My stepfather, Mitchell, treated me and my mother like shit. He now wants to make things right. He claims he isn't drinking anymore and got religion."

Chris got up to grab another beer and pulled out two, figuring Will needed another one also. "Man bro, you know you could have told me all this. I wouldn't have thought any less of you."

Will accepted the offering, unscrewing the cap and downing more of his alcoholic beverage. "Who wants to talk about stuff like this anyway? I'm sure you haven't told me everything about your family."

"Well I've tried... but you never seem interested. I just found out that my folks are separating and I'm not too happy about it. Mom claims my dad has a girlfriend on the side. I begged her not to do anything until I get back home for a few days before school starts again. I just need to hear both of their sides and maybe I can talk some sense into the both of them."

"Why even try?" Will asked with a loud belch, as the front door swung open again. In came Tyler and Matt with Brooke and her friends in tow, all proceeding towards the living room for answers.

"Heard your old man was in town," Tyler said casually with a laugh, trying to act jovial.

"He fucking isn't my old man, Tyler! My old man is dead as you know, and so is my mother! If anyone even cares!" Will yelled on his way to the bathroom, slamming the door loudly behind him.

"What just happened here?" Brooke asked, totally confused.

"I think the subject is better left unsaid. The guy with William tonight was his stepfather and not his dad. It's pretty apparent they don't have the best of relationships."

"No, we don't," William admitted coming back out into the living room, adjusting his shorts and wiping his hand over his mouth as he looked longingly at Brooke, feeling the after affects of the beer. *"Baby, let's get naked,"* he called out to her now, being mostly intoxicated as

she giggled back at him. Everyone else began to laugh too, realizing Will was not being his normal self and acting overly bold in front of them.

"Sure sweetie. I'll be right there," Brooke answered demurely, grabbing a few more beers before joining William. He wrapped a protective arm around Brooke and pulled her in close, swooping down for a passionate tongue kiss that left her weak while the others watched.

"Don't…. wait… up… on … us… " He said slowly with slurred, drunken speech, as they slipped behind William's bedroom door, locking it to the outside world.

Mitchell changed into his own set of athletic shorts and a t-shirt, climbing into the comfortable queen sized bed that he wished Jennifer was there to share with him. He picked up his phone, knowing he needed to text her back after she questioned his sudden departure. *Coming home tomorrow. Concluded my business. Hopefully, I can see you tomorrow evening. Love and miss you. Mitchell.*

Jennifer answered back. *Love you too. I guess you will explain when you get home, but this is not like you to just up and leave. Kisses. Jen.*

Mitchell stared at her message, not wanting to keep secrets from her, but feeling justified just this once. He laid the phone down, but picked it up once more just to text William before he went to sleep. *Can we talk one last time before I leave town tomorrow? I can meet you at Beach Dreams at 8 a.m., if that would be convenient. Please let me know. Mitchell.*

Will heard his phone chime with the familiar incoming text alert while he rode Brooke hard and fast, reading it while he orgasmed loudly. "*Damn, I'm sorry. I forgot to turn it off,*" he confessed, as she looked up at her spirited lover who was suddenly distracted but fulfilled.

She moaned, ready to explode. *"Please just put it down, silly!"* she demanded, as she screamed out her pleasure. The others in the living room could hear them, as they lifted their eyebrows and giggled for what was occurring close by, turning them all on in the process.

"Come here, Mia," Chris beckoned, as she cuddled in closer on the couch and he French kissed her boldly in front of the others, just as Will and Brooke had done earlier. *"Why don't we go to my room and we'll have some fun?"* he whispered against her neck. She was already hot, although not necessarily just for him, but she was willing to comply and join him in his bed. He pulled her off the couch, walking hand in hand to his room, slamming the door behind them as playful giggling was heard.

All that was left in the room was Matt and Tyler along with Amber and Rachel. As they sized each other up Matt paired off with Amber and Tyler with Rachel. It wasn't necessarily that they liked their chosen partner and desired a long-term relationship with them, but lust and sex were the order of the evening for all present. College would be starting soon and the friends would be going their separate ways – maybe to continue with a friendship again the next summer if they chose to come back to Marlin Beach, or maybe just for that summer and for that night. It really didn't matter as the two remaining couples grabbed a few more beers and departed to their perspective bedrooms - lost in the moment and only desiring hot and passionate sex.

As Will held the contented sleeping beauty in his arms, he suddenly remembering the text that remained unanswered. He picked up his cellphone reading the message again that had come in earlier from Mitchell - asking to meet back up in the morning. *"Geesh, should I do this?"* he said aloud, waking Brooke from her slumber.

"What is it, Will?" she asked, rolling over to face him now.

"Nothing… " He answered, kissing the top of her head. *"Go back to sleep. I'll figure it out."*

He began to type, not really wanting to deal with Mitchell again, but knowing it was probably necessary just to get him off his back. *Sure. I will see you tomorrow at 8 a.m. at Beach Dreams.* Will placed his cellphone back on his nightstand, turning Brooke over and spooning her again from behind, feeling like he was starting to get aroused until he remembered his early wakeup time. He fell asleep thinking of many things - his girlfriend who he had fallen in love with, but also his stepfather who he hated and despised.

The requested wakeup call came through at 6:30 a.m. giving Mitchell enough time to shower and grab a quick breakfast in the coffee shop on the main floor. He checked out, taking a refill of coffee with him as he said his goodbyes to the early morning, friendly staff at the front desk, along with Mr. McHenry who was also there.

"I enjoyed my stay."

"Well that is good to hear! We look forward to you staying with us again real soon," Mr. McHenry politely extended, as Mitchell waved his farewell to the group.

He approached the valet parking stand, handing his ticket over to Matt who was already working, trying to make as much extra money as possible for his time remaining in Marlin Beach. He slipped from his bed early after a night of having sex several times with Amber, not even caring if he felt tired now. She still slept as he showered and dressed quickly, kissing her lightly on the forehead before he left.

"Here you go, Mr. Robbins," Matt offered with a friendly smile, realizing it was Will's stepfather that was leaving. "I wanted you to know that I am William's roommate at college and also here at the beach."

Mitchell's eyes lit up with the realization. "Well that's great to hear!" he offered, as he slipped into the car. "I'm meeting up with him now, before I leave town."

Matt nodded and smiled, surprised to hear that Will was seeing him again after the way he reacted the night before. "Safe travels back to Alabama. Nice to meet you!"

"Thank you. Nice to meet you too," Mitchell replied handing him a $10 tip, pulling away from Matthew onto Beach Road.

Matt stared down at the money, surprised by the amount. "Well, he might be a bastard, but he sure as hell tips well!" he said with a shake of his head, shoving the money into his pocket before getting the next car.

Mitchell pulled into Snyder's Beach Dreams Real Estate finding William already parked and sitting in his Jeep waiting. He slid in beside of him, rolling down his front passenger window and talking to Will through it. *"Do you want to go inside or just talk out here?"* he asked.

Will looked tired, still feeling the after affects of the beer from the night before, trying to act normal even though he was suffering from a major hangover. Mitchell recognized the symptoms, being surprised that William would even drink.

"You feeling okay, William?"

"I'm fine, and we can just talk out here for a few minutes, and then I got to get inside for work. Lance will be here soon and I don't need him getting involved again."

"Understood," Mitchell answered. "Do you want to get in my car? The air conditioning is cool," he offered.

"Sure," Will agreed, walking over to the passenger's door and getting in before rolling up the window.

"I appreciate you meeting with me one more time before I leave. How are you feeling about things after sleeping on it for the night?"

Will's head was thumping, but he realized that the only thing he had really slept on for the night was Brooke. He hadn't given any more thought to Mitchell or the wedding. *"When are you guys even getting married?"* he asked quietly, trying to get his bearings.

Mitchell paused, not knowing how to answer. "Well to be honest, I'm not sure. We hope to have the wedding within the year, but we haven't come up with a firm date yet."

William took a deep breath, trying to clear his rambling thoughts that kept haunting him from his past. *"Okay, Mitchell. I guess the answer is yes. I will be there - as much as it causes me concern,"* he said with a pained expression, "you do seem like a different man from what I remember, as much as I don't want to admit it. So when you have everything ironed out with a date and location for the wedding, let me know. If it happens to be planned during a time when I'm back in college though, it may be hard to break away from my classes."

Mitchell beamed brightly with a happy full smile, hoping and praying for this outcome. "Thank you, William, from the bottom of my heart. I can't be more pleased - as I'm sure Jennifer will be also. I will let her know about your classes."

"No problem, Mitchell, but I really need to go now," William responded impatiently.

"I understand," Mitchell answered, as Will left the car and walked back to his Jeep to grab his backpack lying on the seat. *"You may want to try a big glass of water and some Tylenol. It used to work for me,"* he suggested loudly, as William looked up in surprise, realizing he hadn't fooled him - he knew he had been drinking.

CHAPTER 47

"Coming!" Jennifer yelled, as she ran from her bedroom to answer the front door that was being knocked on repeatedly. Mitchell stood on the other side smiling, as she opened it widely to his view with only a towel wrapped around her. *"Why didn't you use your key, silly?"* she questioned, as she caught her breath.

"What fun would that have been? Now that I see you out of breath and wrapped only in a towel," he grinned, with love and passion etched all over his face.

Jennifer just giggled and shook her head as he entered the living room, closing the door behind him with his foot, grabbing her possessively and kissing her deeply for several moments.

"I missed you…. " He groaned. "No kids for a few days yet. Let's make the most of the time we have together."

"Sure… but I do have some questions as to where you went?" she pressed, leading him back to her bedroom and dropping the towel along the way.

"I will explain later…. " He answered, barely able to maintain from seeing her taunt nipples, firm smooth legs and the fringe of public hair now totally exposed to his view. He scooped her up in his strong arms, falling beside of her on the bed, as Jennifer helped undress him too.

As they lay together entwined after an intense *welcome home* lovemaking session, Jennifer's curiosity got the better of her. *"So now can you explain where you went?"* she insisted, looking steadfastly into Mitchell's brown eyes. He propped up on one elbow, admiring the woman he adored.

"I went to Marlin Beach to see William."

Jennifer sat up with her breasts being exposed again, as the sheet barely covered the rest of her. *"No way, Mitchell. That's impossible!"*

He smiled, knowing she would react this way. "God makes the impossible - *possible* - sometimes, Jennifer," he answered practically, sitting up now too while they both relaxed against her gray tufted, upholstered headboard. "I know I totally caught him off-guard and surprised him when I showed up at Beach Dreams, but luckily I was able to speak with him while I was there."

Jennifer was in a daze as she listened to the whole conversation, just shaking her head in disbelief. *"Why would you do such a thing? And honestly I'm surprised you didn't go over this idea with me first,"* she added logically, feeling somewhat hurt.

"I knew you would throw up a red flag for me not to go there, but I went with my gut instinct, which as you can see - did paid off!"

"How so?"

"Lance was there to run interference when Will got upset, and thankfully, he was able to calm him down. I greatly needed and appreciated his help."

"Well I'm sure you did, but what was the conclusion to all of this?" she inquired anxiously, being totally mesmerized and hanging on to his every word.

"We had dinner last night at The Dexter and today I met up with him one more time at Beach Dreams before I left. I asked him to come to our wedding and believe it or not - he agreed to do so."

Jennifer's hands went up to her face in surprise from hearing the unexpected news, as tears began to stream freely down onto her bare legs. *"You can't be serious? He actually agreed to being there?"*

"Yes, my dear, he did," Mitchell proclaimed proudly. "His only request is that you don't plan the wedding during the time of the year when he is in college. So that may be somewhat of a challenge."

Jennifer rose from the bed, opening her dresser drawer as she slipped into a pair of clean pajamas. Mitchell gazed at her lovingly with his hands clasped behind his head. "I think we should plan for next summer. *Maybe a beach wedding since you have now ventured to Marlin Beach without my knowledge,*" she teased with a grin, casting him a sideways glance.

"You want to wait that long?"

"Honey, it takes awhile to plan a wedding anyway, and venues fill up rather quickly."

"Whatever you say, sweetheart," he agreed as he joined Jennifer, wrapping her in his arms for another time and planting a kiss on her lips again, before replacing his discarded clothing also - that were left lying on the floor.

They walked to the kitchen and Jennifer filled up the teakettle with water, placing it on the stove as she took out two large mugs and added tea bags before joining Mitchell at the table. She reached over to grab his hand, squeezing it fondly. "I was so confused when you just up and left. I really didn't know what to think."

"I know... I didn't mean to cause you any alarm. I'm sorry I wasn't totally honest with you, but my worry was that you would try to intervene in some way, and I wouldn't get my chance to speak with William. I just felt driven to do this for us, and for Eva and Jackson too, for that matter. I wanted them to have their brother back in their lives."

"Speaking of Eva and Jackson, two more days to ourselves and then they will be home from church camp. I heard from them yesterday and they seem to be having a great time. They even made a couple of new friends."

"They contacted me too and I told them I was out of town on business and would see them soon. They wanted to know all of the details, but I changed the subject. It wasn't worth discussing a visit with William if things didn't work out."

The teakettle whistled a non-ending, high-pitched familiar squeal as steam poured out of the spout, making Jennifer leap from her chair to silence the noisy metal contraption. She filled each mug, adding honey and milk, offering one to Mitchell and then taking the other for herself. It was their nightly ritual together before retiring for the night, and one that had brought about many meaningful conversations that had made them fall in love.

"Are you ready for round two?" Mitchell grinned devilishly.

Jennifer gulped down the last of the decaf tea, putting her cup down with a delighted smile. "Well Mitchell, maybe you should go away more often," she teased, reaching out to grab his outstretched hand that was pulling her to her feet, as they walked together again towards the bedroom.

He nuzzled her neck making her giggle. "No thanks. I'd miss you too much, love. I'm better off here - never too far away from your arms."

Mike unlocked the door to The Dancing Seahorse, with Nancy close behind, clutching a few bags of groceries that they had just picked up along the way. He flipped on the lights, casting a warm glow around the living room and kitchen.

"Open the patio doors, Mike," Nancy requested as she took the bags of food into the kitchen, placing them on the granite countertop. "The place needs an airing out. I can tell we haven't been here for two weeks with that musty smell present."

Mike walked over to the doors, pulling back on the vertical blinds, before sliding back the heavy glass, and opening the hurricane shutters afterwards. The breeze from the ocean immediately blew in, clearing the room of any offensive odor that Nancy had noticed. *"Is that any better?"* he grinned.

"Yes, dear," she answered, placing the fruit and milk in the refrigerator.

He joined her in the kitchen, assisting her with the last of the bags, placing the chips and pretzels, along with the cereal, on an empty shelf of the pantry. "William knows we are in town and he said he plans to stop by yet tonight."

"Oh, really? I hadn't planned on making dinner tonight," Nancy confessed.

Mike planted a light kiss on her lips. "That's why there's pizza," he laughed. "You know William never tires of pizza!"

"Well, that makes two of you!" she replied cutely. "Would you be so kind as to bring in the suitcases now, and then I will order a couple large ones? That way William can take some back to his place when he leaves later."

"He's not even here yet and you're trying to get rid of him already?"

Nancy shook her head, always being entertained by her husband.

"Seriously, Mike?" she said with a pretend pout as she placed her hands on her slim hips. "Hurry before William gets here. I want to be all ready when he arrives."

"Your wish is my command," he bowed, as he walked towards the door to grab their suitcases, making Nancy giggle. She in turn, ordered the two large pizzas – one with pepperoni and cheese and the other with mushroom and sausage. Mike brought in the suitcases as Nancy hurriedly unpacked them just in the nick of time, hearing William opening the front door without knocking first.

"I made it!" he announced, just as his grandparents reappeared from their master bedroom. *"I'm hoping you ordered these two pizzas since some guy just handed them to me?"* he questioned with a grin.

"We sure did," Nancy replied, happy to see her wonderful grandson as William placed the pizzas on the table by the paper plates that she had laid out. "We also have soft drinks in the refrigerator if you would like one," she reminded, even though they were always there.

William reached out to warmly hug each one of them, planting a kiss on Nancy's cheek besides. "I missed you guys. I'm glad you made it down one last time before I go back to college. I wasn't sure if it was going to happen or not."

"Of course we were planning this trip to see you!" Nancy smiled as she gave Mike and William each a paper plate. "And I'm hoping you will come home to Baltimore a few days before you go back to Towson."

"Of course, Nan. How could I say no to a few days of your pampering?" Will teased, fondly looking at both of his grandparents.

"Have you enjoyed your time here this summer?" Mike asked, biting into the chewy crust of his pepperoni pizza.

"I have…. very much. The job has been great and I have made some new friends," Will added, taking a big gulp of Coke.

"Any female friends?" Nancy pried.

"Actually, yes, Nan. I have a girlfriend and her name is Brooke."

Nancy looked up, studying William in surprise with her pizza still hanging from her hand. *"A girlfriend? Like in a steady girlfriend?"*

Will began to laugh, as Mike joined in along with him. "Yes, Nan, there is finally another female in my life that makes me happy, *but no one will ever compare to you!"* he over-dramatized.

Nancy began to shake her head, enjoying William's humor. "Flattery will get you everywhere, dear boy."

"I certainly hope so…" he grinned, getting up to get a second soda. "Her name is Brooke and I didn't set out to get involved with anyone this summer, but it just sorta happened. She is really cool."

Mike walked to the kitchen and found his bottle of Tanqueray along with some tonic and lime. *"No one plans to fall in love,"* he mentioned matter-of-factly, while pouring a healthy libation into the large glass in front of him.

"Who said anything about love?" Will commented, not wanting to admit his true feeling about Brooke already. "We're taking things slowly. She goes to Maryland – which isn't really that far away - so I guess we can still hook up from time to time."

"Hook up?" Nancy asked, looking puzzled.

"Yeah, it means we will see each other, Nan."

Nancy's face lit up with an idea, looking warmly at her grandson. "Why don't you invite her to dinner tomorrow night? Sarah, Lance and twins will be here also, and it would be nice for everyone to meet her!"

William glanced over at Mike, as he was finishing up his cocktail. "There is no sense arguing with her. You know she always gets her way!" Mike shrugged.

"Michael Miller! I am not that bad!"

The guys began to laugh and shake their heads – *yes* - in unison, as Mike rejoined the table and Nancy sat in silence pondering things.

"Yes, Brooke will be invited. I already gave her the heads up you were coming to town and that you would probably want to meet her. So don't worry, Nan, I will see if she is free for dinner tomorrow night."

Nancy suddenly lit up, patting William lovingly on the arm. "I only want what's best for you, Will. I hope you realize that."

"Of course I do, Nan."

Dinner was over and the extra pizza was placed in a large plastic Ziploc bag, with the directive from Nancy being *that the remainder needed to go home with Will for him and his roommates.* They made their way to the living room with Nancy grabbing the sofa and Mike and William choosing the recliners. The sound of the waves could be heard in the distance as the group relaxed and talked, and Mike turned on the TV.

"Do you mind keeping that off for a bit?" Will requested, looking at his grandfather. "I have something I want to speak with you about - if that's okay?"

"Of course!" Mike agreed, turning off the television again with the remote. *"What's on your mind?"* he asked, turning his attention completely to William.

Will paused, taking a deep cleansing breath before beginning. "I had a visit from someone who I haven't seen in quite a long time."

"And whom might that be, dear?" Nancy asked sweetly, waiting patiently for the answer, thinking it was one of his college friends that had showed up unexpectedly for a beach visit.

"Mitchell Robbins... my mother's husband - if you remember him. He came here all the way from Birmingham, Alabama to talk with me."

Nancy's eyes widened and her hand went up to her mouth in surprise and shock, not knowing what to say, as Mike looked on silently in pure disbelief, ready to hear more.

William glanced at both of them, knowing they were not prepared for the news. "It's okay guys. He was only here for two days and he is gone now. So stop worrying. Everything is okay!"

CHAPTER 48

Nancy began to cry, suddenly fearful and very concerned that Mitchell Robbins had been around William. *"Did you call the police?"*

"Nan, stop worrying! No, I didn't call the police. We talked and actually things seem somewhat better now between us. He claims he's a changed man. I guess time will tell if it's for real, but for some reason I do believe what he is telling me to be factual. His old temper didn't flare once, and he definitely wasn't drinking."

Mike looked at Nancy, concerned with her emotional state. "It's okay, dear. Will is an adult now and I'm sure he can handle Mitchell."

"Yeah, G-Dad, I can. He wanted my blessing to marry my aunt Jen and I hesitated, but finally said I'm cool with it. Lance was around when he first showed up at Beach Dreams, and then the three of us talked in his office. Things got somewhat tense, but Lance kept it civil between us. I agreed to have dinner with him and then we met one more time at Beach Dreams before he left town."

Nancy gulped, trying to regain her composure. *"You can't honestly be considering going to that wedding are you?"*

"I am considering it, Nan. I know I have you guys now in my life to lean on if something were to come up. Plus, I want to be there for aunt Jen as well as Eva and Jackson too."

Nancy rose from the sofa to go to the kitchen, ready to wash the last remaining few dishes that were left in the sink, with Mike and Will trailing close behind. "Can I help you, Nan, with anything?"

"Not a thing, William," she answered, trying to control her emotions as she looked down at the sudsy water of the sink, realizing the dishwashing helped to relax her.

"Thanks for dinner," he said giving her a quick kiss on the cheek goodbye. "I hate to leave, but I gotta get home and get to bed because I work early in the morning. You definitely don't need any help?" Will asked a second time, just to make sure.

"I have everything covered," she lied with a smile. "Please take the pizza along with you."

"Why don't you guys keep it and have it for tomorrow's lunch?"

"Nonsense!" Mike replied, finding the large Ziploc bag filled with pizza in the refrigerator, handing it over to Will before he left. "We will see you tomorrow then? Dinner will be at 6."

"I will be here," Will grinned at his grandfather. "And yes, Nan, I will be bringing Brooke along as long as she is free."

"We are looking forward to meeting her," Mike answered, knowing Nancy was upset, so he needed to do the speaking for the both of them. "Drive safely. I'm going to have one more drink and enjoy my deck now."

"You do that," Will chuckled and waved. "Have a good night."

Will pulled out onto Beach Road and reached for his cellphone, realizing he had a missed call from Brooke and he needed to call her back. "Hello beautiful," he said with a smile, as he returned the call.

"Well aren't you being sweet," Brooke answered.

"I try... Hey, I'm sorry I didn't answer. I was with my grandparents at their place. We had dinner and then we were talking."

"I understand," she replied, as she slipped into some shorts and a t-shirt after just getting home from work. *"Did you want to do something tonight?"*

"If you don't mind, I think I'm going to go to bed early. I'm beat from my long day, but I do have a question... "

"What's that?"

"My grandparents are hosting a picnic tomorrow evening at their beach house - The Dancing Seahorse. Would you like to join me or do you have to work?"

Brooke thought for a moment before answering, knowing she could pick up an extra shift. The summer was coming to a close and some of the wait staff had already left for the season, but then she also wanted to be with Will. "It is my normal day off, so yes, I can make it. I would love to join you for a picnic!"

"My aunt and uncle with be there also, along with their twins. Still okay with all of that?"

Brooke began to laugh, as she propped herself up with several pillows on her bed, realizing she should have changed into pajamas now instead of the shorts she had on. "I think I'm up for the challenge of meeting your family - as long as they are as nice as you," she teased, hoping that to be the case.

"They're the best!" Will boasted, honestly feeling that way about his family. "I will pick you up by 5:45 at your place since dinner will be at six o'clock."

"Do I need to dress up?"

"Nope. It will be very casual. I can't wait to see you again!" Will confessed, suddenly having second thoughts and wishing he could see her now, even though he was too tired to do so.

"Me too…." Brooke sighed, feeling her own fatigue. "Sleep well, babe."

"Yeah… You too… " He answered tiredly, drifting off to sleep soon thereafter.

William sat in his Jeep with the motor idling, waiting on Brooke who was already five minutes late. She slammed the front door of the townhouse that she and her friends were renting for the summer, making her way over to the passenger's side of the car before jumping in. Will looked up from his cellphone, as he busily typed a text message to Mike, explaining *that they were running a bit behind and would be there soon.*

"I'm sorry, Will. My roommates were arguing over something that required my input," Brook said giving an excuse, as William quickly pulled out and headed towards The Dancing Seahorse.

"No worries," he smiled, looking quite handsome and polished with his khaki shorts and white polo shirt on. Brooke noticed he had showered and his hair was still wet and combed back, and his arms looked tan and muscular as he clutched the steering wheel.

Will turned to look at her for a second time, once he was out on the busy tourist-filled Beach Road, finding her very captivating in her white spaghetti strap sundress with her blonde hair flowing freely. "You look amazing!" he complimented as he maneuvered quickly through the traffic.

"Do you think so? I'm just a little nervous about meeting your family."

"Don't be," he said with a sideways grin. "They will love you."

Brooke smiled back, trying to contain her nervousness. "Should we have brought something to eat or drink? Or maybe flowers?"

Will reached out to touch her knee, squeezing it lightly. "Not necessary. My Nan always makes too much food and she could care less about flowers."

"Okay... " Brooke answered, hoping Will was right.

He pulled quickly into The Dancing Seahorse gravel driveway, stopping with a jolt as he parked beside of Lance's Jeep that was already there. "Sorry about that," he confessed, running around to open the door on Brooke's side of the car. He grabbed her hand, helping her down, before planting a quick kiss on her lips. "You look very pretty."

"Thank you," Brooke gushed, loving his compliments as much as she loved him. They made their way towards the beach house and the smell of barbeque filled the air. The still warm, but turned-off gas grill was sitting off to one side and now empty, from whatever was just being cooked. Will didn't hesitate as they climbed the steps together and he opened the door, seeing a room filled with his noisy relatives deeply engrossed in conversation with each other.

"Well hello," Nancy beamed, realizing it was William and his beautiful girlfriend that she was seeing for the very first time. *"Welcome to The Dancing Seahorse,"* she greeted, as Will steered Brooke into the kitchen for his family's scrutiny.

Sarah sat at the table holding and bouncing Abigail on one knee trying to calm her down as she spoke with Nancy, as Lance stood off to one side - deep in conversation with Mike - with Alexander positioned on one of his hips, as Will and Brooke approached.

All attention turned towards Brooke as she broke into a pleasant sunny smile with Will's introduction. *"Everyone, this is my girlfriend, Brooke Hatfield."*

"Glad to meet you," Lance grinned, not quite sure she was one of the remaining partygoers that had been hiding and needed to be kicked out, from the notorious summer party at The Happy Crab that left the place in shambles.

"You too," she smiled back timidly; thinking she vaguely remembered him also from the same earlier summer event.

Sarah stood and walked around the table, introducing herself as well as the twins, reaching out her hand in Brooke's direction. "It is so nice to finally meet you," she smiled politely, as Abby grabbed Sarah's ponytail and gave it a tug.

"Well, you too. Your children are beautiful."

"And so are you, dear," Nancy piped in, making Brooke blush by her sweet compliment.

"Thank you, Mrs. Miller," she answered, feeling somewhat embarrassed, as Will put a protective arm around her waist, pulling her in closer to his side. "Your home is lovely," she added, trying to make conversation as she looked over in Mike and Nancy's direction. Nancy was organizing everything with Mike's help as the food was being scooped out into bowls and arranged on serving platters, being set up in a buffet-style line, making it super easy and relaxed for everyone to help themselves. Hamburgers and hotdogs were offered, along with the side dishes of pasta salad, corn on the cob and deviled eggs. Nancy cut up melon - especially for the twins - and baked chocolate cupcakes with chocolate buttercream icing for desert.

"Grab a plate, Brooke, the rule here is the newest guest to The Dancing Seahorse gets to go first," Mike explained, as he gestured for her to come his way. "And we have room out on the deck for everyone to sit," he added with a friendly smile.

She approached the *food line* with Mike handing her a disposable, oversized oval plate. "Thank you," she said shyly as she accepted it, with Will following close behind, focused on the food only. She sampled each dish, not wanting to be impolite for not trying everything, but not wishing to look unladylike either by taking too much.

"It's okay to take whatever you would like," Will whispered against her hair, for the others not to hear.

Brooke shook her head with a nervous, self-conscious smile, knowing he had read her thoughts. She balanced her plate as Nancy handed her a sweet tea in the other as she waited on William. He did not hold back, filling his plate to full and overflowing - without concern as to what his family was thinking.

"It's okay to get seconds," Nancy gently scolded him, looking at her grandson's generous libation.

"I know, Nan, but it is hard to resist taking everything right away when it's you doing the cooking," he complimented, making her take notice to his kind words.

"Oh, William, what am I to do with you?"

Will smiled, with Brooke noticing the fondness between them. She wished that she had the same, since she rarely got to see her grandparents now, and two of them had already passed.

They made their way out to the deck with the others not far behind. The beach was still active with beachgoers who were in the ocean or sitting in their chairs, grasping the last rays of the sun and watching their children at play. It was a beautiful day and one that was worth enjoying – either with a summer picnic or for spending lingering moments on the beach.

Sarah and Lance strapped the twins into their high chairs and then presented them with finger food, which they greedily devoured, keeping them occupied and distracted for a few minutes. Will and Brooke took their seats close by, as Nancy and Mike joined the others. She brought out a pitcher of iced tea, setting it down in the middle of the table, while Mike waited patiently holding on to his plate and hers, waiting for Nancy to sit down and finally relax.

"It's time to eat!" Nancy announced, after Mike placed the plate of food in front of her and he said a quick prayer of thanks.

They ate in silence, until Sarah broke the ice after finishing her ear of sweet Silver Queen corn. "So Brooke, where do you attend college?"

Brooke wiped her mouth on her napkin, before she answered. "I attend The University of Maryland - College Park campus."

"So did I! Go Terrapins!" Sarah yelled, giving Brooke a broad smile, with both of them now realizing what they had in common.

"And what is your major?" she continued, with her same line of questioning.

"Right now I plan to go into teaching."

"Very good!" Nancy jumped in. "Did William ever tell you that I was a elementary school teacher at one time?"

"No he didn't," Brooke answered, looking at Nancy and then at William.

Will laughed, shaking his head and looking at everyone. "No Nan, we don't typically talk about school that much. We have been trying to forget about all that for a few weeks, especially since we are going back to college soon."

"We get it," Lance interjected, shaking his head and placing some more of the cut up watermelon and cantaloupe on each of the twins' trays. "Just look at that sky and those brilliant colors," he marveled,

trying to change the subject as the sun began to dip low towards the horizon. "It doesn't get any prettier than this in Marlin Beach."

Will felt content after sharing such a wonderful picnic with his family and girlfriend, admiring the sunset that Lance had just pointed out. He reached for Brooke's hand as they sat closely together, gazing at her beautiful face as she smiled sweetly back at him. William sighed, feeling there was only one thing prettier than the brilliant colors displayed in front of them – Brooke Hatfield – the girl that he loved.

CHAPTER 49

"Are you almost ready?" Will asked impatiently, as he idled in the gravel parking area of Brooke's place.

"Sorry hon, I'll be right out. Just running a little behind," she confessed, grabbing her beach bag that was already stuffed with her brightly colored stripped beach towel and SPF suntan lotion.

Will smiled as he saw his girlfriend who was dressed in very short, cut-off blue jeans that were frayed and faded, and a black string bikini top, jogging towards his red Jeep. She jumped into the passenger's side, tossing her bag to the seat behind her, as he leaned in to give her a tender morning kiss.

"It's okay you're running a little late. It gave me a chance to think about what we could get in to today. Maybe the beach and then dinner afterwards?"

Brooke smiled, looking somewhat down. "Anything works... but of course I want our beach time together."

Will pulled out onto Beach Road, taking in her demeanor. *"Why the sad face?"*

She sighed, thinking how she should answer him. "I don't know... we are all leaving soon to go back to college. I guess that's it," she replied distantly, looking at him with a faint smile.

Will reached out to pat her knee as he drove off a side street towards the beach. "Babe, we're a couple now. I will see you as much as I can. Don't worry, I'm not going anywhere," he winked, as he pulled the Jeep to a sudden stop near to the beach access path directly in front of them. "I brought a cooler with ice and water, and already picked up a couple chairs and the umbrella from my grandparent's place since she insisted on hooking us up with sandwiches and fruit."

Brooke broke into a sunny smile, suddenly happy for the day ahead. "She's a real sweet lady, Will. You are lucky to have her in your life."

"Yes, I am," he simply replied, knowing that to be the case.

They walked together from the Jeep, grabbing all the beach items, before heading for the soft sand and shoreline in the distance. "My Nan is very special but so is my G-Dad. I don't know where I would be in my life without them," he mentioned, now the one with the thoughtful look on his face.

Will placed the umbrella securely in the sand, opening it along with the two chairs. The flaps of the umbrella snapped softly up and down from the sea breeze, as they sat down and enjoyed a bottle of chilled water. The seagulls were dipping up and down off of the ocean waves, catching fish and retreating away to another destination, as children and adults sunned themselves or played in the ocean or built sand castles. It was another perfect day to be at the beach with barely a cloud in the azure blue-sky overhead.

Brooke looked at William who was taking in the scenery, studying his tanned muscular physique with his teal bathing suit shorts riding low on hips, exposing a fringe of his public hair to her view.

"What?" he said with sensual toothy smile, realizing she was staring at him, even if behind her black sunglasses.

Brooke smiled back with her equally attractive smile that was perfect in every way - from the braces she wore many years earlier in middle school. "Just thinking that I don't really know a whole lot about you - outside of the few details that you have shared."

Will's smile suddenly turned into a tightly pursed line of his lips, not sure where she was going with things and not sure he wanted to divulge any more of the details of his life. "I can say the same about you…."

"True," Brooke acknowledged. "What do you want to know?"

"Do you have any brothers or sisters?"

"One sister and two brothers," she said matter-of-factly.

"Wow, I would have never guessed!"

Brooke began to laugh. "Well, Will, typically we have had other things on our mind when we have been together - if you catch my drift."

Will leaned in to give her a warm kiss that was already moist from the hotness of the day. *"Has that been so bad?"* he asked enticingly.

"Not at all," she answered. "It's been more than amazing," she replied, opening her mouth for another tongue kiss. "So I know you had a visitor. I guess I am just trying to put all the pieces together. That's all."

William looked over at Brooke, trying to decide if he wanted to reveal anymore of his life to her. He breathed deeply, trying to clear his thoughts, as he looked again out to sea. He grabbed her hand and held it securely as she patiently waited for him to begin. "I will share with you about my past, but I'm asking you to keep what I am about to tell you between you and I. I honestly am a private person and I don't like to talk about any of this. I don't need for your roommates or mine to be talking about all this stuff back and forth."

"You have my word, Will. I would never reveal anything to the others."

"My mother grew up in Baltimore and met my dad in high school where they shared some mutual classes. From what I gather, they became close while doing a school project together after class." He gulped and paused, squeezing Brooke's hand for support. "My mother became pregnant with me during that time, and my mother kept the pregnancy a secret from her family and even from my father, since they were so young. My grandparents, on my dad's side, own a beach house called The Dancing Seahorse – that you were at last night. Many years ago, my dad came here with his twin sister, Sarah, for a vacation."

"Your aunt that I just met last night at dinner?"

"Exactly," Will answered, before continuing. "Dex and Sarah wanted to come to the beach for a few days before their parents arrived. They were to begin college in a couple weeks and they just wanted some time alone to enjoy Marlin Beach without adults supervising and bossing them around."

"That's understandable," she interjected sweetly, fascinated with his tale.

Will sighed, finding it very difficult to continue. "My aunt Sarah and my dad decided to go boogie boarding one sunny, but very windy day. Unfortunately, something very bad ended up happening."

"What?" she asked, now needing to hear the conclusion to the story.

"It was a riptide…. They both got caught up in one. My aunt survived, but my father didn't." Brooke's hand went up to her mouth in shock, from hearing the revelation. "He lingered in the hospital for one week in a coma and then eventually died."

Brooke squeezed Will's hand compassionately, lost with emotion. *"I am sooo sorry Will... I would have never guessed."*

"Who would?" he answered, hiding behind his own black sunglasses. *"There is more though... "*

"Okay... "

"My uncle Lance was the lifeguard that attempted to rescue my dad that day."

"No way! How is the possible?"

"I know, right? It's a miracle my aunt Sarah is even married to him, because she held him responsible for her brother's death for a very long time. But they made peace, obviously, since they are happily married with their kids - Abby and Alex."

"So how does the man that just visited you come into the story?"

Will shook his head distantly, finding it hard to answer. "My mother's father was a pastor and he was very strict. When he finally figured out that she was pregnant – I guess with her stomach getting larger - he sent her off to Birmingham, Alabama to live with her aunt Jean. My mother met someone shortly thereafter at the church where she attended. His name was Mitchell and they got married rather quickly, from what my mother told me – trying to save her reputation. They had two kids together – Eva and Jackson – and that is where I spent my life up until age sixteen when I moved away to Baltimore to live with my Nan and G-Dad."

Brooke looked confused, removing her sunglasses and squinting over in Will's direction. *"I don't understand... Why would you leave your mother and move in with your grandparents in Baltimore?"*

Will ran his hands through his slightly perspired wavy brown locks, knowing Brooke would not be satisfied until he totally spilled his guts. *"You really want to know all this, don't you?"*

"Yes!" she challenged, waiting for him to continue.

"My mother, Claire, got sick with ovarian cancer, and died when I was only sixteen."

"Oh my God, Will, I am so sorry!" Brooke cried out again, feeling totally shaken by his plight.

"Thank you, but I'm fine now. I wasn't then, but I have made peace with things since that time. While my mother was ill, I had decided to find my dad's family that she always spoke about privately to me. My stepfather, Mitchell - who by the way was the one visiting me - didn't like my mom and I talking about my birth father so we would wait to have private conversations about him when Mitchell wasn't around and out of the house, or when he was sleeping."

"It wasn't easy in the beginning when I reached out to the Miller's. I got on a bus without my mother's knowledge, and came here to Marlin Beach to meet my aunt Sarah. She was very angry and said she didn't believe me that I was Dexter's son."

"Dexter - like in the hotel?"

William smiled, grabbing her hand again. "Yeah, the hotel was named after my father. My aunt Sarah and my G-Dad were the architects who designed the resort and that was their one request with the owners - that they would name the resort *The Dexter* in honor of him."

"That is very kind that they agreed to that."

"Yes, it was, but I think it has a great ring to it anyway," he grinned, planting a playful kiss on her lips. "Don't you want to swim instead of talking about such serious stuff?"

"I want you to finish, Will. I am understanding things better now, but not about your stepfather."

"Okay, okay... I will tell you," he sighed, knowing she wasn't going to give up until he got it all out. "Mitchell wasn't nice to me. Matter-of-fact, he was a *fucking asshole!* He was an alcoholic that abused me and my mother - especially when I was younger. His kids - Eva and Jackson - were never touched, but unfortunately for me that was a different story...."

"Will... " Brooke cried out in disbelief, with tears suddenly moistening her eyes from the past world that he was forced to live in and survive.

"You wanted to hear all this, so now I am on a roll," he replied, feeling driven and determined for her to hear the rest of his tale. "Aunt Sarah told my G-Dad about me visiting her, and thank God he hired a private investigator to get to the bottom of things. Because of his persistence, my whole life changed for the better. Yes, my mom died, but thankfully in her Last Will And Testament she spelled it out clearly that my guardians were to be my Nan and G-Dad Miller. Mitchell was in rehab at the time of my mother's death, and my aunt Jen was assigned to be the guardian of Eva and Jackson. My mother did make a concession though, for Mitchell, that if he could get his life together he could share in the parenting duties again along with my aunt."

Brooke sat in amazement taking in his every word, as she and Will began to eat the ham and Swiss cheese sandwiches that Nan had packed for their lunch. *"Did he ever get his act together?"*

Will shook his head, giving it some thought, as he chuckled nervously. "Well, I certainly hope so.... since he came here to tell me just that. He claims he's *a changed man from going to rehab and attending church. He wants to marry my aunt because he has fallen in love with her."*

"You are kidding, right?" Brooke asked in surprise, realizing Will had bottled up so much.

"No, Brooke, I am not kidding. He honestly does seem different - I must admit - and I did promise to give him another chance by attending their wedding."

"This is so unbelievable, Will. My life is so dull compared to yours."

"I would trade *dull* any day, compared to what I have been through in my life."

Brooke stood to her feet, staring down at her handsome boyfriend, trying to ease his worries. "I think I am up for that swim now, if you are?"

"You don't need to ask me a second time," he grinned, jumping to his feet and grabbing her hand as they ran for the shoreline together.

CHAPTER 50

The day at the beach, along with dinner afterwards at Old Bay Café, was memory making for both of them. William felt amazingly cleansed for sharing his past with Brooke, feeling that he could trust her to keep what he said between them. A dinner of crab cakes and peanut fries were ordered by both as they sat hand in hand enjoying the 2-man ensemble crooning out beach tunes and playing their guitars, while they admired the back bay where the restaurant was situated. Brooke did not hesitate to join William afterwards - back at The Happy Crab - for a shower and then passionate sex afterwards before he took her back to her own place and friends.

It was the next day and everyone was up early at the Towson roommates' summer place, each needing to go to their individual jobs that had become more demanding timewise, since many of the other workers had already departed for their homes away from the beach.

Matt poured a steaming hot cup of coffee as Chris was staring at his cellphone and his social media feeds, downing a bowl of corn flakes. William entered the kitchen, dressed and ready for work with his Beach Dream emblem polo shirt and tan khaki slacks on.

"Long night for you again, bud?" Chris slurred out lazily, still trying

to wake up from one too many beers the night before.

"Oh yeah... " Will said, shaking his head up and down with a playful, devilish lift to his eyes.

Matt began to laugh. "You better break this off soon, or you're gonna have one heck of an upset chick when we go back to college."

"No plans for that," Will answered simply, turning towards the counter to pour his own bowl of cereal and milk.

"No plans for what?" Tyler pried, coming into the room last, trying to catch up with the conversation.

"Will and his dick don't want to say goodbye to Brooke before we leave Marlin Beach soon. The poor girl is gonna be heart-broken from the *lover boy* here."

"Whatever... " Will replied while taking a big bite of cereal, rolling his eyes at his *know-it-all* friend - Chris - who was more like a brother. "We plan to keep seeing each other even after the summer. Maryland isn't that far of a drive from Towson."

"True, but she could lose interest," Tyler interjected, grabbing a granola bar and soda from the fridge. "Hey, talking about leaving, I wanted to let you guys know that I plan to roll out tomorrow for Florida. I've been talking to my parents and they want me to come home to Fort Lauderdale for a few days before I go back to school."

"Do they miss, little Tyler Wyler?" Chris teased, being a total ass to everyone and not picking any favorites.

"Chris, seriously, shut the fuck up!" Matt exclaimed, having his fill of his mouthy friend so early in the morning. "Well, we better have some fun tonight if this is the last time that the group will be together here at the beach. God, I hate to think that our summer in Marlin Beach is almost over and we gotta go back to college soon. I feel like we just got here."

"Yeah, I agree... " Will admitted sadly, rinsing out his bowl and putting it in the dishwasher, just in case Lance showed up to do a surprise house inspection, which he was known to do from time to time. "Why don't you guys talk to Brooke's friends about meeting up with us after work, and then we can all hang out on the boardwalk and come back here for some beers later? I will also mention it to Brooke when we talk."

"Sounds like a plan!" Matt replied, adding his bowl to the dishwasher too. I can always hit up Amber and let her know.

"Yeah, and I'll say something to the others once I get to work," Chris chimed in, not wanting to be left out.

William pulled into Beach Dreams realizing that Lance as well as his parents - Alison and John - were already there and parked. The real estate agents, that Lance had hired, were nowhere to be found and were probably out on showings. Will made his way back to his office, passing by the others with a hand wave in their direction, seeing that they were all preoccupied with phone calls.

Will started his computer with more papers waiting on him that needed to be added to the system. Lance had agreed to giving him the day off prior, after he explained that h*e just wanted a total day to hang out with Brooke alone, since they had never gotten a chance to do so the entire summer.*

It was well worth the cost of having to catch up with work now after the amazing day he had just spent with her. To be able to open up and tell Brooke his story with any judgment, besides getting to know her better outside of the bedroom, was a turning point in their relationship. It still amazed him that he had met her at the beach and how well they clicked. It wasn't the ideal thing to continue seeing her since they were attending different colleges, but Will was focused on continuing the relationship after the summer, as was Brooke.

After all, she is beautiful, kind and loving – and the way she listened to my story and then showed me how much she cared – I will do anything to make this work! He thought as he daydreamed at his computer thinking about her.

Lance poked his head around the corner, seeing William in a daze. "Earth to Will," he laughed. *"You seem deep in thought."*

"Oh, sorry uncle Lance. I was just thinking about my day yesterday with Brooke."

"Is that a good or bad thing?" Lance asked, trying to pick his brain.

"Oh, very good! Matter-of-fact, you could say it was perfect!" Will confessed, breaking out into a very pleased grin. "Brooke is the best. I'm still pinching myself that I met her here. What were the chances of that?"

Lance was the next to smile mischievously. "Marlin Beach is a very special place. That is for sure... Remember, I met your aunt Sarah here too - which I am very grateful for."

Will's cellphone began to ring as Lance nodded and slipped away, remembering he hadn't called Brooke as he had planned. "Hey babe, I'm sorry that I haven't call you," he explained after she greeted him. "It's just been a crazy morning with lots of paperwork that I'm trying to catch up on since I was off yesterday."

"No worries," Brooke replied, while taking her lunch break. "Mia said that Tyler is leaving town tomorrow and that you guys wanted to get together tonight. *Is that true?"*

"It most definitely is!" William answered, reaching for his own packed peanut butter and strawberry jelly sandwich, as he continued to work and eat at the same time. "I'm honestly surprised that Tyler has a sudden urge to leave for Florida, but I get family wanting to spend time with you before college starts again. My Nan is asking the same of me."

Brooke thought of William's words, also desiring to go home for some quality family time before college began, but being torn about leaving Will all the same. "I don't want to leave Marlin Beach or you…. " She said distantly.

"It will be okay, Brooke. *We will work this out.*"

"I know we will," she replied happily.

"Why don't we all meet up at The Happy Crab tonight, and then we can eat on the boardwalk and get on some rides? Maybe even play some Skee-Ball and walk out on the pier - if everybody wants to."

"I'm up for that and I'm sure the girls will be also. I will text you when we are ready. If I had to guess, it will be around 7."

"I can't wait to see you later," Will whispered. *"I want a repeat of last night."*

Brooke giggled, now doing the whispering. *"What part – getting your back washed in the shower or the hot sex afterwards?"*

"Both," he teased. *"See you soon."*

Seven-thirty and Brooke texted William – "Be there soon. Rachel and Amber had to work late. Mia and I have been patiently waiting until the others were ready."

"Everyone is here - present and ready. Can't wait to see you!"

"Me too!"

The car skidded into the gravel parking lot, spraying a few loose stones in the air. "I think they're here," Matt announced, peaking out from behind the blind. *"They're looking hot!"* he added, as the girls made their way up the porch steps, sashaying all the way.

The door flew open to an array of scantily dressed females who were obviously trying to allure the males on the other side of the door of The Happy Crab. Each had on very short shorts, with see-through tank tops and barely-there lingerie type bras underneath. The guys took notice as the females pranced around in front of them, much like *bitches in heat.*

"Whatcha say we get goin now?" Will suggested, after grabbing Brooke and kissing her openly with the others watching as they were starting their evening out with a beer.

"Sure," Chris replied, ready and willing to pair off and do his own intense kissing later with Mia.

They made their way to the boardwalk, enjoying the walk and the camaraderie between them. The tram was still boarding passengers as they all climbed on board and chose their preferred seats. The gentle rocking of the trolley cars, relaxed everyone on board as they passed by the many tourists that were walking past the famous eateries, shops and hotels along the way. Finally, they made it to the other end, where the majority departed, ready to begin their night of fun activities.

"I'm starving!" Chris groaned, looking at the long line in front of the pizza stand.

"Why don't we get fries first?" Will suggested, with his arm already wrapped around Brooke's waist. "Surprisingly, that line isn't that long."

"Cuz we don't normally do so in that order," Chris answered, as he grabbed and rubbed his empty, hungry belly.

Everyone laughed, looking at Chris and shaking their heads as they walked towards their favorite French fry stand.

"Go with the flo, bro," Tyler leaned in and mentioned quietly to Chris as they stood in line now for fries first instead of the pizza. "You

don't want to look stupid in front of the girls if you want *some pussy* later at the end of the evening."

"Whatever," he answered with a shrug, acting as if he couldn't care less.

The fries were purchased with Will paying for Brooke's. They ate quietly as they looked out over the seawall towards the ocean in front of them, tossing a few fries in the sand for the seagulls, which dipped down and fought for them greedily before flying away. It was already past eight and the beach was still very active with people who had not packed it up for the day or were just now venturing down to the water's edge. Pizza was gotten next, before they made their way to the rides and then finally to The Sun And Fun Playhouse to play some Skee-Ball, as rock music from a few bars could be heard playing in the distance. The *swirling cone* sign of the ice cream stand beckoned as they each chose their favorite flavor with a few getting sprinkles besides, walking together afterwards out to the fishing pier with their cones still in hand. The fishermen were busily casting out their lines and cleaning their fish, with everyone watching and being fascinated. After some time, Tyler insisted that they return to the boards so that he could purchase an assortment of taffy and candy corn for his family back home in Florida.

"Why don't we get on the Ferris Wheel before we go back to the beach house?" Brooke suggested, looking at everyone for their approval. "Those would be some great pictures to show your family," Brooke hinted, looking in Tyler's direction.

"I agree!" Tyler replied with his bags of candy corn and taffy now in hand, as they made their way towards the large circular ride that Marlin Beach was well known for.

Each of the friends paired off, side by side, male to female, as they stepped together onto the platform of the Ferris Wheel – Brooke with William, Mia with Chris, Matt with Amber, and Tyler with Rachel. The merry sound of a pre-recorded pipe organ played loudly, as the bright colorful lights twinkled around the sides of the ride, raising them high in the air above the Marlin Beach boardwalk skyline.

Will wrapped his arm securely around Brooke's shoulder, hugging her in closely as she laid her head contentedly on him, taking in the beauty of the night sky and picturesque beach town below.

"Everything is so peaceful and perfect up here, don't you think?" she asked Will, as he gazed out over the ocean that held many memories from times past of being up there. He remembered when he moved in with his Nan and G-Dad, how they had brought him to Marlin Beach and introduced him to the Ferris wheel. As he was on it for the very first time, his thoughts wandered to his mom and dad – hoping that somehow they were watching out for him from heaven above.

"Yeah, it's a great place to be – especially when you're in love with someone," he reminded, hugging her closer.

Brooke smiled, looking serenely into Will's vivid, steel blue eyes. "Can we just stop time and stay up here forever? It's our last night together with everyone - and I wish it wasn't so."

Will reached down to give Brooke a deep, passionate tongue kiss as the ride made another rotation. "Hopefully, we will all come back next summer and be together again."

"I hope so too…." Brooke sighed, lost in the moment, as Will's lips met hers again for the umpteenth time.

CHAPTER 51

Will rolled over with a hard-on, realizing it was morning as he snuggled in closer to Brooke's backside. They were still nude and he was ready to go again, even if he was suffering with a slight hangover.

The group had made their way back from the boardwalk and had decided to give Tyler one heck of a going away party, as they emptied the refrigerator of all the remaining beer and several bottles of wine that were still uncorked in the pantry.

They had learned after a season of being at Marlin Beach, that it was better to have *unannounced* low-key parties, if they wanted to stay out of trouble with Lance. So they drank and lit the outdoor Tiki lights, trying to be quiet and stay off the neighbor's radar. In time, everyone paired off for *make-out* sessions on the beach and ultimately sex afterwards - throughout the night.

Chris and Matt had given Tyler his choice of females to hang out with, but it was pretty well known he was favoring Rachel every time they were in a group and he was around her. He wasn't taking it to Will's level of announcing his intentions for a serious relationship with Rachel just yet – still craving the attention of the Towson chicks - but he also enjoyed the time that he spent with her too.

William and Brooke were the first to say goodnight, with Will promising to say his goodbyes to Tyler in the morning before he left. Now that the morning was upon them, he was tired and not sure he could keep his promise as he heard the moving of suitcases in the hallway just outside his bedroom door.

He sat up, rubbing his eyes, trying to chase his pounding headache away.

"You okay," Brooke asked sleepily, looking over at Will with only one eye open.

"Yeah, I'm fine. My head just fucking hurts, but I'll live," he grinned painfully, getting up to grab his underwear and shorts off of the floor. "I think I heard Tyler moving around with his suitcases. I just want to say a quick goodbye and then I'll be back," he promised, leaning down to kiss her softly on the cheek.

"I'll be here waiting," she said drowsily, drifting back off to sleep as William tiptoed quietly from the bedroom.

The house was still silent except for Tyler who was gathering his last remaining things, while he waited on the Uber driver to pick him up.

"I wanted to say goodbye," Will whispered.

"Thanks," Tyler answered quietly, suffering with his own hangover.

"Who's picking you up?" Will asked, taking a seat on the couch by his friend.

"An Uber driver."

"That will cost you some bucks going the whole way to BWI."

"I'm not paying for the fare. My parents are," he shrugged, knowing that they could afford it. He planned to sleep the whole way to BWI, and then again on the direct flight to Fort Lauderdale that would only take two and half hours more. Tyler's mom would be at the airport waiting on him, and once she picked him up she would suggest they have lunch somewhere by the water, which was always the norm. She was a caring and thoughtful mother and one who adored her son.

A horn honked in the driveway as Tyler's cellphone began to ring at the same time. *"Hello? Yeah, I'll be out in a minute."* He rose off the sofa with his backpack already strapped on, grabbing hold of the pull handle of his suitcase with one hand and carrying the bags with the taffy and popcorn in the other - ready to leave.

"Hey, take care," Will called after him.

"That's the plan... and I'll see you soon, bro, in a couple weeks when we are back at school."

"Have fun visiting with your folks," William smiled.

"I'll try... " Tyler nodded, still too tired to want to communicate properly.

William walked quietly back the dimly lit hallway again towards his room, shutting the door softly behind him, as Brooke slept. He smiled, looking down at her crazy array of blonde locks lying every which way across the pillow and her face. He could hear the Uber car pulling away as he climbed back in bed after removing his shorts and underwear again, snuggling in close with his penis immediately getting hard from the skin to skin contact.

"Wake up, beautiful," he beckoned as he rubbed up against her, now fully aroused enough to make love again.

"Hmmm?" Brooke answered, half disoriented from sleeping, turning to face Will and rest her head under his chin as she tried to get her bearings and wake up.

His hand reached up to grab a breast and then a nipple, massaging it between two fingers until it hardened. She moaned and opened her eyes, looking up at William who was totally lost with in the moment. He began to kiss her repeatedly and spread her legs apart, needing to fill her with his manhood.

"Oh Brooke, I want you," he moaned, as he climbed on top of her, positioning his shaft in her opening, as he rode her with deliberate slow strokes. She reacted to his every movement, raising her hips and meeting each thrust with one of her own.

They climaxed together with a heated fulfillment that left them weak and perspired, knowing that their sex life had reached a new level of intimacy over the past few occasions of being together. *"That was amazing,"* she smiled, as she reached her arms around Will's waist and held onto him tightly.

"Yes, it was… " Will sighed, feeling ready to fall back to sleep for a couple more hours. "Lance expects me in the office at noon. I told him Tyler was leaving, so he gave me a little extra time to say my goodbyes before going in to work today."

"You better set your alarm," she lightly warned, not wanting the job of waking him up.

"Already done," he confirmed, as they drifted off again - wrapped together as one.

"Hello!" Will called out merrily to Patti, as she grunted back at him, before making his way down the hallway and stopping in Lance's office first.

"Did Tyler leave yet?"

"He did," Will answered, taking a seat opposite Lance's desk. "We had a great time last night with our friends - enjoying the boardwalk and The Happy Crab."

"Hopefully not too much enjoyment at The Happy Crab," Lance said over his reading glasses, giving Will the raised *warning eye* glare.

Will began to laugh, knowing what he was implying. "Everything is fine, uncle Lance. The beach house is still in one piece and we didn't have a wild party - if that is what you are worried about."

"Now did I say I was worried?" Lance rebounded, not wanting to admit to his apprehensions. "I just have my concerns after what happened to the place in the in beginning of the summer – that's all."

"We all make our mistakes, but I think I benefited from mine after having to perform community service at Marlin Beach Ambulance. I feel I leaned a lot from being there. Those guys taught me a lot about ambulance workers and everything they do for the community that I never knew about."

"Well I'm glad you enjoyed your time there and learned a few things. I will pass that on to them the next time I am volunteering for ambulance duty. This all a part of growing up, you know; and remember, I was young once too."

"I think I heard rumors to that affect," Will teased, getting back up from the chair. "I know I got things to do, so I will talk to you later."

"If you're lucky," Lance winked, as William walked from the room. He had grown quite fond of him, appreciating the time he had spent with his nephew while they were together at Beach Dreams working. Will had become a real asset, taking pressure off of him so that he could spend more time with Sarah and the kids during the summer months. Now it was almost time for Will to leave for college, and Lance knew his schedule would become a challenge unless his mother was willing to take back some of her old tasks that were always hers before going on the cruise. His dad had fully recovered from his illness and seemed to be back to his old self, even playing golf almost daily now, so there was no reason Alison couldn't take on more of the old workload if she was willing.

William's cellphone rang, that was lying on his desk, just as he was ready to call it a day. It was his G-Dad calling, which surprised him since he had rarely done so since he had been staying in Marlin Beach. *"Is everything okay?"*

Mike laughed. *"Do I need to have an excuse to call my grandson?"* he asked while driving home from Miller's Architecture, stuck in Baltimore rush hour traffic.

"Absolutely not! You know I always look forward to hearing from you, G-dad," Will answered sincerely, while placing a few things in his backpack and heading out of the office. *"So what's going on?"*

"Nan and I are just trying to figure out when you will be coming home – that's all. I was looking forward to a few days of grilling out and spending time with you in the pool - like we have done in the past."

"Yeah, me too, G-Dad," Will replied, immediately thinking about Brooke and having to say goodbye to her and Marlin Beach. Now, he felt conflicted, wanting to extend the time as long as he could, so that he could be with his girlfriend for just a while longer. "I should talk to Lance and see when it's convenient to leave Beach Dreams, and of course I will need to clean up The Happy Crab - with my roommates' help - before I pack it up and come home."

"I'm not trying to pressure you in any way, but just keep us updated as soon as you know something. Nan likes to plan out meals and make a schedule, as you know."

"Yes, G-Dad, I know that Nan likes to do that!" he laughed, realizing that his grandmother always had good intentions for planning ahead. "I would say by the end of the week I should be home – if that helps."

"That does help. That gives me a timetable and I will let Nan know. You have a nice evening, William."

"And you too, G-Dad. Please give my love to Nan."

"Will do. See you in a few days."

Will drove to The Happy Crab thinking about the conversation that he had just had with his grandfather. It was unfortunately time to wrap things up Marlin Beach and he needed to talk to Brooke again about their future together. She had already called earlier just to let him know that she would be working late that evening at The Dexter, and then planned to just lay low and hang out with her roommates afterwards - since she was still recovering from the *going away party* for Tyler the night before.

"Hey, didn't expect you to be home yet," Will mentioned to Chris, who was sitting alone on the couch in the beach house watching TV.

"Yeah, me too," he moaned. "To be honest, I'm not feeling the best. I worked until 4 and then I asked to leave. Just a damn headache and my stomach feels like I'm going to puke at any moment."

Will sat in the chair beside of the sofa that had luckily came clean after Lance's upholstery cleaners worked their magic, looking at his weary friend. "No one told you to drink half of the beer that was left last night," he scolded good-naturedly, knowing not to take it too far with Chris.

"I won't be doing that again for awhile. That is, until we are back at Towson throwing our *first party of the school year,*" he answered, with a pained expression.

"Take it easy, Tiger. Plenty of time to think about our future parties! I do need to discuss something with you though. School starts again in only two weeks and Tyler is now gone. We got this place to clean up and my grandparents want me home for a few days. *What are your plans?*"

Chris sat up and looked at his friend. "God, the summer went by too fast, right?"

"Yeah, I know… "

"Well, I did hear from my folks and they would like some time with me also. I was thinking about leaving Sunday for home. *That damn Tyler got off the hook with the cleaning, didn't he?*" Chris complained, with dawning awareness.

"Let's cut him a break, bro. We'll just make him do more in the dorm when it's time to clean there. We got this here, between Matt, you and I. So I will let my grandparents know that I will be home Sunday also."

"What about Brooke? Does she know you're leaving soon?"

Will sighed, looking over at his friend with a similar pained expression now showing on his face. *"She doesn't.* She wants time alone with her roommates tonight though, so I guess I will fill her in tomorrow about the plans."

"You really like this chick, don't you?"

"Like, isn't the word. *I love her."*

Chris shook his head, so far away mentally from wanting that same thing at this point with any girl. *"You seriously are gonna limit your choices this soon in your life? What about all the hot babes at Towson who want you?"*

"I'm perfectly fine with Brooke, and besides, now there is more for you, bro!" Will laughed, giving Chris a friendly pat on the back.

He walked from the room to change into his running shorts, a t-shirt and sneakers, disappearing to the shoreline for a quick run as he dialed home.

"Hello, William! How are you?"

"Nan, I'm fine. I'm just calling to let you know I will be home this Sunday to spend a few days with you before I go off to Towson."

Her face lit up with the news, as she looked at Mike happily. "We can't wait until we see you! I have already started making my fun list of activities and all the meals that I want to cook for you."

Will smiled, looking forward to a few days at home with Nan and G-Dad pampering him before his classes began. *It feels so good to be loved*, he thought contentedly, as he jogged a few miles down the beach, with the sun setting low over the ocean.

CHAPTER 52

The last week in Marlin Beach was filled with bittersweet discussions amongst all the roommates that remained. Brooke's family wanted her home too, so the girls reluctantly planned to leave a few days early also. The only one whose family didn't care one way or the other was Matt's. His mother worked two jobs and was a single mother, and his father lived in California and had nothing to do with him now that he was remarried with a new family. It didn't matter to anyone if he stayed in Marlin Beach or came back home. He would be alone anyway for the most part in an apartment, waiting on his mother to get home from work because she worked all of the time. He had come to accept this, and had learned at young age to hide his hurt and focus on being tough just like his mother, who was forced to do so after his father moved away, many years earlier.

William and Brooke were now inseparable after they were done working for the day, seeing each other immediately. They walked on the beach in the evenings, having long discussions and holding hands until the sun dipped low. Brooke spent the night after intense love making sessions, being wrapped in Will's embrace afterwards. Promises were made and repeated that they would continue with their relationship, and nothing or no one would keep them apart.

Now, William was closing down shop at Snyder's Beach Dreams Real Estate. It was his final day of working there, as he walked in the front foyer for the last time that summer. Patti sat with her head bowed, looking once again at her cellphone that she always seemed to be totally consumed with. It amazed Will that she kept her job with her nasty attitude that always overshadowed any amount of work that she managed to get done. "Good morning, Patti. It's a beautiful day today," he grinned, forcing her look up with a scowl on her face.

"*If you say so...* " She grimaced, returning her eyes to her cellphone feed quickly.

Alison was in her husband's office going over a contract with him for a commercial property. He rarely got involved with any aspect of the business anymore, preferring golf to work, but in this case his wife wanted his input with some unusual circumstances that were occurring. "*Again I will say it - call the contractor, Alison!*" he barked out loudly, as Will walked by, hearing the exchange. Lance was on the phone with a client, and he waved and smiled as Will passed by his door on the way back to his office. He sat down at his desk and turned on his computer for the final time, realizing he didn't want to say goodbye just yet to the job or his coworkers. Lance had been very accommodating with his time, and he had really enjoyed working there. He liked meeting new people and learning all about the real estate business.

Lance poked his head in around the doorframe, with a cup of coffee in hand. "So it's hard to believe today is your last day. We will miss you here at Beach Dreams, my friend."

Will looked up at his uncle, being at a loss for words. "Yeah, I will miss you guys too. Even Patti... " He laughed, making Lance laugh too.

"She's not that bad when you get past her icy exterior. My parents have known her for years and believe it or not, she does a good job when push comes to shove."

"*If you say so,*" Will answered, rolling his eyes and shaking his head.

"Sarah and I would like to have you over for dinner one last time before you head out. We know you are leaving in two days, so why not stop by tonight? You can bring Brooke along too if you would like. We are keeping it simple - with just some burgers on the grill."

"I would love to join you guys! And I'll let you know about Brooke once I call her," he added. "I just wanted to take the time to thank you for everything that you did for me and my friends this summer. Without you, I realize I wouldn't have had a nice place to stay or a decent job. I also know you had my back when I got in trouble with the police. I owe you a lot, uncle Lance."

Lance stood quietly, taking it all in, smiling warmly at William with his kind brown eyes. "That's what family does for each other – they have each other's backs. I'm lucky to have you as my only nephew. Well, I got a few calls to make, but we are planning on dinner at six, so if you need to leave a few minutes early today, feel free to do so."

"Thanks, uncle Lance."

"You got it, buddy. Now get back to work!" he teased and pointed at the computer screen, as he walked away.

Will smiled as he picked up his cellphone, ready to call Brooke. "Hey babe, we got a dinner invite tonight at my aunt Sarah's place. Can you make it?"

"Sure! I worked the breakfast shift, as you know, so I should be free to leave at four - even though they always ask me stay later. I will just tell them I have other plans tonight."

"I would appreciate it," he grinned. "Dress casual and I will pick you up at five thirty."

"I'll be ready."

The last few hours went by quickly as William finished the last stack of file folders that needed to be entered into the MLS. He also reviewed some contracts and upcoming settlement paperwork that Lance had just recently showed him how to look over and check for mistakes. Will cleaned up his desk and then looked around the room one last time before turning out the lights and walking down the hall to Lance's office. "I completed everything that you wanted me to do today, and my office is now totally cleaned up."

Lance tilted his head to the side, studying and approving of William's professional appearance, dressed in the Beach Dreams logo shirt and his khaki slacks. "You have really made some great strides in this business over the summer. *Do you know that?"*

"Well, thank you. I appreciate that. But you taught me everything I know," he praised.

"I know you have some time to think about things, but if you want to come back next summer and work here again, we would love to have you!"

Will was pleasantly surprised by the news. "Well thank you, uncle Lance. I will keep that in mind and discuss it with G-Dad and Nan."

"There's no rush in letting me know. Now get going. Aunt Sarah won't want you showing up late!"

"Yes sir!" he saluted, knowing he was teasing him.

Brooke was waiting as William pulled into the driveway, dressed in a pair of white capris and a black tank top with her blonde hair hanging lose and flowing. "Hi gorgeous, would you like a ride?" he grinned, as she jumped into the passenger's side of the Jeep.

"Hey baby," she smiled, reaching across the seat and kissing him sweetly. "I'm a little nervous about going here tonight," Brooke confessed.

Will pulled out onto Beach Road feeding in with the evening tourist traffic. "No need for that since you've already met them. My family loves you!" he answered with a warm smile, looking her over from head to toe. "You look great, by the way."

"So do you," she replied, noticing his light blue polo shirt and tan shorts that he had changed into.

William parked the Jeep in front of The Playful Starfish, escorting Brooke from her side of the car, as he opened the car door.

"My word, is this place big and beautiful!" Brooke stated in surprise with her mouth hanging open, at seeing the beach house for the very first time in all its glory.

"My aunt and G-Dad designed it, and it was featured in an architectural magazine. *It is quite the house!"*

"I can see that..." She mentioned as she continued to admire the beach house. Will rang the doorbell after they walked onto the large expanse of a porch that held beautiful urns on either side of the solid wooden door, with a wide variety of flowers boasting a color palette that exploded and almost looked fake and too pretty to be real.

Lance answered, holding Alex protectively in his arms. "Come in," he smiled. "Sarah is doing the last minute touches to dinner right now," he explained, as he walked the both of them towards the kitchen with Brooke staring on in amazement at each detail of every room, with her mouth still slightly ajar as she looked on. Abby played contentedly in the play yard nearby, totally fine with being left alone, unlike her brother who demanded to be held by his father whenever he was around.

"Well hello, Will and Brooke," Sarah greeted happily, as she grabbed the mac and cheese from the oven with some potholders, placing the hot casserole on the granite countertop in front of her. "The burgers are done and I have corn on the cob and watermelon too. I hope that will suffice," she smiled, being dressed casually in shorts and a Marlin Beach tee with hair pulled high in her signature ponytail.

"That sounds great," Will answered, walking over to give her a warm kiss on the cheek. "Thanks for the invite. I was hoping to see you and the twins one more time before I left for Baltimore."

"Of course, Will! We would have been disappointed if you hadn't made it. And that goes for you too, Brooke," she added sweetly, looking in Brooke's direction as she was timidly standing off to one side waiting for Will to join her again.

"Thank you both for the invite," Brooke answered shyly, looking at Sarah and then at Lance with a slight smile.

"Please grab a plate and help yourselves. Iced tea and lemonade, along with cups and ice, are over there," Sarah pointed towards the other end of the large counter.

Lance put each energetic twin in a high chair as they cried out to be fed. They kept bouncing back and forth until he gave them some cut up fruit and diced chicken and vegetables on their trays, that Sarah had specially prepared for them.

"Doesn't the twins have their birthdays coming up soon?" Will asked, as he finished off his second ear of Silver Queen corn.

"Yes, in ten days. But you will already be back in college or I would have invited you to their birthday party that we are having for them," Sarah explained, as she spoon-fed the rest of the food to the twins.

"Well that is too bad, aunt Sarah. What would you like as a present for them?" William asked, concerned that he almost forgot the date and would now not be there for their special first birthday celebration.

"Will, they are in need of nothing!" Maybe a nice suggestion would be for you to make a donation to a local food bank in Baltimore or Towson in their honor."

"That's an excellent idea, honey!" Lance agreed, bending down to give his wife a kiss and then wipe off the mouths and hands of both twins, before Sarah lifted them back into the play yard. "I may even suggest that also to my parents since they didn't know what to buy them either."

"May I help you with the dishes?" Brooke asked, finally loosening up and feeling more relaxed, looking at Sarah and wanting to pitch in.

Sarah smiled, liking Brooke immensely. "Thank you, but I am fine with Lance's help. You and Will should relax out on the deck. It is such a lovely night."

William led Brooke around the entire house, giving her a tour of each room while Sarah and Lance bathed and put the twins to bed. Brooke was fascinated with each detail, realizing she had never been in a house of that grandeur. Only The Dexter mimicked that sort of elegance, which now made sense since Sarah and her father had designed that resort too.

They sat out on the deck together holding hands, admiring the sunset as the waves roared and cascaded in to the shoreline nearby. "Who wants strawberry shortcake?" Sarah asked, carrying a tray of four desert dishes filled to overflowing to the oversized, outdoor patio table.

"I sure do!" Will grinned, breaking free of Brooke's hand to grab a bowl of the delicious desert.

Brooke was quick to follow, taking a dish also before joining the others by the deck railing that overlooked the dunes and sea. The moon was glistening off of the ocean in front of them, and a dolphin jumped playfully in the air. *"If I lived here I would never leave... "* She sighed, being in a trance from the tranquility and beauty of it all.

"Well, thank you, Brooke. We are very blessed and thankful that we live here in Marlin Beach," Sarah replied. "I wouldn't want to live any place else."

"It would be my dream come true to live in Marlin Beach one day."

"Then I would say you should focus in on that dream and make it a reality, because you never know if one day it may come true!" Sarah challenged, looking in her direction and then at William with a pleased smile.

CHAPTER 53

It was the last full day in Marlin Beach. William had said his goodbyes to Sarah and the twins after a lovely evening at The Playful Starfish, and knew he would see Lance one more time on Sunday when he handed him back the keys to The Happy Crab after cleaning the beach house. Brooke had spent the night again, and she shed a few tears knowing that they had only two more nights together before they both went their separate ways - back to their homes and families, and then off to separate colleges. William held her tightly and told her *it would be okay* as he tried to suppress his own set of tears and emotions.

With a cleaning bucket in hand, Will scrubbed down each tub, sink and toilet as Matt vacuumed the entire place and then washed up the floors. Chris cleaned up the outside, discovering a discarded red Solo cup hiding here and there, and stacked up the beach furniture and closed and locked the hurricane shutters.

"Man, I need a break," Matt whined, plopping down on the sofa that he had also just vacuumed, finding a forgotten, discarded bra under one of the couch cushions from an unknown female guest.

"We still got a six-pack of beer in the frig if anyone is interested?"

Chris suggested, making his way to the kitchen.

Will collapsed beside of Matt on the sofa. "I say we order a couple of pizzas tonight if you guys are up for it."

"How about inviting Brooke's friends over tonight? I could use one more *sexy time* with Mia," he laughed.

"If you want to have sex, you can go to her place!" Will warned, giving him the eye.

"Hey, why are you suddenly acting like a jerk?"

"Cuz I want things low key tonight and I don't want to clean this place up again in the morning before we leave. Got that?" Will yelled, acting irritable.

"Calm down, Will. No one is going to mess up your precious uncle's place. We know all about his damn rules!"

"Seriously, Chris! You're gonna talk that crap about my uncle Lance after everything he has done for us this summer?"

"Now, calm down!" Matt jumped in, adding to the conversation. "Your uncle has been great, and I for one, really appreciate him allowing us to continue staying here after what happened with the party."

"Thanks, Matt," Will answered, as he looked at him and then stared back angrily at Chris. *"At least some of us get it!"*

Chris got up and grabbed a beer and walked out the front door, slamming it behind him, making the pictures rattle on the wall.

"You know how hot headed he can be, bro. Don't let him get to you. He is feeling the emotion of leaving here, just as much as the rest of us. I get it that you don't want a big party. I plan to get up and out of here early tomorrow morning. My mom wants to have lunch with me before she goes into work."

William looked sympathetically at his friend, knowing what he shared about his difficult home life. He felt somewhat guilty that he hadn't done the same, and had only opened up entirely to Brooke about all the details. "If you want to get out of here tonight feel free to go. I will cover things with Lance if something more needs to be done."

"Are you sure?"

"Sure, I'm sure! Get outta here and enjoy some quality time with your mother before we go back to school. It will surprise her and make her feel happy if you arrive home early tonight."

"Thanks, bro. I think I will take you up on that," he grinned happily.

Within thirty minutes Matt was all packed and ready to roll - with one suitcase and a duffle bag. "I will see you in a few days at Towson."

"I still want my old bed if you get there first," Will teased, knowing Matt had tried to claim that spot when they first became roommates in their freshmen year.

"Then you better beat me there, bro," he threw back, knowing he would never really do that to his best friend. "Enjoy your last night with Brooke and don't let Chris ruin your fun."

"Things will be fine," he promised, walking Matt out to his car. "Treat your mom to dinner on me," he offered, handing him five, twenty-dollar bills.

"I can't take that, bro."

"Oh yes, you can. I insist! My aunt and uncle just gave me five hundred dollars to go towards clothing and other things for school, and I honestly don't need it. I know my Nan and G-Dad will probably hook me up with more money when I get home. Take it," Will insisted, wadding it up and stuffing the money through the half-closed car window before walking away.

"You're the best!" Matt yelled, as he began to pull away from The Happy Crab. "It's been quite the amazing summer!"

William turned to give him the *thumbs up sign* before going back inside the beach house. He sat at the kitchen table running both hands through his wavy brown hair, thinking about the evening ahead. He needed to call Brooke and figure out what was going on with Chris.

The front door opened again and this time closed more quietly than when Chris first left. *"Where is Matt?"* he asked, taking a seat at the table and glancing around the kitchen and living room, not paying any attention to the fact that is car was no longer there.

"He just left for Baltimore. He wanted to get home early and surprise his mother."

"Really? Am I the only one left here - out of the four of us - with any sense?"

"What is that supposed to mean?"

"It means that we have one last night here at the beach and now two out of the four of us has left, and you might as well be gone as attached at the hip as you are to Brooke. *What am I supposed to do now on my last night here, since I know you will be hanging out with Brooke?"* Chris asked in frustration.

"Hey, man, I'm sorry... I really didn't think about things quite that way. Hang with me and Brooke, or invite her roommates over here and we will all hang out together."

"You would do that for me?"

Will looked at him in surprise, not sure where he was going with things. *"I'm calling Brooke and we will all hang out tonight. Okay?"*

"Yeah... okay!" Chris perked up, suddenly feeling much better.

The girls all showed up after cleaning and organizing their place. Three pizzas and sodas were bought, with Will treating everybody and tipping the delivery driver generously. Scrabble was played as teams of two were chosen, with the final winning team being Rachel and Amber - with the highest mutual score.

"We need to get back to our place since we are leaving early tomorrow," Rachel finally announced, glancing at the girls, wanting them to leave also.

"I'll catch up with you guys in the morning," Brooke interjected, hugging close by William's side and planning to spend the night again, as she routinely did now.

"What else is new?" Mia joked, giggling as she watched the two cozied up. "How about driving me home, Chris? *I need to give you a fond farewell.*"

"Oh, really now?" Chris answered suggestively with a lift to his voice, knowing what she was implying. "Let me grab my keys and I will be right with you!"

Amber, Rachel and Mia said their final goodbyes to Will, hugging him a little too closely to the point of making Brooke slightly jealous. "Okay girls, Will gets it that you will miss him. Now it's time to leave," she insisted, showing them to the door with Chris right behind them.

Once everyone was gone, Brooke closed the front door and leaned up against it, making an alluring picture for William that he loved seeing. Brooke in her short shorts that always rode up, exposing the beginning of her derriere. *"I never thought that they would get out of here,"* she confessed, almost in a breathless sort of way.

Will walked over and began pressing up against her, bringing his lips down to hers for a soul-searing kiss, as his tongue darted in and out her mouth. He picked her up in his arms and carried her to his bedroom, undressing her as soon as her feet hit the floor. *"I've wanted you all evening too, my love."*

"Then I guess the feeling is mutual," she whispered seductively, hurrying to undress.

Their lovemaking was unhurried and free to touch and taste, without anyone else in the beach house. Sleep was not the priority on their last night together, as they would dose off for short periods of time and then awaken to make love again until streaks of morning light peaked through the blinds.

"Do you realize we had sex all night?" Will whispered with a contented smile, nibbling on her ear.

"Yes, I do... and it won't be easy making the trip home now... " She sighed, feeling ready to finally fall off to sleep.

He pulled her to her feet, still damp from their lovemaking, standing nude in front of her. "I want to show you something," he beckoned, encouraging her to dress as he started to do the same.

They walked together from The Happy Crab, going towards the shoreline hand in hand, as they watched the sun begin to rise over the horizon. "It's so beautiful, Will... " She sighed. "What a perfect way to end our time here in Marlin Beach."

"I agree... " He answered reflectively, planting a kiss of promise on her lips for the now and the future.

Brooke left William's embrace after tears and hugs and endless kisses of goodbye were shared. He watched her pull away and then he finally shed his own tears without her seeing them. Chris showed up a short time later after a passionate night of his own, with Lance joining the two roommates that remained - with a cup of coffee in hand - ready for the final inspection.

"Well you guys did an excellent job of cleaning up the place - inside and out!" Lance praised, as the four house keys and the single shed key were handed back over to him.

"That means a lot, uncle Lance."

"Yes, thank you for letting me stay here, Lance," Chris added.

"Maybe we can talk about next summer... but we will see as that time approaches again."

"Really?" Will remarked in surprise. "I didn't think that was even a possibility to stay at The Happy Crab again."

"Time will tell," Lance winked as he drove away down Beach Road, heading back home to Sarah and the twins. He left Chris and Will in the driveway of The Happy Crab, packed and ready to make their journey back home now too.

"It's been a great summer, bro. Sorry when I've been a jerk."

Will ignored the comment, playfully punching Chris in the arm instead, before getting in his Jeep. *"I'll see you back at Towson."*

"Yes, you will... " Chris yelled, as he pulled out of the driveway way too fast, throwing up some gravel in the process. William could hear his noisy muffler off in the distance, hoping he didn't get pulled over for another time that summer.

Will took the drive slow, as he left Marlin Beach. He passed by Beach Dreams and Old Bay Café, and then paused to look one last time at The Dexter Resort and Spa – his father's namesake. He remembered picking Brooke up there several times after work, and it was the place he and Mitchell had shared a nice dinner. He crossed the bridge that was already busy with jet skiers who were darting back and forth underneath, and then stopped at Mom and Pops - leaving with a bag of sweet corn and tomatoes for Nan and G-Dad. The Chesapeake Bay Bridge was next which held a few large cargo ships and a flotilla of sailboats that were gliding across the bay water and enjoying the day.

Several hours later, he was back in Baltimore and pulled into the familiar driveway of his grandparents' house where he resided at least part of the time now. Nan and G-Dad were there to greet him with warm and loving hugs that he came to appreciate after his mother's passing. Nan made the promised meals on her list, and they followed the schedule by watching movies and swimming in the pool sometimes late into the evening, as Mike and William talked about *what he wanted to do with the rest of his life after college.*

More tears were shed as Will packed it up for another time several days later, and headed for Towson, waving his fond goodbyes to his Nan and G-Dad as he pulled away from their beautiful brick colonial in Highland Estates.

His phone rang and he realized it was Brooke calling. "Hey baby, I was just ready to call you. *Did you make it there yet?*"

"I'm already in your dorm room waiting, silly, and I gave the guys strict orders that they needed to leave after saying *hello* once you arrived."

"Really?" Will laughed, having a hard time believing that his roommates would even listen to her, especially if they had already started drinking. He turned off the exit that led to Towson, knowing he was only ten minutes away from seeing her now. "I'll be there very soon, *my hotness.* We got some major catching up to do!"

EPILOGUE

10 months later......

It was a beautiful day for an outdoor June wedding.

William and his friends had just finished another year at Towson University and had returned to Marlin Beach for a second season for work and for play. Lance extended an invite to them once again to stay at The Happy Crab, *with the familiar warning that if anything was destroyed or out of place they would have to leave.* William, Chris, Matt and Tyler eagerly signed the lease agreement with all the promises made that Lance wanted to hear - even if he didn't entirely believe they could tow the line for the entire summer season. This time around, Mike and Nancy - or G-Dad and Nan - as William so affectionately called them, were in favor of his return to Marlin Beach since he was now no longer a teenager and had just turned twenty.

Brooke, Mia, Rachel and Amber came back too, but this time they chose a different place to stay, picking a location closer to the Towson guys and the beach. They all picked up where they left off, working at their same jobs at The Dexter Resort and Spa, and of course William was working for his uncle Lance at Snyder's Beach Dreams Real Estate. Will's spare time was spent enjoying the beach and the boardwalk, but was mostly spent hanging out with his girlfriend Brooke - who he had continued dating throughout his second year at Towson, and he still loved and adored her.

William looked at his beautiful aunt Jennifer who looked radiant and ready to walk outside to the beach, ready to be married on the first official day of summer. She wore her brunette hair loose, just the way Mitchell loved it; and was dressed in a strapless, mid-length flowing white gown with white matching flip-flops that were encased in rhinestones, being well suited for the beach. She chose a pearl necklace and a bracelet that Claire had given her, and tucked a small Bible of her father's beneath the wild flower bouquet.

"Are you ready, aunt Jen?" William asked, giving her a gentle kiss on the cheek as he reached out his elbow for her to grasp on to.

"Yes, William," she smiled back tenderly, being caught up in the special moment, as she gazed at her handsome, muscular nephew that was dressed in linen shorts and a teal polo shirt and flip-flops.

They proceeded outside where the small group sat on white chairs waiting, expertly placed by the *special events team* who worked for The Dexter. A local minister had been contacted to perform the ceremony since their pastor in Birmingham *felt the distance was too great for travel.* Everyone rose, as Jennifer and William walked down the center walkway, towards Mitchell and the pastor. A beaming Eva and Jackson already stood up front by their father waiting on their future stepmother and brother to approach.

"Who gives this woman to be married?" the pastor asked, looking in William's direction, as was rehearsed the night previous.

"*I do,*" he grinned, giving his aunt a warm hug and kiss before he released her into Mitchell's care, and then took his seat in the front row beside of Brooke, ready to watch the rest of the ceremony.

Mitchell smiled happily as he grabbed Jennifer's hand, also outfitted in casual attire with white linen slacks, a gray polo shirt and flip-flops. The bouquet was handed off to Eva as the minister began, leading each one in saying their wedding vows before pronouncing them husband and wife. A kiss was given as everyone stood and clapped for their joyous union, with congratulations being given by all.

Sarah and Lance had been kind enough to arrange for a luncheon at The Dexter restaurant afterwards, taking on the entire cost with Mike and Nancy's help. Jennifer and Mitchell were stunned that they would be so kind and generous towards them, but accepted the gift offered along with an invitation to stay at The Dexter Hotel for a - one-week, all expense paid, vacation. It was a time of celebration not only for the happy newlyweds, but also for Eva and Jackson, since they got to return to The Dancing Seahorse for a week of spoiling by Nancy and Mike.

As per Mitchell's promise almost a year prior to William in the parking lot of Beach Dreams, he had maintained his sobriety and was a wonderful father to Eva and Jackson, and a great companion and now husband to his aunt Jennifer. It was obvious they were in love and the family was happy and content.

With a week of fun sharing meals, playing games, the boardwalk and course the beach and boogie boarding, it was time for the family to return to Birmingham, Alabama and for William to go back to work at Beach Dreams once again.

"*I will miss you guys,*" William expressed sincerely, as they were saying their final goodbyes in front of The Dexter, and the rental car was packed and ready to go.

"*We will miss you too,*" Jennifer whispered. "Thank you for coming around and accepting things. I am very proud of you and I know your parents would be too - if they were here today."

"Thanks, aunt Jen, but my mom and dad are always here with me."

"I think you are absolutely right about that," she smiled with a glimmer of a tear in her eye as she got into the front passenger's seat beside of her new husband.

"Drive safely," William nodded, looking in Mitchell's direction. "And you guys behave for your parents," he added, looking in the backseat at his siblings.

"We will," they both answered him in unison.

"Thanks, William," Mitchell said with a knowing look, humbled by his acceptance of him now.

"No problem," he answered with a tap to the car. "Get on the road now or you will miss your flight, and congratulations again on your marriage!"

William turned and walked away as the rental car pulled out onto Beach Road, dialing Brooke on his cellphone as he made his way back towards his red Jeep. "Hey babe, my family just left and I was wondering if you could spare about an hour before I head back to work? I was hoping that maybe you could meet up with me at The Happy Crab?"

"Any particular reason why?" Brooke giggled, teasing him and knowing his real attentions as she locked the door to her place, making her way towards her car, ready to start her engine.

"I was just thinking after a week of being with my family non-stop, it would be nice to be alone so that we can get reacquainted."

"And maybe have some hot passionate sex?" Brooke suggested.

"You read my mine," Will laughed seductively, loving the

brazenness of his hot and passionate girlfriend. "Don't bother ringing the bell. No one will be home anyway to answer it, because the roommates are all at work right now."

"*Seriously?*" Brooke purred, liking where he was going with things as she headed towards The Happy Crab.

"*Yes, seriously.* And by the way... the door will be unlocked, so just come on in. You will find me undressed and nude - waiting on you in my bed for some *serious* lovemaking!"

ABOUT THE AUTHOR

Roberta L. Greenwald lives in beautiful Western Maryland. Beyond being a writer, she is a full time decorator. When she is not working or writing, she enjoys time with her family and fur babies.

The inspiration for Marlin Beach – the third book in the Cutting Tide Saga – comes from her love of the eastern shore of Maryland. Ocean City, Maryland has a very unique boardwalk and beach culture that she invites you to visit and enjoy!